Taking care of baby sister

"You know I'm not crazy. Don't you, Doctor Burns?"

Her mother flinched when he stuck the needle into her arm. Laura was surprised at how quickly her mother went to sleep. Before the doctor could dispose of the syringe, her mother's head lolled on the pillow, and the arm holding the baby relaxed.

Laura held herself in check, until she heard the footsteps go down the stairs and into the livingroom. She sprang to the wastebasket and retrieved the used syringe the doctor had thrown away.

Light glinted off the silver needle. She turned the syringe over in her hand, holding it like a dagger, and plunged it into the baby's white belly. She pulled the needle out and plunged it in again before the baby screamed. As she plunged the third time, her mother opened her eyes . . .

Other Avon Books Coming Soon by
Brenda Brown Canary

HOME TO THE MOUNTAIN

The
VOICE OF THE
CLOWN

BRENDA BROWN CANARY

◆ AVON
PUBLISHERS OF BARD, CAMELOT, DISCUS AND FLARE BOOKS

THE VOICE OF THE CLOWN is an original publication of
Avon Books. This work has never before appeared in book
form.

AVON BOOKS
A division of
The Hearst Corporation
959 Eighth Avenue
New York, New York 10019

First Avon Printing, April, 1982

Prologue

Molly peered over the edge of the cliff. In the moonlight she saw the faint contour of rock outcroppings. They looked small, but having climbed the sheer face of that rocky height many times as a child, she knew their size and the distance to the dry sandrock basin below.

A sudden wind gusted behind her, pushing her forward. She stepped back and drew her ceremonial shawl about her. T.J. had bought the materials—all the colors of the rainbow—from which she had made the shawl with foot-long fringe to sway in the dancing. She had never worn it except for that. Except tonight—she had worn it tonight so there would be something to cover her face when they found her.

Molly looked up at the stars, then closed her eyes. They had made love on such a night four years ago. Made love—not thirty feet from where she was standing, with those same stars standing guard over their first-time fears and fumbling; understanding their need for each other and the deep bond built on a childhood of sharing: hide and seek survival through pastures, woods, and lonely secret caves; daring deeds and daring rescues; injuries received and treated; cavalry maneuvers on ponies; the black eye she had given him in junior high for laughing at her first formal; hours, days, weeks, months, years of talk— sharing ideas, making compromises and commitments. Lovemaking had come in its time, a natural outgrowth of deep, well-formed roots.

That first time had been the result of a pact they made to experiment only once before they married. But it had not worked that way. They had found such pleasure in each other, there was no stopping. She had been as eager as he—every time he came home from college—yet all the while fearful of pregnancy. What she had feared had happened on his last visit before graduation.

Never had she imagined that the next time home he would bring a bride—Kate. Through tears he explained that Kate was pregnant, that he had to marry her.

Molly had let him find out on his own that she also was carrying his child. When news of her pregnancy reached him, he had come immediately, as she had known he would, to stand, head bowed, before her father. T.J. had shed silent tears on their worn carpet and offered the only thing he had left to give—money—which her father had made her refuse.

The screeching night winds swept Molly toward the edge, embracing her as fiercely as T.J. had after Reming's birth. Then he had told her how Kate had been the most sought-after girl at college. She was beautiful, refined, talented. All his friends had wanted her, chased after her, but she had had eyes only for him. Dating her had been a coup, which had catapulted him from near obscurity into the best circles.

His face had spoken his misery while he told her. Molly had no thought about him lying. They had been too close for lies. Their childhood closeness yet unbroken, the wanting between them had been as strong as ever. She had been hungry for his kisses. As hungry for him as she would have been as his happy bride. She *was* his bride. Had been since their first night together. Kate was the intruder.

The memory of Kate's blonde beauty loomed large against the backdrop of stars. Kate. Preening on T.J.'s arm; cool, confident. Kate. Announcing her claim by flashing her big diamonds. Kate. Hiding her pregnancy until the very end; insisting that Harley was premature.

Kate had been protected, sheltered by the marriage that should have been Molly's; while she, the unwed mother, had had to bear the taunts of her tribe, and worse, the whites who called her the town squaw and said she had no idea who fathered Reming.

Her secret meetings with T.J., his constant assurance that, given time, he would somehow find a way to make things right, had sustained her, until Reming, now nearly three, had begun to ask why he didn't have a daddy.

Although they were fast friends and playmates, T.J. had

never identified himself to Reming. Today, she had pressed him for an answer. What was she to tell their son?

He had finally confessed that divorce was out of the question. He loved them both, wanted them both, wanted both his sons.

Sweeping up from the depths of the canyon floor, the wind blasted her. She stiffened against it. T.J. had begged her to let him build her a house on land he owned adjoining her father's. He had described it to her—a lovely big house where theirs would be a permanent relationship open for all the world, including Kate, to see. He'd have his lawyers draw up papers to give Reming his rightful name and a share in T.J.'s estate equal to Harley's.

Molly shuddered. Even in that hot wind, she felt cold, chilled through. What he had offered was a place as the permanent wrongdoer—not the one wronged. His offer had been the final stone that had pressed the life out of her.

There was such a thing as honor. She was the daughter of a chief, the granddaughter of a chief. What pride would there be for the bastard son of a kept woman? Her father had been right all along. Her pride could not be taken from her, only given away. Pride was the only legacy she had to leave her son.

She knew what had to be done. She was resolved. Her people called this cliff The Thinking Place. Why was her head so muddled? Why was she hesitating to take that one last step over the edge?

She had said her good-byes. She had kissed her son good night when she put him to bed. "Be a good boy, Reming. Make your grandfather proud of you." Don't shame him and yourself as I have. She had whispered "I love you" to her father as she slipped past his room and out of the house. He loved the boy. He would take good care of him. She had no worries there. Reming would be better off. Without her the gossip would gradually die down. She owed him that much of a chance.

"Kate!"

She screamed the name over the canyon. With it spewing her hate for the woman who had robbed her of her title as wife and mother; her home at the ranch; her place in the family; and most importantly her earned role as friend, companion—lover—to T.J.

Kate had robbed her! But Kate could never take her place. She had not made that house a happy home nor become the cherished center of a loving family.

After tonight, death would hover over that house like a waiting scavenger bird as surely as it was about to pluck her out of a drudge of days to be gotten through, deposed, as she had been, from her rightful place.

She laughed—relieved—no longer afraid. The wind caught her laughter, swirled it away into the darkness. She stretched her arms wide, spreading out the ceremonial shawl as wings. In her mind's eye she saw herself, the raven-haired Molly Crow, first perched on the cliff, then circling to the four winds; offering, as had her ancestors, a human sacrifice—her own life—in exchange for the destruction of her enemy, Kate!

She stepped over the edge chanting ominously: K-A-T-E. It was a raucous warning call.

The body struck the basin floor, silencing her cry. But the echo carried far down the canyon: K-a-t-e—K-a-t-e—K-a-t-e—K-a-t-e—

September

Hot. The cement step was hot, but Laura gritted her teeth and stayed put. She could take that and more. She would have to be tough, now. Because her clown had already told her that her daddy would lose the argument.

Listening to her parents' voices behind the big oak door, Laura tugged the elastic in her playsuit where it pinched between her sunburned legs.

"Damn it, Kate! Laura has no business in school!"

Her daddy was mad, but his anger had no effect on her mother. She sounded as cold as ever.

"Laura is six years old. She has as much business being in school as other children have."

Her mother's voice made her clown cringe in her arms. Always had. Ever since she could remember.

Suddenly, Laura bent forward and stuck both fingers in her ears. She hated the voice. Hated what her mother said about her and to her. Always trying to make her talk and to keep her away from her daddy.

Laura raised her head and glared at the blazing sun. She was determined not to blink until it blinded her. It forced her to close her eyes. She opened them quickly and focused on the distant twin columns that guarded the opening to the rock wall surrounding the house and grounds like a fort.

Squinting, her eyes burning, she was angry that the sun had bested her; she fought to clear her vision. There were the columns. One on each side where they had always been. Between them, where nothing belonged, was a third. Slightly taller. Broader. Blocking the entrance. She tried to focus the three into two and failed.

The central column seemed to be moving toward her,

5

evolving rapidly into the shape of a man. A giant. With heat waves shimmering skyward, in front and behind, he appeared to have risen out of the hot ground. The devil, maybe. Come to claim her.

She rubbed her eyes, unwilling to believe. The giant loomed ever-larger, striding straight toward her across the island of scorched lawn in the middle of the circle drive.

Shaken, as though lightning had touched earth nearby, Laura cowered, clutching her stuffed clown in front of her for protection. Too frightened to move, she kept her eyes clamped shut until the crunch of gravel directly in front of her jolted them open. Shading her eyes with her clown she looked up into an angular face, still handsome though lined and worn, seemingly molded—over a long time—out of red Oklahoma clay. A face she recognized.

Her held breath exploded in a self-conscious giggle. It was only Reming's grandfather come to fetch him home. She didn't even have to pay attention to him. He knew his way around the place. He would go to the kitchen door rather than ring the bell. He might even have a cup of coffee with Nana. He and Nana were old friends.

She lifted her clown's arm in a wave. The old man grunted a greeting. He took two steps past her. Stopped and turned slowly, came back, and stood towering above her. Watching.

Reluctantly, she met his eyes. They seemed to look deep inside her. Suddenly he gasped as though she had slugged him in the belly. She wanted to look away, but could not. She felt trapped.

"Who are you?" he asked.

Silly old man. He knows who I am.

"You can talk!"

Laura turned away. He knew she had never spoken a word to anyone. Not even her daddy or Nana. She hugged her clown.

"Why do you carry that fool's doll?"

Laura glared up at him. What right did he have to insult her clown?

"I know you now."

He paused. The red gleam in his eyes made her shiver.

He stepped toward her. "Your powers are no match for mine. I can send you back. Send you back and punish you!"

6

Suddenly, the cement burned the backs of her bare legs. Forced her to move up a step into the shade. She scooted backward across the porch and sat trembling against the rough stone wall. The old man disappeared around the corner of the house.

She felt herself gasping, choking for lack of air. She struggled to calm herself so she could breathe. She had never been more frightened. Laura resolved never to be so frightened again.

He *was* the devil. His sudden appearance out of the heat waves had been a warning. He was an Indian healer, she knew. A medicine man. Nana had said he possessed knowledge centuries old and cured people modern doctors had given up on. Maybe his powers were evil, not good as Nana thought.

She never wanted to see him again. Her clown, shuddering violently in her arms, never wanted to see him again. He was dangerous.

Inside, she heard her parents still arguing. Backed against the house, she felt pressed between the medicine man's threats and the loud, strident tones of her mother's voice.

"Dr. Klingman is a specialist. Since there is no physical reason for Laura's not talking, he said we should force her into a normal classroom situation where she'll have to talk to survive."

Her daddy sounded tired and sad.

"You have no feelings for her, do you?"

Her daddy loved her, but he was powerless against her mother.

"What the doctor says makes good sense. I know she'll never learn around here. Not with you and your mother giving her everything she wants."

"It's you badgering her all the time that keeps her too nervous to try!"

Her mother shrieked at him. "Her muteness is just as embarrassing to me as it is to you. After all, I'm her mother."

"No one could tell it from the way you treat her."

Her mother exploded. "She doesn't hide from you everytime you call. It's maddening the way she sneaks around, stalking in corners, listening to conversations she

7

has no business hearing. It's like having a ghost in the house."

If her mother only knew! About the scenes that appeared without warning. People, who were not a part of the present. It was Laura's secret. Guarded by her own silence.

Those scenes puzzled her. They were of a past time. Some as clear as yesterday, others glimpsed only in snatches—dimly—as though through a gauze screen. No matter how she struggled to focus the dim scenes into a clearer view, they remained dark and hazy, not a few of them accompanied by such a feeling of depression that she needed her clown to comfort her. Her clown saw everything. Knew everything. But her clown would only tell her that a terrible secret had been kept from her. And that now it was her turn to be the keeper of secrets.

Inside the house her mother's tone changed, dropping suddenly to a whisper. She sounded frightened.

"Old! Laura's eyes seem as if they've seen everything in the world. I can't bear to look at them."

Laura could almost hear her mother shiver. Her clown wiggled. A happy wiggle. Her mother was afraid. Fear was a weapon to be used against her.

The next morning, over her daddy's objections, her mother scrubbed and dressed her in her Sunday school clothes and trundled her into the pickup to be taken to school. Laura sandwiched herself under her daddy's arm and hugged her clown.

Someone, no one could remember who, had given her the clown when she was born. It had shared her life. Sometimes it even talked to her, usually about her mother. Her clown hated her mother! Especially now, for this school business. Her clown said her mother was trying to separate her from her daddy.

Her clown was no more fooled than Laura was by all her daddy's cheerful talk about how much fun she would have. He knew she wouldn't like it. Her mother had made him take her. He did not want her in school any more than she wanted to go. She could tell by the way he yelled at Harley and Reming, who were wrestling in the bed of the truck.

It was just like Harley to horn in on her first ride to

school. Just then Harley hung over the passenger side and stuck his head in her window.

"Your classmates will all call you a dummy if you won't talk to them."

Laura could hear her mother telling him to say that. She stuck her tongue out at him. He made a hideous face back at her.

Her daddy roared at him, "Sit down, Harley! Or you won't be able to." He gripped the steering wheel, so tightly his hand made a squishing sound against the black plastic.

Her brother hustled to take his place beside Reming on the tool chest just behind the cab. He glanced over his shoulder, his eyes large, his expression hurt.

Served him right. He was always tagging along when he wasn't wanted.

Her daddy smiled at her as he started the truck, but his face looked strained. She knew he was thinking about the same things she was. If she had to go to school every day, she would not be able to go to his office, or ride out to the oil rig or go to cattle auctions with him. He would be very lonesome without her.

Overnight their lives had been turned upside down, all because of that stupid doctor. She had heard him tell her mother that she would talk if she were with other kids, that she would have to talk to get along. That was all *he* knew. He assumed she would *want* to get along. Why should she want to?

The truck jolted to a stop at the end of the circle drive, then her daddy turned right onto the gravel road.

Her talking was only important to her mother because she was worried about what her friends thought. They sat around at the country club, small though it was, comparing what they had: houses, cars, diamonds, their figures, faces, nails, and hair. Her mother was the worst one. She was a taker. She took and took and took. Her daddy tried so hard to please her. It was terrible to see the want in his eyes. He yearned for her mother to love him, put her arms around him, kiss him, and hug him. She never did.

But Laura did. She loved her daddy. He sang to her, and wrestled her on the floor, and hugged her on his lap in the evenings while he watched television. He bragged about the pictures she colored, and helped her cut out

9

paper dolls, and did all the fun things her mother should have been doing with her. And when she saw the need in his eyes, she snuggled close to him and loved him.

The pickup bumped over a pothole, and Laura nestled closer under her daddy's arm. It was hot—Indian summer hot in September—but her hands were cold. He winked down at her, and she pressed her fingers flat against his warm chest.

Her mother wanted her to talk so she could pick her brain, the way she did Harley's, and then use it against her. But Laura had always outsmarted her. There was too much at stake to be forced into talking. She had secret plans for the future. Someday she was going to have her daddy all to herself. She would make the aching look go out of his eyes. When she was grown, she was going to *marry* her daddy.

The truck swerved sideways, and her daddy honked at a careless beagle crossing the road. Laura pressed her head against his chest. With her mother gone, life could be so beautiful. They could do as they pleased every day.

Her daddy ruffled her hair and then kissed the top of her head. "I'll be waiting for you when school is out. I don't want you riding the school bus for a while."

From his tone, Laura knew how hard he had fought her mother about it. Harley had come off the school bus with knots and bruises. Several times he had had his shirt torn off. It was a free-for-all every afternoon, with the big kids picking on the smaller ones. She would not stand a chance on the bus. But her mother didn't care. That was what she wanted—to put her in a situation so frustrating she would have to talk to survive.

Her daddy would never stand for anyone hurting her. Not if he could help it. He wanted her to talk, but he was willing to let her do it in her own time, for her own reasons.

Her daddy smelled so good in the morning, all scrubbed and clean and perfumed with aftershave. Being near him felt so wonderful she could not get close enough.

That was how she knew something was very wrong with her mother. Her mother hated being close to him. Every time he put his arms around her she pushed him away. "Not now, T.J." "Don't do that." "I have things to do."

10

Not wanting him near her was proof that her mother was crazy. Her daddy was beautiful. Laura pushed up on her knees, in the swaying seat. She traced the wave of her daddy's light brown hair around his forehead. She smoothed his eyebrows, which were thick and dark, shading his round blue eyes, giving them a hint of devilishness and mystery.

Everyone said Laura's eyes were like her daddy's. She hoped they were, because his were very beautiful; but she favored his lips. Her daddy's lips were full and pink tinted, and Laura loved the warm, slightly wet feel of them when he kissed her. And he kissed her often, because her crazy mother did not want his kisses.

"You think I don't know what you are doing, Little Lady? Trying a little friendly persuasion, thinking it will get you out of going to school. You're going to be quite a woman when you're grown up." He pulled her against him as they stopped at a stop sign.

Laura stole a glance behind her and found Harley watching. His eyes clouded with the hurt of being excluded. Served him right for taunting her. She smiled impudently at him and he turned quickly away. Harley wasn't stupid. He better not push her too far. She only tolerated him now because Reming came to play with him.

Just then Reming winked at her. Laura knew he didn't approve of the way she and Harley were constantly at each other. He was always playing the peacemaker between them.

Everyone liked Reming: Nana, and Carrie, the maid; even her mother liked him a little. But her mother did not like him as much as she pretended. Laura had often wondered why her mother gushed over Reming in her father's presence but just tolerated him the rest of the time. It was a mystery like so many other things she knew that she knew but couldn't quite bring into focus.

Her daddy sometimes pretended to like Harley better than he did, too. In fact, Laura knew a secret about them. Her daddy liked Reming much better than he did Harley. If her mother ever guessed, she would have a fit, because she wanted him to love Harley more than anybody. Her daddy would probably never admit he liked Reming better, anyway. People never said what was really on their minds. More often than not, they said just the opposite. That was what made talking such a useless game.

A blue Ford Laura recognized entered the intersection from their right. She hit the horn and waved at June, her daddy's secretary. She was headed for the office. Laura pointed for him to follow and even tried to turn the steering wheel herself, but her daddy moved her gently aside and proceeded straight ahead toward school.

Laura hugged her clown. Her daddy did not like what was happening any better than she did, but he was going through with it. No use making them both miserable by causing a scene.

She pictured her mother at home: grinning, smug, thinking she had finally separated Laura from her daddy. She smiled, holding her clown tightly. By tomorrow, she and her daddy would be back together, and her mother would have something else to think about. This day would be the first and last she ever spent in school.

When her daddy parked the truck across the street from the school yard, her smile seemed to surprise him. Hurt flashed in his eyes, and his efforts to hide his jealousy undermined the manufactured cheerfulness in his voice.

"You'll like school so much more than tagging around after me. You'll have new things to see and learn every day."

Her daddy could be so silly. Imagine thinking that a room full of babies would be more fun than being with him.

He lifted her out of the truck and stood her on her feet. She clutched her clown even harder. Harley and Reming jumped off the wheel wells on either side of the truck and disappeared in the crowded school yard.

"Better leave your clown with me, Sweetheart," her daddy said. He reached to take it from her. She held on.

"The other children will laugh at you if you carry your clown to school."

She didn't care whether they laughed or not. Her clown was part of her. As far back as she could remember she had carried it everywhere. She had never been separated from her clown. And not even her daddy was going to take it from her now.

He shrugged as if it made no difference, but Laura could tell it was important to him.

"O.K. It's your choice," he said. "But if the other children laugh, don't blame me."

Laura tucked her clown firmly under her arm and took her daddy's hand. They crossed the street and were halfway across the noisy playground before he spoke again.

"Your teacher probably won't allow you to take your clown to your desk. She might have you leave it in the cloakroom until after school. Wouldn't you rather give it to me?"

Laura shook her head "no." She could never abandon her clown.

"It'd be safer," her daddy said.

She smiled her thanks and trudged on toward the building. If the teacher tried to take her clown, then that was where it would begin. She and her clown were ready. Together, they were a match for anyone.

Miss Glade was short and thin, with a bouncing ponytail that made her look like a teenager. The bell rang while her daddy and Miss Glade were still talking in the doorway. Children scrambled around them on both sides, pushing and shoving to their rowed seats. Laura ducked between her daddy and the teacher to keep from being swept away by the noisy wave. A second bell sounded, and Miss Glade twittered a good-bye and rushed her daddy out the door.

"Thank you for bringing Laura. She'll be fine. It's best not to say good-bye on first days. We know you are in a hurry to get to your office. Laura is a big girl. She'll love being an independent first-grader."

The door closed her daddy in the hall. He looked worried and helpless outside the glass. The teacher took Laura's hand, twirled her toward the class and away from her daddy's locked out face.

"This is Laura Daniels, our new classmate. We are all going to make her feel welcome and help her catch up on the two weeks she's missed."

When Laura looked back at the door, her daddy was gone. The teacher squeezed her hand to bring her attention back.

"Laura's daddy tells me that some of you already know Laura from Sunday school and the country club. She'll feel much more at home if some of her 'old friends' offer to play with her at recess. I know you are all anxious to make her a part of the group."

Miss Glade latched onto Laura's clown.

"I have just the place for your doll," she said.

"Tomorrow, you must leave it at home. But today, it'll be our guest of honor and sit on my desk."

She was jerked to a stop when Laura did not release her clown. The teacher tugged gently.

"What more could a ragged old clown ask for? Guest of honor!"

Laura smiled. Her clown wanted their freedom. Silly-pony-tail-teacher would know that before the day was over.

Miss Glade pried Laura's hands away from her clown, tossed it on her desk, and took Laura to an empty seat at the back of the room. She pressed Laura firmly into the chair.

"Now, this is your very own desk. And what should Laura do, class?"

"Stay in her chair," was the chorused response.

"That's right. Unless you have permission from me to be up."

Laura nodded, smiling.

Pleased, the teacher patted Laura's head, turned, and moved down the aisle toward the front of the room. The moment her back was turned, Laura popped up and dashed to the teacher's desk. She retrieved her clown and sat in the teacher's chair.

Miss Glade cut through a row of seats and moved toward Laura.

"Now. Now. Put the toy down and go back to your seat."

Laura flashed her a loving smile, lifted her clown to her shoulder, and patted its back while she rocked it. The class dissolved into giggles. Laura sat placidly, smiling and rocking, until the teacher was almost within arm's reach. Then, she bolted back to her seat, taking her clown with her.

Instead of pursuing her, as Laura had hoped, the teacher chose to ignore the clown. She stumbled as she turned back to her desk and wound up sprawled in the aisle.

The children clapped and laughed and shouted, oblivious to the teacher's being hurt. Tears welled in Miss Glade's eyes as she sat on the floor, embarrassed. Dazedly rubbing her shoulder, she stared straight at Laura, who radiated her most compassionate smile at the fallen teacher.

Miss Glade glared at Laura through her tears as she pulled herself to her feet. She started to go between the rows, back to her desk, but abruptly she stopped and turned in a slow circle, to stare at the laughing children. She seemed confused by the noise. Her china-white face flushed red. Laura became alert. She saw the tightly clenched, trembling hands.

Miss Glade screamed, "Be quiet!"

The children blinked big eyes at her and shuffled around in their seats to face the green chalkboard at the front of the room.

"Just because Laura doesn't know how to act at school is no excuse for the rest of you. When a person has an accident, it is very rude to laugh! You will apologize immediately by saying 'We are sorry, Miss Glade.' . . . All together now."

The class chorused, "We are sorry, Miss Glade."

With yellow chalk, Miss Glade drew a map of Oklahoma.

"Who can tell me what that shape represents?"

Two girls raised their hands, but Laura tuned out their answers. She counted thirty-three children in the class, not including herself. Too many. The room was crowded and hot. The desks were too close together. There was too little space at the side of the room for games. Large cracks ran lightning-fashion down the walls. The dreary institutional green paint was blistered and peeling in places. There were no screens on the large, open windows and flies buzzed about the room.

It was a terrible place. How could her daddy possibly expect her to stay? Why would he want her to? She had been with him all her life. His business associates were her friends. They were men who talked cattle prices and oil shares. How would her daddy like to be locked in this room full of babies all day, five days a week?

Laura searched the room for the "new things to see and

learn" her daddy had talked about. The bulletin board to the right of the chalkboard had a big square of white cardboard. At its top, lettered in black, was "Color Recognition Board," with the name printed opposite the corresponding color. Laura read the list from the bottom: "violet, green, orange, brown, black, blue, yellow, red." On the opposite bulletin board she read: "See Johnny walk" and "tire-fire, rake-cake, cane-plane" from a card. Another card said, "We like to taste it," and had a picture of a big hot dog. All baby stuff. Laura had always been able to read. She could not remember not reading. But because she never spoke, no one knew. Her daddy thought she was pretending when she picked up the papers on his desk or thumbed through a book or a magazine.

That specialist had known what he was about when he said to send her to school. Her daddy would never make her stay if he knew all she could do. But her mother would be the winner if school made her talk. There had to be a way to get out of it.

Miss Glade had written "OKLAHOMA" on the board and was asking different children to come to the front of the room and point out the corresponding letters on a big cardboard circus train above the chalkboard.

It was a stupid exercise. The word was written on the board in plain sight. Maybe the teacher had forgotten to erase it.

Laura hopped up, skipped to the front of the room, and made a clean swipe with a felt eraser across "OKLAHO-MA."

Miss Glade grabbed her and led her back to her desk. "That was not nice! I am losing patience with you." She pushed Laura roughly into her seat and grabbed her jaw, forcing her to look up. "You will not get out of this chair again without permission." She glared at Laura, then turned and moved sideways down the aisle.

The moment her back was turned, Laura was up, stepping over children's ducked heads from desktop to desktop, keeping one desk behind the teacher, following her.

At the front, Miss Glade turned, and startled, walked backwards into the chalk tray, at finding Laura standing on the first desk, grinning, clown in hand.

The children's laughter exploded in the teacher's face. She had to yell to be heard above it.

"Get back to your seat, Laura."

Laura smiled prettily, turned, and hopped over a boy's crouched head to the desk behind.

"Get down! Get down! We don't walk on the furniture like that."

Laura was too quick. She hopped across the aisle and over three more heads before the teacher could squeeze between the rows. Then Laura reversed course, jumping from desktop to desktop across every aisle until she reached the opposite side of the room.

Miss Glade ran behind the desks.

Waiting for her, Laura tap danced on top of the desk, then feet together, hopped—one, two, three—across to the center row and left the teacher cut off in the far aisle.

The class went wild, clapping and laughing, yelling, "Come this way, Laura." The boys were especially enthusiastic. One stood up on his desk and tried to imitate Laura's tap dance. Two other boys joined him and then a little girl at the back of the room.

Laura snapped her fingers for their attention, then hopped to the desk across the aisle and back again. The others followed suit. A chair overturned and a girl jumped back and forth over it. Laura pushed two more chairs into the aisle. A line formed. They played follow the leader.

Miss Glade stood at the front of the room, screaming for attention. She was ignored. She jerked children into their chairs, only to have them pop back up again when she passed.

Laura walked along the desk tops to the front of the room, jumped to the floor, pulled a little girl out of her seat, and made her skip with her. She went down the rows gathering children, and led them once around the room in an Indian whoop dance. Then she relinquished the group to another leader and returned to a perch atop a desk in the center of the room.

Miss Glade was raging. She grabbed the first two children she came to and shook them by their upper arms. She shook them so hard one boy lost his balance and slid to the floor. She dragged him to his feet and slung him toward a seat. He missed it and sprawled over the desk

17

behind. He was hurt, but he picked himself up, grimacing, rubbing his side, and defiantly got back in line.

To the drum of Laura's foot on the hollow sounding desk, the children were stomping out Indian rhythms. They circled around the room, whooping to the pulsating beat.

"Stop it! Stop it! Take your seats immediately."

The stomping children enclosed Miss Glade in their ring. Circling, circling around her. One brave boy broke the hand-chain and danced forward and back from her, venturing a little closer to her each time. Laughing. Stomping forward and back. Laughing. Laughing. Laughing.

Her face seemed to shatter. Laura watched it happen. She raised her clown over her head, lowering it rapidly three times, as if it were a war lance. She was a chief signaling battle to her laughing warriors.

The teacher charged the circling line. Children fell to the floor; others were shoved against the chalkboard tray. Blood spurted from one little girl's nose and her terrified screams silenced the laughter, but Miss Glade did not stop. She rampaged down the line of children slinging some into the green chalkboard on one side and her desk on the other.

Children tumbled, screaming, into the hall. Miss Glade pursued them, yelling, "Get back in the room. Get back in the room. Do you hear me? Get back in the room!"

The rest of the class emptied out into the schoolyard running, terrified. Dodging teachers and curious students pouring into the hall from other classes, the frenzied first graders stampeded toward the schoolyard. Just then, the principal's angry voice boomed over the noise.

"What's going on here?"

Laura jumped down from her desk perch and walked to the window. The little girl with the bloody nose was being dragged by two friends across the playground. A strange teacher headed them off and made the bleeding child sit and put her head on her knees. Her friends kneeled, crying, beside her, pouring out the details of what had happened.

The young teacher shot them a sharp look. "Be careful! Stories like that can hurt people."

The bleeding child jerked her head sideways out of the

teacher's hands. "It's not a story," she cried. "Miss Glade shoved me into the chalk tray."

One friend screeched, "Miss Glade hurt her on purpose. She wanted to hurt all of us. I'll never go back there. Never!"

"We have to go back," the teacher said. "You belong in your own classroom, and we have to stop this nosebleed."

At her window lookout, Laura giggled when the two girls bolted for the gate. The young teacher looked shocked and struggled to keep the bleeding child from following.

"Come back here," the teacher shouted. The runners ignored her and kept going. Suddenly the bleeding child vomited all over both of them, then crumpled toward her, and she scooped her up on one hip and scurried back to the building.

Laughing, Laura waltzed her clown across the room to her seat. She did not mind being in it since she would soon be leaving. The room was no longer her prison. All that was left was to enjoy the show until her daddy came for her.

When the door banged open she started. The young teacher carried the bleeding, begrimed girl and set her on a front desk. The young woman patted and soothed as she bent the little girl forward until her head touched her knees.

"We have to stop that bleeding," she said. "You are ruining your pretty dress."

Her dress looked beyond help to Laura. So did the teacher's.

"You keep your head down, while I run get the school nurse to have a look at you."

The teacher motioned Laura to the front. "You stay with her, and don't let her take her head from her knees. I'll be right back."

The hall noise swallowed the teacher a beat before the slamming door closed out the confusion. The classroom was hushed and scary.

Round, frightened brown eyes peeped at Laura between matted blond curls. Laura, fascinated by the blood, inched closer to the little girl. The only time Laura had had a nosebleed, her mother had fainted before her Nana had taken charge and stopped it.

The girl sniffled. "Don't stare at me!" She dissolved in tears.

Shielding her clown behind her, Laura backed up, dropped to the floor on her belly, and slithered through the blood pool. Tear blinded, the little girl jumped off the desktop, grabbed Laura by the elbow, and helped her stand. She was trying to wipe the blood off Laura, when the school nurse, followed by the young teacher, came into the room.

"What happened?" the teacher asked.

"Laura slipped and fell in the blood," the little girl said as she backed away from the strange nurse. "What are you going to do to me?" she whimpered.

Sensibly, the nurse stopped where she was and held out her arms for the child to come to her. "Come on, Sweetie. We'll stop your nosebleed and clean you up some. Then we'll call your mother to come after you."

The word "mother" brought the little girl flying.

After cautioning Laura to stay in the room, they all left.

With an eye on the door, Laura crawled on hands and knees through the blood pool; she rolled across it twice; and then wiped up every last trace with the hem of her skirt. She rubbed it in her hair and across her face. Her poor daddy would never let her out of his sight again. When he saw her covered with blood he would be ready to tell her mother, and the doctor, and everyone else what to do about school.

She was drawing her clown on the chalkboard when the principal escorted Miss Glade into the room and closed the door behind them. Laura stood very still. She hoped they wouldn't see her.

"Please try to control yourself," the principal said. "Tell me what happened."

Miss Glade was crying. "They were all so good. So good. Until this morning." She looked up and spotted Laura.

The principal followed her gaze and started when he saw the blood. He rushed forward. "Are you hurt?" He bent toward Laura. When she did not speak he stared at her face and looked embarrassed as he recognized her. "You're T.J. Daniels's little girl."

Miss Glade pointed her finger. "It was *her!* She did it!"

The principal's voice was harsh. "Miss Glade, if you ever want to teach again, you'll control yourself."

"She persuaded them to defy me."

The principal stood his ground, shaking her roughly by the shoulder. "How? She can't even talk."

"She made them laugh at me! They all laughed at me!"

He pushed Miss Glade aside and bent anxiously over Laura. "Are you cut somewhere? Did Miss Glade hit you? Are you hurt?"

Laura jerked her neck and head in an exaggerated fashion. She could tell she must look strange by the principal's startled expression.

"Any teacher of mine better not ever hit a poor little deaf-mute thing like you," he said. The principal walked to the door and spoke to someone in the hall.

"Send the school nurse down here immediately, and call Mr. Daniels. Ask him to come after his daughter."

The nurse came. She explained about the other little girl having a nosebleed, and that Laura had fallen in the blood. The nurse pointed to the spot where the blood pool had been and, finding the floor clean, eyed Laura suspiciously.

Laura hugged her clown, ducked her face shyly. She was relieved when the nurse shifted her attention to Miss Glade and asked if she wanted a mild sedative.

From his position behind Miss Glade's chair, the principal frowned at the nurse and motioned her to leave.

"We don't want to muddle our memory with drugs," he said. "There are questions to be answered, accident reports to be made out and signed."

The nurse slipped out quietly.

"We don't want to muddle our memory with drugs," he repeated. "Do we now, Miss Glade?"

She looked as though she would have been grateful for anything to get away from him.

The principal moved around to the side of the desk and looked down at her. "Laura's father will be here shortly. What are we going to tell him?"

The teacher tossed her head defiantly. "Tell him the truth! Tell him his kid is the most evil human being I've ever met!"

"Miss Glade!"

"Tell him that if I were in his place, I'd never close my eyes at night for fear that little monster would burn the house down around me."

"Did you hurt that child?"

Miss Glade glared from the principal to Laura. "No! But I'd like to! I'd like to very much."

"Not in *my* school you won't!"

"You weren't here. You didn't see the way she corrupted the other children."

The principal turned his angry glare to Laura, who was now sitting on the floor. She clasped her shins and gave him a limp smile over her knees.

"Look at her," he said. "Docile as a newborn kitten. The little thing can't even talk."

"She doesn't need to talk."

"I can't see one trait in her that would make your story plausible."

"Because she doesn't want you to see!"

The principal exploded. "A troublemaker must have some quality of leadership! That poor child has almost nothing going for her—except her father's money. The fact is, you lost control of your class."

Miss Glade's voice quivered. "She *made* them laugh at me. From the moment she walked into this room, she set out to undo me."

"If anyone had asked yesterday, I would have said you were one of my most stable teachers. Maybe you need a rest."

"All I need is to be rid of that one child. I'm telling you she's dangerous! No teacher could cope with her," Miss Glade screamed.

"I want you to know, I intend to keep an eye on you."

Miss Glade stood. "I did not *lose* control. That 'pitiful Polly put-on' against the wall over there, *took* it from me. Smooth as could be."

Laura kissed her clown. Miss Glade deserved this calling down for trying to take it.

"Do you expect me to believe a handicapped six-year-old walked in here and took over thirty-four children—without saying a word?"

"You saw the result. My sweet babies running wild in the hall."

"Running from you, Miss Glade. Not from Laura. And

I deeply resent your trying to use that poor mute child as a scapegoat. She can't defend herself."

The teacher collapsed in confusion into her chair.

Laura bit her knee to keep from laughing. The silly woman would never be able to see that her own mind—the pressure she had felt at being laughed at—had defeated her.

Laura made her face look sad for the principal, as though she sensed the unhappiness in the room. When she looked up, her eyes met her daddy's staring at her through the door glass. She knew her expression was perfect. His face went white.

Realizing the others had not seen him, Laura sprang to her feet, so that he could see the blood on her dress before they had a chance to explain. He threw the door open, quickly crossed the room, and grabbed her. She clung to him, wringing out tears. She twisted about to hamper his search for the source of the blood.

"She isn't injured, T.J." the principal said. "Another little girl had a nosebleed, and Laura slipped and fell in the blood."

Her daddy stood her on a desktop and turned her around, checking the blood on the front and back of her dress. "That doesn't look like what happened to me."

Laura held on to his shirt front feigning terror.

He halted his examination and asked, "Are you bleeding, Sweetheart?"

She shook her head.

Her father held her face between his two big hands. "Did somebody hurt you?"

Laura nodded, concentrating all her acting skills on weeping.

"Who hurt you?"

She cast her glance toward the teacher.

Miss Glade jumped up from her chair. "That's a lie! I never touched her."

Laura recoiled and grabbed her father around the neck. His voice was loud.

"I brought you a little happy, trusting girl this morning. All smiles. Ready to love you. I'm called back before noon to find my daughter covered with blood, terrified by the sound of your voice. And you tell me nothing happened?"

Laura turned to look at the teacher.

Miss Glade squared her shoulders, nervously adjusting her dress. She started to speak, but the principal cut her off.

"There was a great deal of confusion in here after Laura came in this morning."

T.J. scowled at the overturned chairs and scattered desks. "It looks like there was a riot."

Despite the principal's efforts to silence Miss Glade, she blurted out, "Laura caused it. She made the other children defy me. She had them all laughing at me."

"Go ahead and tell us how," the principal said, angrily. "Since you are so determined to make a fool of yourself. Just how did that poor little mute child *make* the whole class misbehave?"

"It was her clown. She refused to give me that filthy doll."

The principal stared in disbelief.

"What if they all brought something?" Miss Glade asked defensively. "School is no place for a rag doll."

"I'm more concerned about whether or not this is the proper place for Laura," the principal stated.

Her father ignored him. "Where are the other children?"

"Gone!" Miss Glade howled. "Run away."

The principal hurried to explain. "Most are in the gym with another teacher. Only two little girls left the school grounds."

"Why?"

"I haven't been able to piece it all together yet."

"You can be sure I will!" her daddy said.

"We can't have this kind of confusion here," the principal muttered. "I have to be concerned with the majority. Public school is no place for a mute child."

Laura felt her father's muscles tighten. She knew he hated the word "mute."

The principal looked flustered when there was no response. "If Laura had been able to explain her feelings for the clown," he continued hurriedly, "Miss Glade would probably not have been so intent upon taking it from her."

Her father disliked people who made excuses at her expense.

"If your teacher could not *feel* Laura's attachment, she

24

has no business teaching. Evidently the children understood. That's what happened here, isn't it? They came to her defense."

"That's not what happened at all," Miss Glade screamed. "She manipulated them. She intended to make a fool out of me."

The principal stepped in front of her. "We do have certain rules about toys, T.J."

Miss Glade refused to stay back. She placed herself firmly at his side as she stated, "I'm a good teacher! The children all loved me, until Laura came and deliberately made me a laughingstock!"

The principal shouted "Be quiet, Miss Glade! You lost control. That's the plain truth of it!"

Laura shook from the exchange. When the principal spoke to her daddy, it was in a completely different voice.

"I'm sorry, T.J., but you see the dangers here. Without speech, Laura is defenseless. She needs a more sheltered environment. We don't have the staff to provide it. I cannot accept the responsibility for putting her in a classroom where she might be misunderstood again." He looked sadly at Laura, and back to T.J. "We can't accept her as a student here. For her sake, please don't force the issue."

Her father lifted her off the desktop and headed for the door. "I didn't want to bring her in the first place. It was her mother's idea. Her fancy doctor suggested it."

The principal followed them to the door. "I knew you were a reasonable person."

"I'm also a proud father with friends on the school board."

The principal grimaced. He opened his mouth to say something, but T.J. slammed the door shutting out whatever it was. "To hell with them!" her daddy said to her. "You have *me*, Sweetheart. I can do more for you than all the schools in the damn state."

Real tears rolled down Laura's cheeks. Her daddy loved her.

He held her tightly as he loped across the schoolyard to the pickup. Opening the door, he set Laura on the edge of the seat. He pulled out his handkerchief and began to clean her face. His hand shook as he wiped away her tears.

"Don't cry God only knows what that madwoman did to my poor Baby, but she'll pay for hurting you. I promise you she will. I'll fix it so she'll never get another teaching job."

Laura clapped her hands in the staccato signal she used for "positively no!"

"You don't want me to?"

She clapped again.

Her daddy stroked her tangled hair and kissed her dirty face. "My sweet, forgiving little angel! Straight from heaven, that's where you came from." He slid her across the seat and got in beside her. "Don't you worry about that teacher!" As he pulled away from the curb, he announced, "We are going to forget all about her—and school!"

Laura snuggled close. T.J. did not mean to forget Miss Glade. He was too mad. She knew he would talk to some of the children, but she was not worried. None of them would be able to tell how everything had happened.

The September sun shimmered heat waves off the red-painted hood of the truck. Laura closed her eyes to shut out the brightness. She was tired, and the heat made her sleepy. Her eyelids fluttered shut.

Laura squinted sleepy eyes against the noon sun when her daddy lifted her out of the truck. Carrying her like a baby, he hurried up the sidewalk. On the porch, he smiled down at her.

"We're home, Sweetheart."

Laura bucked, stiff backed, and screamed. Both hands were empty. Her clown was missing.

Her daddy understood. He set her on the step and dashed back to the truck after her clown. Behind her, the wide front door opened, and Carrie waddled out.

"My God," she roared. "What happened?"

T.J. motioned with the clown for Carrie to be quiet.

"Hush!" he said. "Where's Mother?"

"In the kitchen."

Laura grabbed her clown out of his hand and ran for the kitchen. She wanted her Nana. Nana had to see the blood.

T.J. chased her and, giggling, she ran from him.

"Laura! I don't want your Nana to see you like that!"

She stopped at the end of the hall between the stairway and the swinging kitchen door. Scooping her up, her father took the stairs three at a time. Halfway to the top Nana came out of the kitchen.

"T.J.! What is Laura doing home?"

Her daddy rushed ahead, shielding her body so her Nana could not see her dress.

"The school had me come after her," he called, sweeping Laura into her room. He closed the door behind them. "I didn't want your Nana to see you all bloody," he said to Laura. "It'd be bad for her heart."

Laura counted to herself. One. Two. Three. Four. Nana opened the door on five. She saw the bloodstained clothes and quickly knelt to take them off and check for cuts.

T.J. hurried to explain. "She isn't hurt, Mother. At least she isn't cut."

"What happened?"

"They said another little girl had a nosebleed, and Laura slipped in the blood."

Nana examined the dress. "Do you believe that?"

"No! I think her teacher went crazy and rolled her in it. The classroom was torn in pieces. All the children had run away. The principal and her teacher blamed Laura. Asked me not to bring her back."

Suddenly her mother was standing in the doorway. "But you *will* take her back! She's going to go back in the morning."

"No she's not!" her daddy said.

"She is! They can't keep her out."

Her daddy got to his feet, grabbed her mother's wrist, and pulled her closer to Laura. "For God's sake, Kate! Can't you see the blood? Don't you care what's happened to our child?"

Her mother shook her hand free. "I'm sick and tired of her manipulating everybody around here."

Her daddy walked into the bathroom, turned the water on in the tub, and yelled back, "Get out of here, Kate. Laura doesn't need to hear that."

Laura smiled sweetly at her mother.

"The way you two wait on her," her mother said, "she'll never learn to talk. Do you want her to be dependent for the rest of her life?"

Her daddy came to the bathroom door. "You're in one damn big hurry to get Laura out of the nest. What about your precious Harley?"

"He's your son too!"

"Not so I notice it!"

"You're too busy with your daughter."

"Only because you can't cope."

"I'm going to the school, to find out what happened."

"The principal told me not to bring her back. She is not going back to school no matter what you find out."

"We'll see about that!" Her mother slammed the bedroom door, then opened it again to slam it harder.

Her daddy started after her, but Nana caught his arm and stopped him.

"Let her go, T.J."

"She'll make a fool of herself at the school."

"Better there than here, in front of the child. Now what happened this morning?"

"Her teacher tried to take her clown."

Nana's wrinkled hand fluttered to her hair. "Of all the stupid things! The woman should have sensed her dependence on that clown!"

"Evidently she went crazy when Laura wouldn't give it to her. Before school, I tried to get her to give *me* the clown. She wouldn't. I should have known there would be trouble if a teacher tried to take it."

Nana squeezed his arm. "It's over now, and I'm glad. Stupid idea in the first place—sending her to school."

"Kate is going to push it."

" 'Horses don't shy from a snake down the hill.' That's what the Indian used to tell me. You can't worry about what Kate might do. Laura needs at least one parent's love and comfort."

Laura hugged her clown and shivered. She was cold without her clothes, but her fears were even more chilling. She knew that when her mother found out her clown had caused her to be kicked out of school, she would try to take it. That was not shying from a snake down the hill. That was sure fact. Her mother had tried to take her clown before, because it was dirty and worn.

Nana's warm hand pressed against Laura's leg, making Laura jump.

"This child is freezing, T.J. Get her in the tub."

Her daddy scooped her off the bed and tossed her to his shoulder like a sack of flour. Her clown nearly slipped from her fingers. Laura pushed forward to grab.

"Careful, Wiggle Worm." He laughed and plunked her into the tub. Water sloshed onto his pants and the floor.

Laura splashed water in his face. He ducked her and she came up spluttering.

Nana had followed them to the bathroom door. "You're as much a child as she is," Nana said. "Look at the mess you're making."

"Go away, Mother. I'll clean it up."

"Wash that blood out of her hair. Be sure to rinse it good."

"Yes'um. We'll be starving, time we're finished here."

Laura knew he had said that so Nana would leave and they could play together.

"I'll fix a tray," Nana said, bustling across the bedroom, picking up and straightening as she went. From the hallway she shouted over their laughter, "T.J., that child has had enough excitement for one day."

He grabbed the soap and a rag, worked a lather, and applied it to her skin hard enough to have made Harley holler "uncle." Laura was not about to yell. She clamped her teeth together, froze a smile on her face, and let her daddy scrub her until she was beet red all over. Finally he took pity and eased up.

"Wish your big brother had some of your grit!"

After that he was tender with her as he poured shampoo on her head and worked the shampoo into stiff peaks and styled it into fantastically high swirls on her head.

Laura laughed and kissed him. Her daddy loved her, and she loved him more than anything.

Her daddy lifted her to her knees while he rinsed her hair. He dried it, lifted her out of the tub, and fashioned the towel into a sarong around her.

"And now you are a South Sea Island princess."

He led her to her bed and then started cleaning up the mess. Laura hung her head off the edge of the bed to watch him. They were happy together. Always happy. He loved her; he would never take her clown. Her clown—

Laura tumbled off the bed, ran to the bathroom.

"We better leave him in the tub, Sweetheart. Until he dries."

Laura clapped her hands "no."

"You're home now. No one is going to take him from you."

Laura nodded.

"Your mother does things we don't like, but she wouldn't do that. She wouldn't take your clown. He belongs to you."

Laura nodded again. Her mother *would* take her clown! Her daddy must have understood, because he held her clown over the tub, squeezed it as dry as he could, and gave it to her.

Nana carried a tray full of food into the bedroom. Her father invited Nana to eat with them, but she said she had work to do and went back downstairs.

Halfway through the meal, her mother burst into the room. She glared contemptuously at their party.

"Laura makes us a laughingstock and instead of giving her what she deserves, you reward her."

"She deserves a loving mother."

"Why did you let her take that stupid clown into the schoolroom?" She didn't give him a chance to answer. "She has carried that filthy thing long enough! I tried to get rid of it before, but Carrie gave it back to her. This time I'm going to burn it. Give it to me, Laura."

Laura clutched her clown and scrambled into the bathroom. She slammed and locked the door behind her. Her mother shook the knob.

"You're going to give me that clown. You're too big to play with toys like that. You're taking advantage of us all."

Laura dropped to her knees and looked through the keyhole. She could only see her parents' hands and bodies. She saw her daddy jerk her mother away from the door.

"You're being ridiculous, Kate. Let things cool down."

"Just leave and let me handle this," her mother said.

Her daddy did not budge. Instead, he knocked on the bathroom door. "Open it, Sweetheart."

Laura trusted him. She turned the lock as he spoke to her mother.

"I promised Laura her clown was safe in this house. You will honor that promise, Kate, or there'll be some drastic changes around here."

"I want to talk to you in private." She stormed out. He frowned, following her into the hall.

Laura was disappointed to be excluded from their conversation. Her clown was curious to know what they said. Listening near the door, she heard her mother's voice, tight with anger. "Damn it! Can't you see that child is using you?"

"Better that than taking her security toy, badgering her about talking, and all the other idiocies you've tried."

Laura heard two pairs of running feet on the stairs and Harley's excited voice.

"Is it true what I heard at school? That Laura led the other kids against Miss Glade. That they tore up the classroom and she got expelled?"

Her mother's voice, loud and angry. "See there, T.J.? That's a lot closer to the truth than your version. Children tell things as they are."

"We've all been sent home early because of her," Harley said.

Anxious to see if Reming had come upstairs with Harley, Laura peeked around the door. It was Reming. He had stopped near the head of the stairs. Clutched under his arm was the old battered shoebox, tied with dirty string, that he carried everywhere. Leaning there against the wall, he was watching T.J. with that familiar adoring expression that always made Laura anxious for T.J. to notice him.

Her clown was angry because T.J. had his back to them, and they couldn't see his face. Laura knew though that he wasn't paying attention to Reming. Just then he had all he could manage with her mother, who looked as angry as Laura had ever seen her. Really angry! Yet her hand caressed Harley's upturned cheek. Harley's eyes were shining.

"All of a sudden, everyone at school wants to be my friend."

Laura knew Harley didn't have many friends. She knew why. He was too bossy and mean. Only Reming seemed to be able to tolerate him.

"The kids say Laura's a witch," Harley said. "They're saying she has magic powers."

T.J. laughed. "You're right, Kate. Children tell things as they are. Witches. And magic. Powerful stuff."

"I don't see anything funny!"

"Nothing to get so upset about, either. It's just kids' gossip."

"And if the children are talking, what will their parents say?"

Harley edged forward as though eager to get back into the conversation.

"This morning when it happened, our teacher went to see about the big commotion in the hall. She came back and told the class that a little girl had gone berserk in the first grade. I didn't know she was talking about Laura."

"Doesn't matter now," her mother said. "True or not, it will be all over town. I'll never be able to face my friends again."

She hurried, crying, to her room. Laura was more than a little disgruntled when her daddy followed. Why didn't he just let her steam.

Laura retreated to her bookshelf. Harley and Reming were headed for her door. Harley rushed at her, landing a playful punch on her shoulder.

"You're a hit, Little Sister. One day in school and you're famous. Everyone thinks you're a witch, and I told them you surely were and they better not cross me or you'd put a spell on them."

Laura forced a smile. Harley was just like her mother, trying to use people to gain his own ends. She ran to the bed, fashioned the bedspread into a witch's cape, and swooped around the room.

The look on Reming's face stopped her, made her feel as if she had pulled her panties off in church. She let the bedspread fall to the floor.

"I brought my soldiers. Want to play war?" Reming asked her softly.

Laura had always been excluded from their war game. She had watched the two boys play hour after hour, arranging and rearranging the tin soldiers Reming carried in his shoe box, acting out make-believe battles. Harley was the one who never wanted her to play. He always tried to chase her off, and she kicked him when she could; she would scream until Reming picked out the prettiest soldier and gave it to her to play with.

The soldier he gave her was the smallest one and carried a drum instead of a rifle. Most of the red and blue paint was still on his uniform because the boys did not play with him often. He had an empty hole through his upraised fist where he was supposed to be holding a drumstick.

That missing stick always brought pictures to Laura's mind. Pictures of a dark-haired little girl about her size who had broken the stick out because the drummer boy would not be quiet. The little girl had been sorry after she broke it and had tried to put it back, but it would not stay. It kept falling out, and for safe keeping she had hidden the stick in a scooped-out place under a rock.

Laura could feel the girl hiding the drumstick. Feel the smoothness of the rock as she rolled it away. Feel the damp earth under it. Digging. Dirt under fingernails. All feelings—surrounded by darkness. Someday she would find the stick and return it to the little drummer boy. But only if he would promise not to make too much noise on his drum.

She felt a need to be with the little drummer. He had become her special friend. Laura was glad when Reming sat cross-legged on the floor and dumped the contents of the battered shoe box. She spotted the drummer the moment he tumbled out. Grabbing him, she retreated to her bed, where she sat smiling and shaking her head at Reming's invitation to command his whole company.

At any other time she would have been eager to command, to move the soldiers anywhere she wanted them; but she was tired and sleepy, and she did not feel like playing with Harley. He talked so much it made her head hurt. She wondered how Reming could stand being around him all the time.

With effort she managed to tune Harley's droning voice out and sat rocking her little drummer, daydreaming about the time she would return his missing stick and how happy it would make him.

She had heard Reming tell Harley that the soldiers had belonged to his grandfather. It was hard to believe the scary old medicine man had played with her little drummer when he was new and shiny, long before the little girl had broken his stick. A child then, the old man must have looked something like Reming did now—tall for his age, with smooth olive skin. But she could only picture the old man the way he had looked—mean and menacing—when he threatened her on the porch. "I can call you back," he had said. "Call you back and punish you." Crazy old devil man. What was he talking about?

When it was time for Reming to go home, he asked her if she was ready for her soldier to rejoin his company. He never let her keep the toy overnight. The drummer was part of his set, and he liked to keep them together.

Sometimes, for pure meanness, because he was so close to Harley, she ignored him. He would wait patiently until she was ready to give the drummer up. Reming never grabbed things away from her. He was very kind and quiet. He seldom talked, but when he did, what he said meant something. He never chattered like Harley.

This time Laura gave up the little drummer immediately when Reming asked for him. After all, he had invited her to command his troops. She smiled when she handed the drummer back to him, hoping he would let her play with it again. His smile said he would.

As soon as the boys left her room, Laura crawled into bed with her clown. Her new popularity felt warm and nice. She went to sleep thinking about her little drummer, who belonged to a company even though his drumstick was missing. As sleep overtook her, she tried desperately to hear what her clown was saying. Something about soon she would have her own company made up of her daddy, and Nana, and Carrie, and Reming.

Sometime later Laura was awakened by an uneasy sense of present danger. Her door was open. A figure stood silhouetted against the hall light. She hugged her clown to make sure she was not dreaming. She knew she was awake when she felt the clown's cool dampness. It still hadn't dried from being in the tub with her.

Her mother turned on the table lamp. Laura blinked and pushed the clown under her back to get it out of her mother's sight. Kate's night-bird eyes peering over the lamp made Laura shiver. She was more dangerous than any bird. Her mother could fly to pieces at the slightest provocation. Laura was afraid for her clown, but it was laughing at Kate for sneaking around.

The night-bird eyes closed, then opened slowly. "I won't give you an excuse to scream for your father. All I want are answers."

Laura forced her friendliest smile. Her clown snickered.

"Miss Glade said you walked on desks and made the other children defy her. She said everything you did was intended to make them laugh at her. Is that true?"

Laura hesitated, wondering what her mother hoped to gain. She probably had a plan, but her clown was laughing so hard it made Laura feel reckless. She nodded.

"Miss Glade believes you can talk, and maybe even read. She said she saw your eyes moving left to right when you looked at the bulletin boards. Can you talk?"

Her mother was up to something. Her mother leaned toward her over the lamp and whispered, *"Can* you talk, Laura?"

From under her back, her clown was chanting, *Tell the truth. Tell the truth.*

Laura nodded.

Her clown's chant changed to *The truth will kill her. The truth will kill her.*

"I don't understand you. Why won't you talk?"

Laura traced an arc with her arm and brought her extended finger level with her mother's chest. She sighted down her arm, pointing at a spot between her mother's breasts.

"You hate me, don't you?" asked her mother.

Laura smiled. Her mother knew the answer to that.

"What if I tell your father what you've admitted to me? How would you like that?"

Her clown whispered that her daddy would never believe her. Laura nodded enthusiastically. Her clown was right. Her daddy would never believe her mother and both of them knew it. Kate whirled, headed for the door, then turned and spoke softly to Laura. "I'll fight you with all the strength I have. For your own good."

Laura smiled. Her mother did not care about Laura's good. She only cared about herself and Harley. But Laura's clown cared about Laura and hated the other two. It would never let them get the best of her. Harley was the only one who would believe her mother. Nana, Carrie, and her daddy would call her mother on anything she said about Laura. Her mother, like Miss Glade, was defeated and did not have sense enough to see that her own weaknesses would be the weapons turned against her.

"You can't win," her mother said. "I don't know what you are fighting for, but you'll never win over me."

After her mother left the room, Laura counted to three, took a deep breath, and screamed. She screamed again. Kept screaming until her daddy was at her bedside.

Frantically, she thrust her clown into his hands as if putting it there for safe keeping. She pointed accusingly at her mother, who stood—amazed—in the open doorway.

Her daddy looked sleepy and stunned. He seemed not to understand. Laura hopped out of bed and pantomimed her mother trying to take her clown.

"That's a lie!" Her mother hissed. She sounded as guilty as Miss Glade had.

Her daddy tucked Laura back in bed and placed her damp clown beside her. "If your clown comes up missing, Baby Girl, so will all the checkbooks in this house."

Her mother looked as if she wanted to hit him. "I'd just go to the bank and get a new one."

"Not if the account was closed."

"If you humiliate me with a stunt like that, I'll divorce you, take the ranch and everything you have."

"The ranch is Mother's. You can't touch it. And you are a stranger here."

"After ten years?"

"Folks stick by home boys. I'd get both children; you'd be lucky to get fifty dollars a month alimony."

"You're bluffing."

"Try me!"

Her mother ran to her room crying. She slammed the door, sliding the bolt home so hard they heard the wood splinter.

Laura moved her clown to the opposite side of the bed, near the wall, and slid over to make room for her daddy. He was so warm and comforting she went right to sleep and dreamed that T.J. and she were married and kept her mother locked in a tiny room in the unused servants' apartments, where she and her clown could torment her whenever they were bored.

The next morning a crowing rooster woke Laura at dawn. She left her daddy sleeping, climbed out of bed, and tripped downstairs, with her clown, to visit Nana and Carrie. They were always up before daylight.

She was about to push through the swinging kitchen door when she heard Carrie's voice, loud and angry.

"People like her always get their way. She *needs* another baby! For us to raise just as we do the other two while she's off playing tennis and golf or tanning herself at the club."

Laura snatched her hand away from the swinging door. She knew they would stop talking if she went in.

"It takes two, you know," Nana said. "T.J. would never consider having another baby. Not with all the problems they're having now."

"She'll trick him. You wait and see. It's become an obsession with her."

"I can't understand it. She can't cope with the children she has, much less another one."

"I'm sure she's not thinking about the baby. Because of the way she treats Laura, her hold on T.J. is slipping every day. What she wants is more insurance."

"There are easier ways. She could start by being more of a wife."

"I don't think she has those kinds of feelings for him. Never has."

"Surely she did in the beginning."

"Not that I could see. Seemed she wanted the status more than him."

Laura heard a chair pushed back from the table, followed by Nana's voice.

"Since when have we stooped to gossiping before breakfast? It's up to them to work it out. None of our business." There was a pause, then Nana said, "I have to give Kate credit. I honestly believe she has tried to do what she thought was best for Laura."

"The love was missing. Has been from the beginning."

"To be fair about it, I'd have to say Laura was the one who did the rejecting. Her mother tried hard with her when she was first born. The child just never liked her. That has always been a puzzle to me."

The familiar creak of the upstairs banister made Laura realize that someone was watching her. She looked up to find her mother, in robe and slippers, leaning against the rail. Her mother knew Laura had been eavesdropping.

Laura could tell by the disapproving look on her face. Laura smiled and waved, amused by the thought of the hell that would have broken loose if her mother had overheard what Carrie had said. Her mother and Carrie had always been at odds. Carrie made it no secret that she did not approve of the way her mother treated her daddy.

Laura bowed low to her mother, pushed through the kitchen door, and almost collided with Nana, who grabbed and hugged her.

"My Baby Girl is up early this morning. Ready for breakfast?"

Laura nodded. Nana spooned three saucer-sized pancakes onto the griddle. "Go wake your daddy for breakfast. It will be on the table time you get back."

Laura left her clown propped safely in her chair. Her mother would never dare to take her clown from the kitchen with Nana and Carrie guarding it.

Her mother's door was closed, and she was nowhere in sight when Laura went to wake her daddy. Climbing the stairs, she laughed aloud thinking about her mother's expression on finding her eavesdropping. Her mother could look superior if she wanted. She was the one who had slept alone last night, while T.J. was with Laura.

Her daddy slept with her for over a week before her mother even spoke to him. Those were happy days for Laura, because her mother didn't speak to her either. No lectures about talking, no punishments for hiding. Laura was able to do exactly as she pleased, which meant going everywhere with her daddy. They were together day and night. During working hours he introduced her as "My Business Associate, keeper of the keys and checkbook."

Some of his business associates remarked on Laura's attachment to her clown at her age, but her daddy told her not to pay attention to people like that. Even so, Laura knew that someday even her daddy would think she was too big to carry her clown. She could feel that time creeping up on her, and she was frightened. Her clown only laughed. It said the power was all hers anyway.

From then on she was careful about letting strangers see her clown. She intended to protect it as long as she could. It was a marvel at coming up with ideas to torment her mother. It was her clown that had insisted she carry the checkbook that her daddy had entrusted her with in her front shirt pocket every evening for her mother to see.

From the look on her mother's face it was clear that she did not mind the rift with T.J. half as much as she minded seeing Laura with his checkbook. Laura made sure to keep it in her pocket all during supper.

She did not understand exactly why it upset her mother so. But her clown thought it was funny, and Laura did not trouble her head about the reason.

After supper her daddy always changed her title from Business Associate to Lady Friend. "There is a good movie on television tonight, Lady Friend," he would say. "Want to snuggle with me?"

At bedtime, she became his Baby Girl, and he read to her until they were sleepy, then hugged her until she fell asleep.

Just when Laura was beginning to believe it would last—that her daddy was exclusively hers—her mother destroyed her dream.

It was Saturday night. Her daddy's night off from reading stories. Instead, he let her stay up with him to watch the late movie on television. They had curled up on the couch to watch. Usually she was bright-eyed until the last flicker on the television screen; but the movie was boring, and she began to drowse. She was almost asleep when her mother appeared in the doorway.

At first Laura thought she was having a nightmare. Since the big fight, her mother had not been in the same room with them except for meals. Now, not only had her mother sought them out, she was barefoot. Laura had never before seen her barefoot. She always wore a robe over her nightgown, and that was missing, too. Her nightgown looked new. Yards and yards of filmy blue material gathered to a ribbon that circled her waist, crossed between her breasts, and formed straps over her bare shoulders. It was exactly like a picture of the Greek temple dancer that hung in the study. It was T.J.'s favorite picture.

T.J. forgot about the movie. He kept his eyes on her mother. Kate turned, smiled briefly at the two of them, sat down opposite them, and began to buff her fingernails. Laura took her smile as a declaration of war. Behind her, T.J. barely breathed. He watched her mother as she drew her long legs onto the cushion and casually slipped her gown further up her thigh. Laura strained to see in the half-light. Her mother was naked under the gown. Why? Even more puzzling was her daddy's reaction to it. She felt him shift his position. He seemed to feel uncomfortable with her being snuggled next to him.

Suddenly he asked, "What do you want, Kate?"

Her mother whispered, "You," without taking her eyes off her hands. "Take Laura up to bed."

Laura pressed closer to her daddy, moaning in protest. He patted her stomach, absently.

"I'd like to pretend it really is *me* you want, Kate."

"Hurry and take Laura to bed."

"Kate, if I thought you were doing this purely for my pleasure, I'd be the happiest man in the world."

"Why else would I be doing it?"

"You want a baby."

Laura felt as if she had been slugged in the stomach.

Her mother smiled. "That's no secret."

"And tonight is the night to make babies. Your temperature is up?"

"I haven't taken it."

Her mother was lying. Laura was sure of it, but she was not sure what the lie meant. What did her temperature have to do with babies? Surely her daddy had heard the lie in her voice.

"Stay right where you are," he said, "while I put Laura to bed."

Her daddy stood up and scooped her off the couch. She clung to him. Maybe he hadn't heard the lie. Something bad was happening. Her mother was playing some horrible trick on both of them. Carrie had predicted that she would. Laura wanted to kick her.

"Good night, Laura. Sleep tight."

He carried her upstairs, whistling her favorite tune. Her daddy seemed happier than ever. She could feel his excitement—the lightness of his step. His eyes were shining.

The hurried way he put her in bed beside her clown

made her feel like an orphan. She remembered what her mother had said about fighting her. Maybe winning her daddy for good was going to be harder than she had thought.

"Sleep tight, Sweetheart," he said and flipped the light out. She listened to him pad back down the stairs to the living room. He was in a hurry to get back to her mother.

She heard the click of the television being turned off. Her mother giggled—a high-pitched, false sound. Her mother never giggled. It had to do with her daddy threatening to take her checkbook. And that had something to do with her wanting a baby. But that did not make sense. She was the only baby her daddy had. Her clown was being strangely silent about the whole business.

Laura heard the front door lock snap. Her daddy always locked it the last thing before he came upstairs at night. He was laughing now. Laughing as though he and her mother had never been angry with each other. The marble floor distorted and amplified the sound. It became a demon's laugh, mocking her for believing she had her daddy all to herself.

Her mother giggled again. "Stop it, T.J. You'll wake your mother and Carrie."

"They know we're married. They'll be glad you remembered."

"I've never forgotten for a moment." Her mother sounded breathless, wheedling. "I thought maybe you'd come to me."

Laura ground her teeth together. Something crazy was going on. Her mother liked to fight. She never backed down from a fight. The evening was full of discarded nevers.

How could her daddy toss her in bed to rush back to her mother? Her mother did not love him. She did! Her mother was using him. She was probably going to try to persuade him that they should have another baby.

Laura was sure he would not want a baby. *She* was the baby. It would be terrible having a baby in the house. Her daddy was kind. He would have to pay attention to it, as he did to Harley. And that would mean he would have less time for her.

Once her mother got her daddy into the bedroom and

closed the door, she would not be able to hear what was said. Her mother was full of tricks. She would do anything to get her way.

Clown in hand, Laura slipped out of bed and tiptoed across her room and down the dark hall. She peeked down the stairs. Her parents were at the bottom, coming up. They did not see her. Her daddy had his arm around her mother's shoulders and was whispering in her ear. Laura slid past the stairs, and crossed the hall to the dark side. If they looked up they could see her, but they were too engrossed in each other.

She felt her way along the wall, keeping her eyes on them. Her daddy traced the neckline of her mother's gown with one finger. Her mother giggled. That fake giggle. *Couldn't her daddy hear it?*

Laura reached their bedroom door. It was half open. She eased around it. The bedside lamp was on, the top sheet turned down. She could feel her parents approaching. Her clown was urging her to hurry as she looked frantically for a place to hide. Her mother's closet door was open. As they came into the room she eased behind her mother's long evening dresses. If either one of her parents had been looking, she would have been caught. It was too close.

Through the crack of the closet door, she heard the bedroom door being shut. She saw her daddy unbutton his shirt. Laura picked up one of her mother's high-heeled shoes and set it gently on top of its mate to give her more standing room. She moved very slowly, concentrating on making her movement smooth. She and her clown were hiding. The closet door, directly opposite the foot of the king-size bed, was wide open. Her only concealment was the thin material of her mother's dresses and the closet shadow, but she was not afraid. Getting in and out was the hard part. Hiding was easy. She and her clown could stay there for hours without making noise.

Laura made a peep hole through the clothes. Her mother was sitting on the edge of the bed. She looked pretty in the pale blue gown. Her mother took great pains with her makeup. Usually she took her makeup off, put cold cream on her face, and rolled her hair before she went to bed. But she was not doing it tonight.

T.J. noticed it too. "You look lovely, Kate. Without all that junk on your face."

Her mother smiled her "best actress" smile and switched out the light. Laura was disappointed. Luckily the night light cast enough light.

It occurred to Laura that her daddy might close the closet door. She always had him close her closet door. When left open at night the shadow shapes inside made her have nightmares. Laura felt relieved when he stretched out beside her mother without closing the closet.

Her mother rolled on her side, put her arms around her daddy's neck, and kissed him. She was playacting. Softening her daddy up so he would buy her a baby. Her clown whispered something about her mother having trapped her daddy the same way before, but Laura only half paid attention.

The kiss lasted a long time. She could tell that her daddy was enjoying it. Her mother appeared not to feel anything. Her movements were practiced and mechanical like the dancing doll on top of Carrie's music box. She broke away and sighed. The sound grated on Laura's senses. Laura pushed it out of the way and tuned her ears, expecting her mother to whisper something syrupy about happiness and sweet little babies. Nothing was said. She seemed to be waiting for T.J. to say something.

He was pulling the hem of her nightgown up. "Take that off, Kate."

Her mother slid off the bed, tossed the gown on a chair, and slid back into his arms. They kissed again, and the next several minutes were filled with sounds: rustling sheets, unintelligible murmurs and moans.

Her daddy kept changing positions. He seemed to be all over the bed, while her mother stayed on her back. Whatever her daddy was doing, it was clear that he liked it much more than her mother did. She was tolerating him.

Laura felt like rushing out of the closet and making him stop. If he wanted to tussle, she would play with him. She liked to play with him. He finally rolled from her mother.

"Talk to me, Kate. Tell me what *you* need."

She would ask him about a baby now, for sure. Laura held her breath, easing her clown up her body until their faces were side by side—watching.

Her mother did not move. She had one arm across her eyes, the other straight at her side. Both hands were clenched.

"I don't *need* anything!"

Her voice was so cold, Laura felt sorry for her daddy.

"If you'd only try. I'd do anything—"

"Just give me a baby, T.J."

Laura strained to see exactly what was happening, but all she could see was her mother's knees and her daddy's bottom moving between them. Something made her feel uncomfortable. She wanted to look away, but she could not.

Finally he took a deep breath and held it. Then he groaned softly. He stretched out on top of her mother, and she patted his back three times. Then he whispered, "I'm sorry, Kate," and rolled over to his own side of the bed.

Laura squeezed her clown tightly. It was quiet in her arms, seemingly as shocked as she was by what they had seen.

A few moments later, her daddy started snoring. She saw her mother sit up in bed. She called his name twice, but he only snored louder. Her mother began clicking her thumb and fingernails together, the way she always did when she was angry. Finally, she got up, went into the bathroom, and slammed the door. Her daddy moaned and turned over.

Laura clamped her clown under her arm, slipped quietly out of her hiding place, and eased the bedroom door open. It squeaked like a frightened rat. Something dropped in the bathroom. Quickly, Laura squeezed around the door, pulling it shut behind her. The latch snapped as loudly as a Halloween cricket. She heard the bathroom door open and flew down the hall to her room.

She jumped into bed, stuffed her clown safely under the cover, and turned to face the wall. She had stilled her breathing to simulate sleep by the time her mother came to stand in her doorway. Finally, her mother went away. Laura giggled under the blanket. But her clown was not laughing. It was as serious as Laura had ever known it to be.

After that night, her mother underwent an enormous change. She became quiet and withdrawn, ended phone calls abruptly, and spent most of her time lying quietly on her bed.

Much to Laura's delight, her daddy's visits to her mother's room stopped completely. For several weeks he tried. At bedtime he would knock on her door and receive a "no" or total silence. After the rejection he would come to Laura's room. She had him to herself once again.

One night, after her mother had locked him out, he was particularly sad. Laura sat up in bed and hugged him tightly until she felt her neck wet. She looked up and found him crying. He started to leave, but Laura held onto his pajama top, and he lay down beside her.

"Seven years ago a lady died," he said, half-choking. "And I am feeling sorry for her, and myself, and you. If she had lived, I wouldn't be with your mother now. We would have divorced years ago, and I would have married the other lady, as I should have in the first place." He turned his back to Laura.

She wanted to hear more—the lady's name and what she had looked like—but her daddy would not say another word, even though she shook him, trying to get him to talk, until her clown told her to stop. Her clown said she was acting like her mother and that her daddy needed to be left alone.

Laura left him alone, hoping that he would tell her more the next morning. But the next morning he acted embarrassed and told her to forget what he had said, that they both had to make the best of the situation they were in now.

He had gone off to work then, and left Laura daydreaming about how nice it would be to have a new mother. One who did not try to make her talk, or to trick her daddy into giving her a baby.

There was no more talk of babies from Carrie and Nana, or anyone. Laura figured her mother must have been angry or sick about not getting her baby, because she began to take her meals in her room, alone.

The only person her mother wanted near her was Harley. He visited her room every afternoon after school. Their laughter could be heard all over the house. Once Laura, eager to join in their fun, had marched into the room behind him. He, very promptly, had pushed her out.

When her mother did not stop him, Laura made a face at both of them.

After that Laura did not see her mother for a month. Nor did she miss her. Nana and Carrie and her daddy were busy with Christmas: cutting a tree, putting up decorations, shopping. It was the most exciting time of the year on the ranch, and Laura trailed a sack of Christmas candy everywhere she went, passing it out to ranch hands and horses alike.

Her mother came downstairs briefly on Christmas morning with her robe all bunched up in front of her. She kept clutching her belly. And she went back to her room without opening her presents or showing even the slightest interest in Harley's reaction to his gifts. That had always been important to her. Her place at the table was empty during the family feast. But Laura was now used to her being absent from meals, and she herself ate so much and had such a good time that she hardly noticed.

During the months following Christmas, Laura, with her clown, observed mysterious comings and goings to her mother's room. Dr. Edwards came once a week, sometimes more often. Nana and Carrie took up special trays and carried medicine in between meal times. Once or twice Laura tried to open the door, but her mother kept it locked.

Other than being a little curious, Laura had never been happier, her daddy more attentive. They spent long, toasty evenings in front of the fire. She liked to put her head on his chest where she could listen to his heart beat, and he would sing a sad, silly song for her about a lady in a long black dress. In the spring they took long morning walks, and her daddy pointed out signs of new life, telling her Indian stories about why fawns have spots and where June bugs come from.

Just as Laura was beginning to have faith in their future together, her mother appeared at the breakfast table on Easter morning, her stomach preceding her, her skin a pale yellowish color.

To Laura's annoyance, Nana and her daddy both rushed to her mother's side. Nana took her arm. "Are you well, Kate?"

Her daddy held a chair for her. "You know you shouldn't come down alone."

Laura smashed her cinnamon roll with her fist.

After Easter her mother appeared daily. Each day she looked uglier and more grotesque than the day before. It was as though the last few happy months had never happened. The bigger her mother's stomach swelled, the more irritable she became, and the more determined to make Laura talk.

She denied Laura her treats. Because she would not say "ice cream," there was no ice cream in the afternoon. Because she would not say "cookie," there were no cookies at bedtime.

In the sewing room one sunny April afternoon, her mother emptied a thread spool. Laura reached for it. Her mother held it away.

"Say 'spool,' Laura."

Laura glared and considered carefully what she was about to do, how lovely her world had been before, and how ugly it had become with her mother's return. Now, maybe, just maybe, she had it in her power to send her mother away again. She stood up, squared her shoulders, and looked her in the eye.

"Kate, you are a fat pig!"

She closed her eyes in self-satisfaction. To her shock and horror, instead of being angry, her mother was delighted. Her fat stomach brushed against Laura, making her shudder, as Kate grabbed her hand and hauled her into the kitchen.

"Tell Nana what you said, Laura."

Laura smiled impishly.

"Say it, Laura. Tell Nana what you said to me."

Nana dusted flour off her hands and bent down, giving her granddaughter her full attention. "Tell Nana what you said, Baby Girl."

Laura swiped across Nana's floured dough board and printed a perfect five-fingered pattern in the middle of her mother's protruding belly.

Nana grabbed her hand and wiped it with the dish towel. "Now, now. That wasn't nice." She brushed the hand print off the front of her daughter-in-law's smock.

Inexplicably her mother was crying, hugging Nana around the neck. "She can talk. Laura can really talk. There's nothing wrong with her."

Tears rolled down her mother's face, but she was laughing. "I honestly thought she was retarded."

"This baby is the brightest thing ever born in this family. How could you doubt it?"

"I believe it now."

"What did she say?"

"She said, 'Kate, you are a fat pig!' "

Nana stared. Then stammered. "Now, Daughter. She's smart. I know. But I think you're overexcited. You want her to talk so badly that—" Nana stopped, and started over. "The child has never spoken a single word. I never heard of a baby starting out with all of that. You must be mistaken."

"She said it. She did! Tell her, Laura. Say 'Kate, you are a fat pig.' "

Nana had broken it up then and sent Laura outside to play with Harley.

Thereafter, Laura had a new game, one she liked to play even more than hide and listen. Once each day, when they were alone, she spoke a whole sentence to her mother.

The response was always the same. Her mother grabbed her hand and whisked her off to find another adult for her to repeat it to. Laura never did.

One afternoon at the beginning of summer, she and her mother had been napping together on a narrow day bed on the south sun porch. It was hot and sticky, and Laura dreamed that Harley had her pinned down in her sand box.

She awoke, feeling herself wedged uncomfortably against the wall, with her mother's big stomach pressing in the middle of her chest. She tapped on it as she had seen her daddy test watermelons. It had the same ripe, hollow sound.

Her mother half opened her eyes.

Laura leaned closer and whispered, "Why don't you poot and let the air out?"

The big belly began to jiggle up and down.

"What?"

Laura became much more emphatic. "Poot, Kate! Why don't you poot? And let all that air out!"

Her mother laughed so hard she rolled off the daybed and sat on the floor, still laughing.

Nana ran in, followed by Carrie. Together, one on each side, they lifted her mother back up onto the day-bed and stood in front of her to keep her from falling off again.

For a long time she laughed so hard she could not talk. Finally, she stammered what Laura had said.

Carrie looked at Nana and shook her head. Neither one laughed.

Her mother glanced from one to the other, awaiting their response. Nothing. She repeated the account word for word, then her voice trailed off at the end into silence.

Nana patted Kate's shoulder. "It has been so hot," she said solicitously. "You had a dream, dear."

Her mother slapped Nana's hand away. "It wasn't a dream."

Laura did not like the sound of her mother's voice or the way she hit at Nana.

"The child can talk," her mother said. "You don't believe me, but it's true. The child can talk as well as any of us." She reached behind her and jerked Laura off the bed. "Say it! Tell them what you said to me."

Laura had never seen her mother so angry, but she was not frightened, although she pretended to be.

Again her mother ordered her to tell them what she had said.

Laura looked pitifully from Nana to Carrie and back to Nana. When she did not speak her mother squeezed her hand, crushing the knuckles together. She whimpered, and Nana stepped in and tried to free Laura from her mother's grip.

Her mother pushed Nana away and squeezed harder.

"Say it, Laura. Say 'Poot, Kate! Why don't you poot? And let all that air out.' Say it!"

The pain in Laura's hand was so terrible that her knees buckled and she dropped to the floor. But she was determined that her mother would never *make* her talk.

"Say 'Poot, Kate! Poot, Kate!' " her mother screamed.

The pain was unbearable. Laura screamed.

Nana pulled at her mother's squeezing fingers with both hands. "Stop it, Kate. Can't you see you are hurting the poor baby. Turn loose of her hand."

Carrie locked her flabby arms around her mother's chest and tugged.

Her mother hung on tenaciously. "Say it, Laura," she said. "Say 'Poot, Kate!'" She dug her long thumbnail into Laura's middle finger. Blood oozed.

Nana stopped trying to break her mother's grip and slapped her hard across the mouth. The blow knocked her off balance long enough for Carrie to throw her weight forward and pin her onto the daybed.

Laura escaped and ran from the terrible commotion behind her.

Everything was different after that. Her mother tried to make up to her, but she shied away, remembering the pain in her hand and the frenzied look on her mother's face. The game was ruined, too, because now they were never alone together. Nana was always there, or Carrie.

Two weeks after the incident on the sun porch, her mother went away for a few days. Nana told her that her mother would have a surprise for her when she came home. Laura went into hiding to think about what the surprise might be.

She guessed that it would be something to get her to talk. Probably a piece of fancy equipment, like the tape recorders she had seen in the specialist's office. Her mother would love to grill her through some stupid exercise for hours each day. She was not about to stand for that any more than she had intended to stay in school. Machines could be broken. If her mother brought her a present like that, it would *stay* broken.

The day her mother came home Laura was making mud pies in the flower bed beside the front porch. She looked up and saw the Cadillac pull into the circle drive. Her mother was on the passenger side. Her daddy was driving. Her mother always insisted that her daddy drive her big fancy car instead of his pickup, when she went places with him. Her daddy slowed to a stop at the end of the sidewalk. Laura scooped up a handful of red mud and skipped toward the car. She smiled and waved. Watching her daddy through the tinted glass, Laura drew back to throw. He gasped, swallowing a smile, before he motioned for her to stop.

Her mother had not seen their exchange. She was too engrossed in something wrapped in a pink blanket that she held tightly clasped to her chest.

50

Laura saw her daddy lean across the seat and speak to her mother, who opened the car door and called her.

"Come here, Laura. Come see what I've brought you."

It was too small for a recording machine. Her mother was holding it, all wrapped up and tight against her, as if it was something rare and fragile. Laura started to run. Maybe it was a cuckoo clock like the foreman's wife had. She had always envied her that clock. When it chimed, a mother bird came out and fed a nest of openmouthed babies.

Laura hit the open car door at a run, grabbed the window frame, and hung on it, swinging. Her mother ignored this. Maybe her mother *was* trying to be different.

After pulling herself to a standing position, Laura took her muddy hand off the door. She held her hands behind her back, passing the mudball back and forth. It oozed between her fingers instead of packing tight. She wanted to be rid of it, but there was no place to put it.

It was just her luck to have a handful of mud when she was about to be given something she had always wanted. She would not be able to touch her clock until she washed her hands. It was probably very old. She had heard the foreman's wife tell her daddy that old cuckoo clocks were the most valuable. Her mother would never buy anything but the best.

From the careful way her mother was holding the bundle, she was sure the surprise was a clock, even though it was much smaller than Mrs. Acres's clock.

Size did not matter. She would be pleased with even a very tiny clock—especially if it was a "Let's-make-up-present" from her mother. For a chiming clock all her own she would even try to get along with her.

Her mother leaned out of the car toward her. Laura danced on tiptoe, vowing to herself that she would pull the chains very carefully to wind it, and dust it every day. Her mother folded back the corner of the pink blanket. "Laura, this is your baby sister. Her name is Melissa."

Laura stared. . . . For a moment she could not understand what she was seeing. Her brain tried to make the bundle be a clock. . . . Slowly, her eyes focused on the skin: ugly, red, wrinkled. Oblong-shaped head, like an egg. Red. Bald. Without eyebrows or lashes. It wriggled, like a half dead fish, startling Laura. Immediately ashamed of herself for being frightened, she took a giant step forward, putting herself almost in her mother's lap.

Her mother smiled at her. "Isn't she beautiful?" She pulled the pink blanket back further to reveal a ruffled pink dress trimmed in delicate white lace. It moved again, catching a tiny finger in the lace.

Laura stood her ground and did not shy, even though she felt as if her stomach was floating up to meet her throat. She was dizzy and felt nauseous.

Her mother's eyelids fluttered in that prissy way Laura hated. "Isn't this the best surprise you ever had? Aren't you lucky to have such a beautiful baby sister?"

Laura wanted to smash her mother's face. She gripped her hands together behind her back and felt the mud ball ooze between her fingers and palms.

Her mother disentangled the baby's finger from the torn lace. "See what tiny hands she has? Isn't she the prettiest little thing you've ever seen?"

Laura wished her daddy would shut her up. She looked at him across the front seat. He was very still, his face solemn, watching her. She knew he understood what she felt. He was not the stupid cow her mother was. He knew that this ugly baby was the last thing she wanted and the worst surprise anyone ever had.

Without taking her eyes off the baby, her mother rattled on. "I know you are anxious to touch her, but you're too dirty now. After you've had a bath this evening, I'll let you hold her little hand. We have to be very clean with her to keep her from getting sick."

Slowly, Laura looked up into her mother's face. Dirt meant sickness, maybe death. With her hands still clutched behind her body she lathered her mud ball. Then, quickly, she thrust her hands forward, coating the red smooth face with red drippy mud.

Her mother screamed. She saw her daddy jump from the other side of the car. Her mother tried to kick her away from the baby. Laura dodged nimbly. She was delighted to see that her mother's efforts caused her a great deal of pain. She bent forward—howling—clutching the muddy, screaming baby to her.

Laura ripped the woven pink blanket off the mud-slippery baby, almost pulling it from her mother's arms.

She wiped her red, slick hands on it and flung it back over the baby's face. She heard her daddy yelling, "No, Laura! Don't!" Yet she continued.

She saw him coming around the front of the car to defend her mother and that mud-baby against her. She turned her back on him, tossed her head, and galloped toward the garage.

"Laura," he shouted. "Come back." He sounded both angry and sad. "That's no way to treat your baby sister!"

"Damn it! Shut up and help me out of the car," her mother screamed. "Look what that brat has done to my baby."

From the garage door Laura watched as her daddy carried the baby and helped her mother to the house. Carrie met him at the front door, taking the baby in one huge arm, supporting her mother with the other. He turned and vaulted the porch rail to the ground. Her mother yelled at him over the baby's squalling.

"That's right! Run and console your little darling. Reward her for being such a good girl so she'll be sure and do it again."

"Laura's miserable," T.J. yelled back. "Couldn't you see that?"

"She's crazy! Dangerous. Thanks to you."

Only too happy to escape the angry voices, Laura ducked inside the garage and closed her eyes, anticipating the visions that came to her each time she opened the garage door. Back when she was very little she had learned that no one else saw what she saw there. She saw an old Indian with his horses. Sometimes he would be walking them, sometimes brushing them, sometimes just sitting on a bale of hay, staring at her. At first it had scared her, but one day Nana had shown her some old pictures out of her blue velvet scrapbook. And there he had been, that same Indian, only younger, posing with an old man wearing a funny, gray, pointed beard. Nana had said that the man with the gray beard was her father, Laura's great-grandfather, who had raised racing quarter horses. The Indian, named Charles Crow, had been his trainer.

She heard her daddy's footsteps behind her. He was at the door. Quickly, without wasting a motion, she ducked behind a stack of lumber beside her daddy's table saw. She wanted to be left alone to remember what Nana had told her about the Indian.

It was such a good story. Nana's voice had grown soft with fondness as she talked about Charles Crow being a proud and good man who had been chief of his tribe. He had been the father of John Crow, Reming's grandfather. Nana and Reming's grandfather had grown up together while their fathers worked to breed the fastest horses in Oklahoma and to make their stable the most modern of the time. Long after her father died Nana had kept the stable going for Charles Crow because horses were his whole life. He had lived to be an old man and had taught Laura's daddy to ride, as well as other things about nature and living. He had died when her daddy was nineteen and Nana said he had missed him so much—spending hours moping in the stable—that she had sent the horses to the ranch barn and had the stable made over into a garage. But Laura knew all about the way it had been: the brick floors and big stalls that opened into the central walkway.

The old Indian was always there. She never pictured him doing the same things. Each time he had on different clothes and was doing different things, and he was growing older. Slowly but perceptibly older each time she came into the garage.

Laura wondered what would happen when the pictures reached the end of his life? Then, if she kept coming to the garage, perhaps the episodes would start over again. She was glad he could live in the time he loved. The garage, now, would have made him very sad—with cars parked in the stalls instead of horses. There were places for her daddy's truck; her mother's, Nana's, and Carrie's cars; and in the fifth stall was her daddy's big new boat—which he never used. Plenty of places to hide.

When she opened her eyes the old Indian greeted her, with a worried half-smile, over the back of one of his horses, a fat mare with heaving sides, wet with sweat and foam as though she had been running hard.

The old man stroked and talked to her. "Easy now, girl. Give it time, my poor, beautiful pet. It won't be long now."

At that moment, her daddy stepped into the garage,

calling her. She wished he would go away and leave her alone.

While he stood blinking in the semidarkness, Laura eased around the side of Carrie's car and peeked at him. She was annoyed by his presence. She wanted to find out what was wrong with the old Indian's mare. Her daddy could go back to the house and play with that ugly mud-baby he had brought home. She had her own play-mates.

If only her daddy knew that the old Indian he had loved so much was less than a dozen steps away in the empty stall where he sometimes parked his truck. Laura held her breath, hoping her daddy would see him. But he stared right past him, looking for her.

"Come out, Laura." His voice had lost the anger of before. It was only sad. "I'm not mad at you."

He had nothing to be mad about. She had not brought a new daddy home.

"I saw you come in here, Laura. Please stop hiding from me, and let's work this through together."

There was no way he could work it out. It was done. He had given her mother what she wanted. She would never let him take the baby back now.

But he did not go back to the house. He walked further into the garage.

"Melissa was sent to us to be part of our family."

Her daddy's boots clicked closer down the bricked center aisle. Laura crawled under the trunk of the Ford and popped up, jack-in-the-box fashion, on the opposite side. She stole a quick look, over the stall's half-wall, at the back of her daddy's head as he passed.

"The baby belongs to you as much as any of us. Melissa is as much your sister, as she is my daughter, or Nana's granddaughter."

His words, "Melissa . . . my daughter, Nana's grand-daughter" displaced her as the *only* daughter and grand-daughter. She felt uprooted; a staggering pain surged up her legs and back and down her arms to the tips of her fingers, which clamped shut into tight fists. Her daddy's voice became an enemy broadcast, sending out false information. Tuning him out became a matter of survival.

She forced her attention back to the image of the old

man's mare in the corner stall. Its straining black sides were spotted with white foam. Suddenly, the animal bellowed an agonized sound, not a horse sound. It was more like the sound she had heard her mother make when her daddy had carried her down the stairs and rushed her away in the middle of the night less than a week ago.

Her daddy's voice was drowned in the frantic thrashing and moaning of the mare that Laura knew he could neither see nor hear.

The animal fell heavily to its knees, head down, hind quarters up. The old man's face was wet; sweat dripped from his chin onto the mare's rump as he pulled with all his strength at something hidden from Laura's view. He stopped pulling. The mare quieted. The old man lifted his arm and wiped his dripping face on his rolled-up shirt sleeve. His hand was bloody.

"Please come out, Laura." Her daddy was looking for her under the tarp covering his boat.

Ducking low, Laura made a dash up the aisle and into the stall with the old man and his horse. She lifted the lid of an unused feed bin, built into the outside wall, and tumbled inside. She lay very still, listening for her daddy coming after her.

His boots resounded on the brick aisle. She held her breath. His quick footsteps grew louder; they matched Laura's pounding heart. She was about to spring out of the bin and make a run for it when she heard the door of Carrie's Ford open.

"Laura, please don't hide from Daddy. I'm not mad at you. What you did to the baby was wrong, but I'm sure you're sorry now that you've had a few minutes to think."

She was not thinking about her daddy or the baby now. Peeking through a crack between two boards, all her attention was focused on the mare. If only her daddy could see it, he would not care about the baby either. What was happening to the mare was far more exciting.

"Melissa is a stranger to you now," her daddy was saying. "But you'll learn to love her, as we all will. Babies are fun—"

But Laura was still not listening. Her whole attention was focused on the vision that only she could see. At that moment, it was more real to her than that mud-baby or her daddy. She heard a loud thud near her. She scrambled to a kneeling position inside the bin, lifting the lid with the top of her head for a better view. The mare had fallen to its side. Her shoed hooves were pawing wildly in the air as she tried to get up.

"Easy now, girl," Laura heard the old man croon. "Maybe we'll have better luck with you down."

A spasm gripped the mare's bloated belly. The pawing ceased, as though all her strength was concentrated in her knotting stomach muscles. Laura gasped as the old man thrust his arm between the mare's thighs into her body, nearly to his shoulder. He pulled and twisted, matching the animal's groaning efforts with his own. The mare shivered from head to tail as a large blue bubble emerged. The old man caught it fiercely with both hands. He sat in the wet bloody straw, bracing his feet on the mare's rump. Leaning backward, he strained until his face was red, pulling it out.

Slowly, the bubble emerged, and half-out, the bluish skin broke, revealing small hooved feet, legs, and rounded hind quarters.

Laura had never witnessed a birth before. She was aware of her father still standing a short distance away. If only he could see what she was seeing. Of course she and her daddy had come on calves newly born, but she had never dreamed it happened that way. She was shocked, fearful; her body was as rigid as the mare's.

Once more the horse gasped and heaved. The old man tugged, falling backward into the straw with the colt in his lap as it came free, followed by a mess of green slime and blood.

The old man hollered as though in celebration, as if he was unable to contain his excitement. Laura was amazed. The foal was alive. She saw it breathing. It tossed its head to the side, as the old man pushed it gently off his lap, and scrambled to his knees.

Laura saw the excitement and pleasure drain from his face as he examined the foal. He picked it up, and Laura saw that its forelegs were short and withered. One knee was twisted and malformed, so that the hoof was facing backward.

"Laura?"

It was her daddy again, trying to coax her out of hiding. But she still could not break away from what was before her. If only someone could see it with her.

The old man sat down, stroking the colt's perfectly formed head in his lap. He looked tired and old as he held the foal's muzzle in his hands. It nibbled at his fingers, trying to suck. Suddenly, he pulled back and up and broke its neck with one clean stroke.

At the sound of the bone snapping, Laura ducked. The lid on the feed bin banged shut. She heard her daddy's heavy boots cross the bricked aisle and knew he was coming for her. It was too late to move. Slumping in the darkness, her hands limp at her sides, Laura brushed the dust in the bottom of the bin and wished she could go back into the past with the old man.

When her daddy opened the bin, she turned her head, refusing to look at him. He lifted her out and set her on the stall wall. The old man, with his mare and the dead foal, was gone.

Her daddy hoisted himself to the wall beside her. He seemed as sick and hurt as the old Indian had when he snapped the colt's neck.

Laura studied the place where the old man had been sitting with the dead colt in his lap. The cement floor was smooth and dry where moments earlier it had been covered with wet, bloody straw.

Laura heard her daddy talking to her, but whatever he was saying did not register. Her mind was racing, remembering the night she had hidden in the closet: hearing her mother say "Just give me a baby, T.J."; watching what had followed. It was all connected, somehow, to the foal and how it had been born.

Her mother had had the ugly, red mud-baby in the same way as the mare: sweating and straining and screaming. All that! Her mother had gone through all that just to displace her, to crowd her out of her rightful place with her daddy and her Nana.

But the foal was dead.

Her daddy lifted her onto his lap. "You are still my baby, Laura. And you always will be."

She hugged him, then.

August

Three weeks later, people were still coming to see the baby, and they all brought presents. But the presents were only for the baby, not one was for Laura. In fact, some of the people who used to stop and play with her passed right by without even noticing she was there.

Laura climbed up in her daddy's bookshelf to think about it. She had not changed. Nothing had changed except that her mother had brought that baby home.

Why was everyone so interested in that baby? It could not do anything but sleep and cry and cause everyone a lot of extra work.

There had to be a way to make people notice her again. Laura ran a mental check list of all her skills. The only thing she knew how to do that was the least bit spectacular was the tumbling she had learned from Harley. She could do three somersaults in a row without stopping. Tumbling was not exactly right for the occasion, but it would have to do.

She climbed down from the library shelf and began to practice. Her daddy came and sat in his big chair and watched her. When she was finished he applauded, and she went and sat on his lap. He always made her feel comfortable about herself and smart. She never felt that way with her mother.

The very next time people came to see the baby, Laura went into her act. She rolled back and forth on the living-room carpet, back and forth until her head was dizzy and she was sick of doing it. Still the visitors ignored her.

They went right on talking to her mother and smiling and twitching over that stupid baby, without paying any attention to Laura. It was almost more than she could stand. She wanted to scream at them to watch. But she could not talk. She had to find a way to attract their attention without talking.

Laura sat in the middle of the floor, angrily picking at the carpet pile. From the conversation she gathered that the two visitors had once been her mother's schoolteachers. One was squat and fat, and Laura wanted to tell her how fat she was. How silly she looked from the back with her big flabby hips hanging off the little chair on both sides. The other woman was tall and very thin, and she sat with her back as straight as a board against the couch.

Her mother had the baby propped on a pillow between her and the straight-backed lady, who was making a fool of herself, picking at the baby's toes and reciting, "This little piggy went to market." She ended the chant with a screeching, high-pitched giggle. The baby slept through it all.

Laura carefully eyed the distance between her and the skinny lady. She found a magazine, placed it on the floor to mark her starting place, and put her head on it. She gathered herself into a ball, pushed off with both feet, and tumbled directly toward the couch. Her form was better than ever. She ended the third revolution in a perfect sitting position two feet in front of her target. She posed with her hands gracefully outstretched like a dancer and waited for the recognition she deserved.

The fat lady said something about enjoying her retirement and began describing some foreign place she had visited. Laura looked up at the skinny lady. Her droopy, cobwebbed eyes were locked on her fat friend's face. Her mother was zeroed in on her, too. And the stupid baby was still asleep.

Laura got up and marched back to her magazine. She moved it forward two and half feet, put her head on it, and pushed off with all her might. She ended with her feet in the skinny woman's lap. Laura smiled pleasantly.

Instead of saying something nice about her tumbling, the lady pushed Laura's feet off her lap, grabbed her roughly by the shoulders, stood her up, and shook her.

"Shame on you," she said. "You might have landed on your baby sister and hurt her. You know better than to do things like that in the house."

"She is just impossible," her mother said. "I've never been able to do a thing with her."

"Nonsense!" The skinny, droopy-eyed old school teacher shook her again. "The child needs discipline, that's all. Laura, leave the room. You go think about the bad way you've acted this afternoon. The next time I come, I want to see your behavior much improved."

Laura walked out of the living room, holding herself as straight and stiff as the skinny old biddy behind her. Out in the hall, she turned a corner and marched like a majorette lifting her feet high in the air, then bringing them down as hard as she could on the reverberating marble. Her shoes made a lovely, loud clomp which bounced off the mirrored walls, and met her in the middle, completely surrounding her in the echo. The sound was so good, so effective, that she stopped and pranced in place until her mother yelled, "Laura!"

Then she scooped her clown off the hall chair where it had been waiting for her and scooted out the massive front door, slamming it behind her. The noise was even more satisfying than the echo, so she opened the door and slammed it a second time, hoping her mother was thoroughly embarrassed. She was about to do it the third time when she heard angry footsteps in the hall. She dashed to the side of the porch, slid over the banister on her stomach, and dropped, with her clown, into the safety of the shrubbery. A second later her mother burst through the door to the front of the porch. She yelled toward the giant cedar tree near the circular drive.

"Laura! I'm going to blister you. Do you hear me! I'm not going to have this! You are going to straighten up if I have to beat you three times a day."

Her mother looked so silly screaming at the empty tree that Laura had to cover her mouth to keep from laughing. Her mother surely was dumb to think she would hide in the same tree where she watched for her daddy to come home most evenings.

Laura slipped around the side of the house and flattened herself against the cool brick. After her mother went back inside she ran for the garage. She stepped in backward with her eyes closed, and was immediately transported from the miserable present into the welcome past. The old

Indian was currying the black mare who had lost her foal. He was talking to the horse and seemed not to notice Laura.

The old man was always talking to himself. Most of what he said made no sense to Laura, but she liked to listen. He was not a man to waste words on unimportant things.

"I've seen the way you look at T.J. There's no mistaking that look. The same look his mother gave your father years ago. We did them an injustice, her father and I. Me for keeping still when I should have stood with my son. But I'll stand with you, granddaughter, if you want him and the Lord spares me until that time."

The old Indian seemed to be looking straight through Laura when he said, "Life is only good when you make up your mind what you want and go after it. Don't let anything stop you from having what you need to be happy. Whether it's a man, or a horse, or both."

He always talked as though to someone older and taller than Laura from the way he always looked a little over her head. What he said had never bothered her, but now, she had the eerie feeling she had heard his speech before. She wanted to ask him who he was talking to, but he led his mare past her, out of the stall, and disappeared out the door into a shaft of bright sunlight. Laura wanted to follow, but remembered that her mother was mad and would probably send her to her room if she saw her.

The garage was a lonesome place without the old Indian. Only the tack room remained as it had been in his time. It was filled with dozens of molding saddles that smelled like horses when it rained. Laura loved that room and the loft above with the big hay door and the rusted pulley that was so much fun to swing on.

If her mother came after her she could always climb the pulley to the roof and shinny down the pecan tree around back. Laura took a leather thong from the tack room, tied it to her clown's wrist and ankle, and slung him across her back like a guitar. She climbed the ladder to the loft, eased the squeaking hay door open, and sat with her feet hanging out. It was a long way to the ground, but she was not afraid. Harley was scared of everything. But her mother had always liked him best, until the baby came. She still liked him pretty well. She was always hugging and kissing him and listening to his long-winded stories.

Her mother surely thought talking was the most important thing in the world. That was probably the reason she liked Harley so much. He never shut up. He went on and on and on about things no one cared about. But her mother listened to him.

She did not really care whether he had caught a green lizard, or climbed a dozen trees, or beat Reming to the mailbox two out of three times. And he did not care whether she knew.

If he had to talk, why didn't he tell her what was really on his mind. Why didn't he say, "Stop what you are doing. Belong only to me for a few minutes. I want you to smile at me and touch me. I want to be the most important person in your life for a while."

Laura wanted to say those things to Nana and her daddy. But her mother would never *make* her talk. Nana and her daddy already *knew* how Laura felt, and she had never spoken a word to either one of them. Blabbermouth Harley was just wasting everyone's time.

Harley chattered to Nana the same way he did to their mother. But Laura knew that Nana liked her best. Half of what Harley told Nana he made up, and Nana knew it, but she listened anyway, because it was so important to him.

His whole face would light up, his eyes would shine, and he would wave his hands frantically as if the words could not come out fast enough to suit him. He always made the telling ten times more exciting than the experience had been.

It was so important to him to say things that made Nana smile and nod her approval, or scold him and say he should not take such chances, or tell him he was much braver than she. He colored everything his own way to get her to say caring words.

No matter what Nana did otherwise, no matter how much she hugged, or patted, or tussled his hair, he went right on talking until he made her say the words, as though only the words had meaning. Harley's whole world seemed to amount to no more than one big string of empty words.

Sometimes, when Nana was very busy, she would only half listen, then say the words Harley wanted, and he would go off as pleased as ever—not knowing the difference. When that happened Laura always laughed at him, and Harley would look at her like she was crazy, but Nana would wink, and they would keep it as their secret.

Words reminded Laura of the hollow tin soldiers that Reming carried around in the battered shoe box. They looked heavy—like words sounded important—but they were light because they were empty inside.

The garage door squeaked, and Laura knew it was the wind, but she pretended it was her mother coming after her. Her heart beat faster, and she became alert to every rustle and creak inside the old building.

A pigeon cooed softly. Another bird answered. Under those sounds imaginary footsteps moved toward the loft ladder. Her mother would love to sneak up on her. Catch her off guard.

Laura waited, barely breathing. Her mother would never trap her anywhere. Not ever!

The ladder cried out a remembered warning. Dry wood against rusty nails. With her clown secured on her back, her own papoose minus the cradle board, Laura bolted for the loft door. She grabbed the pulley and swung up to the steel beam which held it and onto the steep, slanting roof. Then she dropped to her knees and crawled to an over-hanging branch of the pecan tree. Voices drifted up from the front of the house, and Laura swung from branch to branch to the ground. She ran to the end of the garage, where she could see the porch.

Her mother was saying good-bye to that hateful skinny woman and her fat friend. They both stopped to moo—one more time—over that stupid baby. Laura would like to have thrown rocks at them all.

Instead, she sprinted straight across the yard and climbed to the top of the rock wall that surrounded the lawns and gardens. When she was safely concealed behind a tall shrub she looked back. They were all laughing and talking. No one had seen her.

Those two old ladies talked on and on, and Laura could tell her mother wanted them to leave. Finally, after much fidgeting, her mother made a production out of finding the mud-baby wet. Laura knew it was a ruse to get rid of them.

The road back to town ran parallel to the wall, passing within a few feet of where she stood. She wanted to be very sure the two old hags saw her, so she did a running

64

war dance up and down the top of the wall from one square-topped pillar to the next.

When she was certain they were both watching, she ran to the nearest pillar, jumped up in the center with both feet, smiled as big as she could, and extended both hands toward the brown Ford—with her middle fingers raised. Those ladies would never get another finger salute as good as the one she gave them!

Her mother and Nana did not know she could do it. It was supposed to be a secret with her daddy. But if he knew those two old ladies, Laura was sure he would not care. Two men on his oil rig had taught her—out behind the metal shed—while her daddy was busy talking to the foreman. But she knew it was not nice because her daddy had told her never, never to do it at home where her mother or Nana could see her. He said it was "strictly an oil field joke," and that ladies would not think it was funny.

He was right. The two old ladies coughed and spluttered inside their brown Ford. The skinny one's cob-webbed eyes almost popped out. And the fat one's mouth stretched as big around as an inner tube. They looked like goldfish inside a glass bowl. And the fat one even ran the wheels of her ugly Ford clear off the road, trying to look back over her shoulder.

Laura held her pose until they were completely out of sight, then slapped both knees and laughed and laughed. If only the guys from the oil rig had seen her. Those ugly old women would never ignore *her* again. They were sure to keep an eye on her whenever they saw her.

The afternoon sun was very hot. Laura's arms had turned red, and her head hurt from the heat and so much laughing. Suddenly, she felt very tired. Like she felt when Nana took her shopping in Oklahoma City and they visited four or five department stores in one afternoon.

Nana insisted that she not touch the stair rails, or play with discarded cups, or play with the gray sand where people put out their cigarettes, or sit on public toilet seats. Invisible germs lurked everywhere, and strangers' germs were the worst kind.

At home, Nana still worried about germs. Even when she used her own bathroom, which was always clean, Nana insisted that she wash her hands afterward. Most of the time she supervised the washing, making sure Laura used enough soap and got them really clean. Therefore, rather than go through all of that each time, Laura seldom bothered to go to the house when she was playing outside.

It usually made her feel a little guilty, because Nana would certainly not approve. But today she had a perfectly good excuse. She was not about to risk an encounter with her mother just to go to the bathroom.

Laura climbed down the wall, pulled her panties down, and wet behind a spreading juniper. While she was squatting behind the bush, she heard her daddy's pickup turn into the long drive. He parked in front of the house, and Laura was pleased when he stopped to look up in her tree and call her name. He seemed disappointed because she was not there.

Her daddy loved her for sure. And Nana loved her. Even Carrie loved her. And Harley was all right at times. Her mother would be sorry about bringing that ugly mud-baby home!

Laura climbed back to the top of the wall. Using her clown as a pillow, she stretched out in a shady spot, promising herself that she would move only her head until someone came and found her. Within an hour she amended her resolution to exclude her hands and arms. Being still was boring.

She made a telescope out of her hands and focused on the mountain at the end of the valley. It was the only mountain anywhere around, and with the sun going down behind it, it looked like a big baked potato on a flat gold plate. The sun turned the brown potato skin pink, and red, and orange. Right on the very top was a big square rock. With the sun on it, it looked gold like a giant pat of melting butter. It looked so real she could almost smell it.

Surely someone would come for her soon. Laura's stomach told her it was suppertime. It had been a long afternoon, and she could not even remember what she had had for lunch.

She adjusted her make-believe telescope, and watched the big pat of butter melt down her Potato Mountain. Her legs began to twitch and jump, but she had made herself a promise; and already she had broken half of it by moving her arms. She stubbornly refused to move her legs no matter how tired they got. The wall was so hard. Much too hard for a bed.

Finally, the back door opened, and Nana called across the yard, "L-a-u-r-a. Suppertime."

Laura caught herself just in time before she answered. Her reaction frightened her. It was the first time she had ever done that. The first time she had even come close.

Nana spotted her on the wall and came toward her. The closer she came the more Laura wanted to say something to her. Nana certainly deserved to know she could talk—more than her mother. Nana would be so pleased.

"How in the world did you get up there? Someday you are going to fall and break your neck."

Laura stood up and started to climb down. Nana swallowed a big gulp of air, covering the few feet between them with running steps.

"Wait! Wait! Let Nana help you. My goodness, you scare me half to death."

Laura allowed her grandmother to help her down. Not that she needed any help, but Nana was such a worrywart, and it made her feel better to help.

"Aren't you hungry, Baby Girl?"

Laura nodded.

Nana knelt beside Laura. "Can you say 'baby' for Nana?"

Laura could hear the wanting in Nana's voice. She tried to see Nana's eyes, but her glasses reflected only the mountain at the end of the valley.

"Please try to say 'baby' for Nana. It would make Nana the happiest person in the whole world to hear you talk."

A cloud moved in front of the reflecting mountain, making Nana's glasses clear suddenly. There were tears in her eyes.

The pain of seeing Nana crying was almost more than Laura could stand. She was about to blurt "baby" when her clown stopped her, whispering that all they had worked for would be lost if she talked to anyone besides her mother. Then, Nana would know that her mother had been telling the truth the whole time they had thought her mother crazy.

Laura hugged her Nana extra tight and kissed her on both cheeks, trying to make up to her for not talking. Nana stood and brushed her tears out from under her glasses. She took Laura's hand. "You are still Nana's Baby Girl, and you always will be no matter whether you ever talk or not."

Nana's little speech made Laura feel so guilty and bad that she dragged her clown all the way back to the house as punishment for not letting her talk to her Nana.

September

Sleep was the last thing Laura ever wanted. That was what people did when there was nothing left to do. When everyone else in the house was in bed, and all the lights were out, then it was time to sleep. But that stupid mud-baby slept all the time. And her stupid mother sat and watched it sleep.

Every day was the same. The whole world revolved around that baby. Laura spent hours hanging on the side of its crib to see what was so fascinating about it.

Usually she was able to sense what others felt. And to understand why they felt it. But her mother's reaction to that baby completely baffled her.

It slept. It cried. It wet every five minutes whether awake or asleep. It grunted two or three times a day. From morning until night the dirty laundry mounted higher and higher. That baby dirtied more things in one day than Laura did in a week.

Besides all its other nastiness. It spit up all the time, usually on her mother's clothing, so she, too, changed clothes several times a day and further increased the mountain of laundry.

The slosh, hum, and spin of the washing maching became background music for every activity. It ran all the time. All day long. Load after load after load. And sometimes it was still running after Laura went to bed at night. Nana and Carrie hardly had time to drink a cup of coffee. And when they did sit down they were always folding baby clothes.

It made Laura angry to see them do it. If her mother wanted that baby so badly, why didn't they make her take care of it? Why should they work so hard just so her mother could sit and watch it sleep? None of it made sense.

Even worse than the mess was the smell. Her mother bathed it every day and kept it all powdered, oiled, and perfumed, but she was not fooling anyone. Laura could tell there was a baby in the house the minute she opened the front door. The whole place reeked of baby. The tack room in the garage smelled better—even when it rained.

October

After weeks of watching, the only change Laura could see was that the baby had grown some. It had gotten longer and fatter; but other than that, there was no change in its activities. The bigger it got the worse it smelled and the louder it screamed—which could hardly be considered an improvement.

Her mother bragged that she had finally gotten the little "angel" on a schedule. And Laura watched. Determined to find out exactly what "schedule" meant. So far, all she knew was that her mother took the baby to her room six times a day and locked the door.

When Laura tried the knob, her mother yelled for her to go downstairs and play. She never did. She pressed her ear to the door and listened. Sometimes she could hear her mother humming softly. Sometimes she sang songs like "When the bough breaks the cradle will fall, and down will come baby, cradle and all."

That stupid baby did not know what she was singing. Somehow, Laura had to find out what went on in that room. Whatever it was, it must be the reason her mother liked that baby so much.

Laura put her whole mind to the problem. Her mother always locked the door. She had tried the knob every time, hoping she would forget. But she never did. The only way to find out what went on in that room was to be inside before the door was locked.

Biding her time, Laura went downstairs and stood on a chair to watch Nana make pie crust. Nana's wrinkled hands knew exactly what came next. Exactly how to pat the dough into a smooth flat ball, put it in the center of the floured board, and roll it out with the floured rolling pin.

So many rolls forward. So many rolls back. So many rolls to each side. When it was finished, she folded it in half over the rolling pin, then unfolded it in the pan, pressed it in, and trimmed off the extra with a sharp knife. Three strokes on each side while she turned the pan on her fingertips. The way she did it was like a dance without missteps.

Laura heard her mother bring the baby downstairs and put it in its crib on the sun porch. She did not bother to go and see. She knew exactly what was happening. Her mother was changing another stinky diaper. Adding to the mountain of dirty laundry. If it were up to Laura she would let the stupid thing stay dirty.

Nana filled the pie shell with sliced apples and butter and sugar and cinnamon. She rolled out another crust, placed it on top, and fluted the edges. When it was all done she pricked a tree in the top crust with the point of her knife. It was like magic, the quick way she drew things on top of her pies, and she never practiced with a pencil.

As an afterthought Nana added a tiny little girl carrying a basket.

"That's Laura under the apple tree," she said.

While Nana put the pie in the oven Laura wiped up spilled sugar and cinnamon off the cabinet with pieces of dough and ate them. Then Laura grabbed up a fist full of dough, smashed it in the sugar, and stuffed it in her pocket. She climbed down from her chair and pulled it back into place at the table. Nana smiled at her as she went out the back door.

Across the yard, behind the grape arbor, Nana's five pet geese preened themselves peacefully in the shallow fish pool. Once there had been several giant goldfish and dozens of water lilies in the pool, but the geese had eaten almost all the lilies and the fish had mysteriously disappeared.

Laura found a long stick and headed toward the pond. The geese hissed and honked and beat their wings on the water as she approached. The big white gander waded toward her menacingly, and Laura waved the stick in one hand, her clown in the other trying to scare him. He came on in a straight line, screaming rancorously, his long neck stretched out, mouth open.

Out of the water he was almost as tall as she was. And

having been bitten several times before, Laura retreated to the opposite side of the pond.

She beat on the water with her stick. The four gray females waded out on the other side. Laura chased them toward the sun porch, and they ran ahead of her, screaming, honking, and beating their wings, making as much noise as an invading army.

Laura chased them faster. The big gander lifted his heavy body and began to fly, low to the ground. The others followed. They swerved just in time to miss the screened porch. There they turned and made their stand. A screaming, honking, hissing chorus of flaying feathers ready to do battle.

Over the tumult, the baby began to scream from inside the screened porch. Her mother shouted threats, yelling at her to get those geese away from the house.

Laura pretended not to hear. She ran at the geese, then retreated. Ran and retreated. Her mother beat her hands against the screen wire, screeching above the din for her to stop.

"Get those nasty geese away from this baby! Do you hear me, Laura? Get away! Get clear out of my sight!"

The back door banged against the house, and Nana's hurrying footsteps crunched across the dry grass.

Laura dashed through the flock of geese, around to the front porch. The geese scattered in all directions, honking, flogging the air with their huge wings.

During the commotion, while Nana shooed the geese and tried to calm her mother, Laura slipped through the front door and up the stairs. At the top she crouched near the banister, holding her clown's face pressed against her chest to keep it quiet while she listened to the conversation below.

"If you'd show a little patience," she heard Nana say.

"Don't tell me how to raise my children."

"We'll discuss it later, when you are not upset."

"I won't discuss it at all. I'm tired of you meddling in my affairs. If your son would ever correct her. But he is as blind as you—"

The screaming mud-baby drowned out the rest of the conversation. Laura scurried down the hall to her mother's room. Inside, she leaned against the closed door, feeling guilty about the hateful way her mother had talked to

Nana. If she had not run the geese it would not have happened. But it was hard to be sorry about the geese. What a commotion they had made! She was glad they woke that stupid mud-baby. It slept too much, anyway.

Laura hid inside her daddy's closet, leaving the door ajar so she could see out through the crack. It was a big closet. Big enough to put her bed in and still have room left over. Besides clothes there were lots of odds and ends toward the back. Tucking her clown firmly under her arm, she explored with her hands, afraid to risk turning the light on in case her mother brought the mud-baby upstairs early.

She identified her daddy's golf clubs; three rifles and a box of bullets; a long bar with heavy round weights on each end, which puzzled her, and tucked in the very corner behind a big locked metal box, she found a leather bag with beads on the front.

Her clown went stiff under her arm, its cone hat poking at her armpit like a pointed stick. She stuffed it hurriedly between her knees, ignoring what she was sure was meant to be a warning.

The bag was shaped like a light bulb, only a little larger, and had fringe on the bottom. She turned it over, examining every stitch. It seemed familiar to her, like a long-lost toy, but she could not place it. On opening it, she experienced the same blank, expectant sensation she felt each time she opened the garage door. A moment later her mind raced with vague, seemingly unrelated, pictures.

A sandrock cave, not deep, but wide and shallow. A peaceful place between high rock walls that locked out sounds. A high cliff where the wind whistled and roared. A campfire, with many people seated around it engaged in some kind of thoughtful ceremony—like a church service —only different. A tall man, with very dark eyes and skin, sat a little apart from the others at the head of the circle. He reminded Laura of Reming's grandfather, only younger, thinner.

Before that day he had threatened her, she had seen Reming's grandfather many times when her daddy gave Reming rides home. Her daddy had usually gotten out to talk. Laura knew he liked the old man, who seemed fond of him. Always before Reming's grandfather had waved to

Laura in the truck and invited her to get out. Her clown had never wanted her to even then. Since that day on the porch steps when the old healer had made his peculiar threat to send her back and punish her, her clown had seemed even more afraid of him. Somehow he had guessed their secret about her talking. Guessed, even before she had spoken her first words to her mother. But it was only a guess. He had no proof.

Now her clown was shaking between her knees. Or maybe it was her knees shaking. She felt cold.

Whoever the dark man was, she had the feeling he loved her very much. She felt a need to be with him, the way she did for Nana when she awoke from a bad dream in the middle of the night. Laura wanted to cry and reach out for him to take her, but the vision faded and would not come back. She tried to bring it back, but he was gone.

As though the tall man in her vision had whispered it to her before leaving, Laura knew what she would find inside the bag: a lock of her own hair, tied up with a slender ribbon, and tied at the other end of the ribbon, a lock of her daddy's hair.

Her clown wanted her to put the ribbon back, but she was too curious. She hobbled, clown still between her knees, to the closet door and examined it in the light. One lock was her daddy's—the same sandy color, the same texture. But the other, the one she had thought was her own, bore no similarity to her blonde curls. It was dark brown, almost black, and very straight. Disappointed, she stuffed it back inside the leather pouch, which she returned to its place behind the metal box. She had been so sure it was her hair tied up with her daddy's.

Seeing the lock of hair that didn't match her own made her uneasy, as though she had forgotten something important. She *had* forgotten! The tall, dark man *was* important to her! Almost as important as her Nana. If the tall, dark man of her vision and Reming's grandfather were the same person, then he might know what it was she could not remember.

Her clown said to put it out of her mind. But she had never experienced that sad, needy feeling for the old Indian, Charles Crow, with his horses out in the garage. Her clown had always been indifferent to him.

The closet closed in on her. It was too hot. The air was heavy with the cloying smell of mothballs, her daddy's cigarettes, and old shoes. Her clown seemed sick.

Laura pushed the closet door further open and inhaled the fresh air. The bedroom smelled faintly of her mother's perfume. But there was another smell—fully as disgusting as mothballs and stale smoke. She could not get away from it, even in her own room. The smell of the mud-baby was everywhere.

The mud-baby had done something to her mother. Charmed her in some way. She was like a radio that had been tuned to a new station. She no longer operated on Laura's channel.

There was nothing fair about it. She had been there first. It was her house. That mud-baby did not belong.

Laura spent several minutes adjusting the closet door to exactly the right angle. She had an unobstructed view of the bed and dresser; but the chest of drawers, her mother's closet, and the bathroom were out of her line of vision. Satisfied she could do no better, she settled on top of her daddy's suitcase, her clown seated, facing forward between her spraddled legs—waiting.

She remembered the stolen pie dough in her pocket. It was covered with pieces of lint, and tasted a little gritty, like there had been sand in her pocket. She ate it anyway, pinching off a tiny piece at a time to make it last longer.

As she popped the last bite into her mouth, the bedroom door opened and closed. She heard the lock snap. That hated sound. It usually meant she was being locked out. Now, she was locked in.

Barely breathing, Laura put her eye to the crack. If she was caught, her mother would be forever suspicious. She might never get another chance.

Her mother laid the baby on her daddy's side of the bed, propped a pillow on the outside edge so it could not roll off, and went into the bathroom. The baby began to whine and fret, throwing its arms around and trying to suck on its fist.

Laura was tempted to run out of the closet and push it off the bed. Before she could make up her mind the stool flushed. Water ran. The baby screamed. Her mother returned, naked from the waist up, carrying her shirt and bra, which she tossed on a chair.

"Now, now," she cooed. "You can wait just another minute." She wiped both breasts with a damp washcloth, laid the cloth on the night table, and stretched out on her side next to the baby. "That's my little angel." She lifted the baby to her side and put her left nipple in its mouth. The baby sucked greedily.

Laura was outraged. The sight of that ugly mud-baby sucking on her mother's breast made her stomach turn over. She wanted to pull it off, fling it down, and step on it, like her daddy did ticks off his hunting dogs.

What about her mother? Her mother had *put* her breast in its mouth. And now she was humming softly, looking at the mud-baby like it was the most valuable thing in the world.

Her mother stopped humming. "We don't know how to act. Do we, Precious? Without your mean old sister rattling the door and banging around out in the hall. I guess she finally got tired and decided to leave us alone."

She kissed the top of the baby's head. "Why couldn't Laura be a sweet little girl like you?"

How dare her mother compare her unfavorably to that stupid mud-baby! Laura clinched her hands into tight fists. Cold sweat popped out in beads on her forehead. She hated that baby! Hated it! And her mother, too!

Laura clamped her clown under her arm and thrust the closet door open with such force that it banged against the wall. Her mother jumped back against the headboard, clutching the baby protectively.

"What are you doing?" Laura demanded.

"What do you think *you* are doing? Sneaking around hiding in closets!"

Her mother tried to cover herself with the edge of the bedspread, but it was too short.

"Is this why you lock me out? So you can let your stupid baby do that to you."

"Go downstairs, Laura!"

"Tell me why you are doing this!"

"All mothers nurse their babies. You've seen puppies nurse. And mother cows."

"You are not a dog. Or a cow."

"But I am a mother."

"You are *my* mother . . . Did you nurse me?"

"No. You were fed on a bottle."

"Why?"

"Because you would not nurse."

"I want to now."

"Certainly not! You're much too big a girl."

"If you let that baby suck on you—then why can't I?"

"Because you're not a baby. You are a big girl."

"I'm not too big to drink milk. Put that baby down and feed me."

"Be a good girl, Laura, and run down stairs. Nana will give you a glass of milk from the refrigerator. Your baby sister needs all the milk I have."

"That baby is nothing of mine. I won't have it! Put that ugly thing down. You nurse me!"

Her mother was shaking.

"Go downstairs, please."

Laura sensed she had her mother off guard. She threw her clown toward the bedroom door and sprang forward, shoving the baby roughly aside, locking her mouth on her mother's breast.

With her free hand, her mother tried to push her head away. Laura clung to her breast with her mouth and both hands. Her mother tangled her fingers in Laura's hair and tried to pull her head away. Laura bit down on her mother's nipple. Her mother's pain-filled scream made a hard knot in Laura's stomach, but she would not let go until her mother gouged her eyes and forced her head back.

Spots of light swam before Laura's eyes. When she was able to focus again, her mother was wiping drops of bloody milk from her nipple with the damp wash cloth. Tears were running down her face, but she was still clutching that stupid mud-baby in one arm.

Laura stood. "Keep your ugly baby close to you," she hissed.

Her mother's face seemed to explode. She charged.

In one broad sweep, Laura grabbed her clown off the floor and unlocked the bedroom door. But not fast enough. Her mother shoved her into the hall and hit her head with her fist.

Laura grabbed the baby and tried to pull it out of her mother's arms. They tussled and above the baby's fright-ened wails, her mother screamed for Nana.

Laura slung her clown far down the hall toward her

room. Grabbing the baby's leg with both hands, she hung on until she heard Nana's footsteps on the stairs. Then, she twisted the baby's foot as hard as she could before letting go. Her mother chased her down the hall, clutching the screaming baby to her bare bosom as she ran.

Catching up, her mother kicked her in the middle of the back just as Nana reached the landing. The blow sent Laura sprawling. She would have fallen down the stairs if Nana had not grabbed her.

"My God, Kate! Have you lost your mind? What are you trying to do to this child?"

"Get her out of my sight, before I kill her."

"What's wrong with you? Have you forgotten that Laura is your child, too?"

"I'd like to forget. I wish to God she had never been born!"

"You don't mean that!"

"I do mean it! She's not right. She never has behaved like a normal child. All the evil in the world lurks behind that innocent face. I can see it. But you and your son refuse to believe it. Just now, she told me to put my baby down and nurse her. When I wouldn't she attacked me, sucked on my breast anyway. I tried to push her head away. She bit me."

She showed Nana her breast. It was turning purple and blue around the nipple, but the teeth marks were in the brown part and did not show.

"Then she tried to pull my baby out of my arms. She twisted Melissa's little foot."

Her mother bounced the screaming baby up and down trying to quiet her.

"She may have broken her foot. If she ever hurts this baby again, I *will* kill her!"

"You won't do any such thing! I don't know what went on in there, but I wouldn't blame her for biting you! I'm sick to death of you making up what all this child is supposed to have said."

"She can talk as plain as you can."

"These conversations are all in your head. And if you're not careful, you'll find yourself locked up somewhere."

Her mother slapped Nana's face, and Nana slapped her back even harder.

"Don't ever put your hand on me again, Kate. And

don't you ever touch this child again. From now on, Laura belongs to me."

"We'll see about that!"

"Then we'll see in court! Think about it, Kate! You could lose all three of them."

Her mother stormed off to her room and slammed the door. Laura clung to Nana's neck with both arms. She was trembling with anger and exhaustion, bewildered by Nana's actions. Nana had never lost her temper before. Not ever. She was always patient and kind to everyone.

Laura leaned back in her grandmother's arms. She smoothed her wrinkled cheeks with both hands. Her cheeks were wet.

"Everything will be all right, Baby Girl. Nana will see to that . . . If only you could talk. No telling how that crazy woman has abused you."

Nana kissed Laura's scratched face and carried her down the hall to her room. She stripped all her clothes off, put her in a hot tub, and, kneeling on the bath mat, examined every tiny cut and scrape before she washed it. Nana clucked a long time over an emerging bruise in the middle of Laura's back where her mother had kicked her.

"Never again, Baby Girl. Never again. Your Nana has kept still long enough. Now there are going to be some changes made. Today is moving day for you. We are going to move all your pretty things downstairs into the little sitting room next to mine. You'll like that, won't you?"

Laura was puzzled. Nana hardly ever let her go in there. She called it her treasure room. And it was filled to overflowing with old furniture, and pictures, and delicate china cups and saucers, and dozens of frilly doilies.

"I'm going to crate up most of that old stuff and store it in the servants wing. I can move the furniture up here. It's time the past was put away. The present is too important."

Laura reached up and hugged her Nana's neck, dripping water all over her dress. Nana lifted her out of the tub and pressed her close.

Her Nana loved her! Enough to put away all her treasures!

As soon as Laura was dressed, Nana led her downstairs to the kitchen and gave her a piece of her freshly baked apple pie. It was still warm from the oven, but Laura was more interested in Nana's telephone conversation with the ranch foreman. Nana never ordered anyone. She always said "please," or "when it would be convenient." But she told the foreman she wanted two men up to the house in twenty minutes, and hung up.

Before Laura had finished her pie, the foreman, followed by a hand named Juan—one of Laura's favorites—appeared at the kitchen door.

"You didn't need to come yourself, Mr. Acres," Nana said.

"Is something wrong, Mrs. Daniels? You sounded upset on the telephone."

"Everything is fine. I want some furniture moved. Wipe your feet on the mat and come this way."

The foreman turned to leave. "If that's all it is, I'll send two of the boys around in the morning."

Laura squeaked her fork across the empty pie plate. Mr. Acres never did anything he could get someone else to do. Not even when her daddy told him. But she could tell by the way Nana drew her shoulders back that he was about to move their furniture.

One of Nana's eyebrows arched. "I want it moved now, Mr. Acres."

"Then Juan can take me back to the office and bring someone else back to help. I thought there was some emergency. I have a million things to do this afternoon."

"Your domino game can wait, Mr. Acres."

Nana led the way to her treasure room, and the foreman followed sullenly. Laura hung on the banister while Juan and the foreman lugged the heavy furniture up and down the stairs: Nana's things up, Laura's things down. Mr. Acres heaved and sweated and groaned. His fat belly prevented him from getting a good hand hold. Several times he halted the moving in the middle of the stairs to trade places with Juan, always giving him the heavy end.

Juan's black eyes twinkled mischievously. He grinned at Laura when he had his back to the boss. She knew Juan enjoyed seeing him work.

Several times Mr. Acres tried to beg off, saying they needed more help, that the furniture was too heavy, that he was afraid they might drop something.

Nana prodded him gently. Leading the procession up and down the stairs like the grand marshal in the Fourth of

July parade, she cautioned them continuously not to scratch the furniture or bump the woodwork. Each time she turned her back Mr. Acres swore under his breath.

By the time Laura's daddy came home the furniture had all been moved, the men thanked and dismissed. Carrie had taken down the heavy drapes and was hanging Laura's bright pink ruffled curtains in their place. Nana's room was a mess, with crates, boxes, and knickknacks stacked everywhere. But Laura's furniture and toys were in perfect order inside the treasure room.

Laura had lived all her life in the room upstairs. The move was the most exciting thing that had ever happened to her. But her daddy hardly seemed pleased. He and Nana had a long, quiet talk in the kitchen. Carrie would not let her join them. When her daddy finally came out, his eyes were red, as if he had been crying. He picked her up, hugging her so tightly she could hardly breathe.

"Nana has found the perfect place for our very special little girl," he said. "She belongs in the treasure room."

Laura wanted him to stay and play with her, but he hurried up the stairs, three at a time, and slammed the bedroom door.

That stupid mud-baby screamed. Her mother and daddy yelled at each other over the noise. Glass shattered against the wall. Her mother shouted words Laura had heard at the oil rig but never before in her own house.

Their fight was even more exciting than the move, but Nana hustled her outside and would not let her listen. Later, Carrie brought out a picnic supper, called Harley, and the four of them ate under the pecan tree behind the garage.

Nana kept Harley and her outside until things had quieted down. But even after they went to bed—her first night in the treasure room—there were several more outbursts from upstairs.

Her mother stayed in her room for nearly a week after the moving day. She kept Carrie so busy running up and down the stairs, bringing things for the baby and carrying food trays, that she did not have time for her regular chores. She no sooner finished one trip than the servant's buzzer in the kitchen summoned her again.

The buzzer frightened Laura the first time she heard it. No one had ever used it before. She did not know it was there. Nana had had to tell her what it was for. Nana had not been very happy about it. She acted as though she thought her mother was being very naughty using it.

Besides being the maid, Carrie was also Nana's best friend. They were accustomed to doing everything together in a set routine. Now her mother's demands upset their schedule. At first they were good-natured about it. Each time Carrie returned to the kitchen, she gave Nana a joking report about what "Her Majesty" was doing and what she wanted. But as the week wore on, and their regular work piled up, they became more and more irritable.

Upstairs was off limits to Laura, but whenever Nana and Carrie were occupied in another part of the house, she crept upstairs to listen outside her mother's door. The first few days she had cried a lot and talked to that stupid mud-baby. Later, she watched television or talked on the telephone most of the time.

On the sixth day, Laura was having lunch in the kitchen with Nana and Carrie when the buzzer sounded. Carrie started to go up, but Nana stopped her.

"Finish your lunch, Carrie. Her Majesty can wait."

Before Carrie had finished half her sandwich, the buzzer went off three times. A harsh, rasping sound, which irritated Laura almost as much as that stupid mud-baby's crying.

Carrie pushed back from the table. "I better go up before she works herself into a state."

"You're not going anywhere. I've had about all of this nonsense I intend to take." Nana moved her chair across the room and stood on it. She was a little person, short and small-boned; even with the chair she was not quite tall enough to reach the buzzer. She pointed to the stove. "Hand me those cooking tongs." Carrie gave them to her, and Nana pulled the electric wire out of the buzzer.

Laura giggled, and the two women laughed.

Carrie helped Nana off the chair and moved it back to the table. "She'll have a fit, Mrs. D."

"Let her. She knows we always eat at twelve. She has her nerve interrupting your lunch."

"I'm just the hired help to her."

Laura had never thought of Carrie as hired help. If she was hired that meant she was paid like Juan and Mr. Acres. Why would Nana pay her best friend?

"You've been a member of this family for thirty years. You are much more valuable to me than she is. I'm not going to have you wearing yourself out running up and down those stairs any longer."

"In all the time I've been here, I don't ever remember you using that servant's buzzer."

"Yes I did, too. When T.J. was little I used it to signal you that he was asleep so you could come up and play canasta."

"That's the only time. Then, and once when you were sick in the night. Like to scared me to death. You had fallen by the bed and were too weak to get up."

Laura thought their faces looked younger when they talked about old times. It was nice the way they got along.

Her mother's voice boomed down from the upstairs hall. "C-a-r-r-i-e! Where are you?"

Startled, Carrie jumped up, but Nana caught her arm.

"I better go, Mrs. D. She's already mad. And I hate it when she's short with me."

"Has she been rude to you?"

"Sometimes. She's so hard to please."

"She won't be so hard to please from now on, because she'll be doing for herself. Sit down. Finish your coffee."

Her mother shouted twice more. Laura was delighted when Carrie did not move. Finally her mother came barreling down the stairs and into the kitchen. Her face was red. She glared at Carrie.

"What are you doing? I've been ringing that buzzer for thirty minutes."

Nana pointed to the disconnected wire. "The buzzer is broken. And I don't intend to have it repaired."

"*You* don't intend— *You* don't intend— . That's fine. It was outdated anyway. *I intend* to have an intercom system installed all over the house." She focused on Carrie. "Reverend Edwards is coming to see the baby. When he gets here, show him up to my room."

"She'll show him into the living room," Nana said.

Her mother pointed her finger at Carrie. "Remember

that my husband pays your salary. *I* run this house. If you value your job, you'll do as *I* say."

Carrie smiled and looked at Nana. Nana's face was pale. She swallowed hard before she answered. "Carrie has been my companion for thirty years—"

"And she can be fired tomorrow, if she—"

"Carrie can never be fired. This is her home as long as she lives. Perhaps you had better ask T.J. about our business arrangements. In the meantime let me assure you that *I* am mistress of this house and will be until the day I die. The only authority you have is what *I* give you."

"You're a senile old woman. If you're not careful, we'll put you in a nursing home."

"I'm going to forget you said that. And if I were you, I wouldn't ever suggest such a thing to T.J."

"We have already discussed it."

Carrie flinched, but Nana's expression did not change.

"Kate, I'm very sorry you are so unhappy."

"I wouldn't be unhappy if you would stop meddling in my business."

"I've done my best to stay out of your affairs."

"What do you call moving my daughter into the room next to yours without my permission?"

"No child will ever be abused in this house as long as—"

"Abused! . . . Abused! I'm the one that's abused." Her mother pointed at her. "That little monster has tormented me since the day she was born."

Laura tilted her head and made her face blank, like she did when her mother tried to make her talk. It was a direct challenge. She hoped her mother would slap her in front of Nana.

Nana did not give her time. She pushed Laura's chair back from the table. "Baby Girl, run outside and wait for Reverend Edwards. Will you do that for me?"

Laura wanted to stay and see what her mother said about her. But the kind way Nana put things, she could never refuse her. She left the kitchen, ran down the hall, opened and closed the front door—as though she had gone out—then tiptoed through the house to the pantry, where she could listen.

The pantry was one of her favorite hiding places. It was small and neat, with two doors—one to the kitchen, the other to the back hall—that provided easy escape when

85

she was being hunted. She felt secure there. The orderly rows of canned goods lined up like well-disciplined soldiers were her friends. Her soldiers. Ready to defend her no matter what she overheard from the kitchen.

Nana's voice was quiet, but she was angry. "How can you talk like that in front of your child? She understands every word you say. Can't you put yourself in her place? Imagine how it hurts her!"

"Nothing hurts her! What amazes me is how you are so taken in by all her tricks. How can you believe she understands, yet refuse to believe she can talk?"

"Kate, you feel so guilty about that child not talking that you imagine—"

"I don't imagine a damn thing! That kid can talk as well as you can."

Laura peeled the label off a can of peaches, rolled it up like a cigarette, and pretended to smoke.

"If she could talk at all, she would talk to me," Nana said.

"Well, she doesn't!"

"Because she can't! And she probably never will, until you change your attitude. Don't you think she knows that you don't love her?"

"That's not true!"

Laura exhaled make-believe smoke.

"Isn't it, Kate?" Nana asked. Her voice sounded sad.

"I love her, but I can't stand the way she acts. I could straighten her up if you'd keep your nose out of it."

"How? By kicking her down a flight of stairs?"

"It doesn't matter that she bit me and tried to twist my baby's foot off."

Laura chomped down on her label cigarette. Her mother had deserved everything she had done to her.

"What do you expect?" Nana asked. "The way you have ignored her since Melissa was born."

"Is that what you told T.J.?"

"He can see."

"You've done everything in your power to make me look bad."

"It didn't make you kick your daughter."

"No. She did that. And if she ever hurts my baby again, I'll do worse than that to her."

86

Laura moved her mouth and twisted her hips from side to side, silently mimicking her mother.

"Listen to yourself," Nana said. "Do you think a proper mother talks like that?"

"Who the hell are you to judge me? A senile old woman who lets a demented six-year-old make a fool of her. You're the one—"

"You've never tried to kick Harley down the stairs."

"He never needed it!"

Laura flicked imaginary cigarette ashes on top of a can of harvard beets, which Nana kept specifically for Harley. No one else would eat them.

Nana's voice was sharp. "Harley is all right. But Laura needs to be kicked down the stairs?"

"If that's what it takes to straighten her up."

"I never have any problems with her. And Carrie doesn't. Or her daddy. You're the only one who does."

"Because you are all blind. You don't want to see what she is. A sneaking, conniving—"

"She is a perfectly normal child. Except she can't talk."

"She *can* talk. And she *does* talk."

"If she talks, why only to you, Kate?"

"Because she wants to make me look crazy. She planned it. She—"

"Kate! Kate!"

She heard her mother's voice rise to a screech.

"Don't Kate me. She hates me, because I'm the only one who ever tried to control her. The rest of you just let her run wild."

"I don't treat her a bit different than I did Harley." Nana sounded calm again. "Children her age have so much energy. They have to be allowed to work it off. You can't expect her to act like a grown person."

"That's just it. She thinks like a grown person. She plans and schemes. She'll do anything to get her way."

"So does Harley."

"Not like her. He'd never dream of hurting his baby sister."

"I can remember a few times that he wasn't too gentle with Laura. He was as jealous of her as Laura is of the new baby."

"Harley never tried to twist her foot off."

"He never had to. You gave him *all* your attention, and ignored her."

"That's a lie!"

"Is it, Kate?"

Laura could tell that Nana was angry.

"You know you didn't want her," Nana continued. "You were upset the whole time you were pregnant."

"I wasn't ready for another baby. It took me a little time to get used to the idea. But when she was born—"

"When she was born you turned her over to Carrie and me. The only time you acted like her mother was when T.J. was home or someone else was around."

"You *have* lost your mind."

Laura blew imaginary smoke at her mother through the pantry door.

"I suppose *you* are the only sane person in this house?" Carrie asked.

"It looks that way."

"Kate. I don't want this ugliness between us. I've done my best." Nana sounded tired and sad. "You won't let me be close to you," she said.

"You never did think I was good enough for your son."

"That's not true. I was delighted when you married. I thought I'd have the daughter I always wanted."

"You had his wife all picked out. You wanted him to marry that Indian, although I couldn't imagine why. Neither could the rest of the town. Of course I heard gossip, that you were once in love with her father, that old charlatan healer."

That caught Laura's attention. She listened carefully, but for several long moments she didn't hear anything more. It was almost as if Nana was too stunned to speak. Then she heard her mother laugh sarcastically. Laura perked up. The conversation was getting interesting.

"Well, T.J. did date Molly all through high school and every time he came home from college," Nana said, ignoring the remark about her being in love with the healer. "I thought they would marry. I was more than a little surprised when he married you so suddenly."

"You were sick about it. You were as cold to me as everyone else in this snobbish town. Only you were a little more subtle about it."

"How can you say that? No bride has ever been more warmly received than you were. Don't you remember all the parties our friends gave?"

"Sure I do. And *she* was at all of them. Every time I looked up, there she was staring at me with those sad sloe eyes. *She* was the center of attention. Not me. Everyone was so concerned with consoling the jilted sweetheart, they didn't think about me. I was ignored, until it became obvious that she had found some man to console her. When her belly got so big she couldn't hide it anymore, all your *dear friends* finally dropped her from their guest lists. Only *then* did they make any effort to get to know me. And don't think I've ever forgotten it."

Laura danced a quiet jig in the pantry. The idea of her mother being a rejected wallflower thrilled her.

"T.J. was worse than any of them. The whole town was talking about her being pregnant, but he wouldn't hear a word against her. He humiliated me by defending her at the country club. I almost left him over that. Would have. But I was already pregnant with Harley."

"You might as well deal that card face up," Carrie said. "You were pregnant with Harley before you married."

"That's your dirty mind. He was a seven-month baby."

Carrie laughed. "A little nine-pound *preme.*"

"It doesn't matter," Nana said. "Kate, you were an excellent mother to Harley. And now Melissa. But Laura—"

"She gives me the creeps the way she's always sneaking around," her mother said. "Always watching. If that Indian slut hadn't been dead a year when Laura was born, I'd swear Laura was really her kid."

Laura threw her play cigarette on the pantry floor, and squashed it out with the ball of her foot the way her daddy did outdoors.

"That Molly put some sort of an Indian curse on me before she killed herself. A curse to make my own child torment me, as punishment for pulling T.J. away from her."

Her mother's voice had risen to a frenzied pitch that grated on Laura's nerves.

"Sometimes I wish to hell she had gotten him instead of me."

There were tears in Nana's voice. "If only I knew how to help you. T.J. and the children—all three of your children —need you."

Laura felt sick, hearing the silly, insulting way her mother laughed at Nana.

"Why you sanctimonious old bitch!"

"Watch your mouth, Missie," Carrie said. "Nobody talks to Mrs. D. like that while I'm here."

"You won't be here long enough to worry about it. As soon as I have a chance to talk to T.J., you'll be looking for another job."

Carrie laughed.

Kate screamed. "Shut up! Shut up! Shut up!"

The wall telephone was dialed.

"Who are you calling?" Kate demanded.

No answer.

"Put that phone down!" her mother shouted.

From Laura's hiding place she heard the stupid mud-baby bawling upstairs.

"Melissa is crying," Nana said. "Hadn't you better go up to her?"

"Who are you calling?" Kate demanded.

"You're upset. Dr. Barnes can give you something to make you feel better."

"There's nothing wrong with me! It's you. All of you."

Dishes shattered on the kitchen floor. A chair overturned. The heavy table screeched across the tile floor and banged against the pantry door. Her mother whimpered. Carrie's voice. Harsh. Breathless.

"If you ever raise your hand to Mrs. D. again, you won't have an arm. I'll break it off!"

"You fat bitch! You'll be out in the street tomorrow. No one will hire you."

. . . Crying. Not her mother. Laura had never heard that cry before . . . Carrie? . . . No. It was her Nana crying. Her mother had made Nana cry.

Laura tried to open the pantry door, but the table was against it. She pushed with all her strength. The door opened a crack, then stopped. The table was wedged against the cabinet. Her Nana was crying. But she could not get to her that way.

She opened the opposite pantry door. It banged against

the shelves, sending a row of canned goods crashing to the floor. Nana would know she had been listening, but she did not care. She had to stop her mother from hurting Nana.

Laura jumped across the rolling cans, and ran through the back hall, the dining room, the front hall. As she reached the kitchen door, her mother yelled, "Cry! See what it feels like. You've made me cry often enough!"

Laura flung the kitchen door open. Nana was leaning against the sink, her face buried in a dish towel. Carrie had her mother pinned to the wall, but she was about to break free.

Break free to hurt Nana. Laura started for her and tripped over a long-handled metal cooking spoon. She picked it up. It was heavy in her hand. She hit her mother with it as hard as she could. And kept hitting her, until Nana pulled her away.

Her mother struggled against Carrie's bulk. "There's your little angel . . . See how she acts. A little savage is what she is . . . Let go of me. I'll teach her to hit me."

Laura tried to break Nana's grip on her arms. She dug in with both feet and pulled like a cart pony. She wanted to smash her mother's face with the big spoon.

Nana was little, but she was strong. "No, Baby Girl. Your mother doesn't mean it. She doesn't know what she is saying."

"I mean every word, Laura! I'll kill you before I let you—"

Carrie boxed her across the face. Blood oozed out of the corner of her mouth. "Shut up," Carrie said, "before I ram my fist right down your throat."

Her mother clawed Carrie with her red polished nails. Carrie twisted her arm behind her, bent her forward, and forced her toward the door.

Laura managed to free her hand and swung the spoon as hard as she could at her mother's face. Her mother turned her head in time to avoid being hit in the nose, but the edge of the metal spoon cut across her ear. She shrieked like a tormented animal—a high keening sound. Laura loved it.

Another sound rose like a whirlwind from the depths of Laura's belly. A loud triumphant howl—so primitive, so integral that it would not be contained. She had won the battle. Her enemy was being led away in shame.

Nana held her fast, and Laura fought as though her life depended on breaking free. Nana was talking to her; but her voice seemed to come from a long way off, and Laura could not make out the words.

Pictures flashed in her mind. A party. People's backs. She was there, as well as her mother, dressed in a party dress, being led away by a group of women similarly dressed.

The picture receded, and Nana's voice sounded stronger.

"Be still, Baby Girl. Everything is going to be all right!"

Laura looked up. She felt closed in, like she had in her daddy's closet after her vision of the dark man. Seemingly, there was not enough air in the room. It was hard to breathe. Her lungs ached. Nana's wrinkled face was pinched and worried.

"You're safe, Baby Girl. Nana has you. Nana loves you more than anything else in the world."

Laura's arms hurt where Nana was holding her.

"Stand very still, and Nana will let you go."

Laura stood straight as a stick, looking up into her grandmother's face. Nana released one arm cautiously. Laura did not move. She released her other arm. Laura turned, grabbed Nana around the waist and held on. Nana backed up to a chair, took Laura in her lap, and held her tight.

Out in the hall the battle raged on. Her mother was fighting Carrie, but from the grunts and groans Laura could tell Carrie was winning. It sounded like they were tearing the house apart. Glass breaking, furniture being overturned. Everything in that hall had a history. Many of the things out of the treasure room had been put there. And none of it could be replaced. But Nana did not move. She pressed Laura's head to her small bosom, covering Laura's exposed ear with her hand, rocking as though the motion could block out the sounds and blot out the memory of her mother's rejection.

"What is going on here?"

It was a man's voice. Laura placed it in church. Reverend Edwards must have let himself in.

"Thank God," Nana said. But she would not let Laura down off her lap. She held her fast and continued to rock.

That stupid mud-baby was screaming frantically from upstairs.

"Thank goodness you've come," Laura heard her mother say from out in the hall. "Keep that crazy woman away from me while I call the sheriff."

"Surely we don't need the law, Kate," Reverend Edwards said.

"I want her arrested. She assaulted me," her mother said.

"Can't we settle this between the three of us? If you make a formal complaint, it will be in the paper—"

"Why should I care if it's in the paper?"

"Carrie has been here for years—"

"I want her out—"

"At least wait until T.J. gets home. Where is Mrs. Daniels?"

"She's in the kitchen," Carrie said.

Reverend Edwards stuck his head in the door.

"See if you can get her up to her room," Nana whispered. "The baby is crying."

The door closed.

Reverend Edwards's voice. "Come up with me to see about your baby, Kate. The poor little thing is crying so."

Running footsteps on the stairs. The bedroom door banged shut. Carrie came into the kitchen.

"Are you all right, Mrs. D.?"

"We're fine. What about you? Did she hurt you?"

"No. But she can fight like a wildcat."

"Here, hold this baby. Don't let her down."

Nana thrust Laura into Carrie's arms and hurried to the phone. She dialed a number. Laura could hear it ringing.

"June, this is Mrs. Daniels. Let me speak to T.J."

Across the room from the phone Laura could hear her daddy's secretary's crisp voice as plain as if she were right there in the kitchen.

"He isn't here. Could I take a message?"

"Where is he?"

"I'm not sure. Out at the rig, maybe."

"Find him. Tell him to come home immediately."

Nana hung up without giving any explanation.

"Carrie, I want you and Laura to go pick Harley up at school."

Carrie looked at the kitchen clock. "It's too late. By the time we get there, school will be out and he'll be on his way home."

"Then wait for the school bus out at the road. Take the kids to town and buy their supper. T.J. will be here by then."

"I can't leave you here, Mrs. D."

"Reverend Edwards will stay."

"What about this mess?"

"Leave it. I want T.J. to see for himself."

"I hate for you to go out into the hall. So many of your lovely things are broken."

"That's the least of my worries, now. The family is the important thing. Somehow we've got to hold the family together."

"I don't see how. Not with her and Laura and me in the same house. Just looking at Laura or me sets her off."

"For now. But I'm convinced it is a temporary thing. Her pregnancy, and the new baby. Too much of a strain on her. With rest and quiet, I think she'll be herself again."

"If you'll pardon me saying so, 'herself' wasn't so hot in the first place. I had to agree with what she said a while ago. T.J. sure missed the boat when he married her instead of Reming's mother. That child was the prettiest, sweetest little thing. I never have been able to get hold of the idea that she is dead."

"No time to look back."

Laura perked up—listening. So it was Reming's mother her mother had been talking about!

"If they had married," Carrie said, "she never would have died that terrible way. Reming and Harley would be brothers—like they want so bad to be. Not that I'm so sure they aren't—the way T.J. acts over Reming."

"Carrie! T.J. would have told us if that was his child. He wouldn't keep something like that!"

Reming? Her daddy's child? It felt true! Laura resolved to think about it later.

"Maybe she didn't tell him," Carrie said. "You know how proud she was. And her father, too. Don't tell me you haven't thought of it before."

"I've wished Reming was ours. But it never occurred to me that he might be."

"You look at him some time. He has expressions just like T.J. at that age."

"Could be. But most likely it's wishful thinking."

"No one could make me believe she had slipped so far that she didn't know who fathered her child."

"Hush, Carrie. Before you make me cry again. Hurry and pick up Harley. I don't want him to walk into this mess. After you and the children have had supper, call before you come home. You have plenty of money?"

"Sure, Mrs. D."

"Don't you think I should call Dr. Barnes and ask him to come over?"

"I sure do."

Nana was dialing the phone while Carrie hustled Laura out the back door. She wanted to kiss Nana before she left, but Carrie blocked the door and would not let her go back inside. At that moment, kissing Nana good-bye was the most important thing in her world.

Laura pled with her eyes, but Carrie took her hand and hauled her down the steps. She jerked free. Carrie grabbed her again.

"Come on now, Laura. We've got to hurry and meet Harley's bus."

Kissing Nana was too important to her. She fled back to the kitchen. Carrie followed her inside.

Nana said "Thank you" into the phone and hung up. Laura grabbed her around the waist and buried her face in her apron.

Nana picked her up. Laura covered her wrinkled face with kisses. Her cheeks were wet. Though smiling, Laura knew Nana's heart was aching.

Laura felt as she did when the pictures came, only there were no pictures now. Emotions flooded her. Loneliness. Anger. Love. Sadness. Nana's feelings. Not her own.

Nana thrust her into Carrie's strong arms. She did not want to leave her Nana like that. She kicked and screamed, but Carrie took her out to the car and held her down in the front seat while she started the motor and backed out of the garage.

Reverend Edwards had parked his car in the middle of

the driveway, and Carrie had a hard time maneuvering Nana's big Cadillac past it. While she was struggling, Laura managed to get the passenger door open, but Carrie swatted her, then reached across and slammed it shut.

Laura's whole hip stung from Carrie's heavy hand. Her swats were not like Nana's love pats.

"You straighten up, before I stop this car and blister you. Your Nana has enough worries without you acting like a fool!"

Laura climbed into the back seat and pouted.

They met Harley, and Carrie let him choose where they would eat. He picked one of the two drive-ins in town, but when the food came, Laura refused to touch hers. Carrie ate it as she did all the leftovers at home. That was why she was so fat. Laura wished she could tell her so.

After they left the restaurant Carrie drove around town for a long time before she called home. Afterward she kept driving. She and Harley sounded like two of Nana's geese, the way they gaggled and chattered in the front seat. Listening to them bored Laura. She went to sleep.

She awoke in her own bed. At first she did not know exactly where she was. Her room seemed all turned around. It was a shock—going to sleep in one place, and waking in another. She had never slept that soundly before.

Outside her window, stars twinkled in the navy blue sky like the diamonds in her mother's wedding rings. The sparkling rings had always fascinated her. They looked out of place on her mother's big hands. Like they were made for another person. She remembered her mother's red polished nails clawing at Carrie.

Nothing would ever be the same again. Not ever. Laura was sure of it. The change had started when her mother brought that stupid mud-baby home. The scene in the kitchen had further widened the breach between them. Laura no longer fit into her mother's life. That mud-baby had squeezed her out.

It was hot in the room. The windows were open, but there was no breeze. The air smelled of dust and scorched grass. Desperate smells. As desperate and desolate as Laura's thoughts.

She tossed and turned in her bed, whispering to her

clown not to be afraid. She wished for the dark man who had appeared to her in her daddy's closet, but he did not come. Her damp hair stuck to her forehead. She brushed it back and shivered. She felt cold and hot at the same time.

The closet door was open, and the moonlight turned her clothes into ominous, stalking shapes—ready to spring at her. She wanted her Nana. Nana would let her sleep in her bed.

Laura threw the covers off, grabbed her clown, and dashed into Nana's room before the closet shapes had time to follow. She checked behind her to make sure nothing was there. Then tiptoed to Nana's bedside. Her bed was made. It had not been slept in. Laura backed against the bed, holding her clown in front of her so it could defend her against the closet demons if they came out of the darkness.

She heard voices coming from the kitchen. Her daddy's —deep, musical. And Nana's—much higher, and a little cracked, like she was tired.

The hardwood floor felt cool and smooth on her bare feet as Laura crept down the back hall toward the sliver of light under the kitchen door. She stopped outside and listened.

"Dr. Barnes suggested that I hire a nurse for Kate and the baby," her daddy was saying, "someone more her own age, who could also be a companion to her. What do you think?"

"Seems like the only solution. She won't want Carrie or me, not after today. And she can't manage on her own."

"She could if she wanted to."

Nana ignored his statement. "If only we could find someone she got along with as well as Carrie and I have all these years. Someone permanent."

"It won't be easy. Young women aren't satisfied to live in anymore. You can't blame them. No chance for a life of their own. Not stuck off out here at the ranch."

Laura heard a cup rattle against a saucer like a nervous hand had put it down, then Nana's tired voice.

"T.J., I hate to bring it up. But have you thought about moving to the city. You could build a nice home. Kate might be happier in her own home. Of course, Laura could stay with me."

Laura choked her clown in a security hug. The idea of her daddy moving off and leaving her, even with Nana, was staggering. The others could go. She would be glad. But not her daddy.

"You can't run this ranch alone," she heard her daddy say to Nana.

"If I can't, we can close down. Feed was so high we operated in the red last year."

"I don't want to live in the city. I don't want my children growing up in the city. I want them to grow up here, like I did. Like you did. And your father."

"Then what about building a house close by?"

"Do you want us out of here?"

"You know better than that. I think Kate might be happier in her own place."

Who cared if her mother was happy? She and her clown knew how much her mother worried about making anyone else happy.

"Kate knew this was a family operation when we married," her daddy said. "I want my children to have the same security I had. If she can't adjust—that's her problem."

Laura felt her clown's stuffed chest puff out with pride. Her daddy's head was where it should be, even if Nana was not thinking straight.

"Maybe I should build a little bungalow. Carrie and I could—"

Her daddy's voice sounded angry.

"That's ridiculous! I'd move myself before I let you leave this house. You've never lived anyplace else."

"This house is a pile of wood," Nana said. "We are talking about your marriage. And your children."

"Put it out of your mind, Mother. If Kate can't adjust, then she can leave. But you and the children stay here where you belong."

"Don't close your mind, T.J."

"I mean it. Things have been bad between us almost from the first. If she walked out of here tomorrow—"

"T.J.! This is a family, not a business. If things don't go to suit you, you don't close up shop. You cope as best you can, and keep on coping."

Her clown almost always agreed with Nana. But not this time. It stiffened huffily in her arms.

"I don't intend to become a martyr for her. I'm sick of all this nonsense about Laura. Kate talks about our child like she was some kind of evil spirit. I don't understand it, Mother."

"Neither do I. But I'm convinced it's real to her. Try to be patient."

"I can't."

"You can!"

Laura's clown twisted angrily from side to side.

"When I see what she is doing to Laura?" There was real hurt in her daddy's voice.

"Laura will survive. She has me. . . . And Carrie."

"But Kate's attitude is contagious. Harley is picking it up. The other day he told me that Laura spooked his pony. She wasn't anywhere around, but he blamed her when his horse threw him."

Her clown pressed tight against her chest, warning her to be quiet.

Laura turned her back to the kitchen door and clamped her hand over her mouth, sealing off the giggle that threatened to escape. She *had* spooked his horse. But he was too dumb to figure out how. The last time he had chased her away from the war game—after Reming had taken his tin soldiers home—she had buried two furniture tacks in the middle of Harley's fleece-lined saddle blanket. He still had not found them. She had checked. The next next time he got up his nerve to get back on his horse—it would throw him again!

"He was embarrassed," Nana said. "He didn't want you to think he couldn't handle his horse."

"But why blame Laura?"

"They'd probably had a little spat before he went riding. Most likely she was the first to pop into his mind."

"But that's just the point. Kate blames Laura for everything that goes wrong around here."

"I'm sure Harley didn't mean anything by it. His pride wouldn't let him admit failure to you."

"What's Kate's excuse?"

The question went unanswered in a silence so heavy Laura could hear the creaking of the old house. Finally Nana spoke.

"If she had gall bladder trouble, or a bad back, we wouldn't be groping for answers like this. We'd accept it, and do what we could to help her get well. . . . Why do we expect people's minds to be stronger than their bodies?"

Nana's speech made Laura's clown feel very stiff and grow cold in her arms. Her clown was not about ready to accept or excuse the misery her mother had caused them.

"One of the things that first appealed to me about Kate," her daddy said, "was her will to survive. To win. She's always been so much in control."

"She will be again. There's no reason to believe this is any more permanent than gall bladder trouble. Money is no problem. We have the means to get her all the help she needs to overcome this."

"The best help we could ever find lives right across the mountain," her daddy said. "John Crow has cured ailments regular doctors couldn't even diagnose. Patients come to him from all parts of the country."

At the mention of the name John Crow, Laura felt her clown begin to shiver. She bent to study it in the light coming under the closed door. Looking at her hands holding the stuffed clown, it seemed her hands were shaking the clown. She clasped her fingers together and pressed it between her palms to keep from dropping it. One thing was sure. Her clown did not want John Crow anywhere near her mother.

"Kate wouldn't accept help from John," Nana said.

The clown stopped shaking.

"If Indian doctoring is good enough for that crooked Congressman she helped get elected, it ought to be good enough for her."

"Even if she'd admit she has a problem, she wouldn't have John. Because of who he is. That was one of the things she raved about today."

Laura's mind raced, trying to relate what her mother had said earlier to the present conversation. She was brought up short by the sternness in her daddy's voice.

"Did Kate say things about Reming?"

Her daddy was always quick to defend Reming.

"Only indirectly. But she accused me of being disappointed because you didn't marry his mother."

"I wish to God I had it to do over!"

The conviction in her daddy's voice gave Laura the same exultant feeling she had when she pulled a successful prank on her mother. It made her feel she was winning, even though her clown was acting a silly goose.

Laura wondered, though, about all the times Reming had invited her to his house before his grandfather had threatened her. Her clown had never wanted to go, even back then. She had always supposed it was because Harley raised such a fuss with Nana not to let her, but now she knew different. Her clown had some other reason to fear Reming's grandfather.

"The nurse is the best idea," Nana said.

"How should I go about finding one? Dr. Barnes couldn't recommend anyone."

"Advertise, I suppose."

"In the Oklahoma City and Tulsa papers? What should I say?"

" 'Live-in nurse-companion . . . wanted for mother of three . . . with new baby.' Something like that. I'd specify between the ages of thirty and forty-five. Give the office phone number. You screen them before Kate meets them."

"I don't expect many applications. We'll probably have to take what we can get."

Laura yawned and accidentally leaned against the kitchen door. It came open. She stood blinking, rubbing her eyes in the bright light. Her daddy got up and came to her.

"There's my girl. Did you wake up?"

He picked her up and hugged her so hard she could not breathe. She had to tickle him to make him stop.

Nana looked at the wall clock. "It's after two. We should all be in bed."

Laura pointed at the kitchen sink for a drink of water.

"Can you say 'water' for Daddy?"

The hope in his eyes made Laura want to repeat that silly word for him as much as she had wanted to say "baby" for Nana. She was about to open her mouth to say "water" when her clown slipped from between her and her daddy. She almost tumbled headfirst onto the floor catching it. By the stiff way it felt in her arms, she could tell that her clown would never forgive her if she gave away their secret. She buried her face in her clown's chest to keep from looking at her daddy.

He hugged her as though to say "never mind." She

tickled him, and they giggled all the way down the hall to her room. He put her in bed with her clown on her stomach, got in beside her, and cuddled them both until she went to sleep thinking about that lock of hair tied up with her daddy's that she had thought was her own. It must have belonged to his old girlfriend, Molly Crow, Reming's mother.

It was raining when Laura awoke the next morning. Someone had closed her window, but the rain came in driving sheets and pounded on the glass. It was a cold, lonesome sound like the whimper of a hungry puppy. Laura was lonesome and hungry. She hurriedly put on her socks and shoes. She had slept in her playclothes. Nana was sure to make her change into a fresh set for today, but not before breakfast.

The house was quiet and dark as an empty church as Laura slipped down the back hall to the kitchen. She found Nana and Carrie sipping coffee and talking in subdued tones.

When she came in, Nana looked up and tried to make her face cheerful, but her heart was not in it.

"There's our late sleeper. Dirty as a little pig and hungry as a great big bear."

Laura took her place at the table and watched Nana prepare her breakfast. She felt like a stranger who had stumbled into the wrong house. Nana and Carrie, always busy and bustling, were listless and dull-eyed. They seemed much older, and very tired.

Upstairs, the stupid mud-baby cried. That hated noise grated on Laura's senses. It did not belong in her house.

Nana nodded toward the disconnected buzzer.

"Maybe I should get that fixed."

"I doubt if she'd use it now."

Nana set Laura's plate with a cup of hot chocolate in front of her.

"Do you think I should go up and check on her, Carrie?"

"No. We better leave well enough alone."

"You're right, of course. But it's hard not knowing what's going on up there."

The mud-baby screamed louder and Laura left her breakfast and headed for the stairs.

Carrie caught her. "No you don't, young lady. You leave your mother alone."

"After she finishes eating," Nana said, "would you give her a bath and keep her occupied?"

"Surely will." Carrie hoisted Laura back into her chair and pressed her down.

"From now on we'll have to do our best to keep Laura out of Kate's way."

Carrie's firm hands said she would not stand for any monkey business. Laura gulped her hot chocolate and resigned herself to being Carrie's charge.

Carrie would not let Laura play outside, and there was nothing to do in the house but follow the fat old housekeeper around and help her dust the furniture and fold the laundry. Laura liked to fold laundry but she refused to touch anything that belonged to her mother or that stupid mud-baby. Carrie tried to make her fold those things, too, but Nana said, "No. Let it go."

After helping Carrie most of the morning, Laura, with her clown, slipped away into the library, which was also her daddy's study. Really it was her study, too, her sanctuary.

It had been her sanctuary ever since she had managed to get Harley one of her daddy's most important contracts to fold into a model airplane. Of course Harley had tried to explain that its subsequent mutilation had been all her fault. His explanation had only served to further infuriate their father. With barely controlled rage, he had banned Harley forever from that room, just as Laura had anticipated that he would.

Now, with her mother pouting in self-imposed seclusion, it was the one place in the house where Laura could count on being undisturbed. She chose a rancher's magazine from the desk and carried it to the front window.

To accommodate the thick rock walls the window sill was more than a foot wide. It afforded her a perfect seat, where, while reading, she could keep watch on the road for her daddy's truck.

Perched there, Laura saw that it had begun to rain.

November

It rained all that day and the next. Then it turned cold. One gray day faded into another. The cold outside the library window made the leaves turn all shades of yellow and orange. One old pin oak, out near the road, turned bright red as if someone had set it on fire, but the beautiful color did not last. In a few days, it turned burnt orange, then brown, and the leaves began to fall. Then it rained for a week, and the lawn was matted with soggy, rotting leaves.

It was a dreary time. Dampness pervaded the silent house, and there were no cheerful faces to dispel the gloom.

Her daddy looked sad in the morning when he left for work, and sad when he came home at night. Nana scurried around all day long, quietly doing her chores, like a worried ant. And Carrie, usually gay and boisterous, dogged Laura's path every minute Laura wasn't cloistered in the library.

The long days melted into each other with nothing to break their sameness but Harley's arrival from school. He acted as though he was unaware of the change except that he had a new job. Since the big fight, her mother had been paying him a dollar a day to do some of the chores Carrie had done before.

Every afternoon he came barreling into the house at three forty-five, shouting to Nana that he was starving. Taking a sandwich or a handful of cookies, balanced on top of a basket of clean baby clothes, up to his mother's room, he disappeared behind the locked door, where Laura could hear him vacuuming the carpet and splashing water like crazy cleaning the bathroom.

Nana and Carrie always stopped what they were doing

and came out into the hall to stare up at the closed door, listening to Harley and her mother laughing together. They smiled and nodded to each other when they heard her mother's laughter, but Laura did not see anything to smile about. There was nothing happy about the distinction her mother made between Harley and her. Her clown reminded her about it when they were in bed at night. Reminded her that her mother was paying Harley to do chores Laura had always helped with, without so much as an offer of payment.

And Harley was so smug about it, too. Counting his money in the living room every evening for her daddy to see, bragging about what he was going to buy, taunting her—out of her daddy's hearing, of course. He said their mother might pay *her* for doing chores if she was not so lazy and stupid about talking.

Money meant nothing to Laura, but she felt like punching him. Her mother, too. The few times her mother came downstairs during the day—to bring a load of dirty baby laundry, or fix herself something to eat—she glared at Laura and told her how sloppy she looked. She mooed like an old weaning cow about what a good boy Harley was and what a help he was to her. At least once a day she asked Laura when she was going to stop being a liar and talk to Nana and her daddy.

Her mother was the liar. Harley would not have lifted a finger to help her if she had not been paying him. He was not good. He was greedy. Her mother knew it. Laura itched to say it to her face. She did not dare, though, because Carrie was always around. All she could do was pretend hurt feelings, to make Carrie glower at her mother in her defense. Then she would run away to hide on the top bookshelf in her daddy's study, where she and her clown spent hours planning what they were going to do to her mother and Harley and the stupid mud-baby.

Her clown was so clever. It thought up the funniest things to say to her mother. Stuff to worry her, besides making her look crazy when she repeated it. Laura had to save one of her clown's best lines for nearly two weeks before she had a chance to use it.

Her first opportunity to slip away from Carrie came while Carrie and Nana were busy organizing the shelves of home-canned food in the storm cellar. Laura made a real effort to be annoying. Finally, Nana sent her for the kitchen scissors and a pencil. She knew perfectly well what scissors Nana meant, but she dashed up the stairs to her mother's sewing room, hurried to find the good scissors, which she stuffed in her rear pocket, and rushed back to the hall, where she stood listening outside her mother's door.

She felt very smug about the scissors. If she was caught it would be easy to pretend a misunderstanding. She wished for her clown—that it could be there when she delivered its line—but she had left it in the cellar with Nana and Carrie, so they would not suspect she had a plan.

Through the paneled door, Laura could hear her mother saying, "You're the smartest baby girl in the whole world. Look how you are sitting up at only four months."

Laura eased the door open and found her mother, in the middle of the bed, facing the baby, trying to balance the clumsy lumpish thing into a sitting position. Each time she took her hands away it slumped to one side or the other and fell backward onto a stack of pillows. The stupid thing giggled at each fall. Nose wrinkled, tongue stuck out like an excited billy goat, it spluttered and drooled all over its shirt.

Disgusted, Laura stood watching, unnoticed, until the mud-baby saw her, and leaned around her mother's shoulder to stare. It stopped spitting and grew quiet. Its wet lips glistened in the light. Her mother followed the baby's gaze, and Laura noticed how she stiffened at finding her standing behind her in the middle of her bedroom.

"Does your grandmother know you are up here?" her mother asked in her most snippish manner.

Laura marched to the edge of the bed and clapped her hands as hard as she could next to the baby's ear.

It screamed, drowning out Laura's giggle.

Her mother grabbed the baby and hurried around the bed to put it in its crib. She put a pacifier in its mouth before she whirled on Laura.

"Why did you do that?"

Laura ignored her. She turned and walked toward the door, swinging her hips in a mockery of her mother's walk.

"Laura! You mock me all you please. But your baby

sister hasn't done anything to deserve your being mean to her! You are going to keep on until you make me hurt you."

At the door, Laura turned, cocked her head, and stared at her mother's breasts. She covered her mouth with her hand and snickered. Her mother looked down self-consciously.

Laura back-stepped across the threshold into the hall, so she would be ready to run. She wrinkled her nose in distaste and pointed with her two fingers forked.

"That baby has sucked your tits all out of shape," Laura said, wishing her clown was there to see the shock on her mother's face. "They're hanging lower every day."

Her mother cupped her hands under her breasts, lifted them, tightened her bra straps one at a time, then went to the mirror, and looked at her profile.

"They may be a little bigger, but they are definitely not hanging," she said, turning back to Laura.

Laura stuck her hand down the neck of her shirt to tug on her make-believe bra. "Old Floppy!" she taunted.

"Get away from me!" her mother yelled, and started after her.

Laura ran for the stairs and was almost to the bottom when Harley burst through the front door and threw his school books on a hall chair.

Her mother ran to the rail calling, "Stop her, Harley."

Startled, Harley looked up at his mother, then at Laura.

"Catch her, Harley! This time she is going to talk! I'm going to make her talk so you can hear her. Then I won't be the only one."

Laura fished for the scissors in her back pocket. She had a weapon. The long silver scissor blades had poked through her pants. She jerked them out, not caring how big a hole they made in the material.

At the bottom of the stairs, Harley stood blocking the kitchen door. Laura gripped the scissors by their black painted handles. She swiped viciously at Harley, feeling no sympathy for him. He pulled in his stomach and fell sideways to escape being gouged. Laura swiped at him again, and he screamed.

"Help me, Mama. She's trying to stab me."

Laura rushed ahead as her mother came leaping down the stairs.

Harley was crying in her mother's arms when Laura cleared the swinging kitchen door and ran into Nana coming in from the cellar.

"What is taking you so long?" Nana asked. "Can't you find—"

Laura thrust the scissors into Nana's hand and ducked under her arm just as her mother banged through the kitchen door and stood glowering at her, with Harley cowering behind.

"The next time you try to hurt Harley or my baby I'm going to give you something you'll never forget."

Nana looked past her mother to Harley. "What happened?"

"Laura tried to stab me with the scissors."

"What did you do to her?"

"I was trying to stop her, like Mother told me. Laura was running from her."

"I told him to catch her," her mother said, defending him. "I was going to make her repeat to Harley what she said to me upstairs before he came home."

"If the child ever talks to me," Nana said, "I don't know that I'd want to share it with anyone."

"You would if she insulted you."

Nana hugged Laura to her. "Did she insult you?"

Laura bit her lower lip to keep from laughing when her mother answered.

"She said the baby was sucking my tits all out of shape!"

At mention of the word "tits," Laura felt Nana's back stiffen.

"Laura said they were hanging lower all the time and would soon be flopping. How would you like that?"

"I would not feel any compulsion to make her repeat it to Harley. I know that."

"It wasn't what she said. I want someone to hear her talk besides me!"

Nana shook her head sadly. "I do, too, Kate. I do, too."

"You don't believe me. You think I'm making it up."

Nana was silent. Harley looked at her as though begging her to say she believed his mother. Finally, he said, "I believe you, Mother. Laura has always been bad. She likes to hurt people. I believe she said it!"

Laura hugged Nana's waist, to make her think what Harley said hurt her, and turned her head slightly to smile contemptuously at him across the room. He was choosing a hard way to go—siding with her mother.

As though he had some inkling of his mistake, he was tugging at her mother's hand, practically dragging her out of the kitchen.

Following Nana back to the storm cellar, Laura felt pleased about Harley's nervousness. Best that he knew he was her enemy. He would worry about it.

"These are your mother's good sewing scissors. You wouldn't have gotten in all that trouble if you had brought me the ones out of the kitchen drawer," Nana scolded mildly.

Laura snapped on a sad face.

"Not that I believe for a minute," Nana added quickly, "that you said those things to your mother. However, I do believe you took a swipe at Harley with the scissors. I realize that it was two against one, and one of the two an adult at that, but you could have done permanent damage. I know you wouldn't want to hurt your brother."

Laura shook her head.

Nana smiled. "I know you wouldn't, Dear."

After supper Laura slipped off, with her clown, to her daddy's study. She climbed to the high shelf, only to be suddenly overcome with the fear of falling. With her clown balanced precariously on her stomach, she went rigid on her back, eyes closed, gripping the edge of the narrow shelf, fighting the unreasonable fear that the board, which had held her all her life, would give way and tip her over the edge.

She imagined herself falling. Falling. Falling through endless space, never to touch anything solid again. While she was falling she saw a big blackbird appear. A blackbird—circling over her mother—cawing her given name: K-a-t-e—K-a-t-e—K-a-t-e. The bird dove in a downward spiral toward her mother's frightened, cowering head. Her clown joined the bird screaming: K-a-t-e—K-a-t-e—K-a-t-e. It rhymed with hate. Hate. Hate. Hate.

The blackbird disappeared. Her clown grew quiet. But the sound of her mother's name echoed inside her head, and with it the rhyming words: K-a-t-e—H-a-t-e, K-a-t-e—H-a-t-e, K-a-t-e—H-a-t-e. She hated her mother—surely. Her clown knew. But it was more than her mother's nagging and her favoritism for Harley and that ugly mud-baby that made her want to hurt them all. There was a reason she could not remember no matter how hard she tried. She had always suspected that her clown knew. That it had something to do with the clown wanting her to talk only to her mother. But she could not be sure.

There were so many things she was not sure of, like her daddy always calling her clown a "him." Laura was not sure it was a him at all. Sometimes, she had the feeling it was a lady, but she could not say why.

The Saturday before Thanksgiving, Laura and Harley went with Nana to Will Rogers World Airport in Oklahoma City to pick up the nurse her daddy had hired.

They arrived an hour early, and after Nana had inquired at one of the ticket counters and found out where they had to go to meet the flight, she allowed Harley to browse in a little curio shop off the main lobby.

He wanted to buy everything he picked up; but Nana said "no" to everything, and Laura was pleased with the disappointment on his face. He was as stupid as that ugly baby. Laura was not about to waste a minute of her first trip to an airport on toys.

In her excitement she had left her clown in the car and did not even miss him, so fascinated was she by the noise and the crowds of well-dressed people hurrying about. It was easy to tell the travelers from those who had come to see someone off or pick someone up. The travelers had worried faces, walked faster, and usually had too much luggage.

A lady's voice on the loudspeaker announced that Trans World Airline Flight 212 was arriving at Gate Nine.

"That's her flight," Nana said. "Let's go."

Nana took Harley's hand, and he made grumbling noises all the way down the glass-enclosed concourse.

Laura tuned him out. She was too busy examining the monstrous plane parked outside the window.

"Help me look for her, Harley," Nana said. "She is very tall."

"How do you know? You've never seen her."

"I read her application. She is five-eleven. And she listed her weight as a hundred and seventy pounds."

"A hundred and seventy is pretty fat for a lady."

"Not when they are that tall."

"Will she be wearing a nurse's uniform?"

"I think not."

Laura spotted her the minute she emerged from the long tunnel that spanned the distance to the plane. She was taller than most of the men around her, and her face was as flat as her chest. Her eyes were wide-set and small, her lips too thin, and her teeth too big. She looked like a very homely teen-aged football player in a skirt. Laura ducked under the rope, dodged up the aisle, and took her hand.

The instant their hands touched, Laura knew she had an ally. She saw the nurse as a little girl, as handicapped by her ugliness as Laura was thought to be by her lack of speech.

Her looks made Laura happy. She had anticipated problems with the nurse. The thought of having a stranger in the house had been threatening to her. But her mother was now the threatened one. She had been homecoming queen in college. The trophy was on the dresser in her bedroom.

Laura squeezed the nurse's hand and smiled up at the ugly face. Its sternness disappeared in the warmth of her acceptance.

"You must be Laura."

Laura nodded.

"Your daddy told me all about you."

Laura led her to Nana and Harley. The nurse introduced herself.

"Mrs. Daniels?"

"Yes."

"I'm Major Klaris Pledge, retired."

Nana smiled. "This is my grandson, Harley."

Harley shook hands with her. "Were you a real major? In the army?"

"Yes. This is my first civilian job."

"I hope you'll be happy with us," Nana said. "We feel very fortunate to have someone with your qualifications."

"Private duty will be like an extended vacation after supervising a staff of forty nurses."

Laura tugged gently at her hand and started toward the luggage area she had noticed when they entered.

"It seems my guide is trying to tell us something."

"Laura doesn't talk," Nana said. "But she has a way of making herself understood."

Harley made a face at Laura. "She is mean as the devil—"

"Harley! If you can't say something nice, then keep still."

"It's the truth! Mother says so all the time."

"And you know what I think about that!"

"Well, Mother is right! She's always doing mean things to both of us."

"You've acted up since the moment we got here. Right now, those ugly labels fit you better than Laura."

Since the day Laura had had to use the scissors to keep her mother and Harley from cornering her, Harley had launched a campaign of constant criticism against her. She really did not blame him. He had chosen the losing side. He was using the only advantage he had, his ability to talk. He could talk to both sides, while she had set herself to talk only to the enemy.

"Laura has always been your pet!" Harley said.

"Be quiet!" Nana snapped, showing a rare flash of temper.

He stuffed his hands in his pockets and walked ahead.

Nana watched him to the terminal door, when he stopped, before she turned to the nurse.

"That's a small sample of what we are dealing with. Kate's attitude is contagious. You may wish you were back running an army hospital."

They collected the nurse's luggage, and Laura waited with her on the sidewalk while Nana and Harley brought the car around. After it was loaded, Laura crawled in the front seat beside Nana and the nurse; but Harley complained that she always got to sit in the front, and Nana asked her to get in the back seat with Harley.

While Nana threaded her way through traffic to the restaurant where she had made reservations, Laura hugged her clown and thought about how it was going to help her get even with Harley. Her poor clown. They had been friends a long time, but now the nurse was her new friend. If she worked it just right the nurse might be even more helpful to her than her clown.

The waiter led them to a table in the middle of the

red-carpeted room and held a chair for Nana. The nurse seated herself before he had a chance to help her. She looked around nervously. Two ladies at the next table stared at her, whispered something behind their hands, then giggled. Her cheeks turned red. She buttoned and unbuttoned her plain brown jacket and looked at her watch.

Laura knew the ladies were laughing because the nurse was ugly. She had been laughed at because of her clown. Being laughed at had made her feel so sad and embarrassed, but her daddy had been there to comfort her. Wanting to comfort the nurse, she put her finger on the nurse's watch band.

"She wants to see your watch," Nana said.

"Does she tell time?"

"I think so, but we have no way of knowing."

The nurse extended her wrist and pointed. "See. The little hand is on the twelve. The big hand is almost straight up. It's about three minutes until noon."

Laura nodded and smiled.

"She's just a dummy," Harley said, making an idiot's face at Laura. "I could tell time when I was younger than her. She's already turned seven and only been to school one day in her life. She got kicked out of first grade last year. She should be in the second."

"Harley, that's enough!" Nana said. "You're almost twelve, and you still haven't learned to behave like a gentleman."

The waiter came and took their order, then Nana tried to soothe Harley's feelings by asking him to tell about his school and his pony. His narrative lasted until the food came, then Nana had to remind him not to talk with his mouth full. Laura wrinkled her nose at him. He was such a slob.

It was a largely silent meal. Nana did not say much, apparently put off by the nurse's homely appearance. Laura wished she could talk, to put her new friend at ease. Halfway through the dessert, Nana sighed. "I'm just exhausted. The excitement, I guess. Would you mind if we stayed in a motel tonight and started home in the morning? I don't think I can face the drive home."

"I'd be glad to drive, Mrs. Daniels. I'm not a bit tired. And I am rather anxious to meet my new patient."

Harley frowned. "I want to stay in a motel. Besides, Melissa is not a patient. She's just a baby."

Nana ignored him. "I hate to take advantage of you like that."

"I'd enjoy it. I like to drive. Besides, I'm anxious to see the country. I've only been in Oklahoma once before, and that was merely a one day layover at Tinker Field."

"If you really don't mind. I *would* rather get on home."

Laura held the nurse's hand on the way to the car. When the nurse opened the door on the driver's side, she lifted Laura into the front seat and gave Harley a look that said he better not comment. Laura smiled at the dashboard. She was very pleased with the way his conduct was working to her advantage.

In the back seat Harley pouted. He did not say another word all the way through town to the interstate. Laura stood up in her seat to see what he was doing and found him asleep. She tapped on the nurse's shoulder and pointed.

The nurse glanced in the rearview mirror. "Looks like our boy has gone to sleep."

Nana turned and peered over the seat. "Thank goodness. This certainly hasn't been his day. He's really a good boy. But he hasn't been himself the past few weeks. None of us have."

The nurse spoke in a confidential tone.

"While he's asleep, I'd like to hear a little more about the situation. I'd rather not walk in cold."

"I thought T.J. had explained it to you."

"As well as he could long distance. But I'd like to hear it from you."

Laura opened Nana's purse and took out the pad and pencil Nana always kept there for her. She sat down in the seat and bent over the pad, intent on drawing the prettiest lady she could. She pretended not to be listening, so they would feel free to talk.

There was a moment's pause. Nana looked out of the window, and, without looking back, she spoke, keeping her voice down.

"Kate was a wonderful mother with Harley. But her second pregnancy wasn't planned. She was much different. Then, when it became apparent the child was mute, she couldn't accept it."

Laura bent over her drawing and did not look up.

"Have you had the child examined?"

"Yes. Many specialists. Best we could find. They said there is no reason she can't talk. Her hearing is fine."

"That was good news."

"Should have been. But it made things worse. After that, her mother was determined to *make* her talk."

"Worse thing she could have done."

Laura smiled at her drawing pad. The nurse was going to work out fine.

"I did my best to convince Kate that what was needed was time, and patience," Nana said. "Things really got bad during this last pregnancy. Then, just before the baby was born Kate started claiming that Laura was talking to her. Not one or two words, either. But whole long sentences. Implausible, vulgar things."

"Did anyone else hear the child talk?"

"No. Not ever."

"These children usually talk—eventually. But only when it's important to them. The key is motivation."

Adults could be so funny. Because she did not talk, they seemed to forget her presence, that she was listening to what they said about her.

"Have you had much experience with this kind of thing?"

"Unfortunately not with children. However, I have worked with a few soldiers who had lost the power of speech. Shock victims."

"I've often wondered if that wasn't our problem. Shock, I mean. Something may have happened to the child that I don't know about. Her mother might have misused her in some way. That thought gives me nightmares."

"Probably did. It could be something the child doesn't even remember."

The nurse's comment about not remembering brought back the uneasiness Laura had felt after her vision in her daddy's closet. She tuned out their conversation, choosing not to think about it, and put all her effort into drawing her pretty lady. After several false starts she managed to draw an oval-shaped face with large, even eyes, a straight nose, and a big smile. She added curly hair, and her own rather lopsided version of a nurse's cap. It was at least as good as Harley could do. She was pleased.

"Kate has kept to her room since the day of the big scene," Nana was saying. "I haven't even seen the baby."

"Is she breast-feeding?"

"Yes."

Laura stiffened. The memory of her mother, half-naked on the bed, with that ugly mud-baby sucking on her, was still repulsive to her. She reached out and turned the car radio on as loud as it would go.

Nana turned it off. "Laura?"

She stomped her foot on the carpeted floorboard.

"I see what you mean about her making herself understood," the nurse said. "There's no mistaking that statement."

"It's going to be a real problem, fostering good feelings between Laura and her little sister."

Laura glared at Nana until she looked out the window. She would never claim that stupid baby as her sister. Not even for Nana.

The nurse patted Laura's knee, and Laura took her hand.

Laura knew the nurse understood. She could feel it in her touch. The nurse did not like that baby either, and she had not even seen it yet. She never would like it, now that they had become friends.

Laura wanted to do something special for the nurse. Something that would seal their friendship forever. She thought about it while she watched the scenery roll past the car window.

Harley woke up, and Nana started talking to him, but Laura paid no attention to what they were saying. Her gift for the nurse had to be something she would never forget. What Laura had in mind, once she gave it, could never be taken back.

When Nana pointed out the turnoff to the ranch, Laura made her decision. She felt very strong. Strong enough to handle anything that came. She moved forward in the seat, hovering over her drawing so no one could see what she was doing. She had to hurry to finish before the car stopped.

The nurse turned into the circle drive in front of the house just as Laura tore her drawing off the pad. She folded it in half and stuck the pad and pencil back in Nana's purse.

Nana smiled at the nurse and said, "I hope you'll be happy here and come to think of this as your home."

"Thank you very much, Mrs. Daniels."

The nurse opened the door and started to get out, but Laura tugged at the hem of her jacket. The nurse smiled at her. Somehow her smile made her even homelier.

"What is it, Laura?"

Laura put the folded paper in the nurse's hand.

"Is this for me?"

Laura nodded enthusiastically.

The nurse unfolded the paper and stared. She looked at Laura and smiled. But the smile seemed strained. Her thin lips began to tremble. She helped Laura out of the car, closed the door, and walked back to the trunk where Nana was waiting to help with her luggage.

Nana took the drawing. "What's this?"

"Did you write that at the bottom, Mrs. Daniels?"

Nana looked frightened. "Where did you get this?"

"It's Laura's drawing. Did you write 'My Nurse' on it for her?"

"I didn't touch it."

Nana's face turned very white. The nurse took her arm and walked with her to the house. Laura followed along behind, feeling disappointed because no one seemed happy about her surprise.

The nurse helped Nana into the living room, where Carrie brought her a drink of water. Nana tried to introduce Carrie, but her voice faltered. Carrie introduced herself, giving the nurse a hard look before she bent over Nana.

"What is it, Mrs. D.? What's wrong?"

Nana motioned for the nurse to show Carrie the drawing. The nurse handed it to her.

"Laura wrote that," Nana said.

Carrie sat down on the couch beside Nana. She was quiet a minute before she started to laugh.

"I can hardly wait until Her Majesty sees this."

Nana became alert. "We don't dare show her. The shock might be too much. It might make her worse."

"I have an idea it would solve the whole problem about Laura. When she finds out she has a child prodigy, little Melissa will be the one without a mother."

Laura gave Carrie a quizzical look. She was crazy if she

thought she was going to write for her mother. Just then Harley banged through the front door, carrying the nurse's largest suitcase. The nurse took it from him and thanked him.

Laura snatched her drawing out of Carrie's hand and gave it to the nurse. The nurse looked at it again, and patted Laura's head. "This is a wonderful present, Laura. The best anyone ever gave me. I'll keep it always."

Harley tried to look at it, but the nurse put it in her pocket before he had a chance to see.

"I'd like to meet your mother now," the nurse said. "Laura, would you take me upstairs to her room?"

Harley shoved Laura aside. "She makes Mother nervous. I'll take you."

"I asked Laura."

"Harley, you help Carrie get the rest of our things out of the car," Nana said.

"But Laura never goes into Mother's room."

"Lots of things are going to be different now that the nurse is here."

Carrie headed for the door. "Besides, Strong Man, I need all your muscle power to help unload the car."

Harley shrugged and followed Carrie. "Okay. But Mother isn't going to like Laura coming to her room," he said, looking defiantly from Nana to the nurse. "She always makes the baby cry." He stomped across the porch.

Nana sighed and pushed herself up out of the chair. "He's right. Kate isn't going to like it."

The nurse placed her suitcase on the floor near the wall and took Laura's hand. "It's important to get the patient integrated into family life as soon as possible."

"I'm afraid that will take some doing."

"While I'm a stranger to her, she won't feel as free to make a scene. Later, we'll lose that advantage."

"Wouldn't you like to rest and freshen up first? There are four empty rooms upstairs, but I think you'd be most comfortable in Laura's old room."

Laura squeezed the nurse's hand and nodded excitedly.

Nana interpreted for her. "Laura wants you to have her room."

"It's settled then. I'm sure I'll love it."

Laura tugged at the nurse's hand.

"She wants to show it to you now."

"All right. I suppose there is plenty of time to meet her mother."

The nurse picked up her suitcase and let Laura lead her up the stairs. Nana followed, chatting amiably. "You can choose any of the four bedroom suites you like best. Having the furniture moved is no problem. Of course, I'll have the room redecorated. What are your favorite colors?"

"White and army drab are about all I've been exposed to for the past twenty years. I really haven't given much thought to color."

"There's no rush. You may have some ideas later."

Laura pushed the door open and twirled around the room like a ballet dancer. She ended in a graceful bow, then ran to the wall and pointed to the wall paper. It was pink, with little girl ballerinas in white and silver costumes.

Nana smiled. "She picked this wallpaper herself. Out of a catalog when she was two and a half. She wouldn't let me look at anything else. Kept turning the pages back to this pattern."

"It's fine with me. Let it stay."

"I wouldn't dream of making you live in this little girl's room. She won't mind a change. Will you, Laura?"

Laura was looking past them, toward the open door. All the fun had faded out of her face.

"I'm sorry, but this room is taken," Kate said. "I'm going to put Melissa in here."

Laura stomped her right foot. She stomped again, harder. Her mother ignored her and moved forward to shake hands with the nurse.

"I'm Kate Daniels. Your employer," she said formally. "Please move your things into the room directly across the hall. I hope you brought plenty of uniforms. I want you to wear white while caring for my baby."

Laura watched Nana's reaction to her mother's silly speech. She was angry but trying not to show it. When she spoke her voice sounded smooth as glass. Burning glass.

"She can't take that room, Kate. It's not much bigger than most of the closets in this house. It doesn't even have a private bath."

"Small rooms can be very cozy. She can share this bath with the baby."

The glass cracked.

"Absolutely not!"

Her mother picked up the nurse's suitcase, walked across the hall, and opened the door. The room was so cramped there was barely enough room to walk around the twin-size bed. Several cardboard boxes were stacked on the floor, and the bed was piled with dresses and men's suits on hangers.

"Carrie has been using this room to sort clothing for the Good Will, but I'm sure you'll have plenty of time to get it cleaned up before bedtime," her mother said, tilting her chin imperiously, indicating that the matter of rooms was settled. "I'm sure this is far better than what you've been used to in the army."

Laura smiled when Nana sighed heavily and pulled her small shoulders back. "Kate! Your high-handedness is outrageous! Money gives no one the right to belittle other people. You're acting like a spoiled child."

Laura's eyes sparkled as she clapped her hands and jumped up and down. Her mother glared at her, which made her even more gleeful. Nana had spunk. Her mother was foolish enough to think she could win.

In confidential tones her mother said to the nurse, "I'm sure you understand the necessity of your being in this room. You can leave your door open at night so you can hear the baby."

Nana refused to step aside.

"You can leave *your* door open, so *you* can hear the baby. Miss Pledge has not come here to take over your responsibilities to your baby, like Carrie and I did with Laura."

"You'll have to excuse my mother-in-law. She has become quite senile these last few months. It's sad, but my husband and I may be forced to put her in a nursing home, for the good of the rest of the family."

Laura watched the nurse. She had not taken her eyes off her mother's face since she started talking. The nurse's expression in no way betrayed her thoughts, but Laura had the idea she was thinking of Nana's comment, in the car, about having nightmares worrying about what her mother might have done to shock her into silence.

Uncharacteristically, Nana was very agitated. Laura felt

121

sorry for her and angry with her mother. The only reason her mother was being so mean to Nana was because Nana took up for her.

Her mother looked at her watch. "I don't want to seem unduly demanding on your first day. Why don't you relax awhile. Come to my room in an hour, and I'll explain your duties. Then there won't be any reason for misunderstanding later."

"My duties have already been explained," the nurse's voice was firm, matching her mother's tone. "Your husband and I have already discussed them in great detail."

"But there are dozens of little things he probably left out."

"Anything he left out will not be done. I would not have signed a year's contract without first having an agreement about what my duties were to be."

The ugly nurse was more wonderful than Laura had dared imagine. She had snatched control from her mother as effortlessly as Laura could make that stupid baby scream.

"A year's contract?"

"Certainly."

Laura felt exhilarated seeing her mother's anger rising because the nurse had dared to talk back to her.

"He's about as crazy as his mother. I never heard of a year's contract for domestic help."

"I'm not domestic help, Mrs. Daniels. I'm a registered nurse."

Laura grinned. Her mother was furious.

"With a slightly tainted record? Why else would you take this job? Any high school girl can learn to take care of a baby."

"I wasn't hired to take care of the baby, Mrs. Daniels. I have a master's degree in counseling and psychiatric nursing. I'm here to help *you* learn to care for *all* your children and to become a part of the family again."

Her nurse was too good to be true! Laura leaned against the door facing, folded her arms, and waited for the explosion. Her mother's face turned bright red, then white, then red again. She was more angry than Laura had ever seen her. Much more than the day of the big fight with Nana and Carrie. It was funny to watch her. Laura knew she wanted to slap the nurse but did not dare. The nurse was half a foot taller than she was and broad as a man.

"Get out of this house! I don't care what kind of agreement you have with my husband. You get out of this house!"

The nurse's voice was pleasant.

"Why don't we go down to the living room and talk about this like two adults, Mrs. Daniels?"

"I don't want to talk about anything with you. What I need is a lawyer. And that's what I'm going to get."

Nana's shoulders drooped, and Laura knew she was feeling sorry for her mother.

"Kate. Please don't do that," Nana said. "We all love you. We can all be happy again. That's why the nurse is here. To help all of us work out our problems. She is to be an objective mediator, as ready to point out my faults and T.J.'s as yours."

"This is all your idea. You put T.J. up to this."

"You're wrong, Mrs. Daniels," the nurse said. "When I answered your husband's ad, he didn't know what he wanted a nurse for. He just knew that the family was falling apart and he needed help. After I told him about my experience and qualifications, he said God must have directed me to answer his ad. That is, if any family needed my services his did."

"He had no right to bring you here without consulting me."

"I think you are right," the nurse said. "He should have discussed it with you. I just assumed he would. Perhaps I was negligent in not suggesting it."

"Counseling won't make any difference. Our marriage went sour quite some time ago. The only thing I want now is out. As soon as I can find a place, I'm going to take my children and leave."

Laura shrank back against the wall, wanting to join the ballerinas in the wallpaper. Her mother could go. She could take Harley and her stupid baby and go anywhere she wanted. But she would never go with her. Away from Nana's protection, there was no telling what her mother might do to her.

Nana's face paled and she gripped her hands tightly in front of her. It was terrible the way her mother made Nana suffer. There would come a time when she would have to pay for all the ugly things she did to Nana. Reverend Edwards often talked about it in church. "Paying for your sins" he called it. He loved to tell about burning in eternal hell. But there were different kinds of hell. Different ways people could be made to pay. Laura concentrated on the future. Her mother would soon be a different person.

"Kate, please don't talk about leaving," Nana said. "I can't stand it."

"You old hypocrite! You'd like nothing better. You never wanted me to marry your son in the first place. You'd—"

"I think it would be better if we discussed this another time," the nurse said.

"There won't be another time. I'm taking my children and getting out of this house right now."

Kate brushed past the nurse and shoved Nana so hard she fell against the wall. Laura ran to help Nana up, but her mother grabbed her by her hair and started dragging her down the hall.

"You're coming with me," her mother said. "That old lunatic thinks I'll leave you here with her, but she's crazy. In two weeks you'll be a different child, once I get you off by myself where you can't run screaming to your Nana."

Laura was so mad she had not thought about screaming until her mother said the word. She opened her mouth and took a big breath, then let out the most terrifying scream she could manage.

The noise jarred the nurse into action. There was a scuffle. Her mother let loose of her hair, and Laura lost her balance and almost fell. By the time she righted herself, the nurse had her mother face down on the floor, her arms pinned behind her.

"I'll have you arrested for this," Kate screamed. "You butch-acting bitch. This town won't put up with freaks like you. I'll have you arrested for assaulting me."

Kate struggled to roll over and throw the nurse off, but the nurse sat calmly astride her back, holding her wrists together with one hand, like a skilled policeman.

The nurse motioned for Laura to come closer. Her voice was quiet and calm.

"Do you know where your Nana keeps clean sheets?" Laura nodded.

"Then run and bring me two big ones."

Laura dashed down the stairs, passing Harley and Carrie on their way up. Harley broke Carrie's grip on his arm and made a flying tackle onto the nurse's back.

"What are you doing to my mother?" he screamed.

The nurse was knocked off balance, and her mother rolled out from under her. Pushing Harley away, the nurse started after her.

But Harley shoved her from behind.

"You leave my mother alone."

Carrie hauled him, kicking and screaming, into a corner. Her mother bit the nurse's hand viciously when she grabbed her. The nurse spun her around and slapped her face so hard that the sharp sound echoed through the hall.

"That's your first lesson," the nurse said. "You hurt me, or anyone else, and I hurt you worse."

Laura was surprised when her mother tried to hit her again. The nurse blocked the blow and wrestled her to the floor. When she was secured the nurse, a little breathless but still calm, called to Laura.

"Did you find the sheets?"

Laura ran for the linen closet in the back hallway. The sound of Harley's sobs, and Nana's, and her mother's curses followed Laura, making her hurry, afraid she would miss something.

When she got back to the upstairs hall, Nana was holding Harley, who was pleading that Nana stop the nurse. Carrie was on the phone to Dr. Barnes, yelling into the receiver to make herself heard above the clamor.

The nurse smiled at Laura.

"Everything is going to be fine. Don't be frightened. Your mother is sick, but the doctor is coming to give her some medicine."

Her mother was out of breath from struggling, and angrier than Laura had ever seen her.

"He's not giving me anything," she panted. "I won't take it. And I'm going to get you for this. I promise you. You'll regret the day you answered my husband's ad."

Laura imagined how crazy her mother must seem to the nurse, knowing only what she had been told before she came and being unaccustomed to her mother's temper fits. Clutching the sheets like schoolbooks, Laura stooped and stroked her mother's cheek in what she hoped appeared to be the tenderest gesture of concern.

Her mother snapped at her hand and was swiftly punished by the nurse, who exerted a painful twist on her arm. The nurse ignored her mother's curses and spoke to Laura.

"Spread one of the sheets on the floor and then step back."

Laura did as she was told. The nurse got off her mother's back and rolled her toward Laura and onto the sheet as effortlessly as she would a small child. Her mother tried to kick the nurse, but the huge woman pushed her mother's legs down, grabbed the edge of the sheet, and then rolled her over and over until she was wrapped up like a mummy. Her mother's face was covered in the rug-like roll, and she began to scream hysterically.

The nurse let her scream.

"Hand me the other sheet," she said over the noise.

Laura gave it to her, and the nurse rested one hip on her mother's squirming body, holding her down while shaking out the folded sheet. It unfurled with a loud whishing noise. She grabbed it in the center, rolled her mother over on it, and tied it behind her back. When she was satisfied that it was secure, she propped the encased figure on her side, resting against the bulky knot, and then began to roll the top of the sheet over her face. She was very neat and precise with each roll, and when she finished, Laura stared at the white form that was her mother. There were tears in her mother's eyes, but she still wanted to fight.

"I'll make you pay for humiliating me like this in front of my children," she said and spat at the nurse.

"You disappoint me, Mrs. Daniels. I thought you were much too sophisticated to resort to that kind of crude behavior."

The nurse got to her feet and walked down the hall to Nana and Harley, who were huddled together, horrified, trying to comfort each other. She touched Nana's shoulder gently. Harley held his fist up, wanting to punch her, but not daring to. He appeared to be both afraid of her and ashamed of his fear.

"I know you don't understand this, Harley." The nurse's voice was stern. "I'm very sorry you had to see it. But I haven't hurt your mother. And I'm not going to. I've just restrained her, to keep her from hurting herself or anyone else."

She rubbed Nana's shoulder in a firm, comforting way that Laura liked.

"Why don't you take the boy downstairs, Mrs. Daniels? Carrie can help me put her in bed. The doctor will be here soon."

Nana nodded her head and leaned heavily on Harley. "Please help me downstairs," she said. "I don't feel very well."

Harley put Nana's arm around his shoulder and clasped her firmly around the waist. "I'll take care of you, Nana." He glared at the nurse. "My daddy won't like what you've done."

Laura was worried about Nana, but she wanted to stay and see what the nurse was going to do with her mother. When Nana and Harley passed her she stepped into the shadows beside the telephone stand so Nana would not notice her and make her go downstairs.

That stupid mud-baby had cried so long it had the hiccups. Laura could hear it wailing and hiccupping from her mother's room. She hoped it would choke to death.

Harley tried not to look at his mother when he led Nana past her, but she cried out.

"Harley, help me. Please help me!"

He whined helplessly, "What do you want me to do? I can't fight her."

The nurse picked up Kate's shoulders and motioned for Carrie to pick up her feet. Together they carried her into her room.

"Help me, Harley," she screamed. "Please help me."

"Mama!" he cried, obviously torn between following her and supporting Nana. Harley was sobbing as he led Nana down the stairs. If he had not been holding on to Nana, Laura could have wished that he would fall and break his silly neck. Her mother had turned him into a cry baby.

Laura ran into her old room to use the bathroom. Her mind was racing. More than anything she wanted to see what they were going to do to her mother, but Carrie would send her downstairs if she saw her. Even if Carrie left, the nurse was sure to send her away when the doctor came.

She finished and started to flush the toilet, but decided

against it, afraid the noise would attract attention. If only she could slip into her daddy's closet.

The sound of flying gravel startled her. A car was speeding down the ranch road toward the house. It had to be Doctor Barnes. There was no time left to plan. She would have to take her chances.

Laura crept to the door and peeked down the hall. The baby was bawling and hiccupping. Her mother was screaming, "My baby. My baby. Let me take care of my baby. Let me up."

The car turned into the circle drive, and she heard Carrie's voice above the din.

"That must be the doctor."

Carrie came out into the hall, and Laura drew her head back inside the doorway. Carrie's heavy footsteps thudded down the carpeted stairs and crossed the marble hall to the front door. The door opened and closed, and Laura crept around the corner to peer over the banister. Carrie had gone out on the front porch to meet the doctor.

Laura slipped into her mother's room. The nurse was bent over that stupid baby's crib, changing a diaper. Laura liked the way she handled the baby. Her movements were swift, perfunctory. Ignoring its outraged screams, she controlled its thrashing arms and legs with firm hands.

Her mother's eyes were riveted on the nurse. Her hands and shoulders moved furiously inside the sheet. She struggled to get up.

"You bitch! Don't you dare handle my baby that way. I'll kill you for this!"

Her daddy's closet door was cracked. Laura eased it open a little wider and slipped inside just as the nurse flipped the baby over on its stomach and turned around. Laura exhaled slowly, through her mouth. She was safe.

"Mrs. Daniels, it makes me very sad to see a baby as spoiled as yours is," the nurse said. "It's not fair to the child."

"She's not spoiled! She's hungry. It's long past her feeding time." Her mother stopped struggling inside the sheet, apparently trying to compose herself. "Please untie me so she can nurse."

"You're in no condition to be nursing a child. You don't want to transmit all your emotional upsets to her. We'll have to ask the doctor for a formula while he's here."

Her mother screamed. "There is nothing wrong with me. Laura did all this. She wants me to look crazy! That's why she talks to me and no one else. To make me *look* crazy."

"Why would a child do such a thing?"

"Because she hates me. And she's jealous of the baby."

The nurse sat on the side of the bed as if she were her mother's best friend, ready for a chat.

"Jealousy can be a real problem among siblings."

Her mother's face was hopeful. "It's more than a problem with Laura. The first time she saw me breast feeding she flew into a rage and tried to twist Melissa's little foot off."

Her mother was warming to playing the part of a pitiful wronged woman. Laura grinned, thinking about choking the fake tears out of her voice.

"I hadn't heard about her doing anything to the baby," the nurse said.

"There's a lot you don't know. My mother-in-law and my husband are using you, Major Pledge." Her mother's tone softened to sugar-coated candy. "I'm sorry I behaved so badly toward you this afternoon. It's not your fault. *They* put me in this position, by not telling you the truth about the situation with Laura. I'm sure you can understand why I've become so defensive—with everyone against me."

"Surely your own husband— He couldn't be against you."

"He is! Because of his mother. He's never broken the apron strings. He believes everything she tells him."

"But what could she have said?"

"She told him I was imagining things. That Laura wasn't really talking to me. It's all Laura's fault. When I tried to make her talk in front of Mrs. Daniels and Carrie, she acted like a little fool. She knew what she was doing. She planned it. She wanted to make me look crazy."

"She talked to you and no one else, and they wouldn't believe she was talking?"

"That's right."

"All because she was jealous of the baby?"

"She hates the baby!"

Laura glared at the mud-baby in its crib. Since the day her mother brought it home nearly four months ago, the

129

red-mud color had faded to creamy white and the wrinkled skin had stretched tight over plump cheeks and legs. Now it was reaching for things and jabbering nonsense syllables. From the position, on its stomach, where the nurse had placed it, it was holding its head up—gurgling Na, Na, Na, Na! Only a few more weeks until it would be saying Nana—calling Nana to take her up and play with her. That thought brought a fresh wave of anger to Laura. But she held herself still, knowing that the nurse would send her away if she made her presence known.

The nurse stood up and folded her arms. "But by your own account, Mrs. Daniels, all that happened *before* the baby was born. You were hearing Laura talk to you *before* you had Melissa. How could Laura be jealous of a child that wasn't even born? Think about what you just said."

Laura wanted to laugh out loud. The nurse was leading her mother. "It's true," her mother pleaded. "All of it's true. Laura hates my baby. She hurt her. She talked to me. She wants me to appear crazy. Why won't anyone believe me?"

Her mother dissolved into tears, and the nurse stood beside the bed, looking down at her. Laura studied the nurse's homely features, searching for some sign of pity. She found none. The thin lips curled downward and the eyebrows arched sharply above the small eyes. Contempt was stamped in every line of her face.

Laura heard the front door open and close. Voices drifted up from the downstairs hall. Nana and Carrie were talking to the doctor. The nurse heard them, too. She bent over her mother.

"The doctor is here." She slipped her arms under her mother's body. "Let me straighten you up in the bed."

Her mother rolled away from her, pitched over on her face, struggled to turn over again, and tumbled off the bed. The nurse let her fall.

"Now see what you've done. You're not hurting anyone but yourself."

"Untie me," her mother screamed. "Damn it! Turn me loose! You'll all be sorry for this."

Laura watched the scene through the crack where the door was hinged. She was completely absorbed in seeing her mother squirm around on the floor trying to free herself from the binding sheets. Suddenly the baby screamed, apparently frightened by the noise her mother was making. Her mother's jerks and contortions became more violent.

"Help me!" her mother yelled. "Oh, God! Somebody help me!"

Suddenly the bedroom door was thrust open. The unexpected sound startled Laura. She grabbed her daddy's overcoat and clung to it for support. When she was calm enough to peek through the crack again, Doctor Barnes was bending over her mother.

"Kate? What has happened to you, Kate?"

Her mother's face was an agonized smear of tears and streaked mascara.

"Thank God you're here. Get me out of this mess. Everyone has gone crazy."

The doctor struggled with the knotted sheet. He glared at the nurse. "See to that baby."

"No!" her mother screamed. "I don't want her near my baby!"

The doctor had loosened the knot, but her mother's struggling tightened it again.

"Be still, Kate! So I can get this off you." He looked up at the nurse and jerked his head toward the bedroom door. "Maybe you had better wait in the hall."

"You may need my help," the nurse said. "She was quite violent—"

"I'll call if I need you. Please!"

The nurse walked out of Laura's line of vision. She heard the door close. Her mother stared after the nurse.

"If that ugly bitch ever comes near me again, I'll kill her."

"Now, Kate!"

"I mean it! I will! I've never been so humiliated in my life. And in front of my children."

The doctor pulled the sheets off over her mother's head and helped her to her feet.

"Now. Take care of your baby."

She rushed to the crib and the doctor opened his bag. Laura watched him fill a syringe from a tiny vial. He pulled a cotton swab out of a dispenser.

"Bring her over to the bed and lie down."

Her mother swayed back and forth, cradling the baby's face next to her shoulder.

"Poor little girl," her mother crooned. "My poor little angel. It's long past her feeding time."

"Well get her over here and feed her. I can't stand to hear a child scream like that. That's more than hunger. She's frightened out of her wits."

The doctor looked and sounded like a television actor, as though he were playing a part—to get her mother to do what he wanted.

"That ugly nurse threw her around like she hated her. Why would she treat my baby like that? What are they trying to do to me?"

"Come on, Kate. Lie down."

Her mother stretched out on the bed, resting her back against a pillow the doctor held for her. She unbuttoned her blouse and loosened her bra strap, exposing her breast. The baby stopped screaming. Its greedy, sucking mouth sought her nipple, found it, and latched on. It whimpered once. Then groaned contentedly.

Laura dug her fingernails into the palms of her hands. The sound of that baby sucking on her mother's white breast was far worse than its screams. She wanted to barrel out of the closet, grab the needle out of the doctor's hand, and jab it into the baby over and over again.

How could her mother show herself and let that stupid baby do that to her in front of the doctor? He sat down on the side of the bed as if he belonged there. Holding the needle carefully away from him, he patted her mother's hip with his free hand. Patted it as her daddy used to before the baby came. Long before that. Before her mother started trying to make her talk.

"You're much too tense, Kate. Try to relax."

"I can't! I've got to get out of here. I've got to contact a lawyer and get my children out of here. They're trying to convince me that I'm crazy. You know I'm not crazy. Don't you, Doctor Barnes?"

"Of course you're not! We all get upset from time to time."

"T.J. and his mother hired that nurse to make me look crazy. Why are they doing this to me?"

"I'm sure that's not their intention."

"I'm not safe here. I've got to get out."

He took her free hand and held it. "Your first responsibility is to your baby. If you're upset, then it upsets her. You don't want your baby to get sick, do you?"

The word "sick" keyed in Laura's memory. Dirt meant sick, maybe death. And she had baptized that baby in red Oklahoma mud. Now, upset meant sick. She smiled.

"We're not safe here." Again there were tears in her mother's voice, but this time they sounded real. "That nurse said she was going to ask you for a formula. She—"

"That might not be a bad idea."

"She's trying to separate me from my baby."

"You could breast-feed morning and night, then your time would be your own during the day—to get out more."

"I'm afraid to leave Melissa. Laura hates her. I'm afraid she'll do something to her."

"We'll talk about it later. I'm going to give you a shot now. Something to help you relax."

Her mother jerked away from the doctor.

"No! I don't want anything. I've got to keep my wits about me! I'm telling you the truth. My baby and I— We are not safe."

The doctor answered quickly, his voice sounded sincere, but Laura knew he was lying. "This medicine is more for the baby than you. Would you rather I stuck this big needle in her?"

"No. Of course not."

Her mother extended her arm and watched apprehensively while the doctor tied a rubber tube above her elbow and probed with his fingertips at the blue veins on the soft underside of her elbow.

"What is that? What are you giving me?"

"A little nerve medicine. Some vitamins. Trust me, Kate. Have I ever let you down?"

"No. But I don't think you understand how serious this is."

Her mother flinched when he stuck the needle into her arm. He pushed the clear liquid into her vein with the plunger, withdrew the needle, then rubbed the spot with the cotton swab.

"Nothing is going to happen to you. I won't let it. Trust me, Kate."

Laura was surprised at how quickly her mother went to sleep. Before the doctor could dispose of the syringe her mother's head lolled on the pillow, and the arm holding the baby relaxed. The baby continued to suck greedily.

The doctor opened the door and went out. Laura strained to hear what was said in the hall, all the while watching the baby's pulling mouth.

"I've seen your credentials, Miss Pledge. They're quite impressive."

"Thank you, Doctor."

"I realize that you have much more experience in this business of mental illness than I do. I'm just a country doctor. A general practitioner."

"You handled her beautifully. I was listening."

"Thank you. I've known Kate ten years or longer—since she married T.J."

The doctor sounded timid to Laura. Like he was not saying what was really on his mind.

"This business with the sheets. Good technique. Very innovative."

"Effective as a straightjacket."

"I hope you won't use it again."

The nurse sounded surprised and defensive.

"She was violent, Doctor. I felt she had to be restrained."

"Mrs. Daniels, Sr., recounted the incident to me when I arrived. In the future, try to use tact. Let her have her way if you have to. But please don't restrain her again unless she is on the verge of murder or suicide."

The nurse giggled self-consciously.

"I'm quite serious, Miss Pledge. I'm well aware that many mental hospitals break a patient down as part of the treatment—to make them obedient and more tractable. That won't work with Kate. I don't want it used."

The doctor was their enemy. That was clear. Laura listened, fascinated, as the nurse's self-confidence mellowed into subservience. Under that thin veneer, Laura sensed that the nurse wanted to humiliate her beautiful mother. Laura felt like dancing around the room. This nurse was going to be far better than anything she had ever imagined.

"There must be some measure of control," the nurse

was saying. "She's unreasonable. Out of touch with reality. Paranoid. I have to be able to handle her. What about the rest of the family?"

"Medication is the only way to treat Kate. She is very proud. If you humiliate her, she'll fight that much harder."

The doctor was right about that. Laura knew. Her mother would fight. And the more she fought the crazier she would look.

"Doctors I have worked with in the past preferred to use medication only when behavior modification failed," the nurse said.

"I'm not a psychiatrist. I'm just a country doctor. But I have very strong feelings about human dignity. As long as she is in my care, I won't strip her of that."

"I'm not sure I agree with you, Doctor, but I have no choice but to do it your way."

"As long as we understand each other, Miss Pledge."

The nurse followed the doctor back into the bedroom. He fumbled in his bag for a pad and began writing prescriptions. The nurse was reading over his shoulder.

Laura could tell by her defiant expression that as soon as he left, she would treat her mother as she pleased.

"If you don't want her restrained, the medication will have to be very strong," the nurse said. "She was very abusive to Laura."

"This dosage should be quite adequate. It will calm her. You'll find that Kate is a very intelligent woman."

"And what if she does become violent again? What am I to do?"

"Call me. I'll increase the dosage. But I don't think it will be necessary. Kate has been under a strain, because of Laura and the baby, but she is not that far out. You're here to take some of the pressure off so far as the baby is concerned—"

"I was not hired to take care of the baby, Doctor Barnes. I was hired to take care of her."

"I don't quite understand what T.J. had in mind, but I'll have a talk with him. I recommended someone to help her with the baby and be her friend and companion. Like Carrie is to Mrs. Daniels."

"Mr. Daniels recognized that his wife is mentally ill and a real threat to the rest of his family. He did not want her

135

put away. He wanted to care for her at home. That's why he hired me."

"If that's how he is thinking, he is dead wrong. Kate is as sane as anyone could be. What she needs is time and less pressure. She'll work out her problems."

Laura frowned. Her body was tense. The muscles in her legs twitched. Doctor Barnes has purposely set himself against the nurse. Her nurse. She sensed that it was something other than his confidence in her mother. She had never heard him say anything to Nana or her daddy about being a "country doctor" before.

He handed the prescriptions to the nurse and closed his bag. "Kate will probably sleep until morning. Please put the baby in her crib and come downstairs with me. I want to talk to Mrs. Daniels before I leave."

The nurse did as she was told.

The baby had fallen asleep with its mouth still pressed around her mother's nipple. As the nurse lifted it away the suction broke, making a loud sound.

That sound lingered after the two adults left. Laura held herself in check until she heard the footsteps go down the stairs and into the living room. She sprang to the wastebasket and retrieved the used syringe the doctor had thrown away. When she pulled the plastic cap off and held the shiny needle up to the light, there were traces of the clear medicine left inside the tube.

Laura moved around the bed toward the crib. She kept her eyes on her mother, half afraid she would awake. But her face was peaceful with sleep. The angry red had faded, leaving only black streaks of smeared mascara under her eyes as evidence of her ordeal.

The side of the crib was halfway down, and Laura inserted her foot between the wooden slats and stepped up on the bottom rail. She leaned over, supporting her weight against the top bar. Light glinted off the silver needle. She looked back over her shoulder. Her mother's chest rose and fell with her steady breathing. Her exposed left breast looked larger than the other, the brown nipple still shriveled and pointed where the baby had been sucking.

It was sleeping with one fist pressed tight against its forehead. Laura pulled the yellow gown up to its chin. It squirmed as the soft material brushed against its skin. She turned the syringe over in her hand, holding it like a dagger, and plunged it into the baby's white belly. She pulled the needle out and plunged it in again before the baby screamed. As she plunged the third time, her mother opened her eyes and tried to sit up. She fought against the medicine, obviously having trouble making her muscles obey. She could not get up, but she clawed at the bedspread, pulling herself drunkenly toward her terrified baby. Her mouth formed Laura's name, but no sound came out. Laura jumped down off the crib, threw the syringe at her mother's bleary face, then ran toward her old room.

The baby's screams pounded in her ears. A different sound. A hurt animal sound. Laura felt as if she were moving in slow motion. The hall seemed as long as a football field. At last she reached her old room and leaned, panting, against her ballerina wallpaper, listening to the thundering herd of footsteps coming up the stairs. Excited voices. The nurse. Doctor Barnes. Nana. Carrie. All talking at once in her mother's room.

She dashed into the hall. Slid down the banister. Slipped silently across the marble hall, through the kitchen, the pantry, the back hall, to the treasure room. Her heart racing, she forced herself to be calm. She grabbed her clown off her bed, propped it in a chair near her play table, took the chest of miniature glass dishes off the shelf in her closet, and sat down in the chair opposite her clown. She set the table for a tea party and was pouring her second cup when Nana and Carrie hurried into her room. She could tell by Nana's worried face that, even drugged, her mother had managed to tell them she had done it.

Tears welled in the corners of Nana's eyes, which made Laura feel sad because Nana was so distressed. Quickly, to cover her hurt, Laura got out a fresh cup and saucer, filled it with imaginary tea from her teapot, and carried it to Nana. Nana accepted it, but her hand trembled so that Carrie took the cup and saucer from her and set them back on the table.

"Your Nana isn't very thirsty now, but we are very glad to see you're having such a nice party," Carrie said.

Laura smiled and took her clown on her lap. She held its cup to its embroidered lips and watched Carrie lead her

Nana away. Nana looked so frail next to Carrie's bulk. And she dragged one foot a little, like a wounded soldier, or maybe Tiny Tim, in the Christmas story about Scrooge.

Except for the screaming baby, it was one of the best tea parties she had ever had. Her clown laughed and did stunts. Laura wondered if it knew they were spending their last few hours together. She had not told of her plan yet. There was plenty of time. Harley was nowhere around. He was probably hiding like the scared rabbit he was.

Laura carried her clown to the window and looked out. Where was Harley? She could account for everyone else. What if he was hiding somewhere in the house and had seen her come out of her mother's room? He was sure to tell it. He loved to tattle on her just as her mother did. . . . Let him tell! Nana would never believe him now. Not after she had just offered her a cup of tea.

She hugged her clown, remembering how good it had felt to jab that ugly baby with the needle. She had waited such a long time. And it had been especially thrilling with her mother unable to stop her. She had been in control. All-powerful. Energized by her dominance. But that baby had dampened her pleasure, spoiled it for her.

The moment before it screamed it had raised both hands toward her—fingers open, spread wide apart—and its startled eyes had looked directly into hers. Eyes not at all like her mother's. And something behind them. A person lived inside that baby.

That was silly. It was a stupid, squirming mud-baby. A thing that could not think. It could only feel and scream. But she had seen it. It had accepted what she had done and was going to do. And it had been sorry for her. She had seen pity in its eyes and she had stabbed it again. The knowing thing had gone away. Melted away. Then it had screamed.

She did not want to think about it any more. She wanted that moment out of her memory. Her clown wanted to dance. She hopped and skipped to the center of the room and spun around and around and around as fast as she could turn.

The thought of the baby receded. She hugged her clown tight, pretending it was hugging her like a dance partner—a man. Her daddy. His strong arms around her. Holding her tight. Spinning. Spinning. Pulling her tighter and tighter against him. Spinning her around and around in an ever-widening circle. Alone. The two of them alone, on top of the mountain where she had seen the dark man, when she had held the beaded pouch in her daddy's closet.

She felt older and taller, but still small, very small in her daddy's arms. His face was younger. Much younger. As though it was before he was her daddy. There was love in his face. Love. And something else. Need. And wanting.

He combed his fingers through her hair. Then he let go and pressed his arm against her waist to make her lean backward, spun her faster and faster. She felt her long, straight hair fan out behind her. Felt the weight of it pulling her head back, swirling, making lovely patterns in the air.

Spinning. Spinning. Laura fell. She lay on the floor, too dizzy to open her eyes. When she did, she was holding her clown. And her clown told her it had been a daydream. But she knew the difference between memory and dreams, the pleasure of being held, the dancing, his loving face, her pulsing heart beating out drum rhythms. She *had* danced with her daddy on top of the mountain. Back in a forgotten time.

Laura pushed herself up and stumbled to the mirror. She touched her hair; it was now short, blond turning light brown, and curly. But she remembered the weight and the pull when it was long and straight and the dark swirl it made behind her when they twirled.

When Carrie came to call her to supper, Laura was still standing in front of the mirror trying to piece together the present and her sketchy memories about the past. Nothing fit, but all of it was real. She knew it was real.

Laura was amazed when she looked out her bedroom window and discovered it was dark outside. How long had she been standing there?

In the kitchen, her daddy's coat was tossed over a chair in the corner. She had not heard him come home. Harley was already seated at the table staring glumly at a bowl of steaming stew.

He glared at her when she took her place opposite him.

"You did it," he hissed. "They're all up there blaming Mother. But I know you did it."

Carrie dropped heavily into the seat at the head of the table. "That's enough, Harley. Eat your supper."

Laura's arm tightened around her clown. She held it on her lap and fed it with her spoon. Each time she looked up, Harley was glaring at her, his head bent over the bowl, his right hand working mechanically, bringing the food to his mouth. His eyes were menacing. It was the first time he had ever eaten a meal without talking. Words weren't needed; his eyes told everything. He was his mother's son. He was the only one who believed her. His defiant glare declared that he had made up his mind to fight for her.

Laura knew then that he had not seen her slide down the banister after hurting the mud-baby. He would have told. She smiled at Harley. He never planned anything. He only felt and reacted. She knew he wanted to jump on her, but he was too much of a coward to do it with Carrie there.

Laura winked at her brother, just to make him madder, and kissed the top of her clown's pointed hat. Harley never planned anything, but she did. Her clown was going to fix him good, but it would have to wait. Her daddy and Nana were too busy with her mother upstairs. If she went ahead with it, only Carrie would see and that would be a waste. She could wait until the time was right.

Harley sat gripping the edge of the table. He was itching to get at her. She yawned to let him know she was not worried about it.

Carrie saw her yawn and ordered them both to bed. Harley argued that he was not ready to go to bed, and Carrie had to threaten to spank him before he slammed out of the kitchen and thundered up the stairs to his room.

Laura kissed Carrie good night and gave her an extra-special hug. It was important to keep Carrie on her side. The night was filled with dreams about dancing with her daddy on the mountain.

The smell of fried bacon woke her the next morning, and Nana came to her room to help her dress. Her eyes were red and sad, as if she had cried all night, but she smiled and scurried about the room as usual, making the bed and picking up toys while Laura dressed.

When Carrie stuck her head in the door to say that

breakfast was on the table, Nana sat down on the bed and lifted Laura on her lap to put on her socks and shoes.

"Yesterday, your mother had a little accident with the baby," Nana said. "They are both going to be fine, but—" Her voice broke, and her chin quivered like she wanted to cry.

Laura felt sick, seeing Nana so sad. She never would have done it if she had known it would hurt her Nana. . . . But it was not all her fault. Her mother had no business bringing that baby home.

"We must be very quiet today," Nana was saying. "So they can rest. And later on in the morning some of the hands are coming to move the baby's things out of your mother's room into the little room next door. Miss Pledge wants to make that into the nursery. Where your mother can't—" Her voice seemed to fail her. She began again. "So there won't be any more accidents."

Laura was glad that her mother had lost that baby. But it bothered her that Nana was so concerned. Nana loves me, she thought. Nana belongs to me! I'll never let that mud-baby come between us!

Nana finished tying Laura's shoe and hugged her. "We're all going to be very busy today. I want you to stay downstairs and keep out of the way. You have plenty of toys. I know you can entertain yourself. Will you do that for Nana?"

Laura nodded. Nana seemed so sad and sounded so desperate that she would have promised her anything.

When they reached the kitchen, steaming plates were already set in their places. Carrie was clearing away Harley's breakfast dishes.

"Mr. Acres stopped by," she said. "Invited Harley to go with him to the Saturday auction at the stockyard."

Nana pushed her bacon and eggs away and reached for her coffee. "That was very thoughtful of him."

"I got the impression it was T.J.'s idea."

"That's one big worry off us. I'm grateful. Whoever thought about it."

Carrie had already eaten her breakfast, but she sat down and started on the leftovers while she and Nana talked about their plans for the new nursery. Laura tuned them out. That was the last thing she wanted to think about. She finished her bacon and gulped down her orange juice.

They were so engrossed in their conversation that they hardly noticed when she slipped out of the kitchen and went back to her room.

Laura grabbed her clown and flopped down on her bed. She had plenty of thinking that needed to be done, about Nana and that baby, mostly. But it was too early in the morning to be weighed down worrying about problems.

She wanted to feel light and free as she had in her dreams. All night long she had danced with her daddy on top of the Potato Mountain. She closed her eyes, recalling the dream in detail, searching for something new—a clue to the forgotten time. But the dream had been a repetition of her waking memory. There was nothing new in it. Only a promise. Of what?

Laura jumped up. She held her clown tight and started spinning. Faster and faster. Pushing everything out of her mind. Leaving it open to feel. Feel. She was on her mountain. The place was called Table Rock. But it had another name. An ancient name in another language that meant The Thinking Place. She had always lived near it. Always. Pictures flashed in her mind like images on a television screen, but they went by too fast for her to remember them.

She was spinning faster and faster. She could feel her long hair pulling her head back, swirling behind her. She was going to fall. Her head was light. A man whispered that he would never let her fall. That he would protect her. Take care of her. There was such wanting in the voice. It was her daddy's voice. Rich and deep. The same tones. I'll always love you, he said. Never leave you. Never. Never leave you. She believed him. She had always believed him.

Her head was dizzy. Dizzy from the spinning. His hands were slipping. Big strong hands. She felt them slipping. Hold on. Hold on. His hands gripped tighter on her back. Then they were slipping again. Across her back. Something was pulling him. Calling him. A voice. Far away. Calling him. She could barely hear it. She strained to hear. Caught it in the distance. Familiar. Her mother's voice calling, "T.J. help me." That hated voice calling her daddy away.

She felt lost. Hurt. Lonely. She sat cross-legged on the floor and closed out the sounds and smells of the house. Pushed the rhythmic pulsing of her heart and her breathing out of her consciousness and let her mind float free. Higher and higher. Expanding. Reaching up and out into the infinity of white light. Waiting. Expectant. Rushing further and faster than she had ever gone before. Without fear. Higher. Higher. The white light receiving her. Warm. Friendly. She was not alone. Others were there. Pulsating around her. Leading her on. Always ahead. Urging. Coaxing. Up and up. The white light was tinted with blue. Gray-blue. Lighter. Freer. A promise moving just ahead of her. Almost within reach. The answers were there. Waiting for her. She had to know. Had to. She was different. Why? . . . Why? . . . Why?

Blackness blocked out the light. Came between her and the promise. The answers moved off ahead of her. She forced her mind through the dark, searching frantically for the blue-white light. The others were gone. She was alone in the dark. And she was afraid. She wanted to push on. She had almost known. The answers had been there. They were somewhere ahead. The dark grew dense. She was terrified. Lost. Afraid to go forward. Unsure of the way back.

A sound penetrated the darkness. A high-pitched staccato ringing like metal on glass. She drifted backward toward the sound. It grew louder, vibrating inside her head. She became aware of her breathing. Her heart was pounding. She opened her eyes. Reming was outside her window, tapping on the glass with his tin soldier. Her soldier. The little drummer.

Reming's lips moved. His voice sounded detached, lagging behind his lip movements because of the separating window.

"Laura. Laura? Can you come out and play?"

She crawled to the bed, pulled herself up, and staggered to the window. Her legs were weak, the muscles trembling. She looked through the glass into Reming's brown eyes. They were warm and soft, questioning. He had never come looking for her before. He was Harley's friend. But he had not asked for Harley. He had asked her to play. He was holding her drummer up to the window. How did you know I needed you? she thought. You came to call me back.

Reming smiled. "Get your coat and come out. I'll meet you at the kitchen door."

143

He walked away from the window. Laura pressed her face against the cool glass, staring at the triangular tear in the back of his oversized jacket. Reming's clothes never seemed to fit. They were either too large or too small. That jacket was big enough for her daddy. It came almost to his knees, and the sleeves hung down over his hands.

Laura grabbed her coat and ran down the back hall and through the pantry. Carrie was in the kitchen making coffee, but she only smiled feebly at Reming without asking where they were going. Her eyes were red, and she turned quickly toward the stove to keep them from seeing she had been crying.

Carrie had been too slow. Laura knew that Reming had seen her face. He lingered a moment in the doorway, as though absorbing the atmosphere of the house. Then he quietly pulled the door closed as if they were slipping out of church. He grabbed Laura's hand and ran—half dragging her—to the garage.

Inside, they leaned panting against the wall. Laura watched the old Indian, Reming's own great-grandfather, currying his favorite gelding in the far stall. She wished Reming, too, could see him. See how proud and straight he stood, matching the proud horse that was stamping and snorting in the frosty air.

Laura felt Reming watching her, looking toward the last stall, where she was looking, and back to her. Questioning?

She turned and smiled up into his warm brown eyes. Reming was so tall, five or six inches taller than Harley. And she was so little. If Reming held his arm straight out she could stand under it without her head touching. But she felt older. Much older.

Laura scampered to the loft ladder and scrambled up. Reming's climbing was hampered by the box of tin soldiers, and she reached down and took it from him. The box was heavier than she had imagined. When Harley was around he was always too selfish to let her carry it. He only tolerated her because Reming would not play if he was mean to her. Reming had always taken up for her.

The box was tied with the familiar frayed string. She picked at it delicately, wanting to untie it; but Reming had been nice enough to invite her to play, and she waited until he was settled into the hay, then pushed the box toward him.

Reming pushed it back. "You open it."

Now Laura did not hesitate. She pulled the bowknot and removed the lid. She felt as though it were her birthday, having all the soldiers to herself without Harley fussing and pushing her out of the way.

She took her time, picking each one up separately, examining the dents and scratches, brushing the dirt out of its face before she stood it up in the hay. Each face was different. Some were round and smiling, others thin and mean-looking. Their expressions even matched their positions. Those that were kneeling or crouching, aiming their rifles, had strained faces. Only the marching ones, with their guns resting against their shoulders, were smiling. It was a reunion with old friends.

When Laura looked at him, Reming was smiling, sitting there cross-legged with his hands folded and relaxed in his lap. There was no hurry about him. No sign that he was impatient with her for taking her time. He seemed content, sharing her enjoyment. Harley would have been fussing, rushing her, anxious to get on with his own experiences. Reming was like her in many ways. It was easy to be with him.

"These soldiers are very old," Reming said quietly. "They belonged to my grandfather when he was a little boy."

Laura nodded. She had heard him tell their history before. She examined the last two soldiers left in the box, stood them with the others, and looked down the line. Her little drummer was missing.

Reming unzipped his coat, pulled the drummer out of his shirt front, and handed it to her. It was warm from the heat of his body, and Laura pressed it between her hands, protecting it from the cold.

It seemed such a long time since last she had held him. So many things had happened. Bad things. But the little drummer did not know about the ugliness. He would never know about her hurt, and her anger, and the loneliness. Even if she told him, he could not hear, because his tall uniform hat came down over his ears and was buckled securely at the point of his chin. She was not even sure he had any ears. Maybe he was deaf. Maybe that was why he played his drum so loudly, so loudly it made that other little girl she could see so clearly take his drumstick away from him and hide it.

Reming was arranging the other soldiers in battle positions, building barricades out of the hay, setting up an ambush. But now that Laura had the opportunity to be a full partner—without Harley shoving her out of the way—she was not interested in the war game.

Like the evening of her only day at school over a year ago, she felt a strong need for the little drummer. They shared a secret about the other little girl. A partially forgotten secret. But one she wanted desperately to remember.

Reming had the ambush ready. He was waiting for her to march her half of the soldiers into battle. "You'd rather play with the drummer, wouldn't you?" he asked.

Laura nodded apologetically and hugged the little soldier. She kissed the painted cherub face.

Reming reached for the battered shoe box. "Grandfather told me he was my mother's favorite, too."

Laura held the drummer boy next to her cheek and watched Reming put the other soldiers back in the box. He had never mentioned his mother before. Never. She could tell by the thoughtful way he put away his toys that he was thinking about her.

"She died before I was three. I wish she hadn't died." He seemed to be talking to the box. But then he looked straight at Laura. "I can barely remember now. It's as if she was a dream. All beautiful. And sad. And quiet." He smiled shyly, as if he was embarrassed because he had told her. "She was almost as quiet as you." He laughed self-consciously, his eyes inviting Laura to laugh with him. She smiled, feeling warm and glad he had told her.

Laura reached out and squeezed Reming's hand. It was as warm as hers was cold. He did not jerk it away. Harley would have. But then Reming was nothing like Harley. He never talked unless he had something to say. Something he had thought over first. He had wanted her to know about his mother, or he would never have mentioned her. It felt good to have a friend.

The little drummer boy was whispering in Laura's ear.

His voice was soft and sounded far away. He was whispering about his drum and how much he wanted to play. If only he had his drumstick.

Reming finished tying up his shoe box. Twice he had shared his toys with her. She wanted to share something with him. Laura took his soldiers from him and hid them in a corner of the loft under the hay. She looked at him to see if he approved. His eyes were sparkling, wondering what she was up to.

She tried to put the drummer in her coat pocket, but he would not fit. She unbuttoned her coat, stuck him in the waistband of her pants, buttoned her coat back.

Laura slid the wooden bolt that held the loft door and pushed the door open. She grabbed the rusted pulley, swung up to the supporting beam, and pushed herself onto the steep-slanting roof. She dropped to her knees, waiting for Reming to follow her.

He leaned out the loft door and looked up at her. "Wow! I'm lots heavier than you. I'm not sure I can do that."

She cocked her head to one side and gave him a look that said unmistakably that he was a chicken.

Reming grinned at her and grabbed the pulley. She knew all the time that he was not the coward Harley was. But she had to laugh at the awkward way he twisted and struggled, trying to swing his legs up and around the steel beam. He was much stronger than Harley, but she had them both bested at climbing. When he finally managed to pull himself up into a straddling position, he was facing the wrong way on the beam. Laura latched onto his coat collar and helped him wiggle onto the roof on his back. He raised his hands over his head and grabbed the gable to keep from sliding down.

Laura was proud of him. He was out of breath, but there was no sign of fear on his face. It was doubtful that Harley could have made it, without falling. And if he had tried he would have been hysterical and screaming for someone to come and get him down. She let Reming rest a minute, then crawled to the overhanging limb of the pecan tree and swung up on it. The cold air made her feel like showing off a little. She stood up on the branch and walked it like a tight rope to the trunk.

Reming was much more cautious. He followed her down the huge tree, but she had to stop several times and show him where to put his feet. He wanted to rest when they reached the ground, but Laura made for the rock wall and he followed.

She started running. Reming loped easily beside her, his long legs making one stride to her three. He caught her coat sleeve and tried to slow her down, but she pulled away. Reaching the wall became the most important thing she had ever done, the last barrier.

Laura scaled the wall and stood up. Reming climbed up beside her and sat down on the wide ledge. Laughing, they pushed and grabbed at each other. Then Reming pulled her off her feet and dangled her over the edge of the wall.

She signaled him to let go. He did, dropping her straight down, and she landed, using the force of her fall to spring up again. She was on her feet and running across the pasture toward the Potato Mountain before Reming could climb down.

Laura did not stop running until she reached the spreading oak on top of the pond ridge a half mile from the house. Then she sat down with her back against its huge trunk and watched Reming walk across the field toward her.

He smiled and waved. Laura waved back and stretched out on the ground. Her chest heaved from running. The pain in her lungs was terrible. She closed her eyes and tried to relax, but the little drummer boy was whispering to her from inside her coat. He was pleading for his lost drumstick.

Laura struggled to get up, but a twinge caught her left side and forced her back down. Her weakness irritated her. She wanted to move on. There were so many places she wanted to explore. All the places the little dark-haired girl had played.

In spite of the pain, Laura felt good. She was free. Freer than she had ever been before. She had never been outside the rock wall without one of her parents, or Nana, or Carrie, or some other adult. She could have. She had climbed the wall dozens of times, intending to go over, but she had not. And not because she had been told not to. She did lots of things she was not supposed to do. But she had never gone outside the compound. She was safe inside the wall. Outside, she knew there was something waiting for her.

She hoped for an answer to the puzzle about the little girl, the dark man, the lady with long, swirling hair, and her daddy. How did they all fit together? Her daddy was real. Maybe she had dreamed the others?

Reming was standing over her, his face concerned. "You'll make yourself sick, running like that."

Laura started to get up. She was anxious to go on. Reming sat down and grabbed the back of her coat.

"I won't let you go until you've rested."

She glared at him over her shoulder, warning him she would fight, even if he were her friend.

"You're headed for the mountain, aren't you?"

She nodded.

"Have you ever been there before?"

She shook her head. Her daddy owned all the land up to the mountain. He pastured cattle below it, and she often rode in the pickup with him when he went to check them. Maybe her daddy owned the mountain, too. He always looked at it more than he did the cattle, but he never offered to take her up there. Looking at the mountain made him sad and quiet. Maybe he wanted to own it. Reming's grandfather owned the land on the other side. Maybe the mountain was his, and he would not sell it to her daddy.

The instant Reming released Laura's coat she was up and away, racing across the pond ridge. He ran after her, but she was a daredevil, sliding down the steepest part of the dam embankment on her heels, jumping ravines wider than she was tall. Reming could have overtaken her easily on flat ground, but the pasture was scarred with washes that ran into deeper gullies. Laura never detoured and she laughed at Reming for going the long way around, seeking the easiest path.

When she reached the hill pasture, Reming was far behind but loping steadily toward her. Cold, frightening pains stabbed under her ribs and in her left side. It seemed there was not enough air in all the world to fill her lungs. She stumbled and fell.

"Wait, Laura! Wait!" It was Reming's voice.

She pushed herself up and kept going. The little drummer was pleading with her to hurry. Hurry! She had been away such a long time. Laura had the feeling she was going home.

Coming up fast behind her, Reming's running steps, pounding the dry grass, sounded like distant drums. She tried to sprint away from him, but he caught her and pulled her down. She tried to roll away from him, but there was no energy left.

Reming propped her head and shoulders in his lap. She felt silly with Reming holding her, but his body blocked the cold wind, making it a little easier to breathe.

"You have it," Reming said. "I've never seen it before, but my grandfather told me about it."

Laura opened her eyes. Reming looked worried. She managed to pat his back. As soon as the pain in her chest eased and she could get a full breath, she would be all right.

His eyes moved beyond her to the mountain. "My mother had it, too."

What was he talking about?

"The mountain does things to some people. It's like a magnet. It draws people to it. My grandfather told me for the truth. He said the mountain did something to my mother, but he won't tell me what. Not until I'm older."

Reming never talked that much all at once.

"I'll take you there, Laura. But I'm older. I'm responsible. From here we walk. No more running."

Laura smiled. Reming was no baby like Harley. Someday he was going to be a man, like her daddy. She felt proud of him and sure that his mother would have been proud of him.

The little drummer whispered over and over. Hurry. Please hurry. Find my drumstick. Laura listened to him and fought to control her breathing. Each time she drew a breath she held it as long as she could before she gasped for another one. The pain in her side eased and she was able to sit up.

Why was her body weaker than her will? Her mind raced ahead, scheming and planning, while her body struggled to keep up. It had always been that way. She was never able to go as fast or do as much as she wanted. She wanted to be on the mountain exploring all the places where that other little girl had played.

Laura picked up a stick and poked at the cow plop at her feet. It was full of persimmon seeds. She looked across the pasture to a clump of small trees near the creek. The lower branches had been stripped bare, but a few orange clusters remained near the top.

She threw the stick away and stood up. Reming grabbed her coat.

"You haven't rested long enough."

Laura pointed at the persimmon tree.

"I'll get them. You rest."

Reming trotted toward the trees, but Laura did not sit down. She followed him, walking slowly. Every step brought her closer to the mountain.

By the time she reached the trees, Reming had his pockets full of persimmons. He handed her as many as she could hold, and they ate while they walked, spitting seeds along the way.

"The mountain isn't really a mountain," Reming said.

It sounded like one of Harley's stupid riddles.

"No kidding," he continued. "Have you ever seen another mountain?"

Laura shook her head.

"I have. My grandfather took me to New Mexico once and we came back through Colorado. Colorado has some real mountains. Our mountain isn't even a hill compared to those."

Laura spit a mouth full of seeds at him.

Reming dodged. "Of course ours is more important, because it has a history."

That was better. He was forgiven for saying it was not a real mountain.

"My people have a legend about it. A story that came down from the past. Grandfather said that people in olden times used to make up stories about things they could not explain."

Reming was surely in the mood to talk. He had never talked so much before.

"According to the legend, it is not a natural mountain at all. It is a mound, built by my ancestors, so that they could be closer to heaven and to God. It's like a church. A place of worship." He sounded like a parrot, babbling truths he had learned by rote. Repeating words he did not understand.

They reached the barbed-wire fence that marked the end of her daddy's land. Reming climbed through and held the wire for her. On the other side a steep bank led to the creek. Laura slid down, ready to wade across, but Reming took her hand and led her around the bank to a narrow place where they could jump.

Beyond the creek, a path twisted through the blackjacks toward the top. The last dead leaves clung tenaciously to the trees, forming a brown canopy overhead and dimming the morning light.

Suddenly she looked up; they were no longer alone. Standing directly before her was a man, and out to one side another. Beyond them was a line of faces. Brown faces. Some young, smooth. Others cragged and care worn. Warriors with lone feathers. Chiefs in full regalia. A medicine man sporting buffalo horns and one wearing a wolf mask.

She had never encountered them before. Not even in the garage. Quickly she looked toward Reming, who had taken the lead ahead of her. Surely he was seeing them, too. But by the way he forged ahead, forcing them to move to avoid colliding with him, she knew that he wasn't seeing them at all. Friendly hands reached toward him. He marched straight ahead. An old woman wafted her feather fan over his head and chanted some sort of blessing when he stopped in front of her to wait for Laura. Hurrying to catch up, Laura heard him humming his Boy Scout song.

She wanted to scream, "Open your eyes, Stupid!" But she knew that just as her daddy had been unable to see the mare and the old Indian he had loved, Reming was unaware of the love that surrounded him, the friends he was missing. She felt sad for him as he loped off ahead of her.

He had gotten several yards away before she stepped out to follow him. A medicine man, wearing the ceremonial buffalo headdress, barred her way with a gourd rattle. She stopped. The murmuring around her stopped. Fiercely, he shook the rattle in her face. The crowd surged around her. Jeering. Threatening. Pointing the way back down the path. Rough hands shoved her. She was cut off. Surrounded. Afraid.

Staring wildly around her, Laura had the sense of

drowning in a whirlpool of old men's protruding bellies, wrinkled skin, and pendulous fat breasts.

Then, grumbling, the crowd parted. A lone warrior, carrying a spear, strode toward her. Laura stared at the spearpoint, fearing he intended to use it against her. It was not made of metal, as those carried by others in the crowd, but hand-hewn from a black rock that shone like obsidian.

She cowered away from that hideous projectile, back toward the hostile crowd. Someone pushed her. She lost her balance, felt herself falling. In one sweeping motion the warrior reached out and drew her to his side. He steadied her there, caressed her face with a rough hand.

Laura shivered as her cheek touched the furry animal skin he wore as a breechcloth, his only clothing. He was tall, rugged-looking; fierce. Standing close to him, she caught his odor which was of rancid grease, man's sweat, fresh-turned earth and pine. Pungent it was, though not a repugnant smell at all. Earthy. Friendly. Familiar. The smell of some forgotten home.

She couldn't imagine why this warrior had come forward to befriend her, but it was enough that he had smiled so lovingly down on her and was now standing guard beside her, his ancient spear at the ready, pointed toward the hostile crowd.

Laura sensed that he was from some earlier past time. He was not of these people who were angry with her. Why *were* these people angry with her? What had she done?

She could not see Reming. The medicine man towered above her. Behind him was a taller warrior with a fat squaw beside him. . . . They all loved Reming and he could not see them. She *could* see them. Why were they angry with her? Why had they separated her from Reming? She wished for the soft comfort of her clown, left for safekeeping on her bed at home. It seemed her clown was trying to whisper to her across the distance. To jog her memory about this ancient warrior and these angry people. Laura rejected that as silly! How could she be hearing her clown across that long distance from home? Impossible! She was only imagining her clown talking because she was so afraid.

Trembling, Laura felt inside her coat for the little drummer. She brought him out and hugged him. The fat squaw started to cry. She had kind, loving eyes, a grand-mother's eyes, like Nana's. Laura reached out, wanting to comfort her, but then panic seized her, and instead she shoved between her and the medicine man. The rest of the crowd parted to let her through. She heard the grand-mother behind her cry out. "Don't go up there!"

Reming was coming back down the path toward her.

"I thought you were right behind me. If you are tired, we can rest."

Laura sprinted ahead of him. The muscles in her legs felt weak, shaky. She was even more afraid than she had been when Reming's grandfather had appeared like the devil himself out of the heat waves and threatened her. She wanted to be safe home in her daddy's arms. But she felt the mountain drawing her forward, holding forth those secrets she had come to unravel. It had its own force, that mountain. That sacred place. She'd come too far to turn back. Laura sped toward a patch of light further on. There the trees opened into a wide clearing, which was bordered by more trees on the opposite side. Red sandrock glinted in the noon sun. It was the flat rock that had looked to her, from her garden, like a pat of butter atop her Potato Mountain. She had reached the top.

A pole, as thick as a man's head, stood in the center of the slab. It was supported at the base by a pile of large stones. Laura ran to it, locked her arms around it, and held on as though a thousand demons were trying to drag her away.

"What is it, Laura? What's wrong?"

Reming patted her shoulder, trying to comfort her. She shook his hand away, circling around and around the pole until its solidness made her feel more secure.

Patterns. Patterns. Her eyes stamped patterns in her mind. The rock slab was shaped like the top of a hammer with the claws pried apart, the pounding face pointed toward the big rock house. Her house. Her daddy's, and her grandmother's, and her great-grandfather's house. Before that it must have been a fort, or a prison. A place built strong, with high garden walls to keep people either in or out.

The claw end of the rock was a wishbone-shaped cliff over a deep canyon that rolled to the river. The land, level on that side, was much lower, as if a giant road grader had come down through the valley, past the ranch, and dumped its load to make the ridge, but then had dug twice as deep when it started on the other side.

It had all been exaggerated in Laura's mind. From her garden wall, and in her dreams, the ridge had seemed much higher and more expansive. It was disappointingly small. Except for the wishbone cliff that ended in the rock canyon. That was so high and steep she was afraid to look over the edge.

She shinnied up the pole and forced herself to look. A raw wind funneled up from the canyon and gusted across the slab, carrying with it the shrill dying echo of a scream.

Laura eased herself down to where her feet touched the supporting rocks. She was shaken, sickened by the sound. Reming, smiling up at her, obviously had not heard it. Why could she see and hear what others could not? It was like living in two worlds. Once she had thought it a gift, maybe, to make up for the silence she imposed on herself. Today, it was beginning to seem more like a curse!

Reming touched her ankle and pointed to the rundown frame house on the narrow strip of land between the ridge and the river. Several cars were parked in the yard along the edge of the gravel road.

"So many patients come to see my grandfather these days," he yelled over the wind, "that he has no time to farm or to fix up the place. He never turns anyone away, you know, whether they can pay or not."

Laura recognized the pride in his voice and a longing, too, as though he wished the place was in better shape, with fresh paint and a neatly plowed garden.

Reming's announcement brought pictures of the inside of that house. Pictures that caused her more pain. Laura fought them back; she closed her mind like Harley and Reming closed their ranks of embattled soldiers, shielding herself from the aching loneliness that seemed so much a part of that other time.

The homey rooms and familiar furniture receded, only to be replaced by the face of the dark man from the vision in her daddy's closet. His face, disembodied, was superimposed over the white farm house like an image on a giant outdoor movie screen. Seemingly alive, animated, he was not talking, as an actor would, but moving through time, with lines forming between lines in his handsome face as he passed from middle to old age.

Laura felt punished and angry, watching time, condensed into slow motion, destroy the dark, loving face she had felt so close to. Moments passed before she recognized the changed image as Reming's grandfather. Before she had only guessed. Now she knew.

Her first thought was of her clown. Her clown had never wanted to get close to the old man. Maybe because he was a healer, who, by reputation, dealt with strange diseases in natural ways and never seemed baffled by anything. Her clown had always been afraid of him, even before the day he had appeared out of the heat waves and made his odd threat. Now, knowing he was part of the forgotten time was double reason to stay away from him.

Reming was watching her. Laura closed her eyes to shut out his concerned face. She hugged the pole. Hard. Wishing for the nice pictures. The happy pictures of her daddy and the pretty lady dancing—silhouetted against the setting sun.

The pictures came to her dimly through that maddening gauze screen that veiled such an important part of her memory. Laura willed herself through it into the blue-white light, but the scrim and her vision moved further off into remote blackness, leaving her feeling abandoned. Laura climbed quickly down from the pole and grabbed Reming's hand. She gripped it tightly, afraid he too might vanish if she let go.

In spite of her mounting fear, she led him in a running circle around the perimeter of flat rock. Reming ran easily on the outside, while she took the shorter inside space for herself. On their second revolution Laura made a light hop-skip and swung around to face him. She placed his hands around her waist, hers around his neck. With her body she directed his movements, and he swung her around and around. . . . Eyes closed, she could feel her hair. Long. Straight. Heavy. Fanning out behind her.

"This is a traditional dance," Reming said, puffing. "How did you know it?"

Laura looked up into his bright face and was overcome by such a feeling of loss and sadness that she stopped dancing. Then, it came on the blasting wind. Wind howling up from the depths of the canyon. Again arose that blood-chilling scream. But this time she heard clearly the name shrilled with it. A name tangled with orphaned feelings from her daddy leaving her to make the mud-baby with her mother. She heard her mother's name again. K-A-T-E! The wind was spitting cold around her. K-A-T-E! A name that rhymed with hate!

Terrified this time, Laura ran for the trees on the opposite side of the clearing. She clung to Reming's hand, which was but a slender lifeline keeping her from being swept away by that terrible echo of her mother's name.

Around them, lining the downward path, were the same Indian faces. Hostile to her, all of them except the one. Her fierce warrior was there, walking between her and the crowd, alternately smiling at her and snarling at them.

Laura was trembling. Reming drew her close beside him and thrust his arm about her shoulders.

"I wish you could tell me why you are frightened. Don't be afraid. I'll always take care of you."

The mood of the crowd changed. Such adoring looks were cast on Reming that Laura wondered that he could not feel them. Grandmothers and grizzled warriors alike, they all loved him. As he passed them, chests swelled, shoulders straightened, heads lifted as though Reming embodied the hope of them all.

Laura felt calmer, proud to be with Reming. She basked in his reflected glory, consoling herself by pretending they were all friends and loved her, too. She ached for them to turn their smiles on her. Approve of her. Now she felt she had known them all. It seemed that once they had loved her. She was sure of it. Sure? Almost sure.

Nana would say it was make-believe. Her daddy would call it imagination. She would never tell Kate. K-A-T-E! She heard the name still echoing behind her. Eerie. Blood-chilling.

Laura shoved Reming ahead of her, prodding him to make him go faster down the narrowing trail. He trotted good-naturedly ahead of her.

She scowled at his back. Even if she decided to talk, who could she tell about these visions? No one. Not Reming. He had been there and seen nothing. Certainly not Harley. And Carrie would think it was a joke. The nurse might think she was crazy and lock her up with her mother. People refused to believe the truth when they heard it, as they refused to see what was all around them.

Laura could see. She *was* sure these people were not strangers. They were all people she had known. Why couldn't she remember details?

As Reming forged further ahead of her, the faces about her turned hostile once more. In the absence of her clown, Laura clutched the toy soldier for comfort as they closed in tighter around her.

Her lone warrior had moved off a distance to her left and was keeping pace with her, moving outside the crowd. With each glimpse Laura caught of him, he seemed to be crouching lower, snarling constantly now, clearly expecting trouble.

It came. The medicine man, with the buffalo-horned headdress, jumped from a boulder directly into her path. She tried to dart past him, but he blocked her way. He shook his rattle in her face.

"Now you have knowledge! Now you must stay!"

All around her Laura heard the chorused response.

"You must stay!"

The medicine man shoved her backward, pointed back up the mountain.

Angry, Laura thrust the little drummer into his face and shook it as he had his rattle.

Then he did a curious thing. He bowed to her, as did his people. They let her pass.

Reming grabbed her.

"What's wrong? Why were you waving the drummer like that?"

He hugged her as though he was trying to still her trembling with his own strength.

Over his shoulder Laura saw her lone warrior confront the medicine man. They exchanged harsh, guttural words. She strained to hear.

"When she comes back to the mountain," she heard the buffalo man say, "she will never come down again." He turned and climbed toward the top.

Laura shivered in Reming's arms. He patted her.

"Don't be frightened, Laura. I'll show you the way." He took her hand, started her down.

Laura clutched the little drummer tightly to her chest. He began talking to her. He was excited, anxious for his drumstick. When they came out of the trees the crowd disappeared.

Free of them, Laura ran, leading Reming around the face of the towering cliff, climbing over huge boulders, jumping from one to another, working her way down to the canyon floor.

At the bottom the sandrock curved gently into a shallow basin. Laura stopped and stared. It looked as though a rock had been thrown from the wishbone cliff high above, into a pool of water, and the ever-widening circle of ripples had been frozen into the rock. The pattern was beautiful, but it made Laura dizzy and sick. She felt nauseated, hearing the same dying scream the wind had first carried to her at the top of the ceremonial pole. Louder now. A hopeless wail. Colored red. A part of the circle of ripples etched into the basin. With the scream, pain assaulted her. A mammoth, crushing hand of pain reached down and grabbed her. Bruising, smashing that pain-blotted name—K-A-T-E—into silence. Puppet-limp, as though every bone were broken, Laura tumbled into the basin and lay on her side. Still. Still nauseated, choking.

Standing above her, Reming looked frightened. "What are you doing? Get up! You're getting so dirty."

His voice broke the spell, banished the pain. Laura felt the puppet strings pull tight again. She was able to stand. She backed away from the basin, turned, and ran.

Her footsteps echoed off the canyon walls—loud and hollow—with Reming's echo pursuing hers. The canyon curved, then widened. She stopped in the center of the wide space, turned slowly around, knowing she had found the place where the dark-haired little girl played with the drummer. She knew what she was looking for. A jagged crack in the rock face. She spotted it on the south side, and hurried toward it, eager to leave the basin behind and forget the unfriendly crowd on the mountain. She longed to be happy and free like the other little girl had been.

The crack was narrow, but Laura slipped through easily. Reming had a much harder time, and she had to pull and pull to get him inside. He stepped quickly away from the

159

crack to let in as much light as possible, but it was total darkness two feet away from the opening.

Small feet scurried toward the back. There was a strong smell of urine. Laura wondered what animals were living there, but she was not afraid of animals, not after leaving the nightmare of the mountain.

Reming was afraid. His voice sounded so nervous when he asked, "Did you hear that? Something is in here."

Laura heard him fumble in his pocket. Then he struck a match. The flame made a very small light but enough to show that the cave was large.

"Wow! I never knew this place was here. I bet Grandfather doesn't even know about it." Reming's match burned his fingers before he dropped it. "I wish I had my flashlight," he said. "We could explore."

Laura was exploring with her hands. She felt around the wall, kicking one foot in front of the other. Her toe struck a rock. She bent down in the darkness and rolled the stone away.

"We had better go now, Laura. We'll come back another time and bring a light."

Laura could feel how uncomfortable Reming was in the dark. He struck another match.

"No telling what kind of animal that was we heard. Probably a bobcat. They den up in places like this."

Laura felt where the rock had been. There was a small depression the size of her fist. She held her breath, hoping. The little drummer was pleading pitifully. Hurry! Please hurry! It has been such a long time!

She thrust her fingers into the hole and came up with the drumstick. She laughed out loud in the dark, and the sound filled the cave, resounding off the walls in an ear-splitting hyena laugh which mocked her as though she were laughing at herself.

The drummer was singsonging. *Give it to me! Give it to me! Please give it to me!* She thrust the drumstick deep in her pocket, afraid he might lose it in the dark.

Reming squeezed through the crack ahead of her. When she reached the outside, his face was grave.

"Were you laughing at me?" he asked.

Laura shook her head and pulled the drumstick out of her pocket. She held it up.

"You found it in there?"

She nodded.

Reming leaned against a boulder, watching her fit the drumstick back in the drummer's fist.

"Let's go and show my grandfather."

Laura froze. There was a secret hint in his tone. She looked up into his eyes, trying to understand what it meant. He did not care that the drummer had his stick back. She knew he wanted to take her to his grandfather because she had found the stick in the cave.

"Aren't you hungry?" Reming asked, coaxingly. "We can get something to eat at Grandfather's."

Laura shook her head. Once again she was afraid. That old healer knew what she had forgotten. She didn't want to find out from him. She was tired and wanted to go home. Laura tucked the drummer inside her coat, climbed out of the canyon, and headed south toward the road. The road was longer, but she wasn't about to go back by way of the mountain. That buffalo man had said he'd keep her there. She'd believed him.

Reming caught up with her. "I'll walk you back. You can visit my grandfather any time."

She smiled and wondered what Nana was having for supper. Reming could stay and eat with them.

The little drummer played his drum all the way back home. From the way Reming ambled along out of step it was obvious that he could not hear it. But Laura heard, and she pranced as high as she could as a tribute to the drummer.

Marching up the driveway, Laura heard her name— screamed. A muffled scream, carried by the treetop wind. She stopped. Reming was staring at the upstairs corner window. He had heard that scream just as she had. Half-afraid to look, Laura followed his gaze up to Kate's window.

Her mother was fumbling to get the glass up. Her hands were shaking, her face streaked with tears. She tugged at the sash. It would not budge. She examined the lock, pushed it, and pulled the window open. Her pointing finger jabbed the screen, making it bulge out.

"You did this! You wanted them to take my baby away. You think you've won, but you haven't! I hate you, I'll get you for what you have done to us."

Miss Pledge came and dragged her mother away from

the window. Carrie slammed it and motioned for Laura to go around to the kitchen door.

Carrie moved away, but Laura stood staring up at the empty window. She had always known her mother hated her. Now Kate had announced it in front of Reming.

His dark face had turned pale.

"She didn't mean it. She's just mad. Grandfather gets mad and yells things—" Reming stopped the lie in midsentence.

Laura smiled timidly at him. It was sweet of him to try. She took the comforting hand he held out to her and let him lead her across the driveway toward the kitchen.

When they rounded the side of the house, Harley jumped out of the shrubbery and lunged at Laura. He was crying, his face red and contorted. "You did this to Mother. Everyone thinks she's the liar, but it's you." He grabbed Laura by the hair and tried to punch her in the face. Laura pushed him away to avoid being hit.

Reming grabbed Harley. "What in the world is wrong with you?"

"Laura can talk. She talked to Mother. I'm going to beat her and make her tell what she did to Mother and the baby."

Harley was so stupid. Reming was half a head taller and twenty pounds heavier, and he had always taken up for her.

"I'm not going to let you hurt her, Harley."

"You don't know what she's done!"

"It doesn't matter. You're twice her size."

"She has made everyone believe Mother is crazy by talking to her and not talking to anyone else."

"Has she ever talked to you?"

Laura smiled. Reming was smart.

"No. She hasn't. But I know she can."

"How?"

"Mother said so. I believe her."

"But you've never heard Laura talk?"

"No."

"Then you can't definitely say it's true."

Laura was thankful she had not spoken to Reming as she had been tempted to earlier that morning.

"I believe my mother!"

Harley was yelling, which meant he was losing his temper and was going to fight.

"No one else believes her?"

"No! Laura has made her appear crazy. My dad has even hired a nurse to keep her locked up. And they moved my baby sister out of her room."

"Look, Harley. Your daddy loves her as much as you do. He wouldn't have hired a nurse for your mother if she didn't need one. She'll probably be well soon."

"I tell you there is nothing wrong with her! Whose friend are you? I thought you were my friend."

"I am your friend."

"Then get out of my way."

Laura was delighted when Reming shoved Harley back.

"I'm Laura's friend, too! I'm not going to let you touch her, Harley. I don't want to fight you, but I will. I will."

"You're going to have to."

Harley threw a punch at Reming's face. Reming grabbed his coat and slung him to the ground.

Reming backed toward the kitchen door, pushing Laura along behind him. "Don't make me hurt you, Harley. I don't want to fight." Harley bellowed and charged like a bull.

Reming shoved Laura toward the porch.

"Get inside, where—"

Before he finished the sentence he and Harley were on the ground rolling over and over in the grass—puffing and blowing and straining. Harley gave it everything he had, but Reming finally managed to get an armlock on him. He sat on Harley's back, bending his hand and arm up toward his shoulder blade and pressing the side of his face to the ground. Reming was not hurting him, except when he tried to get up.

"What more damage can that woman do?"

Laura whirled and found Carrie standing behind her watching the fight.

"Set her son against his little sister, and now these two boys who have been like brothers all their lives."

Carrie was talking more to herself than to Laura. Her eyes were glazed, staring at the fight.

Reming took his hand off Harley's head. "I'll let you up if you promise to leave Laura alone."

"I promise you that I'll beat her to death if she doesn't stop what's happening to Mother."

Carrie shouldered Laura aside and yanked the door open. She lumbered down the back steps and snatched Harley out from under Reming, dumping Reming sideways to the ground.

Laura laughed and jumped up and down, watching Carrie holding Harley by his upper arms and shaking him so hard his hair flopped down in his eyes and then flew back in slow motion after she had jerked him forward again.

Carrie drew Harley up on tiptoe, eye to eye, and sprayed spit in his face when she talked. "You can thank your friend Reming for saving you from the beating you deserve! If you touch your little sister I'll pound you into mincemeat! Don't think I won't!" She slapped him hard across the mouth, and he tried to sniffle back the tears. "That's for threatening to kill another human being. I heard you."

Carrie would always defend her because she was Nana's favorite, and Carrie loved Nana better than anybody in the world. She spun Harley around to face Reming.

"You apologize to your friend. Help him up."

He hesitated and Carrie lifted her shoe against his bottom. Her voice was loud and impatient. "I said help him up!"

Harley extended his hand, and Reming took it quickly and scrambled up. He gripped Harley's shoulder to comfort him. Laura knew Reming was hurt at the way Carrie was treating Harley.

"He didn't mean it, Carrie," Reming said. "One little fight isn't going to come between us."

Harley started for the house, and Carrie collared him.

"Not so fast, Mr. Hitler, Al Capone, gangster, tough man. You owe Reming an apology. Say it!"

She shook him roughly by the shoulder until his reserve broke. He sobbed out, "I'm sorry, Reming."

Reming looked as if he was about to cry, too. Laura dashed out the door, jumped off the porch, and put her arm around him.

Carrie shook Harley again. "Straighten yourself up and tell your sister you are sorry!"

Harley whirled to face Carrie, shrugging her oversized

hand off his shoulder. She had asked too much. Laura smiled. He could not win.

"I *won't* tell her I'm sorry! I'll never tell her, no matter what you do to me. I hate her! I hate her, and I wish she was dead!"

Carrie slapped him hard. "Get yourself up to your room, and don't you so much as stick your head out the door until someone comes to get you." Harley fled up the back steps, sobbing and rubbing his cheek.

With fists clinched on flabby hips, Carrie watched him go, then she shook her head as though to clear away the unpleasantness and turned a shaky smile on Reming.

"Where have you and Laura been all day? She looks pooped."

"She wanted to see the mountain, and she was so anxious to get there, she ran most of the way. To be so little, she surely can run."

Laura perked at the compliment. She looked up at Reming, smiling her thanks. He appeared not to notice her. He was staring at the door, and she knew his mind was upstairs in Harley's room. He was talking to ease the tension.

Carrie seemed to understand his feelings, because she made a special effort. "You all were gone so long, Mrs. D. got worried. But I told her there was no need to worry about Laura as long as she was with you. That you'd take care of her as well as we could."

Reming was more uncomfortable than ever. Laura could feel it. Since he could not do anything for Harley, she knew he was anxious to be gone. He brushed grass off his coat, seemingly at a loss about what to say and how to get away.

"My grandfather would be proud that you have so much confidence in me," he said at last. "I did my best to take care of her. But I couldn't stop her from running so hard. I was afraid she would make herself sick."

"As far as I know that's the first time she has been off exploring like that."

"She surely wanted to see the mountain, but she didn't seem to want to come back that way. We walked all the way around the road."

"You must be starving, both of you. Come in and eat."

Eating was Carrie's answer to everything. She started

up the back steps, but Reming stopped her. "It's getting late. I better get on home."

Laura moved closer to Reming. She did not want him to leave.

"You've already made that trip three times today," Carrie said. "That's over six miles. Stay for supper, and I'll take you home in the car." Reming edged the grass along the walk with the toe of his scuffed cowboy boots and smiled sheepishly at Carrie. "Can Harley come downstairs and eat with us?"

Carrie patted his shoulder reassuringly. "Don't worry. Harley will be all right. But I think he better stay in his room awhile and consider his actions."

Reming looked so searchingly at Laura she became self-conscious and marched the little drummer up and down the walk, pretending she was not listening.

"What he said about Laura being able to talk—it's not true. At times she has wanted to tell us things. Really tried. Because it was important to her. But she couldn't. How could Harley believe she talked to his mother?"

"He's confused about things that have been happening around here. All of us are. He is searching for a way to explain it. His mother blames Laura. That's the easy way out. I hope he will come to see that after he's had a chance to think awhile in his room."

Laura studied the cracks in the sidewalk. Harley was a coward, a sissy mama's boy, but he was stubborn. His mama was so important to him, Laura knew he would take a lot of punishment before he gave up trying to help her.

"I've never seen him like that," Reming said.

"Don't worry. He'll work it out. Come on inside and let's eat."

"I don't much feel like eating, Carrie. If you don't mind, I'd rather get my soldiers out of the garage and go on home."

"You come and go as you want, Reming. You're always welcome. You know that. And not because you're Harley's friend. Because you're *our* friend. Mrs. D. and I thought the world and all of your dear mother."

Reming smiled, like he did not know what else to do or say. Laura ducked her head when he came over to her, knowing what he wanted.

"Are you ready for the little drummer to rejoin his company?" he asked politely.

Laura did not want to give him up. If only Reming would leave him with her, since he had just gotten his drumstick back. But Reming never left any of his soldiers. They were his most priceless possession, and they were a set. She could not ask him to break up the set. She handed the drummer to him reluctantly.

"Thank you, Laura. I'll take real good care of him, and I'll bring him back after school tomorrow so you can play with him again."

He smiled at Carrie and started off to the garage. She yelled after him. "Get your toys and come back by the kitchen. I want to send something home with you, for you and your grandfather."

Carrie hustled up the steps and through the door. Laura listened to her scurrying around inside the kitchen, opening the refrigerator, putting things in a sack. By the time Reming returned from the garage, she was back out on the stoop, holding a large grocery bag. It was half-full, with the top folded neatly down. Reming was carrying the battered shoebox tucked under his arm and studying the little drummer in his hand. He held it up for Carrie to see.

"Laura found the little drummer's lost drumstick today. It has been missing as long as I can remember, but she led me right to it."

"That's nice," Carrie said absently. She folded the top of the paper sack another time and handed it to Reming. "I put in some fried chicken and a bag of Mrs. D.'s hot rolls. And a jar of my watermelon preserves your grand-dad likes so well."

Reming took the bag and smiled up at her. "Thanks, Carrie. That will be a real treat for us. Grandfather is not as good a cook as you and Nana."

Hearing Reming say Nana seemed so natural. He had always called her that, because Harley did. Laura remembered Carrie and Nana talking about Reming maybe being her daddy's real son. She had not thought of it before, but that would make Nana his *real* Nana.

The idea was pleasant to her and that was very strange. Thinking of Nana and her daddy being grandmother and father to that ugly mud-baby caused Laura such turmoil she pulled up a clump of grass and wrung the slender blades together until they stung her hands. She threw the grass and dirt clod across the yard.

Reming looked puzzled watching her. But Carrie hadn't noticed. She was still beaming at Reming's compliment about her and Nana's cooking.

"It's always a pleasure to do things for you, Reming," Carrie said. "You never take things for granted like Harley. You come back and see him tomorrow. Maybe some of your good will rub off on him."

"Harley loves you, too. As much as Laura and I," Reming said to her.

His brown eyes were so sincere Laura half expected Carrie to melt into a big pile of lard right where she stood. She imagined the white uniform shrinking down to cover the black grandma lace-up shoes, with whitish grease pouring out of the neck and armholes, the way leeches dissolved with salt poured on them.

The picture was so funny, Laura ran laughing to Carrie and hugged her. Carrie swooped down and picked her up.

"Now what upset your tickle box, Missy?"

She seemed relieved that her sentimental talk with Reming had been interrupted. So did Reming.

"She's been real happy ever since she found the little drummer's lost stick. She marched all the way back from the cave, as though she could hear him playing his drum."

"What cave?"

"Where she found the stick. In the canyon on the other side of the mountain. I didn't even know it was there."

"Then how did she know? She's never been off exploring before today."

"I don't know, but she led me right to it. The opening is no more than a foot wide. I could barely squeeze through. It was black dark inside. She scrambled around on the floor and found the stick."

"In the dark?"

Laura scowled at Reming. It made her uncomfortable for him to tell it. Now she wished he would take his sack and go home.

"I couldn't see my hand in front of my face. When Harley can come out, we'll take a couple of flashlights and go back. It's a big place. I could tell by the echo inside."

Carrie shifted Laura to her hip. Holding her there with one arm, she reached her free hand toward Reming.

"Let me see that toy."

He gave it to her, and she brought it up close to her face, examining it carefully.

"Why! That stick is no more than two inches long!"

Laura pushed Carrie's hand and the drummer gently back toward Reming. He took the toy. She kissed Carrie's chin to distract her. The big woman giggled and patted Laura's bottom.

"This baby is just full of miracles. Has been since the day she was born."

"She was happy at the cave, but the mountain frightened her. She acted so weird she almost frightened me."

Laura felt a shudder pass through Carrie. The fat woman cleared her throat as though struggling to control her voice. "The mountain does strange things to some people," she said.

"That's what my grandfather tells me," Reming said, wistfully. Then, "I better be going now, Carrie. Grandfather worries if I'm not home by dark."

"You run along. We'll see you tomorrow."

He was halfway to the corner of the house, walking backward. He held up the paper sack. "Thanks again for the goodies."

"You're welcome. Give your grandfather my regards."

"I will."

Carrie had the door open, ready to step inside, when she called out.

"Hey! Reming!"

He poked his head back around the corner of the house.

"Tell you what I'll do. I'll round up a flashlight from T.J., one that puts out a good strong beam. For your cave exploration. The distraction will be real good for Harley."

"That would be great, Carrie. I think Granddad's needs new batteries."

Carrie clomped to the middle of the kitchen and set Laura on her feet.

"You run along and get washed up for supper. I'm going to call your dad and see if he'll be home in time to eat with us."

Laura marveled at the change Reming had worked in

169

Carrie. She was as cheerful now as she had been glum when they got home. The scene with Harley was all but forgotten.

She started for her room, and Carrie called after her.

"And don't disturb your Nana. She's resting."

Laura went to the bathroom, then carefully flushed the toilet as gently as she could, but the noise came as loudly as ever. She heard Nana getting up and ran to the door that connected their rooms.

"My goodness, Baby Girl. You're as dirty as a little pig."

Laura grinned, and clapped her hands to say that it had been great fun getting so dirty.

Nana came and took her by the hand, leading her back to the bathroom.

"Well, let's get some of it off before we go to the table."

She wet a washcloth and bent over, wiping her face.

Laura could feel the grit on her cheeks and forehead. The pink cloth was brown across Nana's hand when she held it away.

"This isn't going to do. Quick! Off with your clothes and into the tub."

Laura peeled her knit shirt over her head and kicked off her shoes, corduroy pants, and panties all at the same time, leaving them in a heap on the floor. While Nana adjusted the water and poured in the soapy bubble bath, she scooted her white-enameled wooden step stool, cut in the shape of a duck, across the floor, stepped on its wings, the top of his head, and over into the high, old-fashioned legged tub.

She let out a surprised cry when she discovered she still had on her socks. Gripping the rounded edges of the tub, she sat down in a cloud of white foam and leaned back, extending both legs in the air so that Nana could pull off the soaked socks.

Nana's face was the most beautiful in all the world! Laughing, wringing the red muddy water from the socks, the fine lines at the corners of her eyes crinkled merrily. Her cheeks were full and rosy, like pictures of Santa Claus, and her lips were naturally pink. She never wore lipstick, except to Sunday school and church, and then only when she was reminded to put it on.

Looking up at her through her simple metal-framed bifocals, her round blue eyes were the color of the sky on a sunny day, and her short wavy hair, always neat under a white net, reminded Laura of a soft silver cloud.

The heaven the preacher talked about in church could not be half as nice as sitting in a warm bubble bath watching Nana lather her hands with green soap, then holding the bar for her while she washed the grime off feet and legs and scrubbed between toes with her fingers. Nana never used a washrag. She worked with her bare hands, and the feel of her deft fingers, moving quickly, spreading soap, gently kneading the dirt off, was heavenly. She scrubbed across Laura's back, tickled the dirt beads out from under her chin, tickled under her arms, splashed the soap off with a cupped hand, and they laughed and giggled and loved each other so much the world outside the bathroom door seemed very far away and unimportant.

Nana had always bathed her like that. She could do it much faster than Laura could do it herself. Once in a while, when Nana was very tired or had been sick, she would sit on the edge of the tub while Laura bathed, but always before she was through Nana had her hands in the water, excusing herself with "You call that clean?" or "You left more beads around your neck than on Miss Astor's pet horse," because she enjoyed the happy, touching closeness as much as Laura.

"Pull the plug," Nana said, pushing herself up with both hands on one knee.

She held onto Laura's arm to keep her from falling while she climbed out of the tub, then wrapped her in a big towel and hugged her dry.

"You dry between your toes while I get your night-clothes."

Laura hated it when Nana opened the door and left the bathroom. The sounds and the smells of the house came rushing in with the cold air, the clatter of Carrie in the kitchen, the welcome smell of supper, and the lingering, hated powder and sour milk smell of that baby.

She shut her eyes, wishing Nana back. The bathroom door closed out the world again. Magically, Nana was there when she opened her eyes. She dropped the towel and ran naked into her open arms. Nana turned her around, and she leaned against her while she stepped into the pajama bottoms Nana held and then pulled up for her. She thrust her arms into her pajama top and watched Nana button it. Her hands were small like the rest of her, the skin loose and lined from years of work, but the strong, gentle comforting feel of them lingered long after the bath was finished and Laura was dressed. She kept her eyes on Nana's hand when she reached for the glass doorknob. In passing, Laura stopped and kissed Nana's fingers. It gave her courage to march out into the world again.

The world was not the fun place it had once been. Not since that baby came. And it was becoming more and more complicated every day. Laura thought about the little drummer. Finding his lost stick should have made her happy; instead she felt uneasy, as though she had made a mistake. Carrie's reaction to the news had made her uncomfortable—a warning that it might cause trouble later. If only Reming had not told. It was their secret. No one else had a right to know.

When she and Nana reached the kitchen her daddy was at the table. He looked tired. She ran and kissed him. He smiled, but the smile did not go clear through. It was only on his face. Inside she knew he was dark and sad listening to Carrie tell about Harley attacking her and fighting with Reming.

From her place at the end of the table, Nana was listening too, the happiness of the bath fading from her face.

"Reming is such a good boy," Carrie said as she set a bowl of steaming boiled potatoes on the table and took her seat next to Nana. "No telling what Harley would have done to Laura if he had not stopped him. Poor child was so upset. It really hurt him to have to fight his friend."

Her daddy forked a piece of roast on her plate and cut it up. He spooned vegetables, passed dishes, serving her first, then himself. Without his usual bantering chatter the kitchen seemed hollow, echoing the sound of silverware against china.

Her daddy had to reach a long way, across her mother's empty place, and Harley's, to take the dishes from Nana. Carrie served herself before she passed the food back to Nana, where it stopped, untouched.

Nana pushed her chair back. "I'll go up and have a talk with Harley."

"No, Mother. Let him be."

"You know he is always ravenous at supper time, T.J. We can't let him go hungry."

"Yes we can!"

"He's all upset about his mother. What he needs is love and reassurance. I'm sure he is sorry by this time."

"Ha!"

Her daddy's explosion startled Laura. His face was tight and angry, which pleased her. Harley had no one but himself to blame. She would have left him alone if he had stayed out of her fight with her mother. He had not. Now he was in for it!

Laura scrambled off her chair, picked up her daddy's fallen napkin, and placed it neatly across his lap. He patted her head.

"Thank you, Sweetheart."

By the time she climbed back in her chair and turned around, he was brooding again.

"I just bet he's sorry! He's probably up there planning all sorts of misery for his little sister."

Nana started to get up. "He's miserable himself. Leave him to me."

"No, Mother!"

Still gripping the table edge, Nana sat back down.

Laura glanced back to her daddy. She could tell by the vicious way he was wiping his hands on his napkin that he was really angry.

"Coddling is what's wrong with him now. I let Kate make a mama's sissy out of him! What he needs is discipline, and that's what he is going to get!"

"I don't agree with you," Nana answered him.

"I'm sorry. But you let me handle it this time."

Nana bowed her head over her plate and listlessly ate a few bites. The clinking of silverware sounded louder to Laura than it ever had before. Unbearably loud, like the swell of the church organ when the choir marched in. Carrie was fidgeting because of it. She looked up from her plate and spoke. "T.J., you remember Reming's tin soldiers? The set you and Molly used to play with?"

"Sure."

"You know Reming always lets Laura play with the little drummer. The one with the missing stick."

"That was Molly's favorite, too. What about it?"

No! Carrie! No!

"Today Laura found his drumstick. In a cave beyond the ridge. Reming said she led him right to it. He didn't even know the cave was there."

All eyes turned on Laura. She smiled from one to the other, hoping they could not detect her uneasiness. If only Reming had not told Carrie.

Her daddy shook his head. "That's impossible. Molly broke it out when she was no bigger than Laura." He laughed softly, and his eyes looked far away. "I remember she said he made too much noise on his drum. Funny what people remember from childhood."

Laura felt light-headed, dizzy. The table and the room seemed to recede, leaving her isolated, alone with her new discovery. It had to be Molly's memories that were all mixed up with hers. The Molly who had been her daddy's playmate and grew up to be Reming's mother.

She poked at the mystery lightly with the tip edge of her mind. It was too scary to wade further into it.

"It's amazing that Laura found it after all these years," Carrie said.

"I'd have to see it to believe it."

Carrie seemed hurt that her daddy wanted proof. "You'll get your chance tomorrow. Reming will be here. You never doubted my word before."

"I'm not doubting it now. I'm sure you did see a drumstick, but it couldn't have been the original. The kids probably made a new one and showed it to you as a joke."

Carrie bristled. "If it had been Harley showing me I might doubt him, but not Reming. Reming has a code. He wouldn't consider a lie funny."

Her daddy looked across the table at Nana. "You see, Mother. What a sad comment on Harley. He can't be trusted."

Carrie's face turned red, her chin quivering. "I didn't say that."

"Yes, you did, Carrie. And I know you love him like he was yours. We all know about him and have known for quite some time."

Nana's face had grown stern. "He is a normal, healthy boy."

"He's a liar like his mother. He will say or do anything to further his own purposes or cover his mistakes."

"That's not true, T.J.," Nana said.

Carrie tried feebly to change the subject. "Did you know there was a big cave across the ridge?"

Her daddy snapped to attention at the mention of the word "cave," as though he had not heard Carrie mention it the first time. "What cave?"

"The cave where the children found the drumstick. Across the ridge. In a canyon."

Her daddy's and Nana's eyes pinned Laura to the back of her chair. She smiled and laced her fingers together across the top of her head. She felt hot all over, as if their eyes were burning her. What did they want?

Her daddy's lips moved, but his voice sounded disconnected.

"Molly and I found that cave when we were kids." Laura squirmed under his eyes, but he was talking to Nana. "We swore to keep it our secret. As far as I know she never told anyone, and neither did I—until now."

"I wonder how this baby found it?" Carrie asked.

If only Carrie would keep her mouth shut. Hadn't she caused enough trouble?

Her daddy grinned and tussled her head. "Stumbled onto it, I suppose. The way we did. Or maybe she is in contact with the dead."

Nana spoke sharply. "T.J.! You know I don't approve of such nonsense!"

"No disrespect intended, Mother. Whatever Laura's secrets, they are her own. We have no idea what goes on in her head, and we won't until she learns to talk. She could be in contact with the devil himself for all we know."

"T.J.!"

"I'm only teasing! More likely she keeps company with a dozen angels." He combed Laura's curls out of her eyes with his fingers. . . . "How I long for her to talk. I have an idea her brain is full of fascinating things. I've always had the feeling that Laura sees things differently than the rest of us. The world must be altogether different to her. Pleasanter, I hope."

His mood changed from lightness to gloom as he pushed back from the table and stood.

Nana's eyes darted anxiously to his face. "Be gentle with him, T.J. Listen to Harley's side of it. Try to be objective. Put yourself in his place. He doesn't see things as we do. He doesn't understand—"

A new defiance crept into her daddy's eyes. "I've shirked my responsibilities long enough!" he snapped. "I wanted so much to get along with Kate that I turned my back on things. Rather than fight about it, I let her have her way with Harley. Look where that has gotten us. She's turned him into a mama's boy! Worse than that. She's instilled her own prejudice against Laura. It's her fault he's perpetrating violence on his little sister. Following her example. God only knows what he may have done to Laura in the past. Or what Kate might have done, either. We have no way of knowing."

Nana made unintelligible sounds, as though choked on a rush of words, undecided what to say. Laura glanced from one face to another, sensing what was unspoken between them, aware of Carrie, across the table from her, with her head down, eyes fixed on her plate. Laura felt happy. Her imagination filled with fantasies about the misery that was about to come down on Harley. He had shunned her, teased her, excluded her from his games, laughed when their mother punished her for no reason—simply because she would not talk. He had mocked her and called her "Dummy" while delighting in her mother's favor. Now it was his turn to be the outcast. Now he was going to find out how it felt to be lonely. She would see to it. A long time ago her clown had promised her everything would be turned upside down. She thought of all the times her clown had been her only friend and protector. Held close, a cotton and cloth barrier absorbing her mother's and Harley's laughter and their hateful comments, it had whispered to her to hold on, her turn would come. It had promised!

"It's my fault," her daddy said. "In the back of my mind I knew what was happening, and I did nothing about it."

Nana's voice was unfamiliar, faltering. "You're exaggerating, T.J. You've blown it all out of proportion. It's not fair to take all your frustration out on a little boy."

Her daddy went on as if he hadn't heard. "I tried to

make it up to her by giving her all the attention I could. But rejection can't be made up. If it could, she'd be talking. I want to hear her chattering away like other little girls her age. And I will. I swear to you I will, if I have to keep her mother locked away upstairs for the rest of her life. And Harley with her if it takes that!"

He strode out of the kitchen, banging the door behind him. Nana jumped up to follow him, but Carrie grabbed her arm and eased her gently back to her chair.

"Let him be. It will do Harley good to see his dad really angry."

"He's unreasonable. There's no telling what he might do in that state."

"He won't hurt the boy."

"I'm not so sure. I've never seen him like that."

"And high time, too."

"You think he's right, don't you?"

"I surely do, Mrs. D. If you'd seen Harley this afternoon, you'd think so, too. The boy needs a firm hand. A man's hand."

"If he ever gets started on him, he might not know when to quit."

"It's mostly bluster. You know T.J. He has a kind heart."

Nana patted Carrie's restraining hand. "Just the same I'm going upstairs. In case things get out of hand."

"You won't interfere?"

"No. I'll check with the nurse about Kate. Busy myself with something out in the hall."

Carrie stood, moved behind Nana's chair, and squeezed Nana's slender shoulders between her two meaty hands. "Everyone's guardian angel," she said affectionately. "If it will make you feel better. But I'd let T.J.'s mad spell run its course. It's time he put some fear in that boy. Harley has been under his mother's influence way too long."

Standing, Nana tottered backward a step. Carrie caught and steadied her. "Careful. Are you all right, Mrs. D.?" Her homely face was worried.

Nana ignored the question, and Laura was sure she had not heard. At the door she turned a preoccupied gaze on Laura. Her eyes were probing, feverish, as though her mind were struggling to piece together some mystery.

"On the other side of the ridge in a cave," Nana said. It

was a statement made to herself. "You found the little drummer's stick in a cave, Baby Girl?"

Laura made her eyes as round and innocent as possible before she nodded.

Nana smiled and left the kitchen. Carrie looked after her and then to Laura.

"Don't get to thinking too much of yourself, Missy. You can take a lesson from your brother. See what happens to people who start thinking the world centers on them."

Laura wanted her clown. She wanted to spend as much time with him as she could, but it was important what Carrie thought of her. Carrie had such an influence on Nana. She jumped up and carried her dishes to the cabinet.

After the table was cleared, Laura hugged Carrie, pressing her face into her huge stomach, hoping she would be dismissed. Carrie patted her back roughly.

"Run on. Go play with your toys. And don't get into anything."

Laura bolted, but she stopped at the pantry door long enough to send an adoring look back to Carrie. The fat woman smiled gratefully as she waved her on.

Her clown was propped in its usual place against her pillows at the head of the bed. She stopped in the doorway and stood reverently, her hands at her sides, concentrating all her attention on it. One of the black buttons was missing off the front of its red and white polka-dot suit. Its yellow yarn hair was scraggly and matted, most of it missing on one side. Some of the stitches in its embroidered face were pulled, causing its face to appear wrinkled. Its once-white cotton skin was stained from many afternoons outside in the red dirt.

Laura went to the bed and took her clown in her arms. The moment she picked it up, she knew it was angry with her. Finding the drummer's stick had been dumb. A dumb thing to do. Reming was home by now. Probably had already told his grandfather about her finding the cave and the drumstick. The old healer would come now. He would come to the house seeking her. Wondering how she had found part of a toy his daughter had broken and hidden years ago. He would come asking questions.

Silly clown! The old healer could ask all the questions he wanted. He would get only silence. The same silence she gave everyone, except her mother. Maybe he wouldn't come at all. Maybe he would not be interested. Her clown had always worried too much about her.

But her clown said there was little time left. They had to hurry their plan.

The clown had been her true friend. Her only friend other than Reming. She pressed the clown to her chest, sat on the edge of the bed, and rocked—waiting. The clown was calm and relaxed, as resolved as she was. It wanted to settle the score with Harley as much as she did.

Her daddy's voice, calling her back to the kitchen, echoed through Nana's apartment. Laura stood, holding her clown at arm's length. It was smiling at her as always. She kissed its dirty face, tucked it under her arm, and skipped through Nana's room to her sewing box. She fished inside for Nana's small, pointed trimming scissors, found them and, holding her clown steady between her knees, clipped the seam at the top of its shoulder, exposing two inches of cotton stuffing—a space just big enough to get her fingers under the material. Her clown's smile seemed bigger than ever as she replaced the scissors and skipped down the back hall through the pantry and into the kitchen.

Harley was seated in his usual place at the table, his head lowered over a plate of roast and potatoes, his fork trembling in his right hand. Nana and Carrie were also seated, toying with half-empty coffee cups.

Her daddy lifted her into her chair, patted her shoulder, and took his seat at the head of the table. He was smiling, obviously pleased with himself.

"Harley and I have had a long talk. When he has finished eating he has something he wants to say."

Her daddy winked at Nana across the table, leaned back, crossing his legs, and sipped his coffee. All eyes were on Harley, and he was painfully self-conscious, cutting his meat gingerly with his table knife, trying not to hit it on the plate, flinching when he did hit it as though afraid of the noise. Obviously stalling for time, he chewed everything with exaggerated care. Finally, he choked and put his fork down. Her daddy stood to refill his coffee cup and whisked Harley's plate over to the cabinet before he had a chance to recover and start the whole process over again. Coughing, Harley followed the lost plate with his eyes as though his last hope had been snatched away. While her daddy's back was turned, Harley met Laura's eyes, telling her unmistakably that what he had to say was all a lie. He hated her more than ever.

He sputtered and coughed once more, then blurted, "I'm sorry about this afternoon, Laura. From today I'm starting all over. I'm going to try to be the best kind of big brother."

He stopped, looking over Laura's head at her daddy. His eyes were brimming with tears, the defiant tilt of his head clearly saying that he had done enough.

From behind her, her daddy's stern voice commanded, "Finish it! Kiss your little sister. She needs to know that you love her."

Distasteful as it was, before Harley had a chance to get out of his chair, she jumped up, flew around the table, and threw her arms, clown still in hand, around his neck. Robbed of the initiative, poor Harley just sat there trembling. She knew he was fighting the impulse to hit her. She also knew he was too big a coward to do anything in front of her daddy. Laura planted a wet kiss in the middle of his forehead.

"See there," her daddy said. "Your little sister loves you so much she's trying to spare you all the embarrassment she can. You were having trouble coming to her, so she came to you. Helping a person save face is the nicest thing you can do for anyone. Remember that, Harley."

Laura had not expected her daddy to add to her victory. She beamed at Harley and, just for show, planted another wet kiss on his forehead before she took his hand and led him out of the kitchen and across the marble hall to the living room. He trailed helplessly behind, too stunned to jerk his hand away, until her daddy's voice came through the closed kitchen door. "Remember everything we talked about, Harley. I know you're going to act like a gentleman. Play something Laura wants to play this time. Next time it will be her turn to play your games."

Laura switched the television on and adjusted the

volume to the loudest acceptable level before she turned to face her brother.

His eyes were focused on a spot in the wallpaper, behind her. "What would you like to play?" he asked formally.

Laura laughed. Poor Harley! He reminded her of a marionette, obeying commands when his strings were pulled.

Harley glared at her. "What are you laughing about?"

She shrugged and walked around him, trailing her clown by its stuffed arm.

Harley turned in a circle following her. "You stop laughing at me!"

She shrugged again. Facing him, she tilted her nose in the air, narrowed her eyes, and smiled, a gesture she had practiced in front of the mirror in preparation for their final confrontation. She lifted her clown, wagging its crooked smile in Harley's face.

Harley pushed the clown away. "Get that filthy thing away from me!"

Laura hugged her clown to her chest and made mumbling sounds as though whispering secrets in the clown's ear. She pointed at Harley, and giggled.

"Don't you dare laugh at me!"

Laura rushed to her mother's favorite chair, a high, tufted wing-back chair covered in rose velvet, and settled into it at an angle, crossing her ankles. Her feet came barely to the edge of the cushion, but she pretended her legs were as long and lovely as her mother's. She smoothed her printed flannel pajamas primly, playing out her charade as elegantly as possible.

"Don't you dare mock my mother! You ugly little pig!"

Laura smiled beneficently at Harley, pleased that he had caught on. She seated her clown on the corner of the chair, its back resting against her knees, exactly as Harley had sat with her mother every evening as long as she could remember. Laura focused all her attention on the clown, pretending it was telling her about some high adventure. She frowned and laughed and nodded appropriately, stroking its matted yarn hair exactly as her mother had done Harley.

When she looked up, Harley's fists were clinched at his sides, his face red and puckered as though he was about to burst, trying to contain his rage. To humiliate him further, she turned her clown to face him and pointed its stuffed arm, laughing and snickering.

Harley started toward her and stopped, tears brimming out the corners of his eyes and running down his cheeks. "You think you're smart. You're trying to force me to hurt you so I'll get in trouble." He clasped his hands in front of him, fingers intertwined. "I'm not going to do it. You're not going to make me do it!"

Laura bent her clown forward, slapped its stuffed knee with its stuffed hand and laughed and laughed for him. Harley stood foolishly in front of her, unable to do anything but stare and choke back his frustrated tears. Laura stopped laughing for her clown and laughed for herself. Harley could dish it out, but he couldn't take it. He was pitiful standing in front of her crying, but she had no pity for him. She was glad he was crying. It was important that he understand, later, that she had planned his punishment.

Harley sniffled and wiped his nose on his shirt sleeve. "I'll get you for this! No one is going to laugh and make fun of me and my mother and get away with it."

Laura waved both hands and howled. Stupid as he was, he had gotten the idea. She curled her lips under, rounded her shoulders, and scratched at her sides like a baboon, making low hooting sounds to taunt him, in a gesture she had copied from him.

He stepped toward her. "You stop it. Stop it this minute!"

She jumped out of the chair, dragging her clown with her, and stepped bravely up to him. She was aware of his fists, trembling close to her head, barely under control. It did not matter. She expected to get hit before it was over.

Laura lifted her clown and bopped Harley over the head with it.

He stuffed his hands in his pockets and stepped back. "Don't you dare hit me again!"

Laura grinned and whispered, "What are you going to do, Sissy Boy? Run and tell your mama? I made your mama get locked in her room."

Harley gasped. "You talked!" He backed away. "Mother isn't crazy. You did everything she said you did." He ran to the hall screaming, "Daddy! Daddy come quick! Laura talked!"

Laura inserted her hand in the cut seam and ripped with all her strength. Her clown came apart in her hands, its cotton insides spilling out on the floor. She threw it down and kicked it as hard as she could, showering stuffing all over the living room. Three pairs of footsteps sounded in the marble hall as Laura collapsed in a heap on top of her clown's ruined body. Through tears she glimpsed Harley's horrified face. She was sobbing hysterically when her daddy reached her.

"My God! What happened here?" He kneeled and lifted her shoulders. "Tell Daddy what happened."

Laura raised her arm over her head, and brought her finger down like an aimed gun, pointed straight at Harley.

"That's a lie!" Harley said. "Another one of her tricks. She talked. She bragged about getting Mother locked up. When I called you, she tore her clown."

Laura concentrated on her clown, remembering all the nights it had slept with her and comforted her after Harley or her mother had made fun of her for not talking. It had been so warm, snuggled close under her blankets. Now it would never be there again. It was beside her, dying on the floor, with its guts strung all over the room. All Harley's fault.

She pulled away from her daddy and crawled toward her clown's mangled body. Its neck was severed, a wad of compressed cotton protruding from its head. She picked up the head, wrapped her arms around it and rocked it protectively as though defying anyone to take it from her.

Her daddy sat crouched on his heels opposite her, his hands hovering helplessly on either side of her shoulders. "Laura, Sweetheart, don't cry. Daddy will buy you a new clown."

Sobbing, Laura shook her head violently at the mention of a new clown. She did not want a new clown. She wanted her clown. She loved her clown. She loved it almost as much as she hated her mother and Harley and that ugly mud-baby.

Her daddy went on as though he had not understood her refusal. "I'll buy you the biggest, prettiest clown in Oklahoma City. We'll go first thing in the morning."

"Didn't you hear me?" Harley screamed over her crying. "I said she tore it up herself! She deliberately tore it. She doesn't deserve a new one."

Clutching her clown's head to her chest, Laura shot under her daddy's arm like a coiled spring. She grabbed a blue glass bird off an occasional table and made straight for Harley.

Carrie intercepted her and took the bird. She ran shrieking back to her daddy, still clutching the clown's head. He folded her in his arms and stood up. She caught his chin in her hand and made him watch as she acted out her love for her clown. She kissed the torn face tenderly, then hugged it next to her cheek and cried out her broken heart.

"I know you loved your clown, Sweetheart. You don't have to convince me."

She patted her daddy's cheek to reward his understanding. His chin was quivering. Gently, she turned his face toward Harley and pointed.

Harley stepped backward, shaking his head. "She's lying! She's lying about me just as she did Mother."

Laura held her clown's head in front of her daddy's face and made a ripping motion. She repeated it and pointed to Harley. Her daddy patted her back soothingly, and she could tell by his touch that he had decided in her favor.

He turned on Harley. "What happened here? Let's hear what you have to say."

Harley backed toward the hall, and Laura was tempted to laugh he looked so guilty. She sniffled instead and squeezed fresh tears down her face.

"She started laughing at me the minute we came in here," Harley said. "She sat in Mother's chair and made fun of me by putting that clown in my place. Then she got up and hit me over the head with it, trying to make me hit her back. I wouldn't and she said, 'What are you going to do, Sissy Boy? Run and tell your Mama? I made your Mama get locked in her room.' Then I called you, and while I was doing it, she ripped her clown to pieces. I swear it. She had it all planned!"

Laura sandwiched her daddy's face between her hands and forced his attention. She shook her head violently to call Harley a liar. Making a fist, she raised it high in the air, bringing it down in a rush toward the top of her daddy's head. Breaking before she reached his hair, she tapped him only lightly. Repeating the process again, she pointed to Harley, then to the top of her own head, rubbing at the center of her skull, where her hair was thick and her daddy could not check for marks.

"She's a filthy liar," Harley screamed. "I never touched her."

Abruptly her daddy thrust her into Nana's arms. The sudden movement frightened Laura and she cried out.

Nana patted her back to comfort her. "Hush now, Baby Girl. You're all right."

Laura shook her head violently, holding the clown's head for Nana to see. She pressed its torn face to her own, forcing herself to think of sad things so she could cry and resisting with all her will the temptation to watch her daddy.

Nana backed up to the couch and sat down. "Now stop crying about your clown. He'll require a little surgery, but Nana can make him over good as new."

Laura allowed Nana to rock her like a baby.

"You can't believe *her!*"

It was Harley's voice, but the change in it made Laura pull away from Nana to look at him. He had stopped in the double archway that led to the hall and was facing her daddy, looking him in the eye. "I know you don't believe her after the talk we had upstairs. I promised you that I would try to get along with her and I would not fight her. I kept my word. I did not touch her! I did not tear up her clown! And she *did* talk!"

Cold shivers ran up Laura's arms, and her stomach tightened into a hard knot. In her daddy's place, she would believe Harley. For a moment she panicked. Harley was going to convince her daddy, and then his anger might be turned on her. A shudder ran through her body. More than his anger, she feared his hurt and disappointment in her. And she could not bare to think about Nana and the hurt it would cause her.

Laura wished herself in the cool, dark cave across the ridge. A quiet place to think and plan was what she needed. She had to make a plan, but there was no time. Harley was winning. If he won, her mother would have the run of the house again. She would have her stupid, stinking mud-baby back. Nana and Carrie and her daddy would be bowing and pampering, pleading forgiveness. She would be the outcast, shunned by them all, maybe even sent away. No! Nana would never let them send her away.

She moaned, pressing her cheek against her clown's pointed hat, her arms encircling, searching for the warm comfort of its soft body, finding nothing but air. Startled, Laura looked down at her empty arms. The clown's head tumbled off her shoulder, bounced off the edge of the couch, and rolled across the carpet, stopping, face up and smiling, against the leg of the coffee table.

Laura slid off Nana's lap onto the floor. Her clown was dead. She had killed it. She had torn its head off and kicked its body to pieces, and Harley was winning. Winning! She had never expected him to stand up to her daddy. She had expected him to run, like the silly coward he had always been. She had depended on it. Her clown had depended on it, too. The moment she put her fingers in the cut seam her clown had whispered, "Pull hard, Laura." And it had smiled. Was still smiling to her. Only for her.

They were all watching. Carrie and Nana, her daddy and Harley. She could feel their eyes on her, judging, condemning, pitying. None of them had the right. She lifted her head defiantly to Harley. He stood, smirking, two steps behind her daddy, his shoulders back, chest puffed out as if he was about to have a medal pinned on it. He had already declared himself the winner and was awaiting her daddy's confirmation.

Laura steeled herself. Her heart was pounding, her body tense. She swallowed hard, willing herself not to be sick. She would never give Harley that satisfaction. Resigned to a guilty verdict, she let her eyes slip to her daddy's face for judgment.

Her daddy smiled for her, like her clown. His eyes were shimmering and misty soft; Laura stared. There was no hint of judgment on his face. She sensed his openness; the knowledge flooded her mind, spilled over, coursed through her body, relaxing strained muscles. She stopped it. Dammed up the pleasant flow. Openness did not mean victory. All it meant was that she still had a chance.

Laura tore her eyes away from the temporary safety of

her daddy's face and stole a quick look at Nana and Carrie. They were leaning reluctantly toward Harley. She was pushed adrift. Swirling. Alone. Her eyes fell to her clown's dead face. It was still smiling. She reached out and grasped its severed head. It had never failed her. Her clown had always been near when she needed it.

Harley had to be crushed, because her mother would fall with him. It was her last chance. Her only chance.

Time was against her. No time to think. No time to plan. They were all watching her. Waiting. Her clown was all she could think about. Her clown. Her clown. It had hated her mother and Harley even more than she did, promising always to turn things around, to put them in her place. Now it was dead and could not even advise her anymore.

Harley could talk. He had everything on his side. She felt like screaming at him. "Talk! Talk! Talk to Mama! Say 'spool,' Harley. Harley, say 'spool.' Say 'baby,' Harley. Love the stupid baby!"

Words! Words! Words like rocks being piled on her head and her back. Heavy rock-words, piled on one at a time, slowly crushed her, pushed the breath out of her body, squeezed the air out of her.

Nana was bending over her. "Laura, Baby Girl. Nana will fix your clown. I promise you. I'll *fix* your clown. You mustn't grieve so over a toy. I know you love him. We'll put him back together, you and I. No more serious than a bath. He needed a bath. He was all dirty. We'll give him clean skin and new clothes. He'll be so happy, feeling all clean and fresh."

Her daddy grabbed Harley's arm and jerked him toward her. "Do you expect me to believe that your little sister ruined her own clown?"

"She did."

Her daddy pushed Harley closer. "Look at her! She loved that clown more than anything in the world. She has slept with it every night since before she could walk. You expect me to believe that she tore it up just to get you in trouble?"

Harley whimpered. "She did it! She tore it!"

Nana helped her sit up. "We'll fix your clown, Baby Girl. He'll be so happy when he is all clean. Just like you after a bath."

Laura watched her daddy's hand fumbling with his belt buckle. Harley twisted out of his grasp and backed toward the hall.

Nana's back was to them. "Now smile for Nana and don't be sad anymore. Can you smile?"

Laura wiped her nose on her pajama sleeve and smiled timidly. Smiling was no trouble for her with her daddy pulling his belt out of his belt loops and Harley backing steadily away from him.

The smirk was gone from Harley's white face. "She talked, Daddy. She tore her clown so you wouldn't believe me. Mother isn't crazy. She's not! You *have* to let her out of her room!"

Her daddy looped the belt in his hand. "That's it, isn't it? The real reason for this elaborate lie."

"It's not a lie!"

Nana turned her attention to Harley and her daddy. Laura picked up her clown's head and planted a "thank you" kiss in the middle of its smile. They had won!

"Your mother put you up to this, didn't she?" her daddy asked.

"No! I swear it. It happened just as I said it did."

"You didn't plan this alone. You haven't the guts or the brains!"

"Daddy, please! I wouldn't lie to you!"

"Like hell you wouldn't! You're just like your mother. Liars, both of you."

"Mother's not a liar! She's not! Laura is the liar!"

Harley *was* stupid. He was *making* things hard for himself. Her daddy was more angry than she had ever seen him. His face was red, the muscles in his neck standing out.

"You are your mother's son. There's no doubt about that."

"Mother told you the truth about Laura. She *can* talk! As plain as I can."

"You thought you'd trick us into letting your mother out, so you'd be on top again."

"No! It happened! I told you exactly what happened."

"You were laughing at me the whole time I was talking to you upstairs."

"No."

"Promising to be the right kind of big brother. And you had this planned all the time."

Her daddy's anger boiled over, and he swung his belt at Harley. Harley turned and tried to run, but her daddy caught him and bent him over her mother's rose velvet chair.

"I should have done this upstairs and saved Laura this misery. I tried to be kind and give you one more chance."

Harley tried to cover his bottom with his hands. "Laura did it! Laura did it!"

Her daddy brought the belt down hard. Harley's wrists and hands took most of the blow, and he screamed in pain. Laura had all she could do to contain her delight. She bit on her finger to keep from laughing.

"Don't hit me, Daddy," Harley yelled. "Please don't hit me again."

"I haven't even started yet."

Red marks the width of her daddy's belt appeared on Harley's arms and hands. He was gripping the chair, resisting the impulse to cover his bottom again.

As her daddy brought the belt down harder than before, the leather made a loud slapping sound, and Harley gave a pitiful cry like a wounded animal. He shifted from one foot to the other while struggling to stand. Her daddy pushed his head down in the chair seat and hit him again with the strap.

Nana stood. She raised her voice above Harley's screams. "T.J., that's enough!"

"You stay out of this, Mother!" He raised Harley to a standing position in front of him. "Now tell me again what a monster your little sister is and what all she has done."

Harley sobbed, rubbing his eyes with one hand and his bottom with the other. "I told you exactly what happened. Laura talked, and she tore her own clown."

Laura sniffled, pretending sympathy for Harley. She put her head on her knees to keep from laughing when her daddy shook him by the shoulders and, tangling one hand in his hair, pulled his head back.

"So! You are going to try to brazen it out, are you? Tell a lie and stick to it until somebody believes you. We'll see!"

He pushed Harley's face back into the chair seat and

came down on him hard with the belt. Harley shuddered, tightening his muscles as her daddy brought the strap down twice more. Harley rolled from side to side on the chair arm trying to escape the strap, but her daddy held him, pressing his face viciously into the chair cushion the more he struggled.

Nana started forward, but Carrie intercepted her, pulled her back, whispering, "He has needed this for a long time, Mrs. D. You see how he persists in the lie."

Harley was sobbing, begging her daddy to stop, but her daddy acted as if he could not hear. He raised the belt again and again, as though he was doing something he had wanted to do for a long time. Harley's sobs turned to outraged screams and back to sobs, and her daddy went on whipping him, until Nana buried her face in Carrie's shoulder and began to cry.

Laura could not stand for Nana to cry. She jumped off the couch and ran to her daddy. She grabbed his arm as he brought the belt down on Harley, and pulled it away. The end of the belt touched the floor and she stepped on it.

"Your little sister is begging me to stop. Do you have any more lies you want to tell on her?"

Harley bawled, "No."

"Who tore up her clown?"

"I did," Harley said without hesitating. His body was shaking pitifully as though he was cold. "I tore her clown," he said. He was sniffling, trying to control his crying. He had wet his pants.

"And what about Laura talking?"

The little self-control Harley had managed broke, and he cried as though he would never be happy again. "I made it up." He wiped tears out of his eyes with his knuckles, glared at Laura briefly, then fixed his eyes on the floor. "I made it all up."

"Why?"

Harley's body sagged as though the question was more than he could bear. He leaned against the chair for support. "Because Mother shouldn't be locked up. She's not the one," he moaned. "She's not the one."

He could be so stubborn. If her daddy beat him again, she would let him. He was as stupid as that ugly baby.

Her daddy yanked his hair and Harley cowered away, batting his eyelids the silly way her mother did.

"And who should be locked up instead of your mother?" her daddy asked.

Harley sniffled and stared at the floor. "No one. Please let me go to my room."

"I have a feeling nothing is settled. You haven't given up this idea of blaming everything on Laura. It's still in your mind. I know it is."

"No, sir."

"Well if it is, it better stay in your mind. If you do one more thing to hurt your little sister, I promise you, what you got this evening was just a taste of what you *will* get. I'll take you to the garage and give you a going over you'll never forget. Do you hear me?"

"Yes, sir."

"Now get up to your room and count all that money your mother gave you for doing things you should have done without being paid. Get all your counting out of your system, because you're going to give every penny you have to Laura in payment for ruining her clown."

Harley squared his shoulders and met his father's eyes as though deciding whether he was strong enough to take the consequences of protest. He dropped his eyes and a tear fell on one black shoe. "May I say good night to Mother before I go to bed?"

"You're not even interested in becoming a man, are you?"

"Yes, sir. I am. But Mother is up there all alone. And I think I'm the only person in this house who loves her."

Nana lifted her head from Carrie's shoulder. "That's not true, Harley. We all love your mother. We're all very worried about her."

Her daddy looked at Harley like he was a used drill bit out at the oil rig. A used bit was no good for anything. "He's not worried about his mother being lonely. He wants her comfort. Isn't that right, Harley?"

Laura was almost sorry for him. He had no fight left. He seemed too weak and defeated to protest.

"All I know is that I'd like to see my mama before I go to bed."

"Well, you just run right on up to your mama. You can even sleep with your mama if you want to, because I'll be sleeping with Laura. You tell her that for me when you finish telling her how badly I mistreated you."

Pushing past Nana, Harley headed for the hall. She brushed his hair as he passed. "Aren't you going to kiss Nana and tell Carrie good night?"

He glared from one to the other, his eyes accusing them of not preventing his humiliation, of not believing he had been punished unjustly for telling the truth.

Nana staggered backward as though he had struck her. Instead of trying to comfort her as Laura would have done, he marched out of the room, apparently unconcerned that he had hurt her feelings.

Laura thought she heard him crying as he ran up the stairs, and then there was a loud argument with the nurse, who did not want him to disturb his mother.

Even though he had refused to kiss her good night, Nana rushed to the bottom of the stairs and told the nurse that his father had told him he could see his mother and to let him stay as long as he wanted.

Nana was too good. She should have let him deal with the nurse himself. He would not have made it past the door, which would have suited Laura better. She did not like for Harley to be alone with her mother when she was unable to spy. They were her enemies. Separately, they were no longer a threat. Together, she was not sure. It made her uneasy.

Returning to the living room, Nana looked as accusing as Harley. "I know you and Carrie are in agreement about how to handle the boy, but I think you were much too harsh with him, T.J. Much too harsh."

"I'm sorry you feel that way, Mother."

"If you'll remember you were something of a mama's boy yourself."

Carrie was bent over picking the clown's cotton stuffing off the carpet. "Not in the same way, Mrs. D. He was much more independent. And he was never a liar."

"He never had a reason to lie for me. Under the same circumstances I think he would have behaved much the same as Harley. Can't you see he's trying to protect Kate? Being a mother, I have to admire his loyalty."

Laura backed up against her daddy's legs, to remind him of her presence. Nana's sympathy for Harley frightened her. She was Nana's Baby Girl. Nana was supposed to take her part, never Harley's. Maybe tearing her clown had been a mistake. Nana was looking at her the way she had earlier when Carrie had told her she had found the drummer's missing stick. Her eyes were questioning, searching, puzzled, as though she had guessed about her Molly-memories and her visions but was not ready to believe the worst about her.

Surely Laura was imagining things. Her Nana would never believe anything bad about her. Laura made her eyes wide and innocent, cuddled her clown's head next to her face, and thought about the way things were going to be when her mother and Harley and that ugly mud-baby were gone and she had her daddy and Nana all to herself. Nana would be happier then. With the three troublemakers gone, Nana would have no worries. The work would be cut in half with that nasty baby out of the house.

Her daddy pressed her head back against him. His fingers, combing through her hair, interrupted her thoughts.

"No matter how much you admire his loyalty, Mother, you can't condone his treatment of his little sister."

Nana's eyes seemed even more piercing.

"No. Of course not."

"That's what I punished him for."

Laura was relieved when Nana's eyes moved up to her daddy's face.

"But don't you see. Indirectly you were punishing him for his loyalty, for trying to protect Kate, which was natural. He was defending her the only way he knew how, by trying to make her actions credible. I see this whole episode as a last-ditch effort of a very frightened little boy trying to save his mother from something he doesn't understand. He couldn't possibly have any concept about mental illness or its treatment. He doesn't know what to expect. He has experienced all this trauma with the rest of us but with far less insight."

Her daddy took his hand off her head and Laura looked up. He was fumbling in his shirt pocket for a cigarette. He lit one and started talking before he blew the smoke all out.

"So. Because he is frightened and upset, we are supposed to let him vent his anger and frustration on Laura. Making her the scapegoat is exactly the reason his mother is locked away upstairs."

Laura smiled when her daddy returned his hand to the

top of her head and pressed her against him again. She enjoyed the warm closeness of his body, but his fingers were trembling.

Nana took a deep breath as though summoning all her strength.

"Let's get it all out in the open, T.J. Harley deserves our best efforts at objectivity. The whole situation was irrational because too many emotions were involved. Strong emotions pent up over a long period of time. The fact is you whipped him too hard. And after the first two licks, I don't think your mind was on him. You were whipping Kate."

"That's not true!"

Nana rushed on as though she wanted to finish before her strength gave out.

"And what you said about him sleeping with his mother, and you sleeping with Laura, was your protest against Kate's rejection of you—implying that she preferred Harley's company to yours."

"She does."

"But that's your problem. And Kate's. Not Harley's. You were lashing him for something he has no control over. Then you made sure he'd tell her."

"He would have told her anyway. He's up there now, wallowing in a pool of tears and self-pity."

Nana, holding her hand across her eyes, leaned weakly against the door facing. "I think he has a right," she said. Her voice was barely a whisper. "You whipped him too hard. I know you left bruises on him."

Laura slipped her hand behind her daddy's knee, pushing him forward, wishing he would do something to comfort her Nana. Instead, he shouted at her.

"My God, Mother! You make it sound as though I brutalized the boy."

Nana reacted to his tone with a flare of temper, the worst Laura had seen from her. She stepped forward.

"You don't know your own strength! I know you hurt him physically. And I don't call it much of an example, matching his bad behavior with your own. It would have been more honest if you had dragged him upstairs and thrown him at Kate. Told her to take her son, and you'd take your daughter. The breach may never be bridged now. Harley may be lost to us forever."

Carrie lumbered across the room and thrust a sheltering paw around Nana's slender shoulders. "Don't upset yourself, Mrs. D. Things will work out."

The muffled tread of rubber-soled shoes crossing the marble hall made Laura look beyond them. The homely nurse, tall and starched in her white uniform, stopped beside Nana, took her small clenched fist in her oversized mannish hands, and gently opened the taut fingers.

"Carrie is right, Mrs. Daniels. Though painful, this kind of confrontation is healthy, and necessary."

Nana drew up to her full height. "There was nothing healthy or necessary about the beating my son just inflicted on poor Harley."

Laura reeled backward as her daddy slumped into the rose velvet chair. He reached for her absently, and lifted her to his lap.

"Mother, please! Everyone must find his own way." He leaned his head against the chair's high back. "I'd like to hear what Klaris started to say."

The nurse always grinned, showing the pink gums above her protruding teeth, on hearing her daddy use her given name. "Before these situations can be ironed out," she said, "people must be willing to voice their feelings. Emotions must be brought out in the open where they can be dealt with. Sometimes aggressions have to be acted out, hopefully in a positive way."

Nana moved away from the two women and sat on the couch. "This whole evening has been wrong. Negative."

"I don't think so, Mrs. Daniels. You disagreed with your son's actions, and you voiced your opinion. How long has it been since you did that?"

"I always tell him what I think."

"Most of your conversation was audible upstairs. I wasn't trying to listen, but I heard you make several comments about his relationship with Kate and Harley and with Laura. All this should have been discussed years ago. I've never heard you do that before."

"I've tried to stay out of his marriage. I had to bite my tongue many times—"

"Maybe you shouldn't have. You were all living here as a family unit—"

A crash came from upstairs, followed by a scream and repeated pounding on the bedroom door, as though her mother was beating on it with something, trying to splinter the wood. Her daddy thrust Laura roughly off his lap and rushed toward the hall. Laura followed, wanting his protection, as though the pounding noise was pursuing her.

The nurse reached the stairs first, her daddy close behind. They raced each other toward the top, and Laura scrambled frantically after. She was aware of Nana and Carrie standing in the marble hall, looking up through the open railing toward her mother's door. She thought about fleeing back to Nana, but she wanted to stay near her daddy. As she reached the top, her mother started screaming.

"T.J., I'll get you for this. T.J., I know you can hear me. Come here! If you weren't such a coward, you'd open this door. Come here, damn it!"

Laura crouched at the top of the stairs. The stupid baby was screaming from the little room where her mother had wanted to put the nurse. Her daddy was saying something, but she could not hear it over her mother's pounding and the baby's screams. Her daddy held out his hand, expecting the nurse to give him the door key. The nurse thrust her hand deep in her pocket and backed away from him.

"Talk to her through the door, Mr. Daniels. If you open it, we'll have to restrain her, and that won't do anyone any good."

Her mother stopped banging and yelled, "T.J., come open this door! You coward!"

Her daddy banged the door with his fist. "I'm here, Kate. What do you want?"

"Open this door, you son-of-a-bitch!"

"I'd be glad to, but the nurse won't let me."

"Hide behind the nurse, you lousy coward. You're afraid to face me after what you've done."

"What have I done?"

"You know damn well what. You beat your son unmercifully."

"He deserved it. He knows what he did."

"Harley told the truth, as I have. Laura is the liar. She talked to Harley as she did to me. She *can* talk! She can! She's twisted everything. Made fools out of all of us. First Miss Glade at the school. Then me. And now Harley. And you are the biggest fool of all."

Her mother's voice cracked, and the mud-baby's screams drowned her out. Her daddy and the nurse moved closer to the door. Laura strained to hear what was being said over that stupid baby's cries. Her daddy turned and looked at her, a long, searching look, and then to the nurse. The nurse smiled. A reassuring smile, but Laura could not be sure. The nurse said something to her daddy. He nodded. Not being able to hear what they were saying worried her.

That stupid baby spoiled everything. Babies always spoiled things. She had always known that. Harley was her mother's baby. He had always come first. And now this one. Both came before her. Trouble, both of them. Harley had caused Nana to be mad at her daddy.

Poor Nana. She was standing in the marble hall below, wringing her hands. She looked so tired and worried, and it was all Harley's fault. Harley and her mother and that stupid baby.

Her mother's voice rose again.

"Laura is the liar! For every bruise you put on Harley, I'm going to put ten on her!"

Laura ground her teeth together. Kate! She could hear the name echoing on the mountain, rhyming with hate. How she hated her! Hated her as much as she did that ugly stinking mud-baby. Kate wanted to hurt her. That was fine. She would show her what hurt meant!

Laura stood, and slipped toward the baby's new nursery. The crib was pushed in the corner, and she marched toward it. The baby had its arms raised over its head, fists clinched, face red from screaming.

She plucked the baby out of the crib by one arm. Startled, it quieted momentarily, and she heard her daddy yell.

"If you ever put a mark on Laura, you'll answer to me."

The baby swallowed a fresh scream as Laura tossed it to her shoulder. Its head snapped backward. It opened its mouth to scream again, and Laura put her hand behind its neck, pressing its ugly face into her shirt to muffle the sound so she could hear what her mother was saying about her.

"Laura has been nothing but misery to me since the day she was born. I tried with her. I really tried. None of you understand the misery I've gone through trying to understand why she rejected me. But I'm finished with that. She's going to be the miserable one from now on. I hope she is out there listening. Laura? Laura? Laura!"

Her mother, calling her, reminded Laura of her clown singing the silly nonsensical song it had sung to her since she could remember. "Come meet your Molly Dolly. Meet me. Meet me. Come meet your Molly Dolly. We'll fall down."

She crossed the room and stood in the nursery door, cradling the baby gently, swaying and rocking as she had seen the nurse do to try to quiet it. Nana saw her, punched Carrie, and pointed at her. Laura patted the baby's back and kissed the top of its ugly bald head. She was surprised at how soft its head was. Nana removed her glasses and wiped tears out of her eyes with the back of her hand. Carrie put a protective arm around her shoulder and hugged her close. She and Carrie both stood smiling up at her for loving the baby.

Her mother screamed her name over and over until her daddy banged the door with his fist. "Shut up, Kate. If you say one more word to hurt that little girl, so help me I'll break this door down and come in there after you."

"I doubt that!" her mother taunted from behind the door. "Cowards beat up little boys. Believe me, I'd give you some of your own medicine."

Her daddy moved toward the nurse. "Give me that key."

The nurse backed away. "No, Mr. Daniels."

"Give it to me, damn it!"

Stepping close to the banister, the nurse dropped the key over the edge. It clattered on the marble floor, and Nana picked it up. She folded it in her hand, and crossed her arms over her chest, resolving the question of the key. Her daddy shoved the banister with both hands and returned to the bedroom door.

"You're lucky, Kate. They won't give me the key. And you're not worth breaking down a seventy-five-year-old door."

Her mother laughed at him.

"There's nothing more worthless than a coward who beats up little boys. You can't keep me in here forever. I'll get out, and when I do, I'll fix you. T.J., I promise you I'll fix you and that evil little witch you are so fond of."

Her daddy banged the door again with his fist.

"Shut your filthy mouth, Kate."

"I don't have to. That's the only thing left to me at present. But it won't always be. I'll get you, T.J. You and Laura both." Something heavy hit the inside of the door. "Laura? Laura, you went too far, when you caused Harley to be hurt!"

Her daddy hammered the door with his fist.

"Shut up, Kate! I mean it! Shut up!"

"You went too far, Laura. I'll get you for hurting Harley! I promise that I will."

Her daddy grabbed the doorknob with both hands, pulling on it. "Shut your crazy mouth."

Her mother yelled over the clatter of the doorknob.

"Laura, I'll get you for hurting Harley."

Her daddy stepped back, kicked the lock as hard as he could, then ran at the door, butting against it with his shoulder. He hit it so hard the wood made a cracking sound, but the lock held.

The noise made the baby scream louder. It was squirming in Laura's arms, flaying at her angrily with its small fists, striking her the way she knew her mother wanted to. She hated the sight, the smell, and the sound of it, and she hated her mother for bringing it into the house.

She squeezed the baby tightly around the middle, making the screaming subside by forcing it to use all its strength to draw the next breath. Its face was a hideous red mask of gasping protest. Laura was careful to keep its back to the others. Only she could see its struggle, the desperate effort to draw enough air to keep from choking. Survival precluded crying. It was fighting desperately. Fighting as hard as her mother had fought her.

Laura smiled, pleased with herself. Her mother and her stupid mud-baby could fight all they wanted. Her mother would never get the best of her again.

Pacing the hall in front of the nursery, Laura was careful to appear to be gentle. She patted the baby's back, jiggled it up and down, and went through all the comforting rituals she had seen others perform. All the while, she was enjoying the muffled battle going on in her arms.

The baby was much stronger and heavier than she had imagined it to be. It had grown longer and put on weight since Nana had moved her into the treasure room. For all its plumpness, it was not cuddly like her clown. It was wiry and hard to hold, with a will to have its own way, like her mother.

It was nothing like her clown. Her clown had loved her, enjoyed her touch, never resisted the way the stupid baby was resisting. Her clown had never objected no matter how hard she squeezed and petted. It had always smiled its love for her, smiled its happy sunshine smile that made its flat, dirty cotton face beautiful to her.

The baby was so horribly ugly, with its red-mud face all pinched, mouth open, gasping like a half dead fish trying to breathe. It reminded Laura of one of the sinners, suffering the torments of hell, in a stained-glass side window at church. The poor man had been cast in a bubbling pit of red-hot lava, his agonized screams captured forever in the colored glass.

Laura had never believed that picture. It looked the way a lie sounded. Like one of Harley's tall tales. The artist who put that picture in the glass, depicting such torture as God's will, had himself been the torturer for putting that kind of fear in people's minds.

It was not that way and never had been! People punished themselves and each other, and God stayed out of what was bad. Laura had forgotten where or when she learned it, but she knew she was right.

Hell was a made-up place preachers used to scare people into being good and giving money. Reverend Edwards mentioned hell in every sermon, and some Sundays he spent the whole hour telling about the horrors of it. He shouted and shook his fist, then let his voice drop low, as if he were telling a ghost story. People tumbled out of their seats and down the aisle to dedicate their lives, and empty their purses and pockets into the collection plate, while he smiled as though satisfied with himself for delivering a successful "message."

Once Harley had made the trip to the front, and her mother had followed him. The next Sunday they had been baptized together in the glass and cement pool above the choir loft. Nana had said they were dedicating their lives to being Christ-like, meaning to love and do good, but it had not worked. They had gone on teasing and making fun of her, trying to goad her into talking.

For a while, Laura had hoped they would change, but

her mother had continued to pick and criticize, telling her how embarrassing it was to have a child people thought retarded. She always hissed the word "retarded" like a witch's curse. Nana's predicted "change for good" had never come about.

Her mother hated her for being different. When Nana or her daddy were not around, Laura had no support except from her clown. She had cherished its approval, depended on its cuddly warmth, been comforted by its protecting presence when her mother or Harley were particularly cruel, or when she was alone and lonely in her bed at night.

Her clown had loved her. It had never rejected her, made fun of her, or put anyone else above her. It had liked her Nana and her daddy, but it had liked Laura best, even crying for her when she was away, the way the ugly baby was crying for Kate, now.

Laura had loved her clown as much as Kate loved the stupid baby. Yet, as much as she had loved the clown, she had killed it. She had ripped its head off in one unflinching stroke and kicked its stuffing all over the living room.

She had sacrificed her clown to defeat Harley. Sacrificing the mud-baby to defeat her mother would be easy compared to that. Her mother's ugly mud-baby had never worn a sunshine smile just for her.

Her mother screamed from behind the locked door.

"Laura belongs in an institution. You know it as well as I do. Stop protecting her, before she destroys all of us."

Her daddy thrust his shoulder against the door.

"Shut up, Kate!"

Her mother shouted louder.

"You're going to be locked up, Laura! Do you hear me? Locked up! Where you can never hurt Harley or my baby again."

Her daddy looked down the hall toward the nursery. His face softened, seeing Laura cradling the baby. He turned back to the closed door. His expression hardened.

"Laura cares more about the baby than you do! It was screaming, because of *your* noise, and Laura has it quiet now."

The tone of her mother's answer was changed, tinged with disbelief and fear.

"My God, T.J. Tell me you haven't let that fiend near

my baby! Please tell me you haven't." The last was whispered, like a prayer.

"Kate, you should have been an actress, the way you dramatize. Laura is holding the baby like a regular little mother."

The sound that penetrated from inside the door reminded Laura of another sound. One she had heard over and over again in dreams, always the last thing she heard before it woke her, a desperate, last scream for help—one without hope of help coming.

"Get her away from my baby! Get her away! Get her away!"

Her daddy pounded the door with his fist.

"Damn you, Kate! You won't let any normal relationship develop in this house. *Your baby* is also Laura's little sister. She has a right to hold her."

Aware that Nana and Carrie and the nurse were watching, Laura extemporized a sad smile and kissed the top of the baby's head. Her parents' angry exchange became unintelligible, punctuated by pounding and profanity from both sides.

Laura's heart was racing, her face hot as she walked casually in a circle, bouncing the baby, lengthening the distance to the stairs, on her right, by three or four feet—making it more than double her height, enough for a running start.

Remembering her somersault trick, she chose a worn spot in the carpet directly in front of the top step, and focused on it. Shifting the baby to her right arm, she placed her left hand flat against its protruding belly, where she could exert all her strength in pushing it sideways. She had the sensation of moving outside herself, like a spectator, as she waited—ready—for her mother's next word. It was her name—"Laura!"—shouted explosively like the crack of a starting pistol. Her daddy backed up and kicked the door. Laura heard the lock snap, saw her mother in the doorway grappling with him. She sprang forward toward her daddy as though she intended to stop their fight.

Six running steps brought her to the carpet spot where she purposely tripped, thrusting the baby away from her. She used both hands to propel it down the stairs, which made it impossible to break her own fall. Laura was afraid as the top step rose toward her face. Her right shoulder hit first, causing sharp pain. She cried out. As if they had taken up her scream in a round, she heard Nana and then her mother scream.

A flurry of footsteps sounded behind her in the hall as she slid forward down the stairs, head up, on her belly, like a swimmer dog-paddling in water. She reached out, grabbing for the falling baby. It was too far ahead, but she set her mind on catching it. To make her effort seem real, she slid, tumbled, and jumped like a player after a ball.

The ugly mud-baby twisted and bounced, screaming as it careened off the wall, pitched into the banister opposite, and, gathering momentum, plunged to the marble below. Its terrified cry was cut off by the dull thud of impact. Its head split watermelon-fashion, spewing blood and gray sticky matter across the shiny floor.

Laura slid to a stop near the bottom of the staircase and stood to get a better look at the baby. There was no sound in the house except her own labored breathing. Her eyes darted to Nana and Carrie. Both appeared frozen, as though they had been zapped into two granite statues. The color was draining rapidly from their faces—like the baby's blood, spreading in a pool at their feet.

The pursuing footsteps started again—faster, louder. Laura turned as her mother and the nurse came thundering down the stairs, bearing down on her like two race-horses vying for the lead. The nurse was on the outside, holding to the banister, her mother inside, nearest Laura, her face as red and contorted as the baby's had been moments earlier.

Laura flattened against the wall to keep from being trampled under their pounding feet. Out of the corner of her eye, she saw her mother's fist drawn back to shoulder level, saw it thrusting forward, seemingly in slow motion, propelled by her hate and the full weight of her dashing body. Laura ducked, avoiding being hit in the face, but not in time to miss a stunning blow to her left ear. Her head rang like a thousand pealing church bells. White spots swimming before her eyes, she slid down the wall and sat on the step. She shook her head, willing the spots away, not wanting to miss what was happening on the floor.

Slowly, her vision cleared, revealing the nurse squatting next to the baby, two fingers pressed against its neck. Her mother was crouched on the opposite side, her hands hovering above the baby's still body like fluttering bird's wings.

The nurse looked up at her daddy on the upstairs landing and shook her head. He bent over the banister, rocking back and forth on his heels, his mouth wide open, as if he had been punched in the stomach. Behind him, Harley was spewing out his supper on the hall carpet.

Below, her mother screamed and lifted the baby into her arms. Slipping sideways, she sat cross-legged on the bloody floor, clutching the baby to her breast. She rocked back and forth—howling—head thrown back. Presently, she stopped rocking and covered the baby's ugly ashen face with kisses.

"My baby. My baby," she sobbed. "My baby. My baby. My baby—" She said it over and over again. In a monotone at first; then gradually, her tone changed, the heaviness fading into a lighter quality. "My baby. My baby." Suddenly, she was laughing, lifting her tear-wet face to the high-domed ceiling. She looked like a child facing the warm sun—her eyes shining with a crazed, frightening joy. Her long blonde hair now matted with blood from the baby's head, was plastered flat against her cheek. She tossed her head to shake it free, at the same time filling the hall with happy, hysterical laughter. No one else laughed. And Laura sensed that her mother was gone for good, leaving a brittle, transparent husk, as empty as an abandoned cicada shell.

Before her echoing laughter died away, her mother shouted, "My baby isn't dead! She's alive! Do you hear me?" She glared from one face to the next, as though defying challenge. "She's alive. It's only a bump. A little bump."

With no more feeling for the baby than she had had for the calf-killing dog she had seen her daddy shoot, Laura masked her nose and mouth behind a banister post, hiding a smile, as her mother scooped a handful of the bloody gray matter off the floor and stuffed it back into the baby's split skull. It oozed back out between her fingers, like the red mud Laura had lathered it with that first day she had brought the ugly thing home. Her mother clamped her hand tight over the wound, trying to hold the ooze in.

"It's only a little bump, Precious. You'll be fine. Fine and dandy."

She removed her bloody hand from the baby's head as though she had forgotten why she was holding it. The wound gaped open, but she ignored the mess pouring out. She lifted the baby in both hands, extending the limp body toward Laura like a cherished gift.

"You can hold the baby, Laura." Laura gripped the banister tighter. Now her mother would let her hold her precious baby—after it was dead.

"She's not hurt," her mother lied. "Only a little bump on the head. Come here. Hold your little sister for me, so I can get up."

Obediently, Laura crawled down the last four stairs. She felt laughing happy. Her mother looked so silly sitting there covered with blood, trying to stuff the baby's brains back in its stupid head. It was reason for celebration, but she had to finish her charade. As she came close to her mother, she managed to squeeze out tears. The pain in her shoulder and in her head helped make her grief seem real. Her shoulder hurt terribly when she moved, but the pain was a small price for what she had gained. She had eliminated the stupid mud-baby—never dreaming it would give her so great a victory over her mother. The real triumph was that she had managed to do it publicly, yet remain innocent. Her daddy and Nana, Carrie and the nurse, had all seen her caring for the baby, loving it, then endangering herself trying to catch it after the fall. None of them could ever be convinced it was not an accident.

Her mother's voice was insistent. "Hurry, Laura. Take your baby sister."

Laura reached timidly toward the grizzly corpse, her eyes begging the stupefied nurse to do something.

The nurse sprang to life, yanking Laura backward by the seat of her pants. "Get her out of here," she yelled. "For God's sake, someone take Laura away from this."

Her daddy bolted for the stairs, and Laura staggered away from the frantic nurse. She watched her daddy hurrying down toward her. The way he moved—his lean body graceful, in-time—like a fine stallion, running—was a delight. Soon he would be all hers. She lifted her face to him, wishing he would take her up, spin her around as he had Molly on top of the mountain, and kiss her the way they had kissed. She closed her eyes, feeling her daddy's lips on hers, searching, penetrating, in a special new way.

New. But not new, because it was a memory. Real in its time and real now, but not complete, because the lady was gone, and Laura was the keeper of only part of her memories. The unknown part troubled her like a forgotten secret.

Tears were streaming down her daddy's face when he picked her up. He hugged her—hard—as if she had been lost and by a miracle returned to him. From the pressure of his arms, the pain in her shoulder reached out and made everything black.

Laura awoke in her bed. The morning sun streaming through the window behind her head was making her face hot. Sitting up, a pain caught her left shoulder and forced her back down. She started to mop her damp hair from her forehead and found that her right arm was immobilized, bound tightly to her body with a strip of torn bedsheet.

She tried to untie the bandage but could not manage the knot. Angry, she pushed herself to a sitting position on the side of the bed and planted her feet firmly on the floor. Her shoulder throbbed, but she resented being bound. She wanted her hand free.

As she stood, the throbbing pain in her shoulder mushroomed into her head. Laura swayed backward against the bed. She was dizzy, with a sick heavy feeling she had never experienced before. There was a sour taste in her mouth. The taste was like her mother's medicine smelled.

Laura was so baffled by her bandage, the thick medicine feeling, and finding it morning instead of early evening as last she remembered, that she was tempted to cry out for her Nana. The unusual silence in the house kept her still. There was not a sound anywhere: no washing machine, no dryer, no water running.

She listened closely, then staggered through Nana's room and listened again. Halfway down the library hall, just before she reached the dining room door, Laura heard a faint moaning sound, like the wind in the top of the pecan tree. She moved quickly through the dining room and opened the door into the marble hall. The floor was clean, with no trace of the grim mess that had been there. The moaning grew louder. It was coming from the upper reaches of the house. The pitch rose and fell in a rhythmical rocking pattern, ending in a piercing scream. Her mother's scream.

The sound made Laura shiver. She hugged her hurt arm to her body for warmth as she crossed the marble hall toward the living room. She stopped, momentarily, at the foot of the stairs, remembering the baby's splattered body. She smiled. The stupid mud-baby had made a worse mess than her torn clown.

Her clown. Something about the unusual quiet made her want her clown. Cold chills ran up her back when she peeked into the living room. Carrie was standing near the window, fingering a man's white handkerchief, but instead of her usual white uniform, she was wearing a black dress. Nana, seated on the couch, was also wearing black. Reverend Edwards and his mousy-looking wife were there, and a man, whom Laura had often seen in church but did not know by name, was sitting on the couch beside Nana. They were all shaking their heads and picking lint off their black clothes, but no one seemed to be saying anything.

Laura had a sudden weak spell and caught hold of a high pedestal table near the door. A white guest book, with many names in it, clattered to the floor. Stooping to pick it up, her head felt heavier than the rest of her body, and she fell across the book, painfully hitting her bandaged shoulder against the funny table. She had never seen the book or the table before.

Nana rushed to help her, but Carrie muscled in front of her.

"You're not able to lift her, Mrs. D. I'll do it."

"Gently, Carrie," Nana said. "The poor baby is in pain. Look how white her face is."

"I'll take her back to her room."

Laura whimpered in protest and held her free hand toward Nana.

Nana relented.

"Let her stay. Bring her to the couch."

The man with no name moved to the end, making room for Laura in the middle. Carrie put her down with her head in Nana's lap.

"I'll go and get the nurse," she said and left the room.

Laura grabbed Nana's hand and placed it over the knotted end of her bandage, indicating that she wanted her to take it off.

"No, Baby Girl. You dislocated your shoulder. We can't take it off until the nurse says we can."

Laura whined. The bandage was hurting her.

"I know it's uncomfortable. The nurse will look at it, directly. You be very still and it won't hurt as much."

Laura lifted Nana's hand to her head.

"Does your head hurt?"

Laura nodded.

"Your daddy gave you some of your mother's sleeping pills. The nurse was afraid he had given you too many—you slept so long. You were a sick little girl for a while."

Nana patted Laura's cheek and directed her comments to Reverend Edwards.

"Laura blacked out, and when she came to, she cried most of that first night. Wouldn't let any of us near her except her daddy. She screamed when anyone else came into the room. He rocked her for hours. She wouldn't let him leave her even long enough to check on Kate, not that poor Kate would have known he was there."

What Nana was saying sounded like a new storybook to Laura. One that had never been read to her before.

"The doctor was here within minutes after it happened. He gave Kate a sedative that knocked her out completely. T.J. wanted him to do the same with Laura, but he wouldn't. Said it was better for children to fight things out on their own."

Laura had considered the doctor her enemy since he had taken her mother's part against the nurse. It was fine with her that he hadn't wanted to treat her.

"But along toward morning," Nana was saying, "T.J. came out of Laura's room and asked me to get Kate's pills. Poor boy, I knew he'd been crying all night, his eyes were so red and swollen. He had taken all he could, and Laura was still thrashing about on the bed—delirious—and crying bitterly, as though blaming herself for what happened."

Laura pushed her mind backward, trying to remember waking and crying, or even her daddy rocking her. Her memory was a blank space. Black and empty . . . Except for the pills. She remembered the pills. Small red and white capsules, and her daddy's big hand forcing them into her mouth, his long fingers poking them far back in her throat, one after another, making her swallow them with water, spilling it all over her and the bed. Him taking several at once, gulping the water. Shaking the bottle, then crushing the thin plastic in his hand as if he was angry because it was empty.

Laura pressed her face into Nana's black skirt. Her whole body was trembling from the chill that came with remembering her daddy's tortured face as he threw the broken plastic against the wall and slipped to his knees beside her bed. It was as if he had been saying his prayers, only he had seemed to be praying to her.

"What have I done?" she remembered him moaning as he pulled her to the edge of the bed and buried his face in her stomach. He had said it over and over—"What have I done? What have I done?"—until the monotony of it, or the pills, had put her to sleep.

If only she had not hurt her shoulder she would not have lost control. It had been the pain that made her delirious. Now, she had no way of knowing what she had done or if she had talked.

Laura rolled her head back to look up in Nana's face. Nana's eyes seemed locked on the preacher, as though she were avoiding looking at her. Laura wondered if it was true, or was she being oversensitive. Maybe Nana was afraid she would break down if she looked at her. Laura hoped it was only that. Tears were sliding out from under Nana's glasses and splashing on the front of her two-piece black suit. One landed on Laura's forehead. A bullet-sized pool—hot and wet on her skin—punishing her for never telling her Nana that she loved her.

Now it was too late to say it to her. Laura felt Nana's tear roll down her forehead and across the bridge of her nose to mix with her own tears. After what she had done to Harley and her mother and that baby, knowing she could talk would kill her Nana. The opportunity was lost, and Laura longed to have another. Those unspoken words, "I love you, Nana," settled like lead weights in the pit of her stomach and hurt more than her throbbing shoulder.

"Sometimes it's hard to understand what the Lord has in mind when things like this happen," the preacher's wife said. "But keep in mind that He has a plan."

Laura looked up from wiping tears on her pajama top. Any other time, she would have laughed. *She* had made the plan! She was going to have her daddy all to herself the way it should have been all along. So far as she knew, she and her clown were the only ones in on the "plan." The Lord couldn't take credit for any part of it!

Nana didn't answer the stupid woman. She sat quietly, brushing Laura's damp hair back from her face, and let her silly comment hang in the air like it deserved.

"It was a terrible accident. Terrible!" Nana said finally, dabbing at her eyes with her lace handkerchief.

As though he had said "Let us pray!" Reverend Edwards's voice boomed across the living room.

"We can be thankful that Laura wasn't more seriously injured."

"It's a miracle she wasn't," Nana said. "She put herself in such danger, trying to catch the— Trying to prevent what happened."

Nana's words sounded hollow to Laura, making her feel cut adrift—as she had when she thought her daddy and Nana were going to believe Harley about her tearing her clown. She thought she had lost, then, about her clown, but she had won. Maybe her doubts were all unfounded. If only she could remember what had happened that night before her daddy gave her the pills.

The homely nurse, dressed in black like the others, followed Carrie into the living room. She insisted that Laura be put back to bed. Laura kicked in protest, almost hitting the man whose name she did not know, but Carrie lifted her off the couch and started out of the room. Laura held her good arm toward Nana, whimpering loudly, but Nana, who was moving as though in a trance, took no notice.

"How is Kate?" Nana asked the nurse.

"She is quiet now, but I don't guarantee how she'll behave during the service. Do you think it wise to let her go?"

"How could we deny her that? She lost her child. No matter what she does, people will understand."

"Who is going to stay with Harley and Laura?"

"I sent for our neighbor, John Crow, Reming's grandfather. He is a very wise man. Exceptional with children. Harley is very fond of him."

Laura grew rigid in Carrie's arms. Even if the others did not know, the old healer would for sure. What was it he had said? He would send her back and punish her. Laura snuggled closer to Carrie's oversized bosom, seeking protection.

Carrie bent and kissed her in a gesture so uncharacteristic that it frightened Laura almost as much as the prospect of having the old medicine man in the house.

Laura searched Carrie's fat, mole-speckled face for some clue about what was known or had been guessed about her, but her face looked carved out of yellow lard. Reaching up, touching the cheek in a plea for some explanation, Carrie flinched as though she had pinched her. Tears welled in Carrie's eyes, but she stared straight ahead like all the tin soldiers in Reming's collection.

Carrie was concealing something. Laura could feel the tension in her flabby body. Was it only a reflection of the tension in the house, or had she given herself away during those hours she could not remember?

Where was her daddy? She needed him now more than ever. Why wasn't he with her? Maybe he did not know she was awake.

Laura opened her mouth and screamed with all the force her hurt shoulder would allow. She made the trapped animal sound she had always used when Harley had her cornered and was about to tear into her.

Carrie nearly jumped out of her skin and almost dropped her.

"Hush that! You're all right!"

The moaning started again upstairs, and something hit her mother's closed door from the inside, followed by the sound of a scuffle.

"See there. You've upset your mother again, poor thing. Your daddy is having enough trouble with her."

So that's where he was! Laura tried to struggle free, but Carrie clamped her tight against her, causing a blinding white pain in her hurt shoulder. Laura settled down, knowing that Carrie would hurt her again if she made more noise.

The nurse was patting Nana's shoulder. "It's going to be traumatic, Mrs. Daniels, no matter who is here with the children."

"Harley may choose to go to the service," Nana said. "It's up to him."

Either way, Laura knew she would be in danger. If Harley stayed he'd be after her. If he went to the funeral she would be alone with the medicine man.

Carrie deposited Laura in her bed and left the room. Laura wanted to call out to her as the nurse, smiling her pink gummed smile, bent over her; but Carrie's heavy tread was already far down the narrow hall, past Nana's apartment, approaching the library and the dining room.

"Let's have a look at your shoulder," the nurse said.

Looking up at that ugly face, Laura felt like a helpless sparrow in the clutches of a cat. Her cat so far, to be sure, but too new to be completely trusted.

The nurse untied the knotted sheet and helped Laura sit up. She unwound the strip of cloth from her body and forced her back to the pillow with a mannish hand pressed flat against her chest, exactly as Laura had used her own hand to push the stupid mud-baby down the stairs. Even with the nurse's other hand behind her head, easing her backward, Laura had the sensation of falling. She grabbed at the nurse, then screamed as a searing pain stabbed at her right shoulder.

"Easy now. Relax," the nurse crooned. "I'm not going to let you fall."

But Laura was afraid, then angry with the nurse for letting her feel that she was falling. She fought down the temptation to bring her foot up and kick the homely woman in the back of the head. She couldn't do that. Now, with the medicine man coming, she needed all her allies. But just then, she wanted her Nana. Why was she leaving her in the care of a person who was almost a stranger when she needed her Nana so much? Laura took a full breath and howled like a stricken dog.

The nurse clamped a firm hand over her mouth. "Don't! Please! There's already too much confusion in this house." Her voice softened as she took her hand away. "Your Nana loves others in this house, but I love only you . . . I know your shoulder hurts. I'll do my best to fix it without hurting you, but you have to help by being still and quiet."

Laura's eyes fastened on her pink-gummed smile. She tried to recapture the mastery she had felt when the nurse first stepped off the plane, but there was a disturbing element growing between them, one Laura could not identify.

"I'm going to help you sit up," the nurse said, shaking a red and white capsule out of the brown plastic medicine bottle. "We'll do it nice and easy. This pill will make your pain go away."

Laura recognized the medicine. The same medicine her daddy had given her to make her sleep. Sleep was the last thing she wanted, but she let the nurse help her sit up, then reached for the capsule with her good hand. When the nurse wasn't looking she shoved it under the elastic waistband of her pajamas and clamped her mouth shut. Barely opening her mouth, she sipped the water the nurse held for her, then made a big production out of swallowing.

The nurse eased her back down and laid a cool hand on her badly bruised shoulder. "Risking yourself the way you did, you're lucky it isn't broken."

Laura forced a thin smile, wondering how much the nurse had guessed and how much worse a break could hurt? She almost wished she had taken the sleeping pill, but there was too much going on in the house that she needed to find out about.

The nurse rewrapped her shoulder and chest, leaving her hand free. When it was done, Laura slipped that hand inside the nurse's and gave her a loving smile, just to watch her sternness melt. Then, to get rid of her, Laura pretended to drowse.

But the nurse didn't leave. Laura had all she could do to feign sleep through the wet kiss the nurse planted on her mouth.

"My poor mistreated angel," she whispered.

At last the doorbell rang, and the nurse eased her hand out of Laura's and quickly left as if going to answer it.

Laura popped her eyes open and followed the nurse's crepe-padded footsteps back to the marble hall where there was a confusion of sound: Carrie's greeting to someone, a disapproving tone in the preacher's voice, the nurse excusing herself to go upstairs. Laura heard, above it all, her Nana's voice, worried and tired, and the deep resonant tones of a man, a man Laura had always known, now and in that earlier time. It was no accident Nana had invited the old medicine man here. Laura imagined him receiving from Reming the news about the baby's death and about Kate. She knew he had caused himself to be invited. He'd come to make good his threats. He would know what she had done. He'd try to expose her. "I can send you back," he had said. Now, Laura was sure that could only mean to the mountain where the path people were waiting. She heard Nana take him into the library and close the door.

Clutching her aching arm to her body, Laura rolled off the bed and stood up. The pain made her feel dizzy. For a moment she felt she might have to lie down again.

Through the open door to Nana's room, she glimpsed her clown's torn head and some of its stuffing protruding from the top of the sewing basket in the corner near the sewing machine.

Laura leaned against the bed, looking at the familiar embroidered red smile, while she listened to the drone of voices—Nana's and the medicine man's—talking in the library. It had been hard to tear her clown. As hard a thing as she had ever done. At least it had not been a waste. After what it had cost him, Harley would surely remember her clown until the day he died! But that was the trick to it. The ugly baby was dead and gone, about to be buried. Her clown was still alive. Not in the sewing basket where its ripped face peeked over the rim of pink and green needlepoint, but inside her head.

Feeling its presence was a comfort to her, and a puzzle. She had always thought the doll was talking to her, whispering to her about her mother and Harley and that ugly baby. Finding out different frightened her a little. The part she had attributed to her clown felt stronger than ever, strong enough to impel her aching body across Nana's room and down the narrow side hall to crouch outside the library door. She had to hear what Nana and the old man were saying. She had to protect herself. And her clown wanted to know!

Luckily, the door was partially open. Across the room, the big double doors into the main hall were tightly closed.

Laura watched in horror as the burly, craggy-faced Indian enfolded her Nana in his arms. She wanted to stomp in protest as his big brown hands rubbed comforting circles on Nana's slender back. But the clown part of her made her keep still and step into the shadows.

"I've waited forty years for you to need me," he said. "I'm sorry it had to be under such sad circumstances."

Nana tried to pull away; but he held her, and she surrendered to his touch. He kissed the top of her head and pressed his brown cheek against her cloud-white hair.

Laura was shocked. She had never seen two old people embrace. And never in her wildest fantasies had she imagined her Nana in a man's arms.

"The hardest thing I've ever had to do was forgive myself for letting your father keep us apart," he said.

Nana pulled away, raising her wrinkled hand as though to stop him. "John, I—"

"I should have married you in spite of his protest. Instead, we've both had unhappy marriages. T.J. and Molly should have been brother and sister, not lovers. Harley, Laura, and Reming should have been happy cousins."

Nana tried to disengage herself, but he drew closer to her, lifted her chin, and looked into her face.

"When this crisis has passed, we could salvage what is left of our lives."

Nana blushed, but Laura could see that she was pleased. She stumbled awkwardly backward, starting one way and then the other, like a schoolgirl unable to decide what to do with herself. "You wouldn't want an old shriveled prune like me."

He closed his two big fists over Nana's small hand. "More now than I wanted you then. Forty years of wanting more. You're the same person you were."

"My mirror doesn't say so."

"Mirrors lie. Memory doesn't. I can see you on the mountaintop, with your long golden hair fanned out behind you blinding me with the sun glinting on it. I can still feel the weight of you in my arms, as we spun around and around for the sheer joy of motion and closeness."

Laura rested her head against the wall. It felt heavy with jumbled pictures, faces, sensations. She closed her eyes, trying to shut out the memories, but the familiar resonant voice whispered on.

"We have so much more to give now than then. We are stronger, wiser—"

Nana interrupted. "And it is your wisdom I have need of now. Your powers were formidable when we were young. I've heard they have increased over the years."

"As all things do with work and practice. I've done little else but meditate and heal these past years."

"John—" Nana faltered and stopped, her chin quivering.

He thrust a protective arm about her shoulders.

"John, something evil has taken over my house." She pressed close to him. "I'm afraid."

She was crying, and he did not try to make her stop. He let her cry so long Laura wanted to rush in to her Nana, but the clown part of her would not let her move from the peeking spot outside the door.

Finally, the old Indian said, "When you are ready, tell me all you know."

Nana spoke in a rush.

"First Kate, and now Harley. Both have turned against my sweet Laura."

She broke off, sobbing, and he led her to the small leather sofa in front of the double windows that faced the front porch and seated her beside himself. He kept his arm around her and stilled her small, white, trembling hands with his big brown paw.

Laura's resentment, about a man being so close to her Nana, was matched by an excitement she did not understand. Excitement and dread.

Nana spoke with her head bowed. "When it was Kate alone, we thought it was out of frustration, because Laura has never talked. Kate hounded the child day and night, trying to *make* her talk."

Those miserable days were over for good. Her mother was powerless now.

"Then, a few days before the baby was born, she started telling us things that Laura was supposed to have said to her. Vulgar, implausible things. When she tried to force Laura to say those things to us, all the poor child could do was stammer unintelligible sounds, trying to repeat the words after her mother. Kate was so angry she dug her thumbnail into Laura's finger until it bled, and Carrie and I had to drag her away."

The medicine man was probably thinking "Good for her mother!" He had guessed she could talk long before that had happened. But he hadn't had proof. He hadn't risked appearing a fool.

"Later, after the baby was born, she tried to kick Laura down the stairs. She claimed Laura had bitten her and twisted the baby's foot because she had refused Laura's request to nurse. Have you ever heard anything so outrageous? Kate threatened to kill Laura if she came near the baby again. That's when I moved Laura into my treasure room, where I could protect her, and T.J. hired the nurse to take care of Kate."

Laura's mind wandered in a new confusion of images. The old healer's devil eyes the day he had threatened her; her mother's face, red and twisted with rage; the faces she had seen on the mountain path. Faces she could see, that Reming could not. The little girl—Molly—hiding the drummer's stick. Her daddy twirling the beautiful dark lady. The mud-baby shattered. Her clown, torn and scattered. Combined with the pain in her shoulder, her thoughts made her feel weak and shaky. She wanted to return to her bed, but the clown part would not let her move. It was interested in Nana's account and the medicine man's reaction. He possessed a strength, a magnetism, beyond her understanding. Molly had been his daughter. Laura possessed part of Molly's memories. That should make him her friend. But her clown had branded him an enemy even before he had threatened her. Why? Laura was puzzled by her ambiguous feelings for him. She did not like him near her Nana, yet she was aware of deep emotional stirrings in herself: a longing, and a loneliness for him, and a deep fear of what she might learn. She remembered how the cement had burned her legs that day on the porch when he had said to her, "Your powers are no match for mine. I can send you back. Send you back and punish you."

"Later, Harley claimed that Laura spoke to him, too," Nana was saying. "He said she called him a 'Sissy Boy,' and taunted him about Kate being locked in her room.

T.J. whipped him cruelly. He went off to Kate's room. He was with her when the accident happened."

Laura smiled remembering Harley vomiting in the upstairs hall, while her mother sat on the marble below him and tried to stuff the baby's brains back into its smashed head. Vomiting was such a sissy thing to do. It proved she had been right about him.

Nana took a deep breath and hurried on. "Kate and T.J. were arguing through the door. The noise woke the baby. It was screaming, and Laura took it out of the crib and was walking it in the hall, trying to quiet it. It was the first time she had ever held it, the very first time." She broke off, sniffling into her handkerchief. Then, continuing in a rush, as though she wanted to be done with the story, she said, "T.J. was angry, banging on Kate's door. They were screaming back and forth. He mentioned that Laura was holding the baby, and Kate screamed that Laura hated the baby and to get it away from her. About that time, T.J. kicked the door open, and Kate flew at him. Laura started running toward her daddy. Probably to give the baby to her mother. He and Kate were fighting when Laura passed the top of the stairs. She tripped and fell . . . Oh, John—"

It was a plea for help, and he wrapped both arms around her Nana and held her close. "I'm here. Let it all out."

"I'll never forget that helpless little baby, bouncing down the stairs. And Laura, terrified, tumbling after, trying so hard to catch her, while Carrie and I just stood there rooted to the floor. Neither one of us made a move to help. It was horrible. Horrible! And Harley believes Laura did it on purpose, that she intended to kill the baby."

The medicine man did not speak, but Laura knew what he believed.

"Harley is worse than Kate ever was. You should see the hate in those young eyes. Last night I went up to tuck him in bed. He was crying, and he said, 'I'm going to pay Laura back for what she has done to Mother!' "

Laura rubbed her sore arm, which only increased the pain. She rubbed harder, clamping her teeth together, thinking about Harley. She had gotten rid of the baby, only to be haunted by Harley, always Harley. The clown part of her screamed that he had caused her more trouble than that stupid mud-baby ever had. But he was bigger than she, and he could talk, and Reming loved him. Not even her ruthless clown was willing to hurt Reming to be rid of Harley.

"I tried to explain to Harley that his mother is sick," Nana said. "That Laura had nothing to do with it. And he said, 'She had everything to do with it. She killed the baby to make mother sick, just as she tore her clown to get me in trouble.' He believes it. He believes my sweet Laura deliberately killed that innocent little baby." Nana pressed a white handkerchief to her mouth with a shaking hand.

Laura wanted to run and hug her. To talk to her. To say, "Nana, I love you. I love you. Please don't cry." But she heard her clown whispering, *No. No. No,* over and over. Seeing Nana cry hurt far worse than the pain in her arm.

"That poor, innocent little baby," Nana said, her chin quivering behind the white lace. "I'll never be able to walk through that hall without seeing it lying there smashed and bleeding at the foot of the stairs. If only I'd gone up when I first saw Laura holding it. But I was so glad to see her loving it. My Laura did love that baby. She was kissing it, hugging it close to her, like she used to hug her clown. Her clown. Oh, God. Harley insists she tore her clown—"

Laura could feel the ugly mud-baby struggling in her arms, and how she had had to squeeze the breath out of it to make it appear placid.

The medicine man placed his hands on either side of Nana's head and pressed gently. "Take a deep breath and relax. You are becoming more and more relaxed. Breathe deeply. With each deep breath this death memory will fade. You will accept what happened. It is over. All guilt erased, you will stop fighting and allow yourself to grieve. After the funeral, you will remember the baby pleasantly. You will be at peace about the baby, knowing that she has returned to a good place."

Nana was completely composed when he removed his hands and kissed her tenderly on the forehead. She smiled at him.

"Your magic incantations always worked, even when we were children."

"No magic in that. Only an old love and a very simple skill."

Laura heard tires on the drive and, through the window behind Nana, saw a big black car pull up in front of the house. Two men got out and came up the walk.

"They are here," Nana said. She started to get up, but the old man stopped her.

"Before you go, I have one question. Think hard before you answer. It is very important . . . When did the loving mother-daughter relationship between Kate and Laura end?"

Nana answered without hesitation. "They never had a proper relationship. From the time she was a tiny baby, Laura cried when her mother came near. She even refused to nurse, and had to be put on a bottle. After that, Kate turned her over to Carrie and me. She was never a real mother to Laura. They've been more like two adversaries in the same house, especially where T.J. was concerned."

The old man took Nana's hand and held it thoughtfully. "All these years, you've given me such lovely dreams."

"It's nice to know your thoughts of me were as pleasant as mine of you."

She eased her hand out of his and stood. "They are waiting, John. I must go."

"Kate needs Harley near her during the funeral. Take him with you. Reming will go to be near him."

"They are so good together. Closer than most brothers."

Standing, the old man towered above Nana. He held her shoulders between his huge hands and made her face him. "Our boys *are* brothers. Half, anyway."

"I was only recently able to believe it," Nana said. Fresh tears rolled out from under her glasses.

"Why are you crying?"

"What kind of man does that make my son?"

"It makes him a man with a deep sorrow. We've talked about it many times."

"It hurts that he did not confide in me. There have been so many things I might have helped, had I known, especially his relationship with Harley. And I feel as if he has cheated me out of my rightful role as grandmother to Reming. Not to mention all that Reming has been cheated out of."

"Reming feels very close to you and to T.J."

Across the room, Carrie opened the double doors and spoke to Nana.

"They are here, Mrs. D. When you are ready, we'll fetch Kate."

"Tell the nurse to bring her down."

Carrie nodded and closed the door, leaving them alone.

Nana's eyes pled for reassurance. "Can you help us, John?"

"I will use all my powers to do so. But in the cure there will be more pain. It is unavoidable."

Laura's breath caught in her throat. Her hands groped around her for her clown before she remembered that she had sacrificed its body to destroy Harley. She shivered in the drafty hall as she listened to Nana's brave defense of her.

"I can take anything," Nana answered him, "but Laura must be spared. My poor baby girl has been through so much. We must find a way to reconcile Harley and Laura. Kate is out of the picture. Her mind is completely gone. It may take years to bring her back, if it can be done at all. But Harley must be led out of his mistaken belief that Laura is at fault."

"We'll talk more later. Put all those thoughts out of your mind. Think about our youth and the time we spent together on the mountain."

"I've never forgotten."

"Keep it firmly in your mind." He raised her small hand to his lips and kissed it. "Now go. They are waiting for you."

Nana stiffened her back and marched bravely out of the room without looking back. Watching from the shadowed hall, Laura wondered what the old man would do next. He stood, for what seemed a long time, staring at his hands. Laura sensed the conflict in him. He could not expose her without hurting Nana. And evidently he loved her Nana from a long time ago.

He bowed his head and quietly chanted some kind of prayer, then walked to the window and watched the cars driving through the gate and the gathering crowd on the lawn and front porch.

Laura's shivering had become tremors. She wrapped her arms about herself in an effort to stop shaking. The medicine man meant to make good his threats against her. She knew it. But she didn't want to think about it. Like him, she turned her attention to the crowd.

Laura had never been to a real funeral before, except the one she and Nana had had for her cat when one of the hands accidentally ran over it with a cattle truck. Then they had taken the cat to the family cemetery, located behind the grape arbor and beyond the pond. There Nana had dug a hole in the far corner and away from the stone markers. They buried the cat and said a prayer for her. Afterward, Nana had read names off the headstones and showed her where her great-grandfather and great-grandmother were buried side by side, with her great aunts and uncles scattered around them. Laura remembered seeing her grandfather's stone with the name Frederick Daniels on it. Nana had explained that he had been her husband, but he had died a long time before Laura was born, back when her daddy was a little boy. Laura had gotten the impression that Nana hadn't been pleased with her marriage by the dry way she said her marriage had pleased her father.

It was the empty grave space next to him that had given Laura a real fright. Nana said it was where she was to be buried. It had started Laura thinking about what she would do if Nana died before she did. The thought was unbearable. She did her best to keep from thinking about it. But the day's events made it hard to keep it out of her mind.

Such a crowd was gathering for the funeral. All those people making the house so busy with death that death had become a tangible thing, like Christmas or the Fourth of July. Both those days had prescribed things to do: laughter and presents on Christmas, salutes and fireworks on the Fourth of July. From what she had seen of a funeral day, it seemed to have its own prescription: tears, and reminiscing about the past, and what was or what might have been. On any other day, Laura was quite sure Nana would call the conversation she had just had with the Indian "feeling sorry for herself." Today, it seemed to be the order of things. Laura felt herself caught up in it. Caught up in the brooding mood of the old man at the window.

While she watched him the diffused light suddenly

solidified into a bright shaft, reflecting shimmering dirt particles all around him.

Laura staggered; she rubbed her eyes, unwilling to believe what she saw. The medicine man—a vision returned—appearing to her exactly as he had out of the heat waves that hot September day he had first threatened her. It had to be a sign, confirmation of her clown's warning. Her fear that day had been as nothing compared to her fear now. This time he had come to make good his threat. He was in pursuit of her.

Suddenly, the medicine man left the window and paced the length of the room. He stopped in front of the desk and punched the gold button which opened a black leather doctor's bag. A bag Laura had never seen before.

Reverently, he stood looking down into its depths, chanting words she strained to hear but couldn't make out. His incantation finished, he lifted from the bag a feather fan and a long, carved stick with a turtle-shell rattle lashed around the middle.

Laura felt her heart in her throat as he crossed the fan and rattle stick on his chest and slowly, ominously, paced back to that shaft of bright sunlight where he lowered himself cross-legged to the floor. There, surrounded again by shimmering dust particles, he sat staring up, unblinking.

New feelings came boiling up out of whatever inside Laura had been her clown. Memories. Sensations of rising, circling, hovering high above that cliff at the mountain. Clear air, clearer thoughts came to her there in The Thinking Place. Below in the sandrock basin lay that beautiful but lifeless form—now discarded. Alone. Dark, blowing hair framed tormented features. Eyes. Molly's eyes. Open. Staring at nothing. All alone. A child cried in the distance. Kept crying. A light had gone on in the healer's house. Then another. But the child—it was Reming—wasn't quiet for a long time.

Hovering there. A soul in flight. Enduring that agony of sound—Reming's crying. Staring down at that abandoned body. That waste of beauty. The resolution had been made. Her clown remembered.

Laura remembered all but that one memory. The one that would make sense of everything. It was still occluded from her. Her clown knew, but wouldn't tell. It told her only that the resolutions had not yet been fulfilled. She struggled to know, but reached only perceptions of betrayal, hate, and an intense feeling of present danger, which she attributed to her fear of the old man.

Softly, he had begun to chant words she could not make out, but the Indian rhythm was one she knew. The same rhythm she had used in the schoolroom to defeat Miss Glade. Laura clinched her fists. It was her own weapon. Now a weapon turned on her. She felt the impact of it resonating louder than her own heart beat in her chest. She fought the terrible gall-tasting fear that nearly choked her. Gasping, clinging to the woodwork for support; weakened, breathing fast, barely able to get enough air, Laura knew the medicine man had begun his attack on her.

There was no time. She had no strength to defend herself. Her skills were in manipulating people. This old man was controlling the inner workings of her own body. Another moment of the terrible pressure inside her chest would bring her to her knees. Mustering all her remaining strength, Laura broke her hold on the doorframe. She pitched backward, turned, and ran stiff-jointed through the dining room into the kitchen, where she collided with a group of ladies from the church.

Backing away from half a dozen outstretched hands, Laura made her way through an orgy of food. More food than she'd ever seen in one place. The table and cabinets were full of casserole dishes, pies, cakes, salad bowls, with more food arriving. Ladies were lined up outside the back door, waiting to hand in their offering. Already weakened, and sickened further by the mixed aromas, Laura tried to figure the connection between death and food. She was sure Nana was in no mood to eat. It made no sense.

Laura hit the swinging kitchen door with a clatter and slammed it back at those coaxing hands and faces. Out in the marble hall guests were crowded everywhere. They were huddled in small groups, talking, and strung out all around the walls. The accumulated noise was deafening. Laura threaded her way through the maze of people. She was heading for the stairs when a hand, flat against the top of her head, pressed her to a stop. She looked up. The two schoolteachers who had come to see the baby and had ignored her somersault trick loomed ahead of her.

The one with the droopy eyes and mannish haircut said, "What are you doing traipsing around in your pajamas in front of company. Go back to your room! Aren't you going to your baby sister's funeral?"

Laura ignored the question, reached up with her good arm, and knocked the woman's hand off her head. Fury flickered across the old woman's face.

"You are mean enough to have killed that baby on purpose! Kate says you are unmanageable, but I bet I could manage you!"

She grabbed Laura roughly by her hurt shoulder. Laura flinched at the new pain but didn't whimper. Instead, she bit the woman's hand to make her let go.

The ugly schoolteacher shrieked and jerked her hand away. Her friend bent to examine the wound. Laura escaped through the bewildered crowd and ran up the stairs. Those two old hags were her mother's friends. She didn't have to be nice to her mother's friends ever again. They wouldn't be coming back after today.

As she reached the upstairs hall, her mother's door opened, and her daddy and the nurse emerged, leading her mother between them. Her mother's eyes were blank, staring unseeingly ahead. Laura stepped close to the banister to let them pass, but her mother stopped. Recognition dawned slowly on her vacuous face, followed by a light of hope.

"Why didn't you come when I called you, Laura?" her mother asked. "What did you do with the baby? I know you have her. Why are you hiding her from me?"

Laura gripped the handrail tightly, afraid her mother might break away from her daddy and the nurse, fly at her and push her over. She remembered the steps rising toward her face as she fell after throwing the baby. She wished fervently that she was on the other side of the hall, next to the wall.

Her daddy, dressed in his best dark suit, his face tired and haggard, tugged gently on her mother's arm. "They are waiting for us, Kate. Laura doesn't have the baby."

Her mother angrily shook her arm free. "I know she does! She's hiding my baby from me."

Downstairs, the buzz of conversation stopped, and Laura could feel the guests staring at her back and beyond to her mother's ravaged face.

Clinging there, watching as her daddy's two hands, seemingly in slow motion, chased her mother's flying, hitting, gouging arm, Laura gripped the banister so tightly her own hands ached. She gritted her teeth to stand the pain her effort caused in her already throbbing shoulder.

Her mother lunged toward her. "You give me my baby!" Then to the crowd, "She has my baby! I know she does!" Kate clawed at the nurse's hands, still valiantly clenched to her other arm.

Laura wondered how much of this was that old witch doctor's doing? Nana would put him out of her house, if only she knew that he sided with Harley and Kate and meant to harm her Baby Girl. There had to be a way to make Nana understand. But without speech, how?

At last the nurse threw her mother against the opposite wall and, with a bear hug, pinned both arms down at her sides.

"Mr. Daniels, if you can't keep hold of her arm," the nurse said angrily, "then for Laura's safety, let's take Kate back to her room." Still struggling with her, the nurse added, "She has no business out!"

Her mother was making deep growling sounds in her throat. Laura crouched lower on the stairs, feeling her knees creak, as she bent them, and a sharp pain run up her back. It was exactly the kind of pain she'd heard Nana describe to Carrie as "the pains of old age." That witch doctor's chanted medicine was already at work on her body.

Suddenly, her mother and the nurse were a flurry of motion again. Her mother spit in the nurse's eyes. While she was blinded, Kate surged free, coming halfway across the stairs before the nurse grabbed her.

Laura wove her arm through the upright rail posts. Kate would have to break either the wood or her arm before she could throw her over to shatter like that ugly mud-baby had on the slab floor.

Glancing down, Laura saw that the crowd had cleared a ring, as though anxious for such a spectacle. One man stepped out like the ringmaster, as if he alone planned to break her fall if she were pushed. Laura fought her terror and the increasing pain in her shoulder to focus on his face. It was her old Indian from out in the garage. Her apparition. This was the first time she had ever seen him in the house. If he really wanted to save her, why didn't he go and stop his son? Tell him to get up off the library floor, quit that chanting!

Her old horseman, her clown's—Molly's—grandfather, melted into the crowd as, simultaneously, the people heaved a great relieved sigh. Laura swiveled around to see that her daddy had roused out of his stupor and recaptured her mother's arm. The nurse was still glaring at him.

"I have her now, Miss Pledge," he said apologetically. Then to her mother he spoke more softly. "Please, Kate. The whole town is here. Please conduct yourself as the refined lady you have always been."

Her mother locked blazing eyes on his face and tossed her head defiantly.

"Laura is a murderess!" she shouted.

Below, from the crowd, Laura heard a great gasp.

"Laura killed my baby!"

Her mother shrieked as her daddy jerked her back away from Laura. She kept plunging, her hands working grotesquely in convulsive choking motions.

Laura drew her arm out of the rails. She felt so small, so alone. This time even her daddy had been ineffectual against her mother. If her nurse hadn't been there, she would be lying dead on the marble floor like the mudbaby. Trembling, Laura tried to stand. Her legs refused to support her. Clawing, desperate to escape before her mother broke free again, she dragged herself along, using the banister. She pulled herself to the top of the stairs, slithered around the corner, and pulled herself another few feet.

She willed the strength to stand. Shakily, moving stiffly with all her muscles and joints impaired by that Indian's death chantings, Laura fled down the hall, only to collide with Harley coming out of his room. Before she could react, she was on the floor, with Harley's hands around her neck, choking the breath out of her. She heard her daddy yell at Harley to leave her alone, but he didn't come to help her. He and the nurse had all they could do to keep her mother off her also. Harley paid no attention to her daddy's command. Laura knew he meant to kill her. She rolled sideways, glimpsing a sea of horrified faces below.

They seemed frozen there, all of them. Why didn't someone help her? Her fear became terror. Her clown. Where was her clown?

At last, Laura heard her Nana scream for Harley to stop. She saw the medicine man, towering above the other guests, rushing for the stairs. Gasping, she tried to move her knee between her body and Harley's to push him off, but her weakened muscles were useless against his superior strength. He sat heavily on her stomach. His hands gripped tighter, thumbs crushing her voice box, making her dizzy and weak, sick with a rising nausea that was cut off the same as was her breath. She pulled desperately at his wrists, her hurt shoulder screaming resistance, as she strained to force his crushing hands apart, but they only clamped tighter. The medicine man was killing her. Harley was but his instrument. Where was her clown now? Her eyes felt as though they were bulging from their sockets. She was about to close them to keep them from popping out, when she recognized Reming coming up fast behind Harley.

Shouting for his grandfather, Reming locked his arms around Harley's neck and jerked him backward away from her. Harley clung tenaciously to her throat, dragging her with him, pulling her up to a sitting position. Then, surprisingly, the medicine man was kneeling beside her, prying Harley's fingers, one by one, off her neck.

Once freed, Laura's first breath seared her lungs. With what little strength returned she scrambled, coughing and retching, out from under Harley, but not fast enough to avoid a solid kick in the middle of her back which sent her sprawling against the wall. She lay there dazed, vaguely aware of Reming and his grandfather struggling with Harley on one side, her daddy and the nurse struggling with her mother on the other, and the horrified crowd, gasping in shocked surprise, below in the marble hall.

"She killed my baby sister!" Harley screamed. "She killed her! And now my mother is sick, and may never be well because of her!"

Kate was sobbing. "Give my baby back, Laura. Give back my baby."

Laura canvassed the faces below. They were all staring at her, some with pity, others questioning. She felt them wondering if it might be true and resented their attention. She wanted to stand up and scream at them. Yes! I killed that stupid mud-baby! I hated it! And I hate my mother and Harley. I hate them all!

She pushed herself up, ready to run to the rail and yell at them to get out of her house. Her knees were weak, her whole body shaking, but she was determined to make them stop staring at her. She stumbled forward, mouth open, forming the word "out." Laura cut it off into a pinched scream, "ow—," as her eyes fell on Nana's upturned face. That beloved face was wet, shining with tears, with a look of dread and the full expectation of speech from her.

Nana. Her poor Nana. She loved her so much, but she could not tell her. Her clown had never let her tell her.

More frightened by her own actions than she had been during her mother's and Harley's attacks, Laura backed into the wall, trembling. She had almost given herself away. She hoped she had covered her mistake in time to convince Nana. Nana must never know she could talk. She could not bear for Nana to know all she had done. To Nana, she was "Sweet Laura," her "Baby Girl." Nothing must ever spoil that!

The medicine man pushed himself heavily to his feet, and Laura retreated from him to a place further down the corridor, away from the prying eyes of the crowd. She watched him draw Harley up, hug him, whisper to him. The old man's deep voice carried to her.

"Your mother needs you now," she heard him say. "You must go to her and help her through this afternoon. Put everything else out of your mind."

Harley pointed at Laura, his eyes flashing his hatred. "I can't forget her! I'll never forget what she did to me, and the baby, and my mother."

"You leave those thoughts with me," the old man said sternly. "We'll talk about those things later. This afternoon you must prove yourself a man by doing what must be done. I want to be proud of you."

Harley let the old man staighten his tie. He tugged his suit coat down, turned and ran to his mother. Shouldering the nurse out of the way, he took her arm.

"Mother, it is time to go," he said, looking back as though for approval from Reming and his grandfather.

The old man smiled at Harley, patted Reming on the shoulder, and sent him along.

Laura watched Harley lead her mother down the stairs and into the crowd. The guests parted to make way for them, and Nana and Carrie fell in behind her daddy, Reming, and the nurse. Comforting hands reached out to them as they passed, but her mother shrugged them off. She was smiling, greeting people like a hostess at a party. They shook their heads and muttered behind her back when she had passed.

While the medicine man stood at the rail, watching the procession file outside, Laura slipped through the double doors past Harley's room and into the unused servant's wing. Those five bedrooms with a common living room had housed a battery of servants when her Nana was a girl, but had been used only for storage since Laura could remember. It was off limits because Nana and Carrie did not have time to clean it regularly. But it had always been one of Laura's favorite hiding places. She knew every inch of it.

Leaning there against the door, listening, she heard the rest of the crowd file outside. The snap of the front door latch made her jump. Her stomach contracted. She was alone with that old devil man.

The old giant's heavy footsteps started in the hall. Were they moving toward her or away? Laura couldn't tell until she heard the stairs creaking under his descending weight. That creepy sound made her shiver.

She bolted away from the door, down the hall, running blindly, fear increasing with every step she took. Laura was brought up short, near the end of the corridor, by a stabbing pain in her chest, followed by the sudden stiffening of her whole body. That old witch doctor had resumed his evil chanting. She knew that he had. All she could do was stand frozen and repel as best she could the waves of agony that she was certain he was projecting on her.

Was it to torture her like this that he had helped Reming save her from Harley? He had threatened that her powers were no match for his. She knew this was his way of proving her helplessness. He was punishing her just as he had said he would.

A rock-hard pain stoned her left breast. If she didn't do

230

something quickly, his chanted medicine would surely kill her.

Laura screamed, "Nana! Please stop him!" to the empty chambers. She stumbled forward, sobbing, dragging herself toward the southeast bedroom, where she would have a view of the cemetery.

The bedroom door, which had never been locked, was locked this time. She struggled with the old-fashioned skeleton key left protruding from the key hole. At last the rusted lock turned, the door squeaked open. Taking the key she closed the door and locked it behind her. Laura threw the key under the bed and went to the window.

Beyond the fishpond, just inside the rock wall, the afternoon sun glinted off a small, blue metal casket suspended in the center of a gold railing set near the edge of the family plot. Laura spotted her Nana in the midst of the family already seated on a row of folding chairs facing the grave. Reming and the nurse were standing behind them, with the other guests gathering about in a straggling semi-circle.

Laura wished for her nurse to minister to her pain-wracked body. She wished for Reming. Reming had always protected her from Harley. Maybe he could do something about his grandfather. But she knew that was only wishful thinking. Reming hadn't yet become aware of his own powers. He wouldn't even be able to recognize what was happening to her. Her only hope was her Nana. Her Nana was old and wise.

New pain assaulted her. Laura pitched forward against the glass. She fumbled with the latch, trying to force the window open. The latch, which had always opened easily, would not budge. Seeking relief at any price, she screamed, "Nana! Nana!" The glass reflected her voice back in her face as the muscles in her hands constricted into locked fists. She was forced to leave the window and pace the room, shaking her hands at her sides to restore even partial circulation.

Suddenly, her clown was there hissing to her. *Nana wouldn't like to do it, but she would let Kate lock you up if you talk to her! She'd know, like the old healer knows, that Kate and Harley told the truth about you. She'd know you killed that mud-baby.*

At that moment it didn't matter what happened later. All that mattered was that there be an end to the horrible pain.

Laura returned to the closed window, pressed close to it, and screamed, "Nana! Help me, Nana!" Below, not one head turned her way.

Again she screamed, "Nana!" only to have her voice choked off by spasmed throat muscles. She tried again to scream, but only a rasping sound came out. Laura felt as though the floor rolled beneath her feet. She fought to balance herself, tried once more to produce a sound. All she was able to bring forth was a breathy whisper, followed by a cutting pain in her voice box.

Laura staggered backward trying to grasp her throat with constricted hands. She tried again to speak her Nana's name. This time not even a whisper could be forced out. A chill ran through her. After all her years of self-imposed silence, now she was truly mute.

Tears streaming down her pain-pinched face, Laura stared down at the cemetery. She saw Reverend Edwards, standing next to the grave, raise his hands for silence. He began addressing the crowd. Laura could not hear what he was saying. She tried again to open the window, and, even though her hands were useless claws with little strength in them, the window pushed up easily.

Laura thought back to the scene she had witnessed in the library. That Indian loved her Nana. He was making it very clear to her that he intended to protect Nana from the truth about her talking. Laura's hands and her face hurt terribly. She had never felt so small and alone. What that old giant was doing to her wasn't fair. She was still her Nana's and her daddy's Baby Girl. She gritted her teeth against the unfair pain and cried.

Three women from the church choir were singing a hymn. Their mismatched voices drifted up to her. They seemed off-key. The discordant sound made her head hurt more. Laura slammed the window. A number of people below turned and looked up at her. She pressed her tear-streaked face against the glass and read the sympathetic expressions on their faces. She knew they thought she was grieving for the dead baby. How satisfying that was, knowing she was fooling them. All except that droopy-eyed schoolteacher and her fat friend. They were watching her, with contempt and suspicion showing on both their faces.

Her clown laughed. *Not those two old schoolteachers, not even that old medicine man can stop us. All those people will be coming again soon for two more funerals. By that time you'll have your daddy all to yourself!*

Laura scowled down at Harley. He had his arm around her mother, comforting her. Neither of them had ever offered comfort to anyone before. Her, least of all. Right then Kate was acting as if she didn't want Harley's attention. She kept shouldering him off.

Suddenly, Laura's skin prickled. She spun around. Listened. She could hear nothing. Not a sound. But she knew. The Indian was coming. She could feel him moving toward her through the empty house. She shook her constricted fist toward the locked door. Immediately, as though for punishment, a pain shot up her arm. She bent over, crying, holding it to her body.

Her clown, angry-sounding, shouted, *Let him come! He is already doing his worst.*

Trusting her clown as she always had, resisting the impulse to crawl under the bed and hide, Laura forced her attention back to the funeral scene below. She could see her mother's face, now in profile. How she hated her! . . . "Say 'spool,' Laura. Say 'cookie' or you won't get one." "K-A-T-E—H-A-T-E!" Laura heard it as an echo from that past time.

The sermon was in progress, but Kate was smiling, waving at friends as if she were on a picnic at the country club. Laura grimaced, knowing that her mother was embarrassing her daddy and Nana.

Another spasm tightened the muscles in her left calf. Laura steeled herself against the screaming pain. She had been hurt before. Her mother had hurt her, trying to make her talk to her Nana. Yet, Laura hadn't broken. She hadn't given in to the pain . . . Now, her resolve crumbled. All those hurts and humiliations had been as nothing to what that old devil man was doing to her now. At that moment, to relieve herself of the constriction in her muscles, she would gladly talk, or crawl, or grovel. Nana was strong. She could deal with full knowledge. Nana would still love her. Protect her. Maybe she would. Maybe her clown was wrong?

Laura sobbed as she shook her ice-cold hands at her sides. They were blue, without circulation in her fingers. She closed her eyes and pressed her useless hands over her ears, listening to the muddled roar inside her own head. Her clown was talking to her, but she couldn't make out the words.

The light on the screen of her closed eyelids shaded dark; further coldness enveloped her. She turned hot. Then faded to cold again. She opened her eyes to find the medicine man towering beside her, gazing down at her mother, who was entertaining herself by climbing spider fingers. Laura shivered. Without a sound he had come right through the locked door. She whirled to find the door standing wide open behind her.

"Look at her," the Indian said at last. "Down there smiling, playing finger games while they are burying her child. Poor, tormented woman!"

The rhythm and cadence of his guttural voice spoke of his doom-chanting. Laura stared at his hands—red, weathered, lined, leathery—gripping the windowsill as though he might rip it off the wall. She edged away from him.

"They spoke the truth. Kate and Harley both . . . You talked. You tore that fool's doll yourself. You killed Kate's baby."

She watched his huge hands rise from the windowsill—thick fingers spreading wide apart like giant claws.

"You cannot be allowed to live among this family."

Kneeling, he grabbed her chin, brought her face around level with his.

Afraid he might snap her neck the way she had seen his father kill the deformed colt in the garage, Laura clawed at his arms. Blood ran. He took no notice. She tried to twist her head to bite his wrist. His hands clamped on either side of her face. She was forced to meet his eyes.

He drew her face closer to his and looked deep inside her. His eyes glowed red, as they had on that day he had appeared out of the heat waves. His force siphoned the energy right from her body. Laura felt her knees buckling. She slumped against the windowsill. The old devil man released her head, grabbed one shoulder, then the sore one. The instant nauseating pain that caused made her knees buckle. He held her upright, moved her over, and pinned her against the wall, out of view from the cemetery.

"Tell me who you are!" he demanded.

Cruel old man. She struggled to free herself, but he had no trouble holding her. Every movement caused agony in her shoulder. His eyes impelled an answer from her.

Feebly Laura raised her hand between them to block out his face.

He gripped his giant paw around her throat and with thumb and middle finger exerted pressure under both her ears. As he mumbled words she did not understand, the strength to hold up that hand drained away. It dropped, paralyzed, to her side.

Laura stared at him. Amazed. Frightened. The thinking part of her felt stronger than ever, more vital, more alive, yet this old medicine man had reduced her body to a useless husk.

"Tell me who you are!" he demanded.

He had taken her voice. How did he expect her to answer?

Then, as though he had read her thoughts, he said, "Your ability to talk is restored as long as you don't try to talk to your grandmother."

Laura tried her voice. "Nana—" It was hoarse and raspy. "I want my daddy!"

Laughing, her clown was saying riddles inside her head. *You've robbed him, too. The power is all yours now. The power belongs to you.*

Laura remembered that day on the porch. Her clown had been more afraid of the medicine man than she had been. Why, in the midst of this pain he was causing her, had her clown lost fear of him?

Once more the old man demanded. "Tell me who you are!"

Then, growling, angry, her clown answered for her.

"You know who I am!"

The old man gripped Laura's shoulders more tightly.

"I had hoped you wouldn't go so far that you couldn't stay. Now, with what you've done to this family, you've condemned yourself. You must be cast out!"

Seemingly, laughter echoed all around Laura as her clown spoke again.

"It is *your* powers that are no match for mine. I have found The Thinking Place. Found it, and remembered."

Laura felt part of her strength returned to her when the old man pulled her into his arms and whispered, "Molly! My Molly!"

Her clown seemed still angry with him from a long time ago. Laura drew away, struggled lamely toward the unmade bed and stood holding onto the footboard for support. Spasmed muscles in her right foot had pulled her arch into the shape of a half-moon. She could not step down on that foot. The pain was all she could bear without screaming.

Angered by her pain, her clown sounded even more hateful when it spoke again.

"As much as Kate and T.J., it was you, with your hollow words—'Pride' and 'Honor'—that drove me to The Thinking Place. But there, listening to Reming cry for the mother who would never be there for him again, I made my resolve. I will have what I pined that life away wanting."

It had to be her daddy her Molly-clown wanted. They had always wanted him to themselves.

"My Poor Baby," Reming's grandfather said.

He sounded like her Nana.

"I closed you in. Gave you no way to go, but to fight."

Laura knew he was talking to Molly. But she was Laura and Molly. He'd forgotten Laura. Laura wanted her daddy, but she also wanted her Nana and Reming. She and her Molly-clown both wanted Kate and Harley destroyed!

"Go home, Old Man. What I came back to do is nearly done!"

Sadly he said, "You know that I have come to stop you!"

She threw her head back and laughed. It was her Molly-clown's laugh, which caused a chain reaction of painful muscle responses. The right half of her mouth pulled off to the side. Her right eye began twitching spasmodically. Her jaws locked open. The laugh turned into a scream of pain and outrage.

With his big leathery paw, the medicine man caressed the tortured muscles of her cheek. His touch made them draw tighter. He withdrew quickly. His face reflected the sternness of a farmer about to slaughter a hand-raised pet for meat.

"Molly, when I punish you, know that I torture myself. I know much of the fault was mine."

Through pinched lips she said, "Then get out of this house. Leave me to do what I *will* do!"

The medicine man made no move toward the door. He stood there stroking the feather fan hanging from his belt.

Her clown flung Laura's nearly rigid body back to the window. Down in the cemetery Kate sat preening beside Harley. She was fluffing her blonde curls in the same way she had in that past time, when she had strutted on T.J.'s arm, flashing her big new diamond wedding rings. Those same rings glittered now as she combed her fingers through her hair.

Laura remembered when her daddy had been so sad because of her mother. He'd told her that if another beautiful lady hadn't died, they'd be with her where they could be happy. She knew now that he'd been talking about Molly. If Molly hadn't left to find The Thinking Place, her mother would no longer be wearing those big diamonds. But there wouldn't have been a Laura. Her daddy wouldn't have had his Baby Girl. It was all so confusing.

She hadn't ever been a Baby Girl. Not really. She and her clown had always felt grown. They had been a match for them all.

Just then her mother bent forward and studied her reflection in the side of the blue metal casket. She blotted her perspiring brow with the palm of her hand and swiped a smudge of lipstick from the corner of her mouth with her finger.

Her mother had asked her to return her baby. Laura's tight facial muscles stretched into a smile. She would do it!

Laura breathed deeply, systematically relaxing the most strained muscles in her face, shoulder, and foot until she was more comfortable. That old witch doctor, watching from behind her, was merely a shadow to her now. From down in the library he had read her mind, locked windows and doors on her, assaulted her body, rendered her mute.

Maybe it was good that he had come. He had shown her things she hadn't thought about before. She'd never stretched herself that far. The laugh would be on him if

237

she used his tricks to accomplish what he had come to stop. If he could control the physical world, she could too! She had been to The Thinking Place, and now she remembered it all. Without doubt or reservation Laura, at that moment, believed she could move the mountain.

As she had seen the medicine man cross his feather fan and rattle stick on his chest, Laura crossed her constricted arms and drew her power inward. New forces surged around her. She felt the old witch doctor step up behind her. She pictured a lance like that carried by the warrior who had protected her on the mountain. More intently, she pictured the black spearpoint driving into the medicine man's belly. Moaning, he backed up. Laura didn't look around. Quickly she concentrated on the lid to the coffin. She pictured it open. Moving outside herself, pure thought without body, she began to lift the lid. It rose slowly. A gasp went up from the crowd. The lid flopped backward—open—exposing the body.

Although the baby's smashed head was covered by a ruffled pink bonnet, still the face looked nearly flat against the pink satin pillow. The skin had darkened from the gray it had been when Laura had last seen it to nearly black.

Laura hugged herself with her crossed arms. She enjoyed the sharp intake of breath from the old man behind her, almost as much as the scene in the cemetery below.

That stupid sissy, Harley, was bent over wretching in the grass in front of the coffin. He never had been anything but a good-for-nothing sissy. Why should the medicine man care what she did to him?

Finally, Harley recovered enough to try to lead his mother away; but Kate shoved him, and he slipped and fell in his own slime.

Laura laughed. Her mother didn't even glance in Harley's direction. Quickly, she moved forward, slid her left hand under the baby, and started to lift it. Then her nose wrinkled. She appeared to gag. She jerked her hand from under it and backed away from the now disheveled corpse.

"Rotten!" she screamed. "My baby is rotten!"

People were straining to see over and around their neighbors. Those who managed it were covering their noses and mouths with handkerchiefs, turning away. Several closest to the front began pushing out of the crowd;

some were already running toward their cars when the next wave moved up to view the body.

Mr. Shrick, the funeral director, yelled at his assistant. "That casket was already supposed to be sealed." The younger man answered him. "I swear to you it was!"

Their faces colorless, both men moved up to close the coffin. They pushed on the lid, bent to check the hinges, and together tried to force it closed. Laura willed it open.

"Let them close it!" the old man said.

"You close it!" Laura challenged him.

The old man pressed close to the window, closed his eyes. He was still clutching his belly. Laura saw the muscles in his neck, arms, even his buttocks tense. His face grew a darker red from straining. The lid dipped once.

Laura tore her attention from the old man, putting all her energies into keeping the casket open.

Finally, with a great explosive gasp, he gave up and leaned gasping against the frame of the window.

"Don't do this! It is cruel!"

Laura laughed. Lifted by her victory over him, her spirit soared, propelled by her newly discovered powers, to reckless heights. She felt unconcerned, even lighthearted, about his presence, unmindful of the danger of him—the damage he had already done her. Her lighthearted mood was quickly shattered when she saw her Nana turn and weep in Carrie's arms.

The medicine man saw Nana, too. He held his spread fingers in Laura's face. Loudly, he chanted five guttural syllables.

Immediately, all Laura's hurts were reactivated with a new charge. Her shoulder began to throb. The muscles all down the right side of her body went into an excruciating spasm. When the pain had subsided enough that she could again look outside herself, she deliberately gazed past the old man in an effort to conceal just how much he was hurting her.

Below, she saw her daddy standing over the baby. His face expressionless, almost somnambulant, he sat back down in his folding chair.

A tight smile lifted the corners of Laura's nearly paralyzed mouth. Her daddy had never loved that mud-baby.

She was his Baby Girl. The only one he loved. Her mother had tricked him into giving her that baby. They were all better off without the ugly, screaming thing, especially Nana and Carrie. It caused them too much work. They weren't really attached to it, either. Her mother had hardly ever let them near it. They were just crying because they were softhearted.

Her mother wasn't crying. At that moment she appeared calm. She was staring at a bright metal object hanging on a branch of the big oak that shaded the graveyard. Laura looked closer. It was a tree saw. Evidently it had been left there by the gravediggers, who had cut away some low-hanging branches.

Kate seemed mesmerized by the bright new-looking blade, gleaming in the sun. She had found it. She could have it!

Laura reached her constricted hand toward her mother. She imagined it placed in the center of her back. She pictured her mother ripping the jagged edge of that saw across her wrists. Laura envisioned blood running, pumping in pools. She pictured it as finished—done! She shoved the side of her hand against the window pane.

Then it was happening. Her mother was running toward that gleaming blade. She reached up for it with her right hand and sawed the jagged edge across her left wrist in the same motion with which she jerked it off the high limb. Blood showered down into her hair. She tried to transfer the saw into her already-cut hand but couldn't grasp it. She paused a moment as though bewildered. Then, gripping the bent tubing frame under her chin, she ripped her right arm down the blade, tearing it open from inside the elbow to the wrist.

The medicine man stared, his face impassive. He began to chant.

The nurse was running toward her, screaming, "Oh, no! Kate! No!"

Evidently unmoved and unmoving, her daddy still sat in his folding chair. He was staring at the blood and Kate's pain-contorted face in the same way that, only moments earlier, she had stared at the blade.

Her mother saw him watching her and screamed, "Laura!"

Many of the fleeing guests stopped to watch. None moved to help.

"Your Laura did this! Laura!" Kate yelled. Then to the crowd she said, "You all saw that casket open by itself. Laura did it! Laura killed my baby! She's killing me!"

Speaking loudly over the old man's chanting and somewhat startled by the unused sound of her own voice, Laura said, "How crazy she looks! Down there screaming that I'm killing her when they all saw her do that to herself."

The medicine man had stopped his chanting to listen to her.

"None would believe her but one who knew," he answered. "You've been very clever. But now I know! . . . Leave her be! And Harley—" His voice trailed off.

The nurse reached Kate then. She tried to take her wrists.

Harley, covered with his own vomit, regained his feet. He outran Reming, shouldered the nurse aside, and tried to hug his mother, whose nose wrinkled as though at his smell. She pushed him violently away. Blood gushed in rhythmical spurts from her mangled arms. Two, three, four long spurts before the nurse regained her tourniquet grip on one wrist.

"For God's sake, one of you, help me!" she screamed. "Can't you see she's bleeding to death?"

Watching from that upstairs window, it seemed the crowd turned en masse and swarmed on Kate and the nurse, who suddenly changed her plea for help to "Get back! Damn it! Get back! Let us through!"

As the crowd parted, the nurse emerged, holding both her hands squeezed around Kate's right arm. Mr. Shrick, his face ashen now, had the left arm. He was watching the nurse and repeating her every move. He appeared to be as much in shock as her mother, who, her knees sagging, was becoming weaker. Both wounds were still pumping blood.

The crowd seemed to be sweeping the trio toward the house. At the back, one on each side, Carrie and Nana were fighting to restrain Harley, who was crying, trying to plow through to his mother. Nana stumbled over a spray of carnations. She nearly fell.

At last her daddy roused out of his stupor and moved to take Nana's arm. When he did, Laura saw Harley surge forth and break free. Near the kitchen door he caught up with them and took her mother's arm from Mr. Shrick. Blood squirted in the transition. Kate stumbled. Laura smiled, pleased with her work.

Mr. Shrick, covered with blood, turned immediately and threw up his hands to the crowd.

"Let them go on in, folks! Everyone, please! Go on home now! The Daniels have all the problems they can handle without company."

Behind the crowd, abandoned in the cemetery, stood the open coffin. Laura tugged the window open, and like the wolf bent on destroying the little pig's house made of sticks, she huffed, then puffed her stale breath into the outside air. The wind picked up, swirled a dust devil of red grave dirt all over the pink satin casket interior and the baby's ruffly, pink dress and bonnet.

Laura took one last look at that intruding mud-baby. With a force that caused the casket to rock between the gold railings, she slammed the lid closed.

That noise seemed to jolt everyone into action. The milling crowd hurriedly broke up. People headed for their cars.

Beside Laura, the old man was fumbling with the belt clasp that held his fan and rattle stick fastened over his hip. Freeing them both, he made a shuffle step, shaking the rattle stick toward Laura. He wafted the fan over her head, then brought it sharply down to make contact with her neck. An axing motion. Clearly a death stroke. Reflexively, Laura threw her hand up, hurting her sore shoulder, but not before he had touched her. A cutting pain slashed across her spine. She saw tears shimmering in the old man's eyes.

"I cannot allow you to win," he said. "You must pay for all you've done!"

Laura glared at him, but it was her Molly-clown who answered.

"I've already paid, Old Man! A year I spent out of body. I heard every word Reming uttered about his Mommy. 'Why doesn't my Mommy come home?' No matter how many times you told him I was dead. And— 'Didn't she love me?' I was there when he cried himself to sleep at night. And me, unable to comfort him. Unable to touch him. Unable to tell him how much I wanted to be back with him. Then, finally, I had to give him up. That was when his mother died. Long after the body was buried."

"You had free choice, Molly. All the way. You blame T.J. You blame Kate and me. What about you?"

"I was betrayed. For my part in it, I told you, I've already paid."

Just then, Laura heard the nurse shouting from the stairs.

"Help! I need help!"

The medicine man was out the door before Laura could move her stiffened body. She dragged herself along, trying to keep up, but he disappeared through the double doors into the family wing.

She heard the nurse struggling with her mother. "Let me help you, Kate! You'll die!"

And her mother's answer. "I want to. Get away from me!"

The medicine man's footsteps went on down the stairs. She heard him say, "Hold her. I'll get my bag."

As she entered that hall, Harley's face popped out of his mother's bedroom. Frightened, wide-eyed, he looked frozen in place between the frame and the door, like a terrified mouse. Gazing at the big blood splotches across the carpet, he acted as though he didn't see her.

Laura slid past him and found her mother hanging half-off the bed, the nurse on top of her. Both the nurse's hands were clamped around her mother's left arm. She was applying steady pressure, obviously trying to cut off the gush of blood that was pooling on the floor.

Her mother was clawing at the nurse's cheek with her right hand; all the while, blood was pumping in spurts from her slashed wrist into the nurse's face, saturating her black funeral dress and spattering the bed.

The nurse shouted, "Quickly, Laura! Grab her other arm. Tight! Until the bleeding stops."

Smiling, Laura backed away from the mess. At the door, she collided with Harley. Then, hate returning to his eyes, he pushed her down and kicked her viciously in the side. He stumbled, screaming, back into the midst of the blood bath.

Through pain-pinched eyelids—writhing, holding her side—Laura saw him tackle her mother, his hands sliding comically up and down her blood-slippery arm, until he squeezed—with more purpose than Laura had ever seen in him—and the spurting stopped.

"No, Mama!" he bellowed, dragging her arm down over the side of the bed, his heels digging into the carpet.

Angry about her own carelessness toward Harley, Laura fought the throb in her ribs and bruised shoulder. The room was spinning; she closed her eyes. When she opened them she found her daddy's heavy boot planted only inches in front of her nose as he stepped over her to help the nurse. He slung Harley into the corner as he heaved her mother back to the center of the bed and pinned both her wrists to the blood-soaked pillows above her head. Her mother cursed him, then breathed a long, exhausted breath, stopped struggling, and closed her eyes.

In the corner, Harley recovered his balance and shoved off from the wall, leaving two bloody hand prints behind him on the asparagus-fern-printed paper. He flew at his father, yelling, "Get away from my Mama! You hate her. Don't you touch my Mama!"

Her daddy elbowed him off, shouting, "Get out of here, Harley! Unless you want her to die. I'm trying to save her life!"

The word "die" stopped Harley, rooted him to the floor, three feet from the bed, like a stunted sapling that had sprouted and grown there.

Laura followed his glazed stare to her mother's face. It was gray against the blood-splotched white pillow cases—the same ashen color the baby's face had been when her mother scooped it off the marble floor.

Slowly, as though he had made the same connection, Harley turned toward Laura.

Her eyes swept the floor around her searching for a weapon; a shoe—anything—

He attacked before, in her stiff and weakened condition, she even had a chance to move. He landed another terrible kick in her ribs and stomped her fingers under his heel in the same swift motion. He dropped astraddle of her, tangling his fingers in her hair, banging her head, repeatedly, against the closet door.

She screamed, only to have the sound cut off by his forearm pressed across her throat, backed by the whole weight of his body. He twisted her head sideways, crushing her between the wall and the floor.

The sound of scraping bone on bone ground inside her head, accompanied by a searing pain in the back of her neck. Her throat felt crushed flat, like a pinched soda straw. No air reached her starved lungs. She fought to throw him off—punching, gouging. She ripped his shirt and pinched, then twisted the bared flesh above his belt. Her efforts only increased his fanatic strength. Clearly, he meant to kill her.

Terror—her need for breath—overcame all Laura's restraint. From the darkness drowning her, her lips moved, forming the word "daddy" in a soundless plea for help.

"She's talking!" Harley screamed as her daddy backhanded him off of her.

Gasping, Laura forced her swollen eyes open, grateful for the light. She felt elated by the sight of fresh blood on Harley's cheek where her daddy's big diamond must have cut him.

Staggering backward, Harley landed against Carrie as she lumbered through the door. She cuffed him soundly on both sides of his head before she dragged him out of the room.

"She talked!" Harley shouted stubbornly from the hall. "Laura talked again!"

Carrie's resounding slap reduced his tattletales to a continuous wail as she towed him down the hall and slammed him into his room.

Over Harley's moans Laura heard the key turn in the lock and Carrie panting her way back up the hall.

The nurse's shout—"She's dead if you don't hold that wrist!"—tore her daddy from her side. Laura twisted painfully to watch him jump to the side of the bed opposite the nurse and press her mother's limp arm between his hands, stemming the weak spurts of blood pumping from the jagged cut below her thumb.

Kate had managed to pull her daddy away from her again. As long as Kate lived, there would be no end to it. Why didn't they let her bleed to death and be rid of her?

Her daddy was sick of her. The nurse had no special love for her, either. Why were they working so hard to save her life? Before, she had only looked crazy; now, without her ugly baby, she *was* crazy. Death was what she wanted. Why didn't they let her die?

Laura felt the floor shake as Carrie knelt beside her. Carrie's flabby face—red and angry from her bout with Harley—softened as she crooned, "My poor Baby Girl. You're safe, now. Carrie's here."

But Laura recoiled, tried to pull away, for there, towering behind Carrie, was the medicine man. She read anger in his solemn eyes. They were filled with resolve. In those slow-motion moments before he struck, Laura knew he meant to kill her!

Struggling, feeling like some wild, trapped thing, trying to break Carrie's iron grip on her shoulders, Laura saw him lift his black bag. He motioned with it like a battering ram aimed toward Carrie's back. Although he never touched her with the bag, Carrie's heavy body toppled across Laura's chest. With the weight and force of a felled tree trunk, Carrie crushed her.

Laura heard the hardwood floor creak beneath the thick padding of carpet. Mingled with that sound was the snap of her own ribs.

Carrie rolled to get up and with that motion Laura felt those jagged bones impale some vital organ. Unbearable pain seized all her senses. Thick, smothering coils of pain squeezed off any possible response.

As quickly as it happened, Carrie was scrambling off her.

"Laura Baby! I'm so sorry," she stammered. "Somehow, I lost my balance."

Her bristly chin quivered only inches above Laura's face.

"Are you all right? Carrie didn't mean to add to your hurts."

Her beloved Carrie, used by that evil witch doctor as a death weapon! It wasn't right!

Laura rolled her head to the side to keep from looking at Carrie's anguished face. A thick, strangling bubble of burning bile rose from her stomach to lodge in her throat. For several seconds she thought it would suffocate her, but little by little she swallowed it back down. All that while, through her fear, she heard her clown screaming, demanding that she not die.

You will not die! Not by his hand! Not yet!

Laura lifted her trembling fingers to her burning throat. Her skin, where Harley had choked her, felt slick and wet in contrast to her parched lips. She wiped the wet liquid across her lips to moisten them. Laura tasted salt and more. A sticky sweetness. She stared at her hand. It was dyed red with blood. Her mother's blood—from Harley's hands.

Laura wiped more blood from her throat and hair and the side of her face. She licked her hand, needing the warm, thick, wild, animal taste. Kate's blood. It was Kate's blood at last. In spite of the debilitating pain, Laura felt a sudden surge of power. Power she had possessed once. Possessed! It was being drained from her by the medicine man. She would have it back! She licked her hand again, only to have it jerked away.

"What are you doing?"

Laura forced her attention from the returning sensation of dominion to look up into Carrie's horrified face.

"Don't lick that blood! I'll wash it off you."

Carrie started to lift her. But the nurse said, over her shoulder, "Don't move that child until I have a chance to examine her. With you falling on her, she may have something broken. How could you be so clumsy?"

Her poor Carrie didn't answer. Laura felt herself being eased back to the floor. Carrie kneeled beside her, looking sadly down on her for some time.

She suddenly asked, "Where is Mrs. D.?"

Laura watched her fat face wrinkle with the new worry about her Nana.

"Go check on her. Please, Carrie! Hurry!" her daddy said, holding one end of the bandage as the old man applied salve to Kate's arm. "It might be her heart."

Alarmed, Laura tried to get up. Carrie pressed her back to the floor.

"You stay still! I'll see to your Nana."

"She is all right," the medicine man said. "Let her be quiet."

Carrie glared at him, then defiantly poked her head into the hall. She turned around and came two steps back inside the room.

"Mrs. D. is sitting on the stairs looking pale as a ghost. What should I tell her about Kate? Is she going to make it?"

As though he were the one in authority, the old Indian grunted assent. Laura saw how her nurse glared at him.

"She's lost about all the blood a person can lose and still live," the nurse said; then to him, "Aren't you going to stitch those cuts?"

"No need. The wounds will heal faster without further trauma to them."

"We'll see," the nurse said curtly.

Laura saw the stiff way her nurse helped him finish bandaging both arms.

"There is still danger of shock," the nurse said, "or more bleeding."

"She will live," the medicine man proclaimed in a monotone.

He sounded so certain of it. That meddlesome old devil man!

Laura recalled her mother in her temple dancer nightgown luring her daddy away from her. And from that earlier past time came sensations, sounds. The eerie whistle of wind gusting around her woman's body, and a chanted echo: K-A-T-E—H-A-T-E. KATE!

Kate *will* die!

Her Molly-clown was snarling, prodding her onward, as Laura pressed her fists against her closed eyelids and pictured blood. Rivers of blood. Fountains of red, thick, sticky blood.

There was a flurry of motion around her. She heard the witch doctor's shuffle step, heard his rattle stick. She opened her eyes just in time to see his feather fan descending quickly toward her throat; and in that same glance, the nurse, behind him, looking disgusted as though by a child's foolishness.

But it was not foolishness. It was real, real power in the old man's feather stroke. The slashing pain closed Laura's eyes involuntarily and propelled her into a long, dark tunnel. It was in that black death tunnel that she met Kate. Laura pushed her forward, fought her own way back.

When she was able to force her eyes open again, that old witch doctor was bent over her mother's body, chanting, wafting his fan with bird-wing strokes from her deathly gray face to her toes and back again.

On both of Kate's bandaged forearms red splotches bubbled through the white gauze. She was dead, or nearly dead. Laura knew what the others could not know. That old healer, with his wafting fan, was actually coaxing her spirit back into her body.

Again Laura closed her eyes. She projected all the pain he had caused her back onto the old man, and in that same thought made his fan a drawing instrument, drawing even more blood from Kate's body.

Laura sustained her effort past her own pain of impalement on her broken ribs, past the muscle spasms in her hands, feet, face, and now her throat. She kept thrusting more and more pain on him, prodding, stabbing, until, at last, he whirled toward her and whacked the edge of the fan against her throat. Her daddy, standing behind him, looked perplexed by his actions but made no move to stop him. Laura was immediately choked by a fit of coughing.

She rolled on her sore shoulder and felt her broken ribs pierce deeper. She lay gasping, trying to breathe while at the same time she forced herself to watch the medicine man. Seemingly, he was working in a haze. Could that be her own tears? Coldly, Laura assessed the damage she had done him.

He seemed less robust than before. His energetic hand movements were more subdued, but he was still working over her mother. What little damage she had done him was as nothing compared to what he had done to her. She knew she was losing this death battle.

Gradually his chanting grew from but a whisper to a full-voiced, desperate intonation of a language she realized she had once known but was now forgotten to her. His motions became more jerky, frantic. He wafted his fan the length of Kate's arms, fluttered it over her heart.

Laura smiled her satisfaction as the blood spots grew on her mother's bandages. Her spell on the fan was working even though the old man had already sent her once into the death tunnel, and she was clinging now, by only her clown's will, to barely enough life-force to keep her body from succumbing. Her head drooped to the floor. She could no longer hold it up. The old man was actually killing her as he had said he would. She hadn't believed that he was that much stronger than she.

Kate must die! Kate must die!

It was her Molly-clown chanting from within her.

Kill her! Kill her now!

Unable to confront the old man's strength again, Laura concentrated on her nurse. She had done it before—forced her thoughts upon that ugly woman until she converted the nurse's will to her own purposes. She had to do it now. Had to!

At last Miss Pledge slapped the healer's rattle stick out of her way. Exactly as Laura had wished, she began cutting through the blood soaked bandages with her blunt scissors.

The old man stopped his chanting only long enough to command, "No! Don't do that!"

Just then Nana came into the room. She stood looking at Kate's gray face on the blood-stained pillows and the blood oozing through her arm wrappings, soaking into the sheets.

"She's so pale," Nana breathed.

"She is dying. I am certain she will die unless you get a real doctor out here." The nurse was standing with her scissors poised, as though ready to finish her cutting, where the old man had told her to stop.

The medicine man's voice was deep, firm. "Kate will not die! I will not let her die!"

"Mrs. Daniels, this man is an untrained charlatan!"

Nana's voice was barely a whisper. "Trust him, Miss Pledge. If he says all will be well, it will be."

Laura saw the nurse reach across the bed and shake her daddy's shoulder.

"Are you willing to trust your wife's life to this primitive person, Mr. Daniels?"

He roused a little, as though from a long sick spell. "I trust him."

The muscles in Laura's throat constricted again, causing her to cough wrackingly. Her daddy was weak! If he'd only stand with her nurse against the medicine man. Let her cut off the bandages. Her mother would bleed to death in seconds. Then the two of them could be together without the menace of her. But where her mother was concerned, her daddy's will melted. Laura recalled the sting of his abandonment the night her mother had enticed him to make that horrid baby. It was no different now. Here she was hurt, unable to get up off the floor, and he hadn't come to her. He'd stayed by her mother's side.

Angry, with great effort, Laura raised her knotted fist. She let it fall with a thump against the floor.

Her daddy looked past the old man to her.

She glared at him.

Without warning the medicine man spun toward her. Laura suffered terror as he suddenly wafted his fan over her head. Immediately her nose spouted blood in two thick streams. She hadn't the strength to sit up. She was choking, drowning in her own blood. Everyone in the room was watching. Would no one help her?

At last her daddy shouldered the medicine man aside. Laura saw him grab a skirt of her mother's off a chair. She felt her broken ribs grind into flesh as he lifted her. Even with that pain dizzying her head, she welcomed that first unimpaired gulp of air. She was grateful to be able to breathe even though through her mouth, as he pressed the skirt under her still spewing nose.

Before the medicine man pushed her head between her knees, causing real agony in her chest, Laura saw him hurl the feather fan against the wall, march to his bag and fetch back another one. He began his chant louder than ever over her mother. The blood stopped oozing from her bandages, and her eyelids fluttered open. Weakly, she called, "T.J."

Laura felt him waver, then lean toward her Kate as though drawn by an invisible noose around his fickle neck. He nodded to Carrie, who thrust a chair near Laura and eased Nana into it. Nana reached down and took her from her daddy. He rushed back to the bed and grasped her mother's hand.

"I'm here, Kate!"

Limp, leaning against Nana's knee, able to sit upright only because Nana's arms were around her, Laura glared at her mother holding her daddy's hand and mooning up at him with eyes that silently pled for help. She looked quickly away, unable to stand the sight of them. Her eyes fell on the discarded feather fan wedged at an angle between floor and wall like a brace. If only she had the strength to reach it, waft it over her mother's head, and watch her life's blood gush from her. But not a muscle, except those of her eyes, responded to her commands. Only her mind was functioning. Darkly, from inside, her Molly-clown was hissing that Kate had better be saying good-byes to her daddy because she would never pull him away from her again.

The nurse finished timing the pulse under Kate's jaw and turned to scowl at the Indian.

"God had a hand in this. You did not one thing of any medical value!"

Laura saw the medicine man smile broadly at the nurse's back as she turned from the bed and rushed to kneel beside Laura.

The nurse's ugly face was wrung with anger and fear as her hands moved deftly over Laura's body, straightening her legs, feeling the back of her neck and down her spine.

Laura nearly cried out as the nurse depressed each rib in turn, but her clown warned her to keep still, that there was no help for her internal injuries, and that she must not be confined to bed as the doctor surely would do. As she always had, Laura obeyed her clown. She bit her lip, tried to transport herself away from the pain by playacting at being brave to inspire more allegiance from the nurse. Her nurse was tough. She respected toughness.

A fine trickle of blood was still coming from Laura's nose. It was dropping onto the nurse's knee. The nurse made no effort to move, yet she was distracted enough that she passed over the broken ribs.

Laura felt torn between her need for help and her allegiance to her clown. Dutifully, she fought down her self-pity and let her clown pump her full of their old hatred for her mother.

Silently, Laura put forward the thought Insist, insist! Finally the nurse said, "This episode is just the beginning, Mrs. D."

She unbuttoned Laura's blouse, exposing her already blackening rib cage. "Kate is dangerous, not only to herself. Her insanity is projected onto every member of this household. Harley's attacks, even Carrie accidentally falling on Laura was the result of the nervous climate created by that madwoman. She belongs in a mental hospital!"

252

Laura heard her mother moan. She saw Nana glance toward the bed, then back to the nurse.

"No!" Nana said firmly. "Kate will be kept here, and as much a part of the family as possible. We must. For Harley's sake."

Laura cried out and cowered away from the nurse's fingertips as she lightly brushed them across the huge, rapidly darkening bruise beneath which the broken bones ground deeper into her with each breath or movement.

"You see for yourself the effect Kate has on Harley," the nurse said. "Look what he's done to his sister!"

Good! Let her blame Harley. No need to place that guilt on Carrie.

Laura saw Nana's eyes fill with tears as she studied her chest. If Nana only knew. It was her old medicine man who had caused most of the damage. Mortal damage on the inside where none could see.

"My poor Baby Girl," Nana said. She sobbed once.

It wasn't like Nana to break down. Maybe she sensed it. Maybe she knew. It was a terrible thought—that her Nana wouldn't stop that witch doctor if she knew.

"Poor Harley is not himself," Nana said. "You must forgive Harley for Nana's sake."

Laura knew that she was struggling even to talk. She seemed so different, so shaky and old. Laura had never meant to hurt her Nana, but she had.

For a moment Laura wished she could forgive Harley, if only for Nana's sake, but then her hatred overwhelmed all feelings of forgiveness. How could she help but hate him after all the pain he had caused her. Replaying his attacks, remembering the feeling of suffocation, her hate billowed into red-hot destructive flame. That flame engulfed the medicine man, too, for putting an end to her dream of having her daddy to herself in this house with Nana and Carrie. She held him accountable more for that than for the smothering hot wave of weakness that was sweeping her so quickly toward that black oven of a tunnel—the death tunnel. It seemed such a shock, coming so quickly. She wasn't ready to die!

Doing battle with her weakness, a wave of resentment rose against all of them: her nurse and Carrie, and especially her Nana and her daddy, for not seeing what that witch doctor had done to her. They had all seen him wave his fan over her, causing her to cough and her nose to bleed, yet none of them seemed to hold him responsible. No one had even questioned him about it. No connection had been made. Seemingly his aggressions against her were already forgotten.

Laura seethed. Then, her anger was tempered somewhat by the realization that she had made Kate look crazy in that same off-handed way.

The nurse pointed to two crescent-shaped marks over Laura's ribs that matched the outline of Harley's boot.

"Next time he might use a sharp stick or even a knife."

"Oh, my God!" Nana said, slumping against the back of the chair. "We can't begin to think like that." She closed her eyes momentarily, then squared her slender shoulders and sat up straight. "I know I'm right in this. Kate must be kept at home for Harley and Laura ever to be reconciled."

Maybe her Nana didn't know after all.

Laura looked to her daddy towering beside the bed. He had let go of her mother's hand. She appeared to be sleeping. Laura saw her daddy flinch, as if he hated that Nana wanted to keep her mother at home. But he did not dispute her. Laura wondered. In all the major decisions of his life had he ever disputed the word of someone telling him what was best for him?

The nurse sighed. "Have it your way. However, there are changes that must be made," she said.

Laura's eyes darted from one face to another: her daddy's, Nana's, Carrie's. They were all watching the nurse as she stood and turned in a semicircle, apparently studying the room.

All eyes were on the nurse except the old man's, and his were on her. Cold. Piercing. Laura could feel them boring into her, constricting her insides. She bent over grasping her stomach, to fight new pain, as she heard the nurse say, "All this furniture must be moved out. Too dangerous. I'll need special locks on the closets and bathroom doors. A hospital bed, one with rails. Emergency restraint cuffs for her hands and feet."

Laura taunted the old man with a grin.

Picturing her mother strapped down like a prisoner to be tortured pleased Laura. Maybe this was better than killing her. Less humane. Especially since her nurse loved her and hated pretty women like her mother. After she was gone her nurse would go on punishing Kate for her and calling it treatment. Laura's stomach tightened for laughing, but the pain that caused was not at all funny. Groaning, Laura rolled toward Nana, who patted her shoulder as though to console her for a minor scratch. She pushed herself to her feet.

"I'll see to all that today," she said without looking at the nurse. She headed for the door, her face like a sleepwalker's.

The nurse called after her, "The windows. We'll need some kind of bars or grillwork on the outside of these windows. And a grilled door going out into the hall."

"All unnecessary," the medicine man grunted.

The nurse glared at him, then rushed to stand in front of Nana. "Make up your mind, Mrs. Daniels, whether you want me here to give Kate professional care, or whether you want to put her in the care of this untrained person!"

Laura was galled by the amused tilt at the corners of the old man's mouth and by his nod to her Nana approving her consent to the nurse.

"We'll order what you want," Nana said sadly and followed Carrie out of the room.

So it was the old witch doctor running the house now. Her Nana was no longer her ally. Nana was taking orders from him. He had defeated her in another battle. He had won perhaps the greatest victory—power, influence over her Nana, who was really the center of her home. Maybe Kate wouldn't suffer under the nurse's treatment for long, but Kate would remember. Always!

Suddenly the medicine man scooped Laura off the floor and was out the door with her before she could make even the faintest protest to her daddy or the nurse. His every movement caused agony to her battered body, but that pain was nothing compared to her fear. She knew she had only moments more to live. From the rigid set of his jaw it was clear he meant to end their death battle now. She wasn't ready to die. Her Molly-clown wasn't ready for her to lose her body. The way she had torn her clown's body came to mind. But her clown had been ready for that, had urged it.

Laura intended to twist out of his arms, but she found that her body would not respond to her commands no matter how much she strained. Only her right hand could move, and that took all her effort. She clawed at his hand to make him drop her. She had barely scratched the skin before her fingers knotted into grotesque talons. Paralyzed! Her whole body was a useless weight. Yet her spirit was a dauntless thing, still strong.

Her clown was whispering to her.

If you let him kill you now, all is lost. One more day. You must have one more day!

Helplessly, Laura watched the spastic muscle tremors in her arms, stomach, and legs, as the old devil man carried her downstairs. Knowing that he intended it to be her last trip through the house she loved, Laura gathered to her all the familiar smells and sights.

As they passed the mirrored panels in the marble hall, Laura glimpsed an ill-looking little blond girl, hollow-eyed, in the arms of a menacing Indian giant. Another child, surely. Yet she recognized the dim image as herself. Had she become that shadow child so quickly? It seemed impossible! That child was dying. Nearly dead now!

Laura suddenly felt as though she were floating, that she could float free if her clown would only stop binding her to that mortally injured image in the mirror—that pain-wracked image. But the pain and her clown kept pulling her back into that body. Such pain! It pulled and repelled at the same time.

As the Indian carried her out of view of the mirrors, and her image was lost to her, Laura felt for one terrifying heartbeat as though she had at that moment died. She screamed! That terrible animal sound—one of the few sounds she'd ever allowed herself to make. Her multi-purpose sound expressing fear, anger, rage, danger. The sound alone convinced her that she was still among the living. She dedicated herself to that scream—all her remaining strength. She wanted to live! Nana or the nurse would hear, surely, and come to rescue her.

Her captor, that horrible witch doctor, tightened his grip on her. He silenced her scream the same way she had the mud-baby's, by shutting off her air supply. He squeezed, and, not only was he choking off her breath, his strength was grinding her broken ribs further into her vital organs.

Nearly strangling, Laura saw him glance once over his

shoulder, as though looking for anyone who might have heard her scream and followed them. No one there, he rushed on down the side hall, past the library, toward her treasure room.

That hall, narrow and dark as the death tunnel she had just come back from, plunged Laura into a storm. The grief of separation from home . . . her Nana. Anger. Fear of monsters—the unknown. There was still so much she could not remember. She couldn't. She wouldn't. She didn't want to die!

By the time he reached her Nana's room, Laura wanted, with her own will, not just her clown's, to fight to stay as long as she could. In spite of her spasmed muscles and the ever increasing throbbing in her chest, she wanted to live.

But she had to have help!

She closed her eyes, picturing herself kissing the nurse's ugly face. Laura set her whole mind to infusing a knowingness in her nurse.

Help me! He's going to kill me! Come now!

The medicine man laid Laura on her low bed. She shuddered, sending even more desperate signals to the nurse, as he pushed her door closed, then squatted in a very Indian way beside her.

Her mind was now on a circuit sending a constant distress signal.

Help me, quickly! Leave Kate! Come to me!

Laura's skin felt like a million stinging ants were crawling between the layers of tissue the moment the medicine man placed his hand over her small chest. It was the end! She knew another moment would bring that devastating death pain and its accompanying pangs of loneliness and loss. It seemed like only a moment ago . . . that last time, crushed on the canyon floor. Desperately, she sent out her silent call to the nurse.

Help me! Come now!

Laura felt suspended in time and space. Waiting. She looked into that old witch doctor's face and recalled, from that past time, his self-righteousness, his uncompromising pride.

She expected him to jam his huge hand down and force her broken ribs, like knife blades, further into her. Instead, his eyes pierced her.

"Why do you make yourself suffer so?"

Before Laura could muster breath to answer, his hypnotic eyes bored deeper into hers.

"Accept that I will finish what must be done. Give up! You remember The Thinking Place. You know that life and death are all the same."

When at last she did manage to speak, her voice was thin and raspy, her breath coming only shallowly from under his burning hand. Hers was a child's voice, full of her fear, yet still possessing a shadow of the marvel of six-year-olds.

"I remember from The Thinking Place . . . One time is much like another."

She was stalling, had to stall, to give her nurse time to find her.

"It's all a game. Isn't it?"

Forced to stop for more breath, Laura directed all that remained of her power, again, toward the nurse.

Come away from Kate! Hurry to me!

Laura actually saw tears in his eyes as he said to her, "You have to be stopped."

Her anger at the witch doctor's judgments, his assaults on her, and her present predicament made her reckless enough to risk attack. She pictured her warrior. He appeared, snarled at the medicine man, and drove his black lance into the old man's gut, quickly retracting it. As he was about to thrust a second time, because she had run out of strength to hold him in thought, he evaporated.

"You made this game. Then, and now!" Laura whispered vehemently.

The medicine man grasped his belly with his free hand and doubled over, but still he did not remove his other hand from her chest.

He would crush her, now, she was sure. Laura took the deepest breath she could. At the same time—defiantly—she tried to call her warrior back again.

"There will be another time for all of us," Laura said, intending it as her death warning to him.

Just then Miss Pledge burst into the room, and disbursed the assembling shadow of her warrior. Keenly Laura felt his loss, though she was grateful when her nurse took three long strides across the room and jerked the witch doctor's hand off her chest.

"Mrs. Daniels may trust you, but I don't. You'll not perform any of your hokey-pokey on this child!"

Watching the old man fight off his pain, trying to hide it from the nurse, Laura saw, too, the deep hurt on his face. His voice was gruff as he spoke directly to her, ignoring the nurse.

"You must give up this time. You are making scars that won't easily heal and will be carried through many lifetimes."

"Who are you talking to?" the nurse snapped. "I don't believe that foolishness about having more than one life."

He didn't answer her.

Laura only frowned, wanting to tell him they were all deserved scars!

"For some, maybe, in your judgment, they were deserved," the old man said aloud.

The nurse, standing protectively between Laura and the medicine man, was looking at him the way she did Kate. Laura suppressed her smile. He did appear to be talking to himself.

"Maybe others would judge differently," he was saying. "What about your Nana? Her only crime has been in loving you too much."

The nurse spread her feet wider apart as though readying herself for defense.

"You are crazy. As crazy as Kate. Carrying on a one-sided conversation with a child who can't talk."

In front of the nurse, Laura could only project her thoughts to the old man. Nana's guilt and yours are shared. I heard your confessions in the library. Maybe it was your older love that foreshadowed the lives of all of us who came after!

She knew the old man had intercepted her reply by the way the muscles in his face grew taut. Laura did smile, then. She felt a returning sense of power, power that for the briefest moment eclipsed the terrible burning pain that was growing in her chest. She had made him draw in upon himself. She had confounded him at last, made him assess his own blame. Realizing she would need time to make a present for her daddy, while the medicine man was off-guard she put forth the idea of a trade: Kate and Harley for one more day.

She saw the Indian's brown eyes snap alert. He scrutinized her face.

"I want nothing more than I want you to resolve your relationship with T.J. once and for all," he said.

Quickly, the nurse marched up and grasped the old giant by his shoulders. She shook him.

"Are you in shock from the sight of Kate's blood?" She peered into his eyes. "What are you talking about, that you want Laura to resolve her relationship with her father? That is a relationship that can never be resolved."

The old man gently removed her hands from his shoulders, placed them together at her waistlevel, and patted the backs of her hands with his big bear paw.

"That is exactly the point," he said to the nurse. Then he turned his gaze to Laura. "Their father-daughter relationship can never be resolved."

The old man made a sobbing noise deep in his throat. It was the most pitiable sound Laura had ever heard.

"I have no choice but to return to my meditation," he said.

Laura understood his meaning perfectly. There would be no clemency. No mercy. He had pronounced his death sentence on her. He planned to proceed with her execution as speedily as possible.

Only her clown had the will to fight him. Exhausted, Laura's instincts for survival propelled her toward conservation of her own strength to fulfill, as she always had, her clown's wishes. She was asleep before her nurse could even comment about what to her must have seemed a very strange encounter with a crazy man.

Laura awoke with a start. It was dark outside. Only the small night-light was burning on her dresser across the room. On the ceiling it cast eerie shadows of the two figures arguing near her. To look at them, Laura painfully rolled her head sideways on her stiff neck.

"I don't care what that old man's ties are with this family," her nurse was saying.

Had she been here all the while she slept?

"He wants to harm Laura. I can feel it!"

"What you feel is Laura's fear of him," her daddy said. "She's always been afraid of him."

"That brave child would never be afraid of anyone

without good reason. You should see the effect his chanting has on her. She writhes in her sleep as though she's being tortured."

"His chanting is for Kate."

The mournful cadences penetrated Laura's consciousness then. Thoroughly aroused from sleep, the full impact of them hit her, causing the pain to swell in her throat. She choked it down, only to have it swell again. The monotonous Indian rhythms drummed in her chest cavity, making it impossible to separate that vibration from the pounding arhythmia of her own heart.

Her nurse's irritated voice cracked across the small room.

"He is making all that racket in Kate's room?"

"No. In his own. The upstairs guest room."

"It's not for Kate he is chanting. It is against Laura! When I came down here he was pressing Laura against her bed. I think he meant to strangle her. I forced him back away from her, but he continued to carry on a conversation as though she were talking to him, all about him wanting her to resolve her relationship with you. Then he turned right around and said the father-daughter relationship could never be resolved. Believe me, he is as crazy as Kate. And the trust you all put in him makes him even more dangerous."

Laura saw that her daddy's hands were trembling so that he stuffed them into his pockets. Her nurse was looking at him as if she were assessing his own competency.

"I've been sitting here thinking about what we witnessed upstairs. I don't believe he has curative powers, but I saw his powers for evil. Your medicine man touched Laura with his fan and she choked with a coughing fit. Then he waved it over her and her nose began to bleed."

Her daddy jerked his hands out of his pockets and displayed them palms up.

"I attribute those things to coincidence. What reason would he have to harm her?"

"I sense that he believes what Kate and Harley have said all along. That Laura killed the baby and did all the other things they accuse her of."

That wasn't what Laura wanted her nurse to tell her daddy. The nurse had done what she had called her to do. Why didn't she leave?

"We've all had a day that could shock anyone senseless. Carrie is with Kate. You go get some rest."

"Are you in shock, Mr. Daniels? Have you heard anything I've said. I'm telling you that Indian means to harm your daughter."

He was backing the nurse toward the door.

"I'll be here with her all night."

"Don't you let that crazy man near her!"

"Thank you, Miss Pledge, for all you've done. Good night."

He backed the nurse into Nana's room. Laura heard the lock snap and thought how odd it was that he would lock that door.

Her clown was laughing, pleased to have him back again. The laughter stopped when he turned and leaned against the door, and Laura saw his face. He had sounded controlled, almost serene with the nurse, but he was not calm.

He saw her awake, watching him. His head pressed back harder against the door, rolled side to side. His cheeks were flushed, his eyes feverish. Abruptly he stepped forward.

"Molly?"

Laura felt the soul of him pushing against her, seeking, absorbing, trying to know. Then, without recognition, as though he had called a stranger by a friend's name, he shuddered and was no longer the supplicant, but a father again. His frenzied face seemed to crumble and the tears flowed.

"My sweet Baby Girl. Somehow you have become entangled in my punishment."

He stumbled forward, scooped her into his arms, crushed her against him.

Laura's broken ribs gouged further into her. She stifled a scream but could not suppress the moan that billowed up into her throat with a pain that made her afraid to breathe.

Her daddy also moaned, an excruciating sound full of bewildered helplessness. He laid her gently back the way he had found her and slipped to his knees beside the bed. Laura saw that he was still wearing his bloody clothes.

He pressed her cold hand to his cheek. "I'm so sorry that I hurt you. So many want to hurt you. If what they believe were all true, it would be my fault. My fault."

262

Then he became suddenly fierce. "Harley will pay for hurting you! He'll regret ever raising his hand to my Baby Girl. From the day he was conceived he has brought nothing but pain."

Laura watched the fierce, reflective look in his eyes turn crazed.

"But then, even that comes back to me. How I regret the day I first set eyes on Kate!" He lowered his head and cried into the bedspread.

Laura tried to raise her hand in order to brush her fingers through his hair to comfort him. Her hand wouldn't move. Neither was there a response in her arm. She stared at it, bewildered. She tried to wriggle her fingers, but they no longer obeyed her signals. She concentrated all her effort on moving just her index finger. No response. Terror struck her. She tried her legs and feet. Nothing there. She was paralyzed. That old devil man was winning. He meant to take her right out of her daddy's arms. Separate them again.

Her clown screamed, *No!*

A tremor shook her as she willed her being outside the ailing body. In the manner she had manipulated the body of her stuffed clown, she willed her limp hand up and flopped it on her daddy's head. Barely able to pinch her thumb and forefinger together, she tugged at a lock of hair to make him move up on the bed with her.

He wiped his eyes and stretched out carefully next to her. Laura bit her lip against the pain his movements caused her. For a time she was still gathering strength. Slowly she maneuvered her head around until she could rest it against his chest. She listened to his racing heart. Gradually his heartbeat slowed and finally settled into its normal beat. It wasn't good for her daddy to be so upset. He needed her more than ever, now. They *belonged* together. They would *be* together!

Laura studied the dried blood spots on his shirt. Kate's blood. Her enemy's blood. Deep within her, ancient instincts stirred. Shadow memories of past times and further past times. Old rituals remembered. From her daddy's white shirt, Laura licked that blood. Her medicine. The proper medicine brought to her by her most loved one. Medicine to break the old man's spell.

The nearest spot clean, she mustered enough strength to

move her head further onto his chest where she could reach the next spot. With the accumulating salt taste she felt a returning surge of power. The old man's chanting from upstairs was fading, becoming a faraway sound. Her fingers twitched, flexed. She could bend her elbow, twist her ankle. All these movements caused pain, but she could move.

Three blood spots were soaked to a faint pink. Laura was able now to move up on her knees to reach a large blood splotch over her daddy's belly. She took the shirt material in her mouth, nibbled at it, sucked the blood. Her daddy's breathing quickened. She looked up at him. Their eyes locked. There were questions in them, but he made no move to stop her.

Breathlessly, her clown whispered to her, *We will win!*

It was her Molly-clown who pushed Laura's consciousness up out of sleep with the will to stand and walk, to move her stricken body where she wanted. She was standing beside the bed even before she had her eyes completely open. It was daylight outside. Her daddy was gone.

She thought at first that his having been there—the medicine he had brought her—might have been a dream. But there was the impression of his body still on the bed.

Recalling the warmth of him in the night, their close silent communion, Laura pulled herself up, fought the pain from the death wound in her chest and in her taut muscles.

From upstairs she heard the medicine man still chanting, his deep voice sounding tired and cracked. Yet he persisted! That monotonous droning bass sent a tremor through Laura. A wave of weakness billowed in her head, coursed downward all the way to her toes.

Reeling, she clutched at the bed sheets to steady herself. There in front of her, thrown to the side as though she had been covered with it through the night, was her daddy's white funeral shirt.

Laura picked it up and examined the faintly pink wrinkled and puckered spots where she had sucked Kate's blood from it. She licked at a small spot and felt better. Stronger. She was pleased with herself and with her daddy's reaction. He must have sensed the strength she had drawn from Kate's blood and not cared about the primitive implications of it.

He had shielded her with his medicine shirt, and she had slept through the night unscathed by the old man's chanting. Laura threaded her arms through the long sleeves, which she rolled above her elbows. Tediously, because of her stiffened fingers, she buttoned each button down the front. The shirt hung past her knees. From among her best dresses she chose a high-necked, puffed-sleeved white blouse and a long indigo jumper. She struggled into them and moved lamely to the mirror.

Her medicine shirt was well hidden, but the mirror told such a sad story that Laura could hardly look at herself. She was bent over at a sharp angle, favoring the left side where Carrie had fallen on her. Her small hands were gnarled, the skin on her forearms pinched into dehydrated wrinkles, like the wrinkles that lined her face and throat. Her eyes were sunken.

The ugly baby in its casket had not looked as pitiful as she did at that moment.

Slowly, with much gritting of teeth, Laura pulled herself erect. Her broken ribs slashed at her insides. She moaned and watched her already pale reflection turn chalky. If Nana guessed how badly she was hurt, she'd be confined to bed, or worse, sent to the hospital. Laura forced one foot to move in front of the other and practiced walking—and smiling—in front of the mirror.

Maybe she could fool her Nana. She would be distracted the day after a funeral day so filled with horror, and with the workmen coming to build Kate's prison.

Painfully, her muscles already contracting from her short walking practice, Laura made her way to the sewing box in Nana's room. She plucked her clown's head out of the scraps, stuffed it tight with extra cotton, and turned under a hem, pinning it with two crookedly placed straight pins. She found a needle already threaded with a long white thread. In Nana's sewing-machine drawer, Laura found a key ring she remembered. A nice heavy one some insurance company had given away for advertisement.

Her clown cautioned her about wasting her energy on unimportant things, and Laura made no attempt to close drawers or put away anything.

That's right. That's good. Her clown encouraged her.

Now find a hiding place in the marble hall where you can watch unseen.

Laura chose the shadowed corner next to the front door. She sat gingerly on the umbrella stand and began to repair her clown's head. It was comforting having it near her again, even though its voice had been with her all the time. Her clown's head would be such a comfort to her daddy. Then, in a moment of self-pity, Laura thought about all the pain she had endured and still faced just to make this present for him.

Laughing—rather derisively, Laura thought—her clown said, *It is the perfect charm for him!*

It was, to Laura, the best possible charm. Men his age carried them all the time: their dead grandfather's old pocket watch with their grandmother's bridal picture still inside; or a rabbit's foot made into a key ring, with the once-soft white fur turned brown and slick from years of wear. Her clown's head would remind her daddy of her childhood. Why was her clown still laughing that mocking way?

Just as Nana called lunch, the workmen arrived. Lunch was forgotten. The men fitted black bars over her mother's windows and made a door out of bars. Laura watched them through the paneled window next to the front door as they cut it specially and welded it out in the yard. They hung it on the outside of the wooden door to her mother's bedroom. It was supposed to look fancy, like the gate to a patio, but from the marble hall looking up, it suggested what it was—a jail door to keep a prisoner locked away. A death-row prisoner.

Laura watched the men make it, thinking it was a waste. A way would open for her to kill Kate and Harley yet. She ran through a list of possessions that only they touched. Something suitable for a proper death curse—her mother's big diamonds, Harley's toothbrush. To be rid of them had been her whole reason for being. That old man wasn't going to snatch it from her just like that!

Nana, with the workmen, came to make the final inspection of the barred door. Laura watched her try to smile as she told them she was pleased with the way it had turned out. Her voice sounded so sad.

From where he had been lurking silently behind Nana,

Harley came suddenly alive and pushed her roughly aside, apparently blaming her for the bars.

Laura was on her feet, ready to defend her Nana. She hobbled two agonizing steps on tightly constricted arches before her clown commanded, *Sit down! Harley could easily kill you now!*

He stood screaming in the upstairs hall, making a fool of himself as the men packed their tools to leave, until the medicine man emerged from the guestroom and coaxed Harley downstairs toward the kitchen.

At the foot of the stairs, Harley spotted Laura. He lunged toward her, but Carrie blocked his way. The old man soothed him, whispered to him, caressed his face until, finally, he let Carrie lead him through the swinging doors toward the smell of coffee and hot bread.

The medicine man strode straight to Laura. Before she could coerce movement from her stricken limbs, one giant hand was on her, searching, feeling out the bulges under her clothing. He lifted her skirt and stared at her daddy's rumpled shirt. He bent closer to examine the faint pink stains.

Gravely, he said, "You remember more than I thought you did. But this will no longer protect you."

That fan he carried as though it were some regal extension of himself, he wafted quickly over her head. He chanted a long string of words that sounded like obscenities to Laura. Such pain assaulted her that she simultaneously hated her body, the old man, his fan, her Nana for bringing him into the house, and her daddy for being the cause of all of it.

Laura didn't see where he had gone. When she fought her way through constriction and fear back to full awareness, she was seated on the umbrella stand, gripping the antique oaken seat with both her gnarled hands, straining, occasionally panting. The pain was cutting a slice through her midline just below the diaphragm. She imagined the old man's bear paw inside her abdominal cavity squeezing her entrails to mush. That evil old devil man! Killing her! Once his own. Just to save Harley and Kate.

Upstairs, her daddy, with Juan helping, was moving her mother's dresser into the nurse's room. Laura managed to

267

focus the haze from her eyes as she watched them make additional trips after her mother's expensive chest of drawers and night tables. They were wrestling the older furniture that the nurse had been using into one of the empty bedrooms in the servants' wing when the new hospital bed arrived.

Unobtrusive in her shadowed corner, Laura sat transfixed as the delivery man demonstrated the bed in the marble hall before taking it upstairs. All electric, it moved up and down—head, foot, and all together.

Urged on by her clown, Laura doggedly dragged herself upstairs to see her daddy and the nurse wrestle her mother into it, but Carrie closed the new door in her face and locked it from the inside with her key. The workmen, before they left, had given Carrie, Nana, her daddy, and the nurse, each a shiny new key. There had only been the four. And all of the four people with one of them were inside the room.

Her clown raged. Laura felt nauseated from the effort of climbing the stairs. She was so much weaker since the Indians' last assault than she had been earlier.

Locked out, she leaned against the wall listening to her mother's screams, musing about how things might have been different if her mother had had a door like that earlier. One that opened only with a key and had no knob. It wouldn't have been quite so easy sneaking into the closet and spying on her with her stupid baby, or escaping after stabbing it with the syringe.

Laura felt the constriction in her abdomen draw tighter. Hot fingers of pain spread over her ribs pressing the jagged bone further into her. Cold sweat oozed from her pores. Her legs felt like jelly.

Behind the locked door the commotion died down. Then, so loudly Laura felt the plastered wall vibrate, her mother screamed, "Harley! Harley, help me!"

Harley exploded through the swinging kitchen door downstairs, followed by Reming and his grandfather. Gasping, Laura's brain sent out the slow-moving message for her feet to move. She felt suspended on a stationary cable, trussed up for her enemy to reach her before she could release herself. She read it in Harley's face. He had already blamed her for Kate's cries for help.

She was relieved when Reming tackled him before he

made it to the stairs. The medicine man looked scornfully at her before he hauled both boys to their feet and led them back into the kitchen. Laura expelled her held breath, then bowed her head to meet the onslaught of pain that caused.

Moments later, with her mother shrieking, "I wish you had married your Indian bitch. You've only brought me misery. Get out! Get away from me!" her daddy fumbled the barred door open and threw his shiny new key behind him. It landed at Laura's feet.

Wondering at the vast, foreboding wilderness to be crossed between the tips of her fingers and the floor, Laura stared at it. She had never wanted anything more. That key was the shiny new sword that would allow her to pierce the sanctuary of her mother's cell. That old witch doctor thought he had beaten her. But she would get Kate yet!

Stooping, Laura felt a broken rib prod a resisting mass of something vital inside her. She froze, afraid of the pain.

Her clown's acid hiss stung her. *The key is necessary. Don't be a coward! Kate is your enemy!*

At once, feeling bone piercing muscle, Laura bent forward and scooped the key off the floor. Straightening, she felt that same bone retract, followed by a gush of weakness. Her consciousness seemed to fade in and out, driven in front of her by waves of red and orange pain.

Finally, when she managed to bring her eyes into focus, it was on the medicine man's face upturned to her from the marble hall. She knew, then, that he had tricked her. He had purposely used the key to make her injure herself further. Now, the key would be useless to her. There would be no time.

The force of her hate for him sent her stumbling forward to crash chest-high into the balcony rail. That, too, she knew he had done to her. This time, behind her eyelids, the avalanche of red and orange pain was tinged with purple futility and finally muddled—all of it together—into a brown waste.

Sobered, her clown whispered to her about her gift.

Somewhere, beyond herself, Laura heard her daddy crying. She forced her eyes open. He was there facing the old man in the hall below her. She had to reach him. Give him her clown's head. It would comfort him.

The medicine man kept her daddy turned away from her

all the while he watched her fight her way downstairs. She clung to the banister with her chin, using her gnarled hands on the upright rails to pull herself along and drag her feet down one torturous step at a time.

When she neared the bottom, she heard her daddy say, "One wrong decision I made at twenty-two, and it ruined us both, Molly and me."

He broke away from the old man. Laura followed him lamely, though she pulled herself up as straight and proud as she could as she passed that witch doctor. He whispered to her.

"Don't fight. Let go! No need to suffer so!"

Just then, from her prison above, her mother screamed, "Laura! Give back my baby!"

It was over between them. Finished! Laura's weakness had brought about a cold apathy toward her mother. She had no more energy to waste on her.

Something stung in Laura's right hand. Slowly she forced her cramped fingers open. There was the shiny new key. She had been clutching it so tightly that it had cut her palm. Blood oozed from the jagged cuts, staining the new metal. She turned and hurled it at the witch doctor's head. The key cut his cheek, then clattered to the floor at his feet.

Laura was smiling as she eased into the library behind her daddy. He hadn't noticed her at all since leaving her mother's room. She narrowly missed being crushed by the door as he slammed it as though trying to slam out her mother's ranting.

Laura took refuge behind an overstuffed chair as her daddy rampaged around the room. He shoved books off of shelves, smashed a framed mirror with a cut-glass candlestick. Finally, he stopped to stare at the picture of the Greek temple dancer. Then, slowly, deliberately, with a blunt letter opener from the desk, he ripped the canvas to shreds. Laura's smile broadened.

Her clown was laughing, deliriously happy, like the grown-up Molly dancing with him on the mountain.

Her daddy dropped into the desk chair, his head in his hands, his whole body quaking. He was hers now. Completely. She knew that in destroying that picture he had finally ripped Kate out of his system.

He took her on his lap—absently—as though his mind had temporarily vacated his body. For the first time Laura noticed that wrinkles had come in his face. Just since her daddy had leaned, rocking over the banister, looking down at the smashed baby, worry lines had appeared, marring his storybook handsomeness. Even his hair was graying at the temples. The sight of him—trembling, solemn, and staring—filled her with pity for him, and a quiet new tenderness to match her passion to possess him totally.

He looked so sad and tired. Now was the time to give him his present. Her clown's head would remind him of her childhood. Why was her silly clown laughing that ugly way?

Laura got down from his lap and swiveled his chair around to where the light was best. She forced herself between her daddy's knees. As though the essence of him had been away somewhere, he seemed to return, slowly, his consciousness surfacing—rising from the depths of his faraway eyes. At last he reached out to her, touched her sore shoulder, as though he had forgotten she had been hurt—as though he could not see that she was hurt—diminished to but a shadow of herself. Laura stood the pain rather than frighten his hand away. She could tell her presence pleased him. He had stopped trembling. He even smiled a little when she handed him the clown's head from her skirt pocket.

The way he looked at it, she knew he understood it was the most precious thing she could give him—the last remnant of her clown. He took his keys out of his pocket, threaded them off his old ring and onto the new one. When the last was in place, he grabbed her to him in a hug that made her hate Harley and the witch doctor for all the damage they had done her body. Then, her daddy began to cry, like her mother might come down the stairs and yank the clown's head away. Laura kissed his neck and cheek, smoothed his hair. Suddenly, he started to laugh—through his tears—louder and louder, and Laura trembled at the hollow, unhappy sound of it.

Less than an hour later, at supper, the medicine man sat across from Laura in her mother's place, on her daddy's left between him and Harley. He watched around the table with quiet eyes. There was no resisting his death power now. His tricks and his chanting, the powers he had invoked against her had done irreparable harm to her body. Laura could feel it deteriorating. That old devil man was going to drive her back to The Thinking Place.

How odd it seemed by contrast that at that very moment he was caressing Nana with such a protective, loving gaze that it made her blush and seem very young. Nana would never know that since coming into the house he had concentrated all his powers on destroying the person she treasured most in all the world—her Baby Girl.

At least his protectiveness toward Nana was some comfort to Laura, since he was bound to separate them. The Indian was so big, his shoulders so broad, there would not have been room for the nurse if she had come to the table. This she could not do until after regular meal time, when Nana or Carrie would go to sit with crazy Kate.

Harley barely picked at his food. His eyes were sunken and watery, with dark circles around them. He had lost so much weight the past week that the bones in his face stuck out. He was pitiful. Harley looked up from his plate to glare at Laura across the table. Laura only smiled—sweetly—at Harley, to make him act worse. That was all she could do. The black nauseating pain where her rib continued to impale her made breathing ever more difficult.

The old man kept his hand constantly on Harley's shoulder. Nana, too, from the other side. As though they were holding him in his chair to keep him from lunging at Laura's throat—which was all he really wanted to do. His eyes said it—*I hate you, Laura!*

Laura knew exactly how much of her sweet smiling Harley could take. She measured it out to make him explode—which made him appear insane, howling "I'll beat your face in!" to a smiling hollow-eyed, pitiably sick-looking angel who accepted his rage and reflected only love for him.

The instant he said it, Carrie reached across the table and slapped him. Nana grabbed her hand. "Don't! Please don't!" And Laura felt Reming draw close to her, ready to protect her in case Harley broke free from his grandfather.

Her daddy put his arm around her from the other side and kissed her forehead, while Nana and the old man patted Harley's shoulder to quiet him.

After Carrie's slap Harley just cried in his plate, and once in a while he would open his mouth and let the old man feed him. He was so pitiful even Laura felt a little sorry for him. But it was not her fault he had been born where he did not belong.

Reming, silently watching his friend, kept glancing at her daddy as though he expected him to do something to Harley.

Her daddy was the one Laura was really sorry for. She lifted her corner of the table cloth and peeked at his pants pocket. It was bulging—tight enough to burst—with her clown's head key ring and her daddy's hand on it, squeezing its comforting softness the way Laura had when her mother made her nervous. She knew he was not really thinking about the clown though. Instead he was looking at Harley being spoon-fed—like the sissy baby he was—by the old man.

Suddenly her daddy blurted, "Harley, I've never been so ashamed of anything in my whole life as I am of you!" Then, he looked hard at Reming and brought blood to his own lip, trying to bite the tears back. When they spilled out the corners of his eyes, he let them fall on the table and did not try to brush them away or hide them.

Reming was crying, too, and the old man was looking sadly at both of them, while Harley played with his food as if he had not heard, or did not care, what his father said.

Everyone in the room, except Harley, was crying. But no one said anything until her daddy spoke to Reming.

"You know. Don't you, Son?"

Reming answered without taking his eyes off her daddy's face.

"I have thought it was true for a long time now. Talk at school. Mostly, the way you treat me better than you do Harley."

"When you were born," Reming's grandfather said to him, "T.J. wanted to claim you then. Give you his name. I stopped him, which was a mistake that cost me your mother's life before I was able to see how wrong I had been."

Laura smiled, imagining a wondrous light coming into Reming's eyes if the old man should tell him the truth, that his mother was sitting beside him at the table.

She wasn't prepared for Reming's question, "Wasn't my mother wrong, too, for leaving me?"

"She died," his grandfather replied softly.

"She killed herself!" Reming said. "Laura acted it out in the canyon. She knew. It took me a while to figure out what she was doing. She saw the past there. That's what frightened her so."

His statement pricked her Molly-clown. Once it would have hurt deeply, had a lasting power over her, but now it was a guilt long purged with her grief in The Thinking Place. It was good to know that Reming was coming into his own powers. One day he would be as strong as his grandfather.

Reming looked away from his grandfather's face to Harley. Then he looked back to her daddy.

"I'm glad to know it is really true," Reming said pointedly, "because my brother needs me."

His remark sent an involuntary shudder through Laura's weakening body. A death chill. A portent of disaster. She had purposely crippled Harley. With full right she still felt! He had been Kate's ally and therefore her enemy. Earnestly she hoped that Reming would never reap the injury she had sown, for there was no time for her to do anything with Harley now.

Laura's pulse throbbed in her own ears. It was too rapid. Thready.

Her daddy stood, walked quickly behind her chair, gripped Reming around the shoulders, and kissed his cheek. Then he pushed through the swinging door and tromped heavily through the marble hall and out on the front porch.

No one else moved in the kitchen until Reming reached across the table and took Harley's hand.

"Come out to the garage with me," he said. "My soldiers are in the loft."

Moving like a sleepwalker, Harley let Reming lead him out the back door. Nana and Carrie and the old man got busy clearing the table. And Laura slipped out of her chair and went down into a squat as the muscles in her legs failed to support her. She grabbed the table edge and dragged herself back to a wobbly standing position before anyone besides the old man saw her.

He was gazing at her sideways as though estimating how much longer she could last. His sad, resolved look of forgiveness reminded Laura of the look she had seen in the baby's eyes when she had stabbed it with the needle.

That made no sense! He was the one doing harm to her. Driving her out of her home. Keeping her from living peacefully here with her daddy, Nana, Carrie, her nurse, with Reming as her best playmate and friend. He'd stopped her from getting rid of Kate and Harley. That old devil man had done exactly what he had threatened the day he had appeared out of the heat waves. He'd been punishing her since he'd entered the house. Now he was sending her back.

Why was her clown laughing?

Laughing!

Glaring at that devil witch doctor, Laura put all her remaining strength into marching straight and tall from the kitchen.

Out in the mirrored hall she leaned against the wall. She was panting. Slowly, she dragged herself along from mirrored panel to mirrored panel toward the front door.

Laura had heard her daddy go to the front porch. She hoped he was still there. The last of her strength was pouring out of her as fast as her mother's blood had yesterday.

Tears streaked her face as Laura leaned heavily beside the door, trying to muster strength to open it. All her lovely plans had been ruined by that one interfering old man! But then, Reming would be left with him. Maybe when Reming fully discovered his powers, he'd do something about the old meddler. She hoped! She'd put thought to that after this was over.

What was it her clown found so funny? Still laughing! Saying riddles again. Riddles about the resolve she had made in The Thinking Place. That resolve taking precedence over all. The medicine man hadn't won, her clown was saying. Laughing! He'd been used!

How?

Laura thought for a moment that she knew. But then she lost it.

She found her daddy sitting on the steps, elbows on his knees, holding his head in his hands. She slid between his legs, thrusting her arms around his waist.

He hugged her fiercely, and she knew he was still crying by the way he sniffled before he said, "My Sweet Baby. Don't ever leave me." His voice cracked. He tightened his hold on her, and she relaxed against him, letting him support her whole weight.

"My Baby. My poor, silent, sweet, Baby . . . How can I make it up? All the misery that crazy woman has caused you?"

Laura leaned away from him and smiled into his haggard, tear-streaked face. She kissed the end of his nose and brushed his hair back from his forehead. He needed her now. Needed her more than all his money, or the ranch, or the big house so filled with misery. More than he had ever needed Kate.

She looked deep into his blue eyes, promising—silently —that she would always be his.

Suddenly, he held her a little away from him, pulled her forward and back, his eyes intent on her features, like the medicine man's had been the day she had mistaken him for the devil and ever since Nana had called him into the house.

"My God! I saw it then. Caught it full! That flickering shadow at the back of your eyes."

His face seemed to pale.

"Is it because I need her so?"

He moaned quietly—closing his eyes—then opened them and again searched her face.

"Because I want to see? . . . Or because I know?"

He shook Laura gently by her shoulders.

"Every time, when I know, I make the knowing go away."

He pulled her to her feet and looked her up and down.

"Other times I've seen, like now, only I convinced myself I was imagining."

Laura dropped back to her knees, between his legs, and nestled her cheek against his arm, feeling the soft hair brush against her face.

He moved his arm a little away; but she pulled it back next to her cheek, and he bent to search her eyes once more.

She settled against his knee. Smiling. Glad. Feeling his misery drowning in the excitement of discovery.

When she was full. . . . The new light in his eyes. Sparkling. Misty. The soft breeze ruffling his hair. Hope replacing the pain on his tired face. . . . Her attention was drawn beyond him by a glorious fireball sun—falling, nearly concealed—leaving only its outer rim, a crowning halo—pulsating behind the mountain.

"What are you looking at?" He pulled her closer, turning to follow her gaze westward, toward the mountain.

Dying sun rays—orange and gold—glinted off the rock called The Thinking Place. A dream place. Real now. Memory now. Beckoning.

She smiled for him. With terrible effort, to mask her weakness, she stood. Took his hand.

He fumbled the clown's-head key ring out of his pocket. And Laura heard her clown laughing more joyously than ever. Her daddy found the key to the truck, picked her up, ran and placed her in the seat. He got in beside her, turned the ignition, and pumped the gas pedal until it started. He gunned the truck down the drive as though they were responsible for the sun fire and were racing to extinguish it.

Laura, beside him on her stiffened knees, held, with the last of her strength, to the back of the seat so she could look through the rear glass at the house. She saw the old man, followed by her Nana, rush out on the porch and come running down the driveway after them.

She could still read his lips when the medicine man thundered, "No, T.J. Don't go with her!"

But the truck windows were rolled up and his voice didn't penetrate over the truck sounds in the cab.

Her clown stopped laughing and screamed in protest as Laura willed her numb lips to move, forming—slowly and deliberately—the words "I love you, Nana!" Her good-bye was mouthed silently against the window.

The medicine man tried to block Nana's line of vision with his giant's body.

Angry, Laura hurled the last of her force against him, a force which dropped him to his knees in the dust.

That old witch doctor extended both hands, palms raised, heavenward. She saw him swaying, his mouth moving, and knew he had resumed her death chant.

Immediately, Laura felt his aura all around her in the truck cab. Thick it was, smothering, wringing the last of her energy from her just to keep it a distance away so that she could breathe.

Her Nana had stepped around him and was still running after the truck. With her will and her Molly-clown's help, Laura clung to the back of the seat in order to read what was on Nana's lips and to keep that beloved face in view as long as she could.

"Stop! T.J.!" Nana was screaming, "Laura is trying to talk! At last, My Baby is trying to speak to me!"

Her face was alight with new hope when she stopped. She gasped for breath, her skin was ruddy as she smiled and waved after them.

But behind her, the medicine man, still on his knees, was swaying in a quickened circular motion. Both his raised hands were knotted into power fists.

Laura toppled sideways against her daddy's arm. Too weak to rise, all she could see was the seam in the seat cover. She stopped struggling and snuggled there feeling her daddy's warmth. He was all hers now. She was going to last! That old devil man wouldn't be able to kill her in time to keep them from reaching the mountain together.

Her clown was laughing again. Smug. Laura knew then what had been hidden from her all along. A long life with her chosen family had never been a part of her Molly-clown's plan. She had come back only for him!

Laura shifted her eyes to stare sideways at her clown's head dangling from the key in the ignition. She wondered who had given her that clown? Her daddy and Nana had puzzled over it often. Neither had ever remembered.

It was smiling at her now, as it had all her life, with its crooked embroidered smile. A triumphant smile! And why not? Her clown had used them all. Even that old devil man!

Her daddy drove the truck straight across the hill pasture, through mud and gullies, right to the foot of the mountain, where the path started up. He jumped out in such a hurry that he left the key in the ignition. With her clown's own strength, Laura removed it and handed him the clown's head.

He waited, watching her. Then, toward the mountain, he said, "If only we could go away. Just the two of us." He held the clown's head toward the path. "Follow the sun, maybe." Then, "Why did you bring me here?" he asked, making a game of it. "To climb to the top and see where the sun is going?"

Lightly her clown lifted her off the seat. She stepped in front of him and skipped up the path. The moment Laura stepped under the trees she felt a change. It was cooler. Darker. Night-black in places where the foliage was thick.

She walked slowly—like a bride down the long aisle of a cathedral church—pacing her steps to the beat of drums instead of organ music. The same dark, grizzled warriors, instead of groomsmen, lined the path. Her special warrior was there leading them. They were smiling this time, pleased with her, not angry as they had been when she had come there with Reming. She turned, seeing them smile at her groom. He was oblivious to their presence.

Running ahead, she twirled around and around, feeling light. Wanting to run and run and run, she was held back by the drum and the dignified faces lining the path. She thought of her little drummer. Maybe it was he playing for her. She closed her eyes, feeling his music. Feeling. Changes. Inside. Each drum beat marked a transition going on inside her body. Baby fat burning away. Fuel, creating a new energy that was pushing her bones upward, stretching her as she danced her way to the top, making her taller and slimmer, leaving her prickly hot, then cool. Tingling. Suddenly aware of the pull of long hair. She tossed her head—proudly. Heard it swish behind her, circling her slim hips.

Eyes still closed, she danced forward, moving up and up, trusting herself to the gentle hands passing her along from one partner to the next. Up. Drawn—like a flower, growing—lifting her head, longing for the top, where she must bloom.

The little drummer gave one last flourishing drum roll. She opened her eyes. Found herself alone in the clearing. She spun around and around. Unfolding to the freedom of fullness. Open. Happy!

She cried, "T.J.?"

He emerged from the trees—blinking—in the sun's

dying brightness. As he looked at her his face took on that brilliant red glow, reflecting—inside-out—a joy not to be compared with earthly things.

He breathed her name, "Molly?" A prayer. A supplication. "Molly . . . Molly."

She ran into his open arms and felt them close her home. Tight—pain-forged bands, claiming her as his bride, never to be pried from her again.

He lifted her, to meet his face, and looked deep into a soul that had never left him.

"My Molly, Dolly. My Molly."

Setting her feet lightly on the rock, his arms, still tight, circling her waist, he danced her around and around the ceremonial pole. Twirling. Spinning away lost time. Celebrating their new reality. They moved in ever widening circles to the melody of her happy laughter, accompanied by his rhythmical breathing and the night wind sweeping them toward the cliff.

Ecstatically he screamed her name once more: "M–O–L–L–Y—" And the echo, M-o-l-l-y, replaced that other hated name neither of them could remember.

Stopped. Near the edge. So close they were one being. Sharing strength and softness. He breathed, "Molly," at last, quietly, as she led him in flight over the canyon.

Epilogue

At first light the next morning Nana and the old healer found their crushed and broken bodies at the bottom of the sandrock basin.

Laura was clamped tight in her daddy's arms, her body resting across his, her head off of his left shoulder.

Incongruously, her daddy was holding the clown's-head key ring behind her back, its embroidered smile showing between his stiffened fingers. He had multiple hemorrhages, and all the separate ribbons of his drying blood had merged with Laura's and collected in a common pool in the lowest part of the basin.

The old healer made no effort to keep Nana from the grizzly sight. He let her kneel and examine the cold, stiff bodies. She wept. And he let her weep. At last he wept with her. And when they were through weeping, Nana sat a long time studying the dead face of her son, and the child—her sweet, silent Baby Girl.

Finally, through tears, she said, "They are both smiling. As sure as that crazy clown smiled its way through little Laura's whole life."

"The dark. An accident, I'm sure," the medicine man said kindly. "They must have been playing a game. Dancing, maybe, to relieve the tension."

"You know better," she said. "No accident in the same spot where your Molly died. T.J. had reached his limit. He took Laura with him. Afraid to leave her—helpless as she was without him."

"That child wanted him to herself," the old man said. "She won him."

Nana choked back fresh tears.

The old man bent to help her to her feet, and, as he

lifted her, she whirled suddenly to look at Laura's dead face.

"What is it?" he asked.

"I thought I heard her speak. Words I longed for all her life."

"Then suspend your disbelief! You wanted a sign. What did you hear?"

"My sweet Laura saying 'I love you, Nana.'"